PROUD CAPTIVE

Her pride was all that she had left. She turned and spoke through rising anger. "Do not touch me! I am quite capable of entering alone." The man drew back, one hand held up before his face, a movement at once duplicated by his fellow. Head high, face impassive, Lia went to confront the lord commander.

His eyes flicked over her casually, then returned to linger on her face. He was very tall and brown, hard-muscled, with a lean tapering body and wide shoulders. He wore only a loincloth of white into which a long dagger was thrust. His hair was the color of polished ebony and clustered in curls over his head. As their glances locked Lia saw that his eyes were the deep brilliant blue of the sea at noon and they glittered under the arching dark brows. He looked to be in his late twenties but his commanding manner and titles made him seem older.

Their mutual assessment took only seconds. One corner of his mouth flicked upward in what might have been annoyance or amusement. "Where were you going? Were you going to meet others? I know Red Bor was here. Were you his woman? Speak up!" His voice was hard and compelling with the brusqueness of one used to instant obedience.

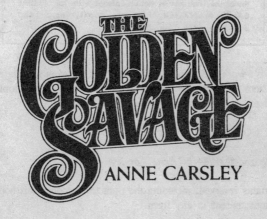

THE GOLDEN SAVAGE

ANNE CARSLEY

PINNACLE BOOKS   ◎   NEW YORK

This is a work of fiction. All the characters and events portrayed in
this book are fictional, and any resemblance to real people or
incidents is purely coincidental.

THE GOLDEN SAVAGE

Copyright © 1984 by Anne Carsley

An original Pinnacle Books edition, published for the first time
anywhere.

First printing / May 1984

ISBN: 0-523-42143-5

Can. ISBN: 0-523-43122-8

Cover illustration by Dan Gonzalez

Printed in the United States of America

PINNACLE BOOKS, INC.
1430 Broadway
New York, New York 10018

9   8   7   6   5   4   3   2   1

THE
GOLDEN SAVAGE

Chapter One

THE EXILES

LIA SPUN DOWNWARD in the warm water, reveling in the silkiness of it against her skin. A black fish glided far ahead and vanished behind a tall cropping of coral. Her ears began to ring as she increased the rapidity of her strokes. She reached for the fronds of a tall undersea plant and looked upward to the slanting light diffused into the clear depths. Lazily she began the long rise to the surface.

She floated there and waited for her breath to return. The early-morning sun touched her bare tanned body and mixed its gold with that of her streaming hair. The swelling waves lifted her toward the glistening white sands of the island but she propelled herself backward. It was so calm and serene here. She would drift awhile longer before returning to the sharpness of Ourda's tongue.

The words of last night flashed into her mind. Ourda had put down the last cooking pot and faced Lia with an air of determination. Her black eyes in their nests of wrinkles searched those of her charge. "When do we go to the mainland, Lia? Your father has been dead nearly a moon and still we linger. The boat is ready and our food packed. You must honor your promise. His old friend, Cithri, will find you a good husband. I may even live to see your sons about you. Your mother was wed at fifteen and you are two summers past that. I have not wanted to press you but now I must."

Lia knew that she should have spoken soothingly. Ourda was

1

old for all that she was still sturdy and her hair only sprinkled with gray. She had loved and served Lia's mother, Ze, agonized over her early death, then wandered with Medo, the father, and the child she cared for as her own. She had come into voluntary exile here on the uninhabited island of Pandos with them seven seasons ago and they had been content. Medo, always a scholar, buried himself in his collection of tablets, scrolls and nostrums, emerging only to treat with certain of the pirates who infested these waters and seemed to hold him in great awe. Last winter Ourda had begun to grumble about this sort of life leading nowhere for a young woman and Lia grew conscious that her father saw her with new eyes. Her freedom was precious to her; she did not mean to lose it.

"I want no husband! That would be bondage. There are things I mean to do, plans to be made." She watched Ourda's face darken but plunged ahead with what must be said. "I promised my father to go to Cithri in his name and ask for protection. I would have said anything, given anything, to ease his pain. He was fevered and tormented, out of his mind, and forgot that we had spoken of travels to far places. Let it be, Ourda. I cannot seek the sort of life that once nearly destroyed us!"

"The goddess will be angered and your father's shade will reproach you, Lia!" Ourda's face wobbled and the tears began. "He thought of you and now. . . !" She wailed louder and began to beseech the ancestors for understanding.

Lia had come to the beach, knowing that Ourda must be given time to calm down. She had always been able to mollify the older woman when necessary but she knew that this time she must go very carefully. A flicker of motion had made her glance up just then and she had seen the clear outline of sails vanishing around the crags at the eastern end of the island.

One ship? Two?

Some of the pirates had come here regularly up until several moons ago but Medo never told her of the arrangements he had with them. His illness had been so sudden and devastating that there was opportunity for only a few gasped words before death took him. Such thoughts had to be pushed back; he would not want her to weep for him. She had begun to walk toward the east, knowing that in the past some of the pirates, harried by each other as well as the forces of Crete, hid in the secret coves and waterlocked caves of Pandos. Perhaps these would be some she knew. In the morning she would watch and see.

Now Lia kicked up spume and laughed as an inquisitive gull swooped low to investigate, then veered out to sea with a raucous cry. Another cried in answer and she thought how very human they sounded. She began to stroke swiftly through the water which was so clean and pure that the individual grains of sand could almost be distinguished far below. Last night she had meant to return to her home but sleepiness overcame her and she rested under a flowering bush just off the beach. It was still very early and she had been unable to resist the lure of the sparkling water. Ourda would not worry; they had all been in danger of their lives and knew how to conceal themselves, secure though Pandos had always been.

The shrill cry rang through the air with such sharpness that Lia paused to listen. Would a gull cry so painfully? Just then the scream came again and this time there was no question of its reality. The voice was human and desperate, filled with mortal anguish. It was suddenly choked off, rose once again in a thin shriek and stopped. The silence was absolute.

Lia fought the water that had previously been her element. It entered her mouth and gagged her. She flailed, momentarily helpless, although she could swim long distances underwater and once bested a huge octopus in battle. Her breath came harshly and then she was moving without being aware of it, her body tense and heavy.

Her feet touched the bottom and she rose to stand silent, listening. A low-pitched voice spoke in a vaguely familiar language and was overridden by a harsher one. Both were quiet and Lia heard slapping sounds. Had Ourda followed her and been frightened by some of the pirates seeking Medo? It might just be that the pirates and their women were sporting here. If that were the case she would need to vanish. She had gone among them with Medo several times in the past but she was always dressed as a boy, considered small for his age, and interested only in learning. Even those who came most regularly, Red Bor, Poldon and Genor, did not know her sex. She had heard snatches of the tales they told and knew the precaution to be a wise one. Certainly the pirates were fierce and dangerous but they had never threatened Medo; on the contrary, they had shown him all deference. Might they show less to his "son"? If properly approached it was highly likely that she might be able to obtain passage to Egypt for herself and Ourda. But the old woman must be persuaded first. Why had she not spoken earlier?

The voices came again, this time on a questioning note, and she heard the rattle as if a sword had been sheathed. One word was repeated several times; the familiarity of it tugged at her mind and a slow dread began to rise although she could not place the language.

Lia ran swiftly to the bush where she had tossed her faded tunic earlier. Heedless of the hampering thorns, she jerked it free and pulled it down over her head. Her dagger, sharp and shining, hung in the twisted cord that served as a belt. She put her hand on the hilt as she slipped along the sand under cover of the overhanging bushes.

Her heart hammered against her ribs and her wet hair tumbled down her back. She should have bound it up under the cloth, she thought, and at a distance she might still appear to be a boy. But there was no time. She reached the boulder closest to the copse from which the voices had sounded and peered cautiously around it. Her eyes burned with the intensity of her gaze and her mouth went dry.

A fat bearded man stood with his back to her as he scanned the craggy hills in front of him. One hand rested on the belt that held his sword and the other was upraised as if for silence. But it was the other man who held Lia's eyes. He wore only a loincloth and his body was supple as he ran his hands over the woman who lay sprawled on the white sand, her head twisted over toward Lia, the mouth open and wide. It was Ourda.

There was a red patch below her ear which was spreading even as Lia watched. It was soaking the loosened dark hair and dripping into the sand. The man who bent over her bore blotches of it on his fingers and wrists. The old brown gown that she wore was pulled far up over the thick thighs and blew slightly in the rising wind.

Lia knew that Ourda was dead; there was not the slightest sign of motion from the crumpled form. She stood looking at the murderers of the one person left to her in all the world. Her sight blurred and tears threatened. Then her dagger was in her hand and a restoring anger poured through her. She heard a far-off snarling and realized dimly that it came from her own throat.

She bent and caught up a stone the size of her fist in her free hand. Then she was in the open, running toward the men and crying out. "Murdering spawn! Filth!" The stone spun out and caught the fat man in the mouth so that he stumbled backward as blood and teeth spattered out. The smaller man jumped up and spoke urgently to her but his eyes flickered toward his cloak and sword which lay near the water's edge. His comrade jerked out his own sword and yelled something incomprehensible.

"For Ourda!" The anger was all-consuming now as Lia reversed the dagger as Medo had taught her long ago and threw it directly into the bare chest of the ravisher. "Die!"

It hit home and he fell over Ourda's body, both hands clutching at the blade as he tried to speak. Lia felt the fierce surge of exultation. Death for death! The fat man lunged toward her with a roar and she saw that, despite his size, he could move swiftly. She sidestepped and looked around for another stone but only the fine white sand was underfoot. The sword whistled down and sliced part of her tunic away as he advanced on her. His face was congealed with fury and he pulled out the dagger thrust in his own belt when he came nearer to Lia. She was being herded back toward the rocks where he would try to hem her in. Now he was so close that she could read the triumph in the little eyes and smell the sour wine on his breath.

Lia bent low as if to cower from the upraised sword, which barely missed her as it slammed down. Then she threw herself past him, her long fingers and their sharp nails raking the arm that held the dagger. He howled and twisted around but she was free and running for the shelter of the woods. Nothing could be done for Ourda now. At least she was partially avenged and Lia must save herself. Later she could weep and mourn, even think of the future, but now a place of safety must be found. She would go to the cave in the high crags where she and Ourda had often been sent by Medo when strange sails were sighted. A wave of pain swept over her but she thrust it back and ran fiercely on, heedless of the shouts behind her. It seemed to Lia then that five winters swept back and once again she and those she loved fled from those who would destroy them. Now she alone remained. Death and disaster had followed them; perhaps that had been the will of the gods all along. "Submission! Yield totally to the great ones! Those who do not shall surely die!" The old chant of the priests and their followers rang in her ears as past and present dangers seemed to merge.

Rocks tore at her bare feet and low-hanging branches slapped her face as she ran but Lia felt nothing. Once she tripped and almost fell, wrenching her ankle sharply before she managed to retain her balance. She stood still for a breath, straining to hear, thin trickles of sweat dripping between her breasts while her heart hammered. Her throat was dry and parched. One hand was bleeding from a surface cut she could not remember receiving.

All was silent around her. She was far enough up on the mountain slope to see clearly the open sweep of shimmering sea. There was no sign of the ships of the invaders. The green woodland drifted in a warm haze and the breeze tossed the heads of some purple flowers at Lia's feet. It might have been any peaceful day on the island. A tiny lizard darted out onto a rock, paused, then fled back to safety. She found herself envying it. Where were the murderers? Surely they did not give up this easily? Fear and reaction mixed with savage anger as she looked carefully about.

Strength was coming back to Lia's body and the pain of her ankle receded. Will of the gods, indeed! Had Medo not taught her that one must fight for oneself, not yielding or giving up? He had fought and lost Ze but time was gained and both lived on in their daughter. "I will survive." The words spoke in her mind and gave her courage.

Lia resumed her climb, determined to reach the sheltering cave by early afternoon. She went carefully, melting behind trees, pausing to watch from time to time and listening for any strange noises. Once in the depths of the wood which would eventually open out onto the bare crags, she became conscious that no birds sang or moved, no insects were visible and the very wind had ceased. All her senses cried alarm and she froze with her hand on the trunk of a large old tree. She had often come here in the past and felt no strangeness. Now she knew, and did not know how she knew, that death and evil were in this place.

Suddenly there was motion in the thicket just ahead and a tall man came slowly into view. He wore only a loincloth on his thin body. His flesh was white and stretched tight. His skull was high, sloping, etched with standing veins plainly visible even across the glade. She could see his face clearly as he revolved about, obviously looking for something. The brows were dark lines that seemed to match the thin pursed lips and his eyes seemed unnaturally large.

Lia was thankful for the instinct that held her still and had led her to peer around the tree rather than venture out. Frail though he appeared, this man was as great a danger as those who had slain Ourda. All her senses told her that.

He turned abruptly and bent to the ground. Lia saw that several small animals and birds had been cut open, their entrails spilled out and arranged. He thrust his fingers down into them and began to paint his chest with the congealing blood. His voice rose in a high humming which gradually altered to short guttural cries. The dappled light reflected off his body as he knelt there and the windless air was weighted with the scent of blood. The very branches seemed to lean toward him as if to do his bidding. His chant began to take on rhythm as he lifted the trailing entrails upward. His face took on the same look of mingled hunger and ecstasy that Lia had seen on other faces before the time of sacrifice.

Revulsion shook her and she knew that she must get away. Priests—and he could be no other—were the same everywhere. Had Medo not told her the truth of that? She stepped backward and a dry branch cracked under her foot. Instantly the chant ceased and the huge eyes lifted to the place where she stood, half concealed though she was. She could not fathom how he had heard her but the fury in his stance as he rose was all too evident.

He called out in words she could not understand and came toward her. Lia turned to run but it was too late. Two burly men were crashing through the wood to intercept her. It was obvious that they had been there all along. They must have observed her earlier but why had she been allowed so close to the rites?

Blocked, she turned in the opposite direction and then the priest was in front of her. He moved so quickly that there was no time to retreat. One bony hand caught her wrist and pulled her toward him. His grip was so strong that her backward jerk

was useless. The cadaverous cheeks were working and the
fierce eyes blazed into hers with such intensity that she felt as if
she were drowning in a black, icy sea. He spat words at her as
the other men came closer.

She kicked out as he swung her around so that the struggle
was useless. "Evil! Let me go, you spawn!"

One side of his mouth lifted and she saw that he was
toothless. The other clawlike hand lifted and slammed down at
her neck. She tried to dodge but could not and pain poured over
her as the world exploded into green fragments. His high
laughter rose as she fell forward.

A commanding voice called, "Zarnan! Zarnan!" It was
filled with anger and as Lia went into darkness she took with
her the memory of the baffled rage on the priest's face as he
turned toward the sound.

Chapter Two

HAND OF THE INVADER

LIA OPENED HER eyes slowly and stared at the woven canopy above her. She felt a gentle rocking motion, then gradually became aware that her body was cushioned by soft mats. A cool cloth was placed against her throbbing neck. She clenched her hands at her sides as she gradually turned her head. Late sunlight glittered on the open sea on one side and she could see the familiar line of the cliffs of Pandos on the other. She sat up so quickly that the world swung before her and darkness threatened to come down again.

A hand touched her shoulder and a low voice said, "Drink this. It will hearten you." The accents were those of the mainland.

Lia looked up into a face so repugnant that her nightmares might have been more comforting. The priest had been fearful enough—but this! The man would come only to her waist had she been standing and the hump on his back rose higher than the squat head which was covered with a shaggy mat of coarse brown hair. One eye protruded grotesquely. The other was sunk deeply in the socket. Both rolled outward. His nose twisted up in a red mass of veins and skin. His jaw appeared to be hung at a slant and a red growth hung beneath the receded chin. Had she fallen into a nest of monsters?

Shock held Lia still as his low laughter came. "You have not entered the underworld, lady. You yet live. I thank you for not screaming. Many do when they behold Naris for the first

9

time." He extended a heavy cup toward her and she saw that it was of beaten gold.

She had to use both hands to hold it because the mists seemed about to envelop her again. The honey-spiced wine eased her parched throat and began to clear her head. She knew that she should drink slowly but could not; the horror of this day was not yet done. Her voice came croakingly, "What pirate ship is this? Why am I here? I would speak with your captain at once in the name of Medo of Pandos."

The hunchback began to laugh, tried to stop, then gave himself up to it. That was so fearful a sight that Lia averted her eyes. Perhaps she was really dead and this was her punishment for ignoring the gods so overtly. Medo's strong common sense rang in her mind. "Certainly the gods exist; humans are their sport and nothing we can do will still their savagery. I have walked in my own way and suffered less than some. You will choose, my daughter." Ourda worshiped her own dark goddess faithfully and lay slain. The hunched one was right to laugh, for was it not all a supreme jest?

He looked down at her and spoke contritely. "Forgive me, that was unpardonable. It is just that the pursuers are not often taken for the quarry." His voice was rich and deep; there was real concern in it. "You are safe now. Rest, refresh yourself. Water for washing, more wine, food and garments will be brought for you. These mats can be let down for privacy amd later you will be questioned."

"By whom? Who are you? I demand to speak with your captain! The matter is urgent." Lia tilted her chin upward and looked boldly at the man. "I must know. . . ."

He broke into her speech. "It is best not to command, lady. You will not be harmed if you obey and answer questions truthfully." He put one hand to his chin and she saw that the fingers were smooth, the nails well tended. A huge green stone was set on a golden band on his thumb. "You cannot hope to protect the other pirates, you know. We are bound to harry them from the seas."

"Other priates! But it is you who are the pirates!" Lia saw from the expression in his eyes and the shaking of his head that he did not believe her. "My dearest companion lies dead. Murdered by foul ones!" She would have said more but Naris made a silencing gesture.

"I am empowered to inform you that you have been taken under the guardianship of Crete. Our mighty commander, the Lord Paon, titled Royal Friend, Scourger of the Seas, Harrier of Pirates, Servant of the Great Goddess, has sailed with his three ships for many days in search of the pirates Red Bor and Genor. We know for certain that they have been here many times before and, further, that they have women aboard. I advise you to be honest with the commander; he is a man of short temper and strong hatreds. One of those is piracy."

Lia knew that he spoke officially to her now for all that he had seemed somewhat friendly earlier. There was no way to prove that she was not a pirate; in Cretan eyes all those who rendered help to them as Medo had done and profited thereby would surely seem guilty. Medo and those few pirates she had known all spoke of the mighty power of Crete with awe. It was the island kingdom that ruled the far seas, upheld the laws it made by strength and force, controlled trade and protected its own. Medo had visited there in his youth but had always been reticent about it. "There is a grace of life, an enhancing like none other." She recalled the comment and the swift way he had parried other questions. He had been talkative enough about his journeys into the northern mountains, far deserts and even several voyages into a distant cold sea.

"The priest who attacked me. He is one of you?" She wanted to get as much information as she could before the commander must be faced. Would the Cretans have slain an old woman? Yet who else? The pirates knew of Ourda as the woman who tended Medo in his chosen exile; there would have been no reason. What could she, Lia, expect except rape and defilement? Her jaw tightened. Much depended on the manner of man the commander proved to be. Let them think she knew a great deal. There were other ways to fight her own battles and defiance would appear to serve her ill. "I will avenge you, Ourda. I swear it." She made her promise to the dead and felt her heart lighten a trifle.

The ship swayed and rocked under them just then as the freshening wind spread her sails. Men called to each other, eagerness in their voices. Naris turned to look and so did Lia. The place where she sat appeared to back onto another section built of wood and partially hung with woven cloth as was the canopy over her. Perhaps the commander or those favored by

him took their ease here. She could see down the long body of
the ship to a curved prow. Places for oarsmen to sit ran along
the sides. Higher up there was a small cabin or private area.

"I can answer no more questions, lady. We are sailing and
the mission cannot be delayed. Remember all that I have told
you." He gave that grotesque smile and called to someone just
out of earshot.

Lia jumped up, ignoring the ringing in her head. "But Ourda
must be buried; she will walk and weep forever if she is not. I
cannot leave her so!"

"The choice is not yours to make." Naris walked away.

She would not weep or call out before the two men who now
came up, eyed her curiously, put down several bundles and
lowered mats to give her privacy. She stood very still, her face
impassive, until they were done. Then she sank to the deck in a
small heap, her hands over her mouth so that her pain might
not be heard. Survival must come first; Ourda would be the
first to counsel her on that. If ever she were safe again she
would find a shrine of the dark goddess and offer many
sacrifices for the woman who had loved and served her so
devotedly. Why had she not left the island with Ourda? They
would both be alive and free if she had.

Her stomach jerked at the thought of food but she forced the
meat cake and bread, drank sparingly of the wine and eagerly
of the water. She washed herself and dressed in the loose brown
gown of a coarse weave that had been provided. Her golden
hair was bound back from her high forehead and plaited at her
neck. She felt the pulse hammer at her temple. Surely she
could play a role for her life's sake, only let it begin soon
before all her courage drained away! Perhaps she should be
humble and fearful, hoping that the arrogant tilt of her dark
brows and blazing green eyes would not give her another
appearance. Lia had never been able to hide her feelings. Now
she must.

Lia stepped outside the area enclosed by the mats, folded her
arms across her chest and stood looking back at the rapidly
vanishing mass of Pandos Island, which had been home and
refuge. Never again. The sun was very low in the sky now and
the tips of the waves seemed to reflect the redening light.
Clouds drifted on the horizon, seeming to melt into the water.
A great fish jumped up far ahead and fell back to safety. The

sails caught the wind and belled out so that the ship began to move more swiftly. She caught sight of another ship, sails spread, just rounding the point. The scents of seasoned wood, growing things and salt sea came to her nostrils. A late gull flapped low over the water. Had it only been this morning that all this began? She clenched her fingers into the flesh of her arms and willed the tears back.

There was a step behind her and she whirled to see one of the men who had brought her the supplies. He pointed at her, beckoned and gestured upward. She inclined her head and said, "I am ready." He did not understand but stood waiting for her. His fellow appeared beside him, motioning that she was to walk between them.

They went down the center of the ship. Men bent to their tasks but paid no attention to Lia. She felt their watchful eyes on her back. A burst of speech rose once but was quickly hushed. They climbed some narrow steps, crossed a shiny flat area and came to an enclosed section built of polished wood that gave off a faint shimmer. Her first escort rapped once and was answered by a gruff monosyllable followed by a sharp command. Lia recognized the voice, for it was emblazoned in her memory. It was the same one that had called out to the priest just as he felled her. Now the man behind her gave a push to the small of her back just as the other stood aside.

Her pride was all that she had left. She turned on him and spoke through rising anger. "Do not touch me! I am quite capable of entering alone." The man drew back, one hand held up before his face, a movement at once duplicated by his fellow. Head high, face impassive, Lia went to confront the lord commander.

The brilliance of light in the room made her blink at first. Candles were massed in jars around a wide chest on which a long parchment painted in several colors rested. The man who bent over it straightened up as Lia advanced a few steps. His eyes flicked over her casually, then returned to linger on her face.

He was very tall and brown, hard-muscled, with a lean tapering body and wide shoulders. He wore only a loincloth of white into which a long dagger was thrust. His hair was the color of polished ebony and clustered in curls over his head. The planes of his face were sharply cut and clear, the nose high-bridged. There was an off-center cleft in the square chin and an old scar made a white mark under one eye. As their glances locked Lia saw that his eyes were the deep brilliant blue of the sea at noon and they glittered under the arching dark brows. He looked to be in his late twenties but his commanding manner and titles made him seem older.

Their mutual assessment took only seconds. One corner of his mouth flicked upward in what might have been annoyance or amusement. "Where were they going? Were they going to meet others? I know Red Bor was here. Were you his woman? Speak up!" His voice was hard and compelling with the brusqueness of one used to instant obedience. He spoke the language of the mainland with an accent that was slightly different from that of Naris. "I have no time to waste!" Mobile lips curled back from white teeth as he took a step toward her.

"I know nothing of the pirates and their whereabouts. I am no man's woman; I am myself alone. Lia of Pandos. Yours are the first ships to come here in many moons. My companion and I lived here alone. She was slain this morning." She was proud that her voice remained level. If his men had murdered Ourda he would surely know. It was well nigh certain that the ships she had seen were those of the Cretans.

"Slain?" The dark brows came together. "Doubtless by the pirates fighting among themselves." Contempt ran in his voice. "They often fight over women."

Lia heard another note in his voice and wondered at it. It seemed that personal hatred mingled with a strange vulnerability. She was aware also that his searching eyes were causing all her pulses to come alive. "She was old. She had never done harm to anyone." It took all her effort to keep the tears from misting her eyes. Something warned her that this man would be pitiless.

"They who serve Minos of Crete do not kill unnecessarily." He shrugged as if to dismiss the matter. "Naris will have told you that you are under the guardianship of Crete; he has a gift for softening reality. Actually you are part of the spoils of this mission. Zarnan has already shown interest in your fate. Our lady goddess has many forms and he is the foremost of her servitors. You might be given to him or perhaps service in the temple of snakes would be to your liking. Then there are the love temples where men visit the slaves regularly. Need I continue?"

"You have no right to take me prisoner!" The words blazed out at him before she could stop herself.

"You mistake me. I did not speak of prisoners. You are property just as that chest of jewels yonder or those coffers of robes."

Lia's palm started upward but she caught the gesture just as his hand went toward the jeweled dagger thrust into his loincloth. His expression did not alter but she felt the coiled fury of him. What madness was this? She should try to conciliate him rather than give way to the pain and anger within her heart.

"That was wise of you to check yourself. I think you will have much to learn of the ways of civilization. But we waste time! Are you now ready to tell me the truth of your presence on Pandos? It will go far better for you if you are reasonable, you know. A word to the king will ensure a comfortable slavery for you." His mouth quirked upward but his brilliant eyes were still flat and cold.

"I can only tell you the truth, Lord Commander, and I will do that right willingly. There is no need for threats or coercion." She guessed that he was a man tightly reined, one who had mastered himself early and remained in control at all times, showing little emotion. She could not doubt that he would give her up to one of the fates he had mentioned without the slightest qualm.

"I will listen. Beware that you do not lie to me." He sat down on a small chest and waved her to another. His gaze did not leave her face.

"Surely you will know truth when you hear it." She looked straight at him as she spoke.

He leaned over and caught her wrist, the fingers digging hard into the flesh. They were so close that she caught the scent of sandalwood and saw the curve of his long dark lashes. His touch burned her skin as a pulse hammered in his throat and his teeth gleamed white through the sensual lips. The air was suddenly stifling. Lia felt the blood begin to roar in her head and she wanted to be even closer to him. Time faded; there was no reality but this man.

He spoke softly. "Truth is not in woman, lady. Speak and I will judge. You may hope that what you say pleases me."

Chapter Three

BOND OF BLOOD

"I KNOW THAT your time is short even as you have said, Lord Commander, but I ask that you hear me out." Lia's mouth was dry as she murmured the words. Behind the rising torrent of her feelings she was half aware that he might actually believe her story if she were careful in the telling of it.

His free hand went to her face and drifted lightly down the side of her left cheek. A shiver began in her body as he cupped her chin. She leaned toward him slightly and saw the dark face change imperceptibly.

"Why not? Surely there is time for easement." He spoke as if to himself, then reached for the clasp on the shoulder of her robe.

"No!" Lia jerked back suddenly, Ourda's crumpled body a flaming memory in her mind.

Incredulity washed over the lord commander's face as his hands dropped away. "You say no to me! You will not say it again!" He towered over her, his eyes now dark and menacing.

Lia faced him without shrinking despite the fact that she knew any chance of softening him was gone. She was now only an obdurate captive to be handled sternly. He would take her, of course, but there would be no yielding in it. She would resist in the only way she could.

There was a hammering at the door just then and a hoarse voice called out in Minoan, the language of Crete, which Lia had once studied with Medo, and the language of the

16

mainland. She could understand a little of it. "Come, Commander, hurry! The pirate!" The rest was unintelligible.

Paon shouted, "I am coming!" Lia was forgotten as he caught up another dagger and a sword, jerked a leather garment around his upper body and started for the door. His face was suddenly younger in his eagerness for the battle. He turned back to her after calling out again to the man.

"Zarnan will deal with you. For now, however, you shall remain locked in here." His voice was brisk and impatient.

"Wait!" She hated that she must plead but the priest was evil's very self; all her instincts told her that. "I can tell . . ."

"It is far past that." He whirled and was gone through the instantly slammed door. She could hear his orders given and felt the quick movement of the ship as it was brought about. A bolt was thrust home on the outside of the door and footsteps moved away.

Lia resisted the impulse to throw something in the direction of her departed captor and began to look about the room for a means of escape. She had no illusions as to how she would fare in a battle. If the pirates saw her they would regard her as plunder; the Cretan meant to give her as a bauble to his king at best. Zarnan's huge eyes flashed in front of her as she recalled Paon's last command. Any other fate would be preferable to him!

She looked at the clutter in the chamber almost blindly as she tried to master the fear that welled up every time she thought of Zarnan. Chests, robes, vases, loose jewels, coffers of scrolls, some heavy weapons, a long roll of some iridescent material and several ornate jars stood along the walls. A raised pallet close by was piled with cushions and a scroll lay open on it. The candle in its horn holder was long since burned out.

Lia crossed to the chest where Paon had been examing the map and spread out the scroll, remembering as she did so that one of Medo's greatest treasures had been the map he obtained long ago in Egypt. She had traced his journeys with him and longed to make them herself one day. Now she unrolled this one as far as it would go and saw Egypt, the outline of mountains, desert, on to the two rivers that fed a fertile civilization and the shape of another great land beyond it. In the other direction she saw that the sea stretched endlessly beyond some great rocks with only the hint of a land mass. She could not interpret the symbols written here. The map was plainly unfinished and she wondered if the lord commander himself worked on it or if the ship carried a scribe. It might be that Naris filled such a function.

A current of cool air touched her face just then and she glanced upward to see a woven brown cover standing clear from the upper part of one wall in the freshening wind. She had to stand on a chest to reach the opening, which was a hole cut for air and light, done apparently as an afterthought, perhaps when the ship was already at sea. With quickening excitement Lia saw that it was just possibly large enough to permit a slender body to slide through and drop to the deck below. But what good would that do? She must get off the ship itself.

The low hum of voices drifted to her and she heard the rattle of swords as someone gave an order. Several words stood out. "Goddess! Snake!" A chill seemed to hang in the air, causing Lia to wonder if their goddess, whoever she might be, had arrived to carry the Cretans into battle. Her glance went to the cloud-obscured moon and down to the nearly calm sea. A dark mass loomed on the near horizon and, even closer, she saw a clefted mass of rock thrusting up. It told of the closeness of the mainland, for she recalled it from Medo's map and from the several journeys she had made with him in the early days of their exile.

"Ship!" The cry came quickly and was silenced almost immediately. Lia was grateful that she could recollect even a few words of the Minoan language, for they were doing her good service now. She heard the stroking of the paddles as their own ship slipped along. They were stalking the prey. Her thoughts went to Paon almost inadvertently; he would be enjoying the chase.

She jumped down and went to one of the chests of treasure, going through it rapidly. There was little time for choice. Several milky pearls, two green stones, one large clear one, a huge red one and a smaller pink oval were crammed into a corner of her skirt which was then brought high and tied securely to leave her legs free. She ran to the pallet and tossed the covers about as she thrust both hands up under them. That search yielded two daggers and a long sword. She smiled to herself. The lord commander slept lightly indeed. Did he fear his own men? She put the smaller of the daggers, black-handled, with a curving polished blade, into her waistband and returned to the opening in the wall.

She could barely hear the slap of the paddles; there was no sound or movement from the men, only silence. The land seemed even closer now and she could smell the freshness. The chance must be taken. She took a deep breath, put both hands to the rough wood and pulled herself up. Her knees were scraped, her palms wet, as she teetered there in full view for an endless moment before dropping to the floor below with a thud that rang in her ears. Backing swiftly into the shadows, Lia edged toward the entrance of the lower deck.

Time seemed to stop as she stood poised, waiting. Discovery could come in the next instant and she knew that she would not so easily win free again. She darted down the small incline of steps, around some coiled ropes and past another stack of weapons, to sink flat on the far edge of the deck. Her palms were raised to lift her upward and her legs were tensed. The drumming of her heart rang in her ears.

Someone called out an urgent word and was answered with a command Lia could not understand. She heard the shuffle of sandals as another man took up the first word. When she twisted her head to the side in an effort to see without totally giving herself away, there was only the expanse of deck. It was growing lighter, however, for the moon was about to emerge from the cloud bank. Just as the last vestiges blew away and radiance poured toward her place of concealment, Lia half jumped, half tumbled overboard and drove downward with all her strength.

She swam underwater for as long as her breath held, trying to get as far from the ship as possible without risking tiredness. There was no way to know what she must face when the mainland was reached but at least she was free of the Cretans. "For the moment, at least." One corner of her mind gave the warning thought but she brushed it aside as the slow rise to the surface began.

Her head broke the water well behind the ship, which was drifting majestically, paddles silent. There was no sign of an alarm and she smiled with relief. When she glanced out to sea she saw another tall shadow advancing slowly; a second stood well off from that one. All had the long delicate curves of the lord commander's ship as she now observed it. But where was

the pirate ship that they were supposed to be pursuing? No
matter, she must take full advantage of this time.

She turned toward the mainland, now even more clearly
visible and began to swim steadily, hoarding her strength.
What were battles to her? She was free and that was enough.
The water was faintly warm and she could smell the odor of
distant flowers. She should be glad that all had gone so well
and yet there was the faintest regret in her that she would never
see the lord commander Paon again. Untouched as she was,
Lia wondered how it would have been to have him hold her.

Her wrist was throbbing and she lifted her hand to inspect it.
Odd, that she had not noticed it before now. Apparently she
had caught the skin on a jagged edge of wood when leaving by
the window and all her movements had opened it, for the thin
trickle of blood was readily visible even in the darkness. The
flesh wound would not hamper the striking power of her dagger
and that was all that was necessary, she thought as she allowed
herself to sink deeper in the waves and resumed her strokes.

It was only moments later that she felt powerful undulations
around her as the water pushed toward her and was thrust
outward. She scanned the area around but could see nothing
but the ships. Suddenly a powerful rushing motion almost drew
her under. Lia jerked around frantically but only the waves
were visible. She gave a few experimental strokes and kicked
out. Almost instantly she could discern the circling motion
caused by the movement of a great body drawing closer to her.

She could not repress the scream that split the air and came
again in reverberations of stark terror that drew her down into
the depths and caused her to rise spitting and coughing even as
she fumbled blindly for her pitifully small dagger. The
momentary flailing sent the creature back in an incredibly rapid
motion and the swirling waves went over her head again. This
time she went deep, holding her breath instinctively.

The huge shape passed directly above and she fancied that
she could see the gleaming teeth, blunt, heavy head and
barreling body topped with fins. A shark attracted by blood and
of a size not to be imagined. Pure panic blurred everything as
she came up and screamed again, blind to anything but the
awful death that waited just beyond the next wave.

The shark came closer and this time she saw the tall fin

rising out of the water as it appeared to contemplate her. She floated motionless, recalling all the tales of how they were attracted by movement and fear. What good would it do her now to prolong the time of being torn apart? Still, the hunger for life held her and she gripped the dagger in one hand as she fought the panic.

There was a splashing off to one side and then something sped past her head to strike the circling fish with a force that made it dive. Lia drew up her legs and pushed away from the vortex that threatened to pull her down again. As she did so she saw a man swim past her and dive downward, his short sword gleaming. Her head turned and she saw the small round boat bobbing a short distance away. Two figures were standing up in it, spears brandished. One of them called to her but she could not understand the words. The meaning was clear enough; the Cretan ship had turned and was now only a short distance away. Another small boat was making its way toward them and she saw the lifted spears.

A wave of relief came over her so sharply that she began to tremble and could barely stay afloat. Captivity, slavery, servitude, all were better than such a death. She began to swim toward the ship and was drawn back by the furious battle that raged with the shark. The men began to shout, and as the brute surfaced a spear slammed into its side. The man who come so boldly into battle was wielding his sword and the water gleamed with blood. She saw his face clearly despite the streaming hair and gore. It was Paon.

The shark bore down on him now, mouth agape, and he could not turn fast enough. Lia saw that one shoulder seemed torn; there was no way he could avoid the onslaught. She lunged at him with all the strength born of desperation and years of outdoor living. She caught him around the hips and they went deep into the underwater chill, clinging together, still holding their weapons, united in this struggle for survival. She felt his free hand on her arm and the clasp was one of recognition. Warmth pervaded her being even at this time when death was in their faces.

Even this deep the struggle could be felt from the surface. Paon shifted his sword to the other good hand and pulled her upward with him while the water swirled and foamed in the throes of what they could only hope was death for their

attacker. As they reached the blessed air and drew deep breaths
Lia saw that the shark bristled with spears on one side. It tossed
heavily in the swells and lashed about but it was dying. The
huge body was bigger than the small boats taken all together
and the evil teeth shone through trickling blood. The shadow of
the Cretan ship fell across them in the fading moonlight and the
cries of Paon's men resounded in their ears.

They swam toward the nearest boat and eager hands reached
down to pull them up. Lia looked at him and saw that his
shoulder still bled and that there was a long gash on his face.
His white teeth flashed in a half grin that was part salute and
she answered it with a smile. They two might have been alone
in that scene of carnage.

"I have cause to thank you, Lia of Pandos."

"As I thank the lord commander."

Over the formal words that did not seem out of place, Lia
read the message of his eyes and silently gave answer.

Chapter Four

THE AWAKENING

WARM FIRM LIPS caressed Lia's face lightly and touched her mouth gently. Fingers played in her hair and a low voice spoke of journeys they would make together into distant lands. She stretched one hand up to reach the unseen face and draw it down to hers. The sense of pleasure faded as she reached out and then she was alone in the chilling dusk. Great rocks rose on all sides of her and she knew that something fearful waited just beyond.

Lia sat upright with a gasp, every nerve alert to the danger. She saw the now-familiar cabin that was Paon's, the open window through which she had slipped, heard the emphatic tread of guards as they went back and forth and felt the softness of the pallet beneath her. The sense of nightmare faded as she expelled her breath softly. She looked down at her body, scantily clad in a soft golden robe, and examined it for wounds. Except for some scratches, a few bruises and several cuts, she appeared to be whole. The stiffness would fade as she began to move about.

Paon had said nothing else to her after their rescue but had devoted his attention to giving orders to his men in such rapid Minoan that she could not follow. She had been escorted to his cabin again, food and wine brought along with salve for her skin. The guards had been posted and the way to escape totally barred. Then she had not cared; exhaustion had taken its toll.

She had caught up the first soft garment to hand, drunk some of the heady brew and tumbled down into oblivion.

Now she rose and stretched lazily. Nothing had been accomplished, her plans lay in shreds and she was still captive. But she was alive and would see the loveliness of the days, feel the wind on her face, know joy, pleasure and pain. If it had not been for Paon she would have died hideously, victim of her own lack of caution. Who would have expected so huge a shark in these waters? Relief swept over her and she stretched again, enjoying the pull of her muscles against each other.

"You seem quite recovered."

The deep voice spoke just behind her and Lia whirled, holding the brief robe together over her nakedness, suddenly conscious of her unbound hair spilling over her shoulders and her face flushed with the heaviness of sleep. Paon stood there in the half-open doorway, sun glinting on the black hair and bronzed skin. He wore only a loincloth of white and his injured shoulder was wrapped in a gauzy cloth. The wound on the left side of his face was a thin red line and already closing. He looked at her and the dark brows winged upward in query as the rest of his face remained closed and still. His eyes were even more brilliant, holding as they did an emotion that she could not read.

His presence shook her and she felt her blood begin to course more warmly. Lia knew instinctively that she stood on the brink of a thing so new and strange as to alter all her life. One glance from this cold, assured Cretan stirred her senses, making her remember love tales she had read and yearnings that came to her in the nights. She had vowed to possess herself alone, belonging neither to man nor gods, and now she felt only the power of what lay between Paon and her once-inviolate self.

"I am much better, sir. How is it with you?" He must not guess her feelings; that would be humiliation in truth.

"I?" He folded both arms across his broad chest and surveyed her without moving. "Oh, splendidly if you consider the fact that the pirates have escaped without a clue as to their destination and that I must now return to Crete with my mission unaccomplished. Other than that, quite well."

"But all this?" Lia waved at the contents of the room. "Surely your king will welcome treasure?" She had the feeling that they sparred on several levels and her skin began to prickle.

His voice was harsh. "I was sent to find and harry the pirates, to bring them back as prisoners, to rid the sea of them. Spoils and excuses will not suffice. So great Minos bade me." He stepped closer to her and his words scorched the air between them. "My man of keen sight spotted the pirate ships, two of them and almost certainly Red Bor's, on the horizon as I spoke with you earlier. They were hidden in the secret coves of Pandos and, had you been less obdurate, we might have had them. Now they have escaped again and my time for search has come to an end!"

"How many times must I tell you that I know nothing of Red Bor! You are obsessed with him!"

Paon caught her arms in both hands, his grip causing her flesh to ache. That corner of his mouth lifted and his eyes glittered down into hers. "Obsessed! You would call it that. You who are of them! Perhaps you were left behind to deflect us? Does your master think that your charms would hold back all the forces of Minos? Surely he knows that I cannot be influenced—he who has the best reason to know my hatred!" His face paled as the blood drained away; the brilliant eyes were suddenly flat and glaring. "And the old woman was slain by his men to make you all the more appealing, was she not? Did you watch? Did you relish your role?" He began to shake her as he spoke.

Lia felt her fear begin to rise. He sounded as though madness touched him. Somehow she knew that he walked in another time and faced another adversary. Just so had Medo, her father, looked when he spoke of those who would have slain them or when his guard fell and he remembered her lost mother. Pity flickered in her even as she tried to pull away.

"I do not know what you are talking about! I am grateful that you helped to save me from the shark but what right have you to hold me prisoner and take me from my home? Go about your business, Cretan, I am none of it!"

He pulled her roughly toward him. She resisted and the robe fell open so that her breasts were exposed. Anger was open between them but another thing lay beneath it, waiting to be ignited. One hand rubbed across her nipples almost casually but Lia felt the trail of fire. His manhood stirred against her and his face grew purposeful.

"My appetite must be slaked. Then you go to Zarnan."

Lia fought as he pushed her toward the pallet but it was no use; he tossed her down as though she were a cloak. He pulled the loincloth away and stood above her as if he were already master. His manhood was long and powerful, pink-tipped, hard. His lean waist tapered into long powerful legs and slim hips, all darkened by the sun. His muscles were ridged and strong. A taunting smile was set on his lips as he surveyed his prey.

Lia braced herself for battle but a warning rang in her mind. He wanted her to fight him so that he might savagely subdue her. She could not have explained how she knew this but she was certain of it. She forced herself to lie quietly under that mocking gaze even though every instinct demanded that she rebel. Memories of the fearful fate of Ourda lashed at her. This man might be no different and he believed that he had reason for his treatment of her.

Paon looked at the spill of golden hair, the defiance in the amber-green eyes, the smooth curves of the slender body and the lushness of her rounded breasts. Her oval face with the high cheekbones and arched brows swam before him and his hunger fought with anger. Lia knew his thoughts and almost wished herself old and wizened. Yet age and weight had not helped Ourda. A woman walked in peril by very virtue of her sex, it seemed. There was no doubt in her mind that he meant to rape her whether she fought or yielded. "Survive!" The word rang in her mind as she lay bare to him.

Paon sank down beside her and gathered her unresisting body to his. She wanted to shut her eyes but dared not. His mouth ground down onto hers and his tongue thrust past her teeth as he settled his weight firmly on her. He put one hand in her hair and the other cupped her face as he drank of her mouth. She held her arms rigid at her sides. Her body he might have but her spirit was her own.

He looked directly into her eyes as he made free with her flesh. Lia allowed all the fury that she felt to show there but it was no deterrent. He would have her and bend her to his will. She thought of the warmth he had first stirred in her and the gentle kisses of her dream before it became nightmare. Pain licked at her for a thing she had never known. Now, if she lived, there would always be the memory of this rape that was her first encounter with the power of the body.

Paon's face was grim as he released her mouth and moved his hands down over her hips. An instant later he was thrusting the whole long length of himself into her tightness. Lia remembered the way Ourda was splayed on the beach and if this was to be her fate also. He was pushing again at her now as he lifted her to meet his demand. Her body stiffened against the interloper and her hands came up to repel him in the same instant that he sank so deeply into her that she thought she would split open. He remained in her for only a moment but, over the pain and shock, Lia felt a slight answering push, a beginning excitement. He withdrew and turned on his side. She fought the feeling back and curled into a tiny ball. There was a smearing of blood on the pallet, the blood of the virgin.

There was a strange ache in her loins and the tips of her breasts began to burn. She wanted to put her hands to them, to touch the obdurate back facing her, to stroke the long smoothness of it, even feel the length of him near her once more. He had raped her and would take her prisoner to Crete where she would face an unbearable fate if all he hinted of Zarnan were true. She must fight against any further feelings for Paon; he was the enemy. Had he not just proven that?

"You were virgin." Paon sat up and looked at her, his glance half rueful as it went from her face to the blood on the pallet. "By the immortal goddess, how was it that you were not taken? I know of no pirate, least of all Red Bor, who would not take such a morsel." His puzzlement made him seem far more human and his anger appeared to have vanished.

Lia pulled some of her hair forward so that her nudity was at least partially concealed. This was not the time to mourn over her lost virginity or cry out angrily at his slighting words. She must do the best she could while he was disarmed toward her. Revenge could wait. Somehow he must be prevailed upon not to give her to Zarnan; she had no illusions about him releasing her.

"Lia." His voice was gentler than she had ever heard it. "I thought you used by those I hate and despise. I did not mean to hurt you."

The words trailed away as she looked up at him. It took little effort on her part to allow tears to film her eyes, although she would not shed them. She forced herself to blank out the contradictory feelings she had toward him and her chin was high as she spoke. "I was reared as carefully as any lady of Crete, Lord Commander. The circumstances were vastly different, I know, but the intent was the same. Do the Cretans maim and kill and pleasure themselves as they wish? Twice now I and mine have suffered at your hands and it is not ended."

He rose, drew on a thin robe, handed one to her and poured wine for them both. Then he sat cross-legged before her. His face was impassive but the hardness of his manner was muted. "Drink the wine. It will revive you." When she obeyed, he continued. "Listen to me. I have spoken with those who returned from patrolling the beach. Two were high on the crags in search of any other inhabitants of the island when you arrived. The other two were with the body of the woman. They came upon her unexpectedly and frightened her. It seems that she fell dead before them. She was not harmed by my men. They buried her later, just as they buried their comrade whom you killed. Neither spirit will wail from the netherworld."

"They lie! Do you think I would not have known if Ourda were ill? It was murder, I tell you!" The passionate words burst out before she could stop them. She seemed fated to anger him further. Why was she not able to be conciliatory even in this time when her need was desperate? "I saw them standing over her! It was obviously murder!"

Paon's eyes went dark. His voice was drained and cold as he spoke. "You cannot believe the truth but it is so. Long ago some of those close to me perished in flame and there was nothing to bury. Treachery, yes, and out of a fair face. They haunt me!" He jerked out of his reverie and looked at her shocked face. "She is decently buried. Let that be an end to it! Now, it is death to slay a soldier of Crete. I wonder that you had the ability to do the deed."

Lia met his speculative gaze without flinching. She was thankful beyond the telling that Ourda was covered by the sands of Pandos but she did not believe Paon. What did it matter? Nothing could bring back her companion of the years.

"I will avenge you." The resolve of blood rang in her mind as her jaw tightened.

Paon said softly, "I spoke the truth." His hand touched her cheek and drifted, feather-gentle, down her neck.

Lia leaned slightly toward him, wondering that he could be so gentle when just recently he had pinned her to his will. A strange, confusing man, this lord commander. She felt her face begin to flush and a tingling began in her nipples. It was growing hard for her to breathe as her skin prickled.

"Will you have me now, Lia? The choice is yours to make." He was so close that his warm breath stirred the soft hair at the nape of her neck.

Refuse him, draw back and coldly demand her freedom? The thought lingered insanely in her mind even though she knew the foolishness of such a course. A captive could only submit and wait for the time to strike. Her tongue touched her upper lip and her whisper was hardly discernible. "Yes. Yes." She knew then that she wanted him with a hunger that could only grow.

Paon turned her to him and set his mouth on hers. Their tongues joined, probed, thrust. She put her arms around him and yielded to the fire that was sweeping over her. She could not think; only feeling remained and it was all-surpassing. He devoured her and she drowned in him. Once she looked at him and saw that his eyes were almost black with passion but his face still appeared shuttered and apart. Then he lowered his mouth to her swollen nipples, flicking his tongue over them until she wanted to scream with the anticipation that heightened into delicious agony. Finally he set his teeth very gently to one and drew the fire upward as Lia arched to meet it.

Paon guided her hand to his stalk and closed it there. The pulsations from it reminded her of the burning ache from her own womanhood and she rubbed it gently, slowly as his mouth locked onto hers again in a heat that melted her against him. They moved together in a rhythm that reminded Lia of the sea swells.

Then they were lying full-length on the pallet, their hands moving over each other, voices murmuring little sounds of query and delight. Lia felt the big body swing up over hers, hesitate and move downward. This time, however, her hips rose instinctively to meet him and his shaft went deeply into

the wet warmth of her. There was pain this time, too, but it was
like nothing she had ever imagined. It was yearning and near
satisfaction, savagery and sweetness. He drew out of her
slowly and she arched, reluctant to let him go. Then he came
down again and this time they merged together from head to
toe, kissing and fused.

Then Lia felt her body begin to pulsate as Paon thrust
upward, back and upward again. His shaft seemed to pierce her
very heart and she felt herself widen to accommodate him. His
mouth drew again on her breasts and his hot breath burned in
her ears. He was everywhere in her and outside of her. Her hips
were writhing now and the fire was reaching outward. Her
arms wrapped around his muscular smoothness and her voice
spoke his name a long way off.

He sat up and pulled her to face him so that they sat joined in
the flesh. Her hands were on his shoulders and his mouth laved
her stomach and breasts with slow hot kisses that never reached
her mouth. Lia felt the tightness in her begin to loosen as the
wave and the fire began to join. Every inch of her flesh moved
in response to his and she felt him blaze inside her.

"Now! I cannot bear this!" The words rushed out of her.

"You can! You can!" He put his lips on hers to silence the
cry and their tongues fused as they moved upward.

Lia was beyond thought or conscious caring. All that
mattered was that his pumping and thrusting should not stop,
that her writhing body should hold him inside and give her
surcease from the engulfing passion. She lifted suddenly as his
longest stroke tore into the very core of her being. Her heels
hammered on the floor and her hands clutched his back with a
power that could bruise. She felt him go hard and still, then his
power flowed loose inside her. In that same breath she rose to
her own crest, held and lingered, then let go into the melding
of flame and wave, glory and light.

She felt the scald of tears on her eyelids and felt his lips
touch them. Her arms went around him as he drew her close. In
the last instant before sleep took her, Lia felt him kiss her hair
and run his fingers through it. Just so had the lover of her
dream done. She did not try to recall the end of that dream—
this was delight enough.

Chapter Five

PASSION'S GOAD

LIA AND PAON, surfeited, slept long. When she woke, it was to his kisses. There were no words for them, only feelings, as both reveled in the long, slow summoning of the fierce fire that burned between them. Paon led her gently to the heights, holding back until she could join him. Her breasts ached for his sure fingers and her mouth molded itself to his. It seemed to her that she could never get enough of this man and that frightened her even as it exhilarated her senses. It was even more exciting to see the way he responded to her touch, the way he grew long and powerful as her fingers drifted downward, the intensity of his eyes as she played her tongue in the open palm of his hand, the hammering vessel in his temple when she moved closer to him. This was all power and they held it over each other in this time-enchanted time of learning and giving.

When the light outside the square of window grew hazy, Paon left her briefly to call for food, water for washing and wine. These were set just inside the door and he brought them to her with his own hands. As they ate cheese, oat cakes and drank the rich, spicy wine Lia felt the beginning soreness in her loins and smiled to herself. How strange that she had ever wondered about love. What more could two people need?

"You might be the very love goddess herself as you smile so enigmatically. Will the goddess deign to tell her humble supplicant what he may do to gain her favor?" Paon, naked,

31

brought the water closer and knelt to look up at her. He was smiling, his face open and gentle, the wariness gone.

Lia laughed out loud and put both hands on the strong arms. "I do not know about the goddesses of Crete but this mortal asks that you wash her back."

"Do the goddesses not sometimes take mortal form? I hasten to do your bidding." He kissed her wrist and she felt the pulse jump there.

Lia wanted then to speak of the future and what it would hold. She wanted to tell him about herself and to know everything there was to know about him. Something warned her to take this time for what it offered and not to question.

"Sit." He indicated the little tub which was nearly filled with fresh cool water. She obeyed and he tipped a fragrant solution into it, which rose up headily. "It is Egyptian; some say Isis herself gave it to mortals."

"And now you give it to me." She dipped her hands in the water and let it trickle over her breasts as he watched. "My back awaits, Lord Commander."

He rubbed her back slowly, lingeringly, his breath stirring her hair. His lips touched her spine and ran a trail of kisses along it until her buttocks were reached. Then his hands went around to her womanhood and began to rub gently. She arched backward, already feeling the fire begin to build. He put seeking lips on hers and their mouths joined. They twisted together and the tub rocked as Paon slipped in some of the fragrance that had been spilled.

He sat down abruptly and they broke apart. Lia began to laugh at the scowl on his face. She dipped down in the scented water and shook with the force of her amusement that was somehow release from the drugged passion of all the hours. Paon looked at her, grinned and reached down in one swift motion to pull her dripping from the little tub. She kicked and made mock struggle but he held her firmly before collapsing on the pallet with her.

"Kiss me and I will let you return to your bath." His tongue tickled her ear as he spoke and his fingers were lazily encircling her already-engorged nipple.

"It is your turn at the bath." She gave him a saucy smile and tried to wriggle free. Her hands sought his stalk and began to move on it. "Are you not ready for the soothing coolness that it offers?"

"Only you, Lia. Only you." The words were not spoken lightly for the laughter left his face and his eyes grew dark. She felt that he did not really speak to her but to a nebulous thing beyond them both. Quickly she said, "I will not kiss you. What is the forfeit?" A foolish game, she thought, and yet they shared laughter as well as passion.

"This." He pushed her back so that she lay flat, then lowered his body beside her and began to trail kisses up and down the length of hers. Little chills ran over her, yet it seemed that the very blood would burn out of her skin. She reached out to caress him but he drew back. "Later. I will show you." He set his mouth to her nipple and drew on it softly at first and then so urgently that she began to shudder with the force of her hunger. He put his whole hand firmly on her cleft and began to massage it while he watched her face. She began to burn and ache as she tossed back under the sustained, loving assault of those all-knowing hands and mouth. Paon smiled and waited.

His hand shifted and his mouth took its place in one smooth motion. Lia twisted away in sudden fright but he held her steady while his tongue tantalized. She was coming alive in a new and different way. This was as if she came into flower, opening in the richness of sunlight from bud to fullness. His tongue went deeper; his lips folded over her and she came out into openess, then floated on a sea of contentment. Lassitude took them both suddenly. Lia's last conscious thought was wonder that Paon did not remain close to her as they drifted into sleep.

It was pale gray light in the cabin when she woke. Paon lay apart, arms pillowed behind his head, powerful body relaxed under the thin coverlet pulled across him. His face was grave, almost stern, and his eyes were watchful. Lia shifted her position and saw that he had covered her nudity with one of the robes. She sat up and met his gaze, wariness coiling in her even as she thought of the pleasures of the night just past. What had happened to change him?

"Tell me how you came to Pandos, Lia. Tell me of your life here. I would know about you." His mouth curved upward and the words were gentle but his tension was obvious.

"Now?" She wanted to touch him, to feel his kisses soft on

her face and know the closeness of their flesh, perhaps begin to
know him beyond their mutual hungers of the body. For all his
soft tones she knew that he commanded her. This was not the
eager lover of a short time ago; this was the lord commander
confronting a prisoner with whom he had dallied. Mutinous
words sprang to her lips and were pushed back. Something told
her that he would welcome them from her.

"Now." He sat up and watched her face with those brilliant,
enigmatic eyes. "This very moment."

She would have some control of the moment, at any rate.
"As you command. But, though short, the tale is painful to
me. Let me tell it without interruption." She held up her hand
as he started to speak. "When it is done, Lord Commander,
you will know the truth."

His face darkened when she used his title but his voice was
still calm. "Speak. I shall not interrupt!" He folded his arms
over his chest and waited.

"My father, Medo, was far-traveled, learned in healing
skills, languages and ancient wisdom. He was a scoffer, a
maker of tales, a wanderer, and already in midlife when he
came to the village where the young Ze, she who would be my
mother, lived with her friend and servant, Ourda. They loved
each other instantly but her family objected and tried to wed
her to another. With Ourda's help she ran away to him; they
settled down briefly when she bore me but my earliest
memories are those of roaming." Lia went backward in time,
forgetting the dark man before her for the moment as she
recited the facts quickly before the nightmare could rise to
confront her as it had done so often in her youth. "I remember
them as beings apart, close to each other in such a way as to
shut Ourda and myself out. She died when I was six.
Childbirth. The son was born dead and Ourda blamed it on our
way of life to my father. I think we were all mad with grief. He
left me with her and went into the wilderness. She took me to a
small village where she had distant relatives and they took us in
for her sake. Some of the younger girls were trained as
servitors of their special goddess and I was one of them. Ourda
told me that my mother had been destined for her before she
chose my father."

Lia's voice thickened and Paon shifted restlessly although
his gaze never left her face. She clasped her hands before her

so that they might not shake and spoke again into the
shuddering silence.

"My father had been gone for three winters when I took part
in my first ceremony. The harvest had been bad, hunting was
poor and something had to be done. The goddess demanded
propitiation." Lia spoke shortly now, unaware that her voice
was becoming thin. The dark grove where the wind brought the
scent of blood, the death dance and the final struggles of the
young victims with whom she had laughed and gamed, the
night bird flying upward with raucous cries, and the cold
fingers of the priest as he touched her own face, the
pronouncement that in three moons the daughter of Ze would
go to meet the goddess herself—all came back with such force
that she seemed to stand there now. "I was unwilling and they
imprisoned me against all of Ourda's objections. It was an
honor, they told us. All the signs and omens continued bad and
the ceremony was to be moved up. A maiden was also to be
given to the goddess at the same time as I."

Strong arms went around Lia and drew her close. Lips
moved across her hair, touched her forehead and the side of her
neck. She felt some of the chill melt from her body but she
stood rigidly against Paon while his warmth attempted to draw
her back. He did not speak nor did he try to dissuade her from
continuing.

"My father returned while the moon was yet a sliver in the
sky. He told me later that he was very mild and meek until he
actually was given permission to see me once more as was his
right. As his servant Ourda came with him. Then he defied
them all, threatening to slay me outright rather than let me die
in that fearful sacrifice of pain and orgy which had given me
nightmares by day and night alike. The goddess would wreak
her vengeance on them, he said, particularly on the priests who
had suggested me. I remember them muttering, calling out as
they, villagers and priests alike, stood around the hut with their
torches blowing in the night wind and hungered for blood. It
seemed to me that the very face of their savage goddess was
stamped into theirs. I never knew how they allowed him to take
me, one man against so many. Ourda told me once that they
believed him mad with loss and passion, that he had sworn to
kill us both rather than live without Ze and that the goddess
could have no one who was tainted. At any rate, he held them

at bay, sending Ourda and me ahead, joining us very quickly while the villagers, many of whom I loved and with whose children I had played, howled for my blood and his."

She relaxed a little now in the arms that still surrounded her. She felt the quick beat of his heart in the broad chest and the intake of breath at her last words. It was far easier to go on now that he was not watching every expression.

There was a sudden banging at the door that made them both jump. Paon roared out something and steps retreated hurriedly. He shouted again and the silence was absolute. His voice was almost a whisper as he said, "Finish the tale, Lia, and let it be done."

She spoke now of more wanderings in the forests and one to a small city beside the sea, a period of dwelling with the fisher folk, even a short sojourn in the far village of Cithri, Medo's friend. There was no peace for him anywhere and eventually they went to the solitude of Pandos Island. There, instead of becoming closer to each other, they drew apart. Medo could not forget that his daughter had nearly died because he had not been there to protect her and Lia suffered the memories that were to haunt her forever. She clung to Ourda for a time, and when he discovered that the older woman still tried to worship the savage goddess and berated her cruelly before destroying the shrine she had secretly set up, unknown even to Lia, she was able to comfort Ourda in shared tenderness. "She taught me how to tend the house, work with herbs and plants, fashion simple garments, care for the few animals we had, the ways of the woodland. She tried to teach me as she believed my mother would have wished. All that she truly wanted was to see me wed to a man who would protect me. Had I left Pandos as she wished all this would not have happened." Lia struggled against the tears that must not be shed in front of Paon.

"And your father?" Paon's fingers moved on the tightness at the base of her skull.

"He was changed from a merry, lively wanderer into a morose and silent man. I learned writing, languages, some medical lore, much of life in the far lands and great cities that he visited but from him I knew nothing about the heart, about the things he cared for. He told me once, 'I took the sacrifice of the goddess twice over and have lived to pay for it. Look to yourself, my daughter, and do not care too well for anything.' I cannot think that death was unwelcome to him."

Little fires were igniting under her skin again as he touched her tense shoulders. She drew back slightly and looked him in the face. "But you wished to know about the pirates, Lord Commander, and here I have not obeyed you."

"Lia, believe me that it has eased you to talk. . . ." He paused when she held up her hand.

Lia did not dare tell him that she had actually seen Red Bor and some of the other pirates as they dealt with her father. Instinct told her it was far safer to know nothing of them at all and to make Paon believe this. "My father was an exile but we had to be maintained. He received some goods from them in return for treatment of wounds and the like but Ourda and I were kept hidden at such times. He was reputed to have knowledge of the future and wisdom known only to the gods. I think they feared him and he played on it. Their ships came here to the secret coves but I was forbidden to go near. When my father died suddenly, we were alone and none came until you." She did not turn away from his searching gaze; she dared not.

"Can I believe you?" Paon seemed half musing, the brilliant eyes strangely soft. "Yet you were virgin and Red Bor or any pirate would take his own sister if he fancied her. You want to be free. Where could you go? What did you think to do?"

"I am learned, as I told you. Egypt has welcomed many exiles." She would not tell him of the small hoard still buried on Pandos and she could not mention his jewels she had taken for all that they had done her no good. "Ourda knew several kinsmen who would have helped us after my father's death but they hated him while he lived. I wanted to go to Egypt."

Paon's eyebrows arched upward and he gave a short bark of laughter. "I have spent much time there, lady, and I can tell you that a fair woman is the same everywhere. Yes, the luring eyes that go elsewhere and bring down destruction! Destruction on the innocent!" His voice grew harsh as the darkness looked out of his face. "But I dealt with her, the slut!"

"Lord Commander! Are you ill?" Lia stepped closer to him as his agony seemed to spurt out at her.

"Ill? Of course not! I assume you plan to sell your flesh to best advantage in Egypt? I can tell—"

"Never!" Lia snapped out the word and started to turn from him but he caught her arm and pulled her close against him in one swift movement. "Release me!"

"I doubt that you mean that. We joined well together, Lia of Pandos, and I will say that you learn quickly. Egypt is not for you but I think I can guarantee that you will find Crete most agreeable in that respect." He lowered his head and fastened his mouth on hers.

Firmly held though she was, Lia struggled against his strength, which had seemed so comforting only moments before. His tongue thrust between her teeth and she felt his member rise between her legs. Her blood began to move more rapidly as she melted to the hunger of his hands. Gentleness was to be no part of this passage between them, for he was caressing her roughly, not caring if she responded. A chill went over her and she tried again to pull back but it was no use. Her desire faded and she went limp in his arms. He did not even notice but ground his mouth all the harder on hers.

He started to pull her down toward the pallet where they had known such pleasure but just then the door swung inward and the harsh voice broke across them in triumph and condemnation.

Chapter Six

TIME'S LONG DRAWING

"SO THIS IS how the lord commander of the fleet has taken to spending his time! Dallying with the pirate whore! I sought to approach you and found my way barred. Reviewing your maps, considering strategy, preparing reports, they said. Excuses all and I knew them for such. I, Zarnan, holy priest of our lady goddess, call you to account. You have been remiss in your duty!"

The cadaverous priest was wrapped in a long white robe and his hairless skull glittered in the sunlight that shone behind him as he stood in the doorway and stared at them. He spoke in the language of the mainland, his flat black eyes roaming over Lia as he did so. He held a shining black staff in one hand, brandishing it as he came to face them.

Paon rose in one easy motion, lifted the topmost robe from the pallet and dropped it around Lia's shoulders. She pulled it close to hide her nudity, shook her hair back and stood beside him. He did not trouble to hide his own naked body but stood easily, both hands on his hips, surveying Zarnan. A half smile played on his lips.

"You exceed your authority, priest. I command here and I only. Would you have me restrain you as is within my power?" His tone was almost conversational.

Zarnan gazed malevolently at them both. He seemed to rise even taller as he brought the staff down three times in succession, then held it like a shield between himself and

39

Paon. The pouring light seemed to dim. Someone cried out in Minoan only to be quickly silenced.

"I represént the Lady of the Snake! I am her shield and the instrument of her power! Minos has seen fit to honor your half-breed blood but I see no captive pirates; no great battles have occurred and there are no clues as to their strongholds. You have had only minor skirmishes and acquired insufficient booty. You have accomplished nothing and now you withhold this woman from me, although, by law, one who defiles the rites as she did shall suffer for it. Now you set yourself high! I shall denounce you, Paon!"

"Do as you wish when we reach Knossos." Paon seemed unaffected by the flood of anger. "My tolerance is low this day. Minos is my friend and my betrothed nears the end of her term of service to the goddess; I have served Crete well. Leave me."

Lia's head spun. His betrothed! But what had she expected, after all? He was powerful in Crete. Only let him use that influence to help her and she would ask nothing more. She lifted her eyes and looked proudly at Zarnan.

"Hirath's family is wise even if she is not. We shall see." Zarnan projected his voice then so that it became a deep-toned bell to carry over the entire ship. Lia wanted to put her hands over her ears but forced herself to remain immobile. "Our Lady of the Snake, the Great Mother Goddess of Crete, she who has dominion over life and death, earth and all the nether regions, she who is all within herself, claims this woman for the holy rites! I, Zarnan, her servant, do speak her will! Who defies it defies the goddess and imperils his life!"

"She belongs to King Minos as the spoil of war!" Paon shifted his stance and the pulse began to beat in his temple. "She is learned and adept in lore. I took her. I rescued her from the shark and I will hand her to my king. I have said it."

"You defy the goddess!" Zarnan's face was incredulous but there was satisfaction in it.

"Not the goddess but those who seek to use her for their own purposes."

At Paon's bold words there was a collective gasp of horror. Lia looked up and saw his men clustered around the door, their faces blanching in spite of the dark tans. One of the foremost men clutched his dagger as his shocked gaze went from Paon to

Zarnan. Once again Lia thought of the waiting villagers of her youth and the way they watched impassively while death was done. Who was to say that Crete was any different?

It was obvious that these two had a feud of long standing. She must save herself. Those who spoke with the tongue of the gods always had the cutting edge. A possibility of subterfuge sprang into her mind but the use of it would depend on whether Paon responded. She must try, regardless of the consequences. Zarnan was darkness and evil to her mind.

"Listen!" Lia heard her own voice ring out boldly, giving no hint of the fear she felt. Zarnan and Paon swung to face her in amazement. She lifted a hand to silence any protest. "As the lord commander has said, I am learned in many things. My dead father traveled far into many lands, even those beyond the cold seas, and saw wonders. Strange cures, walking stones, blue men, statues with eyes and hands of fire all hung with blazing jewels. He gave me knowledge as his legacy." Zarnan's face was red with fury but Paon was inscrutable as always. Lia knew that she held them for this instant only. The men were a huddled menace behind her. "He shared the secret way, the truths embodied in the ancient legends, and said those possessing such knowledge and the wisdom to use it could be among the mighty. I have sworn to speak of this only to King Minos of Crete and vowed by my own gods. I have asked the lord commander to stand as my witness."

Her challenge was flung. Would Paon take it up or would he abandon her to Zarnan as he had threatened? Whatever he thought of her it would seem that he could not pass up the opportunity to face down his tormentor. It was the barest chance she had but she could not yield without a battle.

Zarnan laughed, a high cackle that shook his whole body. "What could a woman know of the great seas and their routes? You lie, woman. Cretans are not such fools as you may think."

Sweat trickled down Lia's back but she forced herself to remain calm. If she offered the slightest hesitancy or fear, the whole gamble might be lost. "I have spoken only the truth." The words hung, cool and contained, in the air.

"The woman stands before Minos with me, there to tell her tale. She shall have her hearing; I have sworn it. The matter is closed." Paon waved Zarnan back.

Lia was dizzy with relief. He had given her some measure of

safety by his words. Doubtless his own cause was served also; he was not wholly a man who did the expedient thing.

"You opposed my presence on this voyage from the first, Paon, although all the portents showed a priest of the goddess was needful." Zarnan clipped his words out now; the flush of anger was fading to cool calculation. "You say that the woman shall speak before the king. You know very well that few can enter in to him and those few specially chosen. How is it that you consider yourself one of those? Least of all with a common captive? Further, you have sported with the property of the king, as I saw. She should have been kept inviolate." Paon started to speak but Zarnan held up an admonitory hand. "This matter will be resolved. The great goddess is not deceived by the foolishness of mortals. I shall be present when you speak with Minos and I shall present when you face the bulls of death. Be warned!"

He strode from the cabin, his staff held before him, his back stiff and straight. The watching men moved back from the door hastily and began to murmur to themselves. Lia felt the very air lighten as he vanished.

Paon called out to the men, "Get to your duties! We must make Crete as quickly as we can!" He was reaching for his loincloth and girding it about him as he spoke. His voice was firm and steady. The confrontation with Zarnan might never have happened.

"Aye, Lord Commander." One of the foremost men gave the reply and the others made mutters of agreement as they began to disperse.

Paon turned to face Lia and she saw that the cold mask was in place, the brilliant eyes hooded. The exciting lover, the tenderly passionate awakener of her senses, was gone and in his place stood the inscrutable captain who would take her to an unknown land as the spoils of battle.

"I had to say what I did. I thank you for your support, Paon. I do not know what belonging to your goddess means but if Zarnan is her foremost representative I do fear her power." Lia clutched the robe to herself and wondered why she felt bare before this man who had stirred her so strongly only a short time ago. "What will happen when we arrive in Crete?"

"Zarnan has ever been my enemy. He and his ilk seek to usurp power from Minos and try to bring down those who are

in his favor. But Minos has honored me and I serve him faithfully. I would use any method to support the true leader of
Crete. This is, of course, a small matter but Zarnan's spies are
everywhere and he has powerful allies. I wonder that he
thought me important enough to come on this journey
himself." Paon swung a dagger and belt around his lean waist,
then ran both hands through his crisp hair. "You must stay
apart now. You shall remain in this cabin and guards will be
posted. Since you seem to be a spinner of tales, look at the
scrolls and concoct one that will not shame me before the
king." His voice was brisk and matter-of-fact as he reached for
a short brown cloak.

"I do not understand. You will not come to me again?" The
words burst out before Lia could help herself and she instantly
loathed the slavish sound of them.

"No. Is it not enough that I protected you from Zarnan and
will see that you are safely given to the king? What else would
you have of me?" Irritation was sharp in his questions as he
faced her.

Pride burned in Lia and lifted her head high. She drew
herself up and folded her arms. "I would have my freedom,
Lord Commander. Cretan struggles are of no interest to me.
You do me no favors, I believe. Zarnan is, as you say, your
sworn enemy. Any gain against him is to your advantage as
well. But he seems to hold a personal thing with you. What is
that, I wonder?" Hurt made her want to lash out at him, at the
very least to prick a response from that icy exterior.

He laughed but there was no amusement in it. "I do not
discuss personal matters. Let it be, I warn you. Further, you
were virgin when you came to me; if I had known that I would
never have touched you. None should know that you were so.
It would be the misfortune of both of us. Far more so for you
than for me, inasmuch as virgins or near virgins are highly
prized in the temples of the Lady of the Snake. I must go now.
Do as I have bidden you and examine the scrolls."

"Paon!" His name was torn from her. The cool, dismissing
voice stabbed at her heart even as she sought composure. "I
did not mean . . ."

"I bid you good day, Lia of Pandos." He touched his hand
briefly to his head and was gone, the door slamming behind
him.

Tears brimmed in Lia's eyes but she was determined not to

shed them. She had endured much and this was certainly only the beginning of a great trial. Was she to weep and wail because of a man when her very life and safety might depend on the artful concoction of a suitable tale to tell a powerful ruler? She dashed the tears back, trying not to think of his face, warm and eager, above her in passion's initiation. Could he give and take in the manner that he had without caring at all? She knew that he could. All the tales of love and loss made that very plain. Always the woman suffered. She, Lia, would not have it. This would be her opportunity and she would use it. She had little doubt that Paon meant to use her.

She caught up the goblet from which she had drunk so long ago and hurled it at the wall. It broke with a satisfying crash that she longed to repeat. "One day you shall pay, my lord commander!" Her flesh longed for his touch even as her mind warred against his power over her. "One day!"

In an effort to distract her thoughts from her plight, Lia spent the rest of that day and the next perusing the scrolls and tablets in Paon's chests. Food and drink were brought by a silent seaman whose eyes on her were watchful. She longed for fresh air but did not deign to ask that she might go on deck. The pace of the ship seemed very slow; still she was not anxious to reach Crete.

The scrolls must belong to Paon, for they seemed unlikely booty. Some were written in the graceful hieroglyphics of Egypt, an art which Medo had once taught her. She could make out deeds of the pharaohs, judgments of the gods and armies pressing into far lands. Egypt, where one day she might live. The thought was heady and lifted her spirits. The written Minoan of the tablets and some scrolls was beyond her but the art was not. She looked for the first time upon a supple, graceful people at the harvest, sailing, in processions, at the worship of a shrouded figure she assumed to be the great goddess Zarnan represented. She saw dolphins and men sporting in the sea, a huge octopus writhing with an enormous fish, a fleet moving before a mighty city and in the distance a tall remote figure over whom the sign of a double ax was superimposed. There were reproductions of sea battles but never any on land. There was never any physical manifestation of their gods or goddesses as in the Egyptian lore. A strange people, Lia thought.

She found several smaller scrolls written in the language of the mainland at the very bottom of one of the chests. The hand inscribing them had been shaky and the words were often confusing as if the writer worked in an unfamiliar dialect. Lia was reminded of Medo's tales, for this man told of the wonders of the cities of the deserts, fierce gods and savage beasts, struggles in the sands and of kings who warred with each other to the destruction of their peoples. In a broken comment that was almost an afterthought, he added, "And I go on the cold land where the stones go down to drink. If I live, I shall see this marvel and the jeweled eyes also. . . ." There was no more. Had he gone? Had he lived? She thought of all the things she would never know and the longing for freedom rose high to mingle with wanderlust, Medo's heart in his daughter. She dreamed as she had always done but now a blue-eyed man walked beside her and by night passion laid its seal upon them. She would wake to emptiness.

On the fifth day of her confinement to the cabin Lia looked up from one of the tablets to see Naris standing just inside the doorway. His loose robe served to hide some of the ugliness of his body but his face was even more fearful than she remembered. He smiled at her and his features slid together in a twisting mass.

"It will not be long until we arrive in Crete, Lia of Pandos. You must be ready." The warm cultured voice held compassion but there was a hint of warning in it.

"You are sent by the lord commander?" In spite of herself her eyes went beyond Naris and her hopes rose.

"He sails on one of the other ships now. The transfer was done late at night. He must inspect them before our arrival. Zarnan remains on board this one and that is why you have not been permitted outside. None shall touch that which belongs to Minos. But I . . . I am Naris and I go where I will."

"I am glad that you have come." Her words were sincerely welcoming as she advanced toward him. The soft yellow robe she had put on earlier swirled around her body and her golden hair flowed free. She saw the pleasure in his eyes and fought her instinctive recoil.

"You are fair." He surveyed her coolly. "In time you might be more than that. I think you will need a friend in Crete. Ah, I know that you think to rely on the lord Paon but he will be otherwise occupied."

"Otherwise?" She could barely force the word past her stiff lips.

"Paon expects to wed the lady Hirath soon after we reach Crete. She is the daughter of a highly placed family and soon to be released from the service of the great goddess, the Lady of the Snake. Such a marriage would greatly enhance Paon's standing at court. He has endured much, you know. Battles in far lands, exile and the loss of everyone close to him. But we speak of now! King Minos ordered the marriage for Paon and naturally her family had to accept it, but they are bitter. The lady herself has many ideas." Naris grinned at Lia as he waited for her reactions.

"It seems that his future is well assured." Her pride rebelled that Naris should think her so transparent. "But what is that to do with me?" The pain ran deep, for she knew that a fierce attraction lay between herself and Paon.

Chapter Seven

WHOM THE GREAT GODDESS HAS TAKEN

NARIS NODDED AS if in approval. Then he paused and drew a small cup from his robe. A stoppered flask followed and he refreshed himself after glancing at Lia, who shook her head. She dared not risk the possible clouding of her senses.

"Sometime I will tell you Paon's history. For now I will simply say that life in Crete is often turbulent. Not very long ago there was an attempt on the life of Minos and Paon was instrumental in warning him. Hirath's service was shortened because of the intervention of the king and there are those who say, Zarnan foremost, that the goddess is greatly angered."

"What do you want of me, Naris?" She took the attack boldly to him and was conscious of the fact that this appeared to please him. It was almost certain that he meant to manipulate her but perhaps he did intend to befriend her. She could only wait and learn what she could.

"There are many plots, for Minos has no heirs—his seed does not hold. Some are mounted against his friends, Paon especially, for he is partially Egyptian and came to Crete only some eight or ten seasons ago. Zarnan hates him and would do anything to bring him down. His is a brutal nature. He wishes to give Hirath to Minos; he is confident that the heir would come from their mating and would have the blessing of the Lady of the Snake since Hirath is her priestess. If Paon should lose the support of Minos, he would die before the bulls. Such is the law of Crete."

Lia stared deeply into the dark eyes. Such was his power that she was already forgetting the hideousness of his outward appearance. "I still do not understand why you have told me all this."

"Then I will be blunt." The man who spoke now was one of authority and determination, a schemer in a cause as yet unknown. "Paon is aware of Zarnan's intentions. It is very likely that you will indeed be summoned into the presence of Minos, there to give the tale of the far land, which will amuse him even if he does not believe you. Properly gowned and jeweled, you would interest him. I have no doubt of it. None can refuse the command of Minos. The lady Hirath could not nor could her betrothed. Is it not likely that the worthy lord commander supports you for a reason? You do understand me now, Lia of Pandos?"

The cabin was suddenly stifling. The bed of the king of Crete and she newly trained to it by Paon! If he thought to use her in such a manner—she jerked her thoughts away and looked at the waiting Naris. He, too, thought it a good idea but he presented it with what seemed honesty. The memory of Paon's arms and warm lips, his power to send her into the heights and depths, came to torment her now. Had all that meant nothing to him?

She tilted her head back and let her lashes sweep down. "Then let the lord commander put the proposal to me or do you speak with his voice in this?"

He shrugged, palms out. "My voice can be many. Think on what I have said and we will speak again." The next words came in a deadly whisper. "You are not foolish enough to disregard the chance you may be offered?"

She allowed him to see that her hands trembled. Fear and confusion mingled as she said, "I am troubled and really do not know what will be expected of me. Paon called me the king's property, you know." The bitterness that flooded her voice was very real. "How can I expect to be given a choice?" Would he see through her dissimulation to the core of anger that had been building in her ever since she was taken prisoner? All her senses warned her to beware.

He grinned and all his face moved in frightfulness. "You are golden, Lia of Pandos. There are very few such in Crete. Think on what we have said."

"Golden?" She could only stare at him. Expecting confrontation, she was given inane remarks.

He made an encompassing gesture. "The sun's own brilliance is on you and the interlude with the lord commander has given you luster. Our king will be a lucky man." He went over to one of the chests and, with the ease of familiarity, rummaged until he found a loose brown cloak with a deep hood. "Put this on and come with me. I imagine you are ready for fresh air. Furthermore, there is something I want you to see."

She obeyed with alacrity and was pleased to see the approval in his eyes. The mild air was fresh and sweet; she drank it in hungrily. The corner to which he took her was deserted. They stood together as she followed his gaze skyward.

Above the billowing sail that shone softly in the fading rays of the sun, Lia saw a banner of rich golden color, which streamed out to show the figure of a woman, faceless, tall, crowned and adorned with snakes that seemed to move over her half-concealed body as the wind lifted. Zarnan, clad in the same gold, stood far ahead, arms lifted as if in supplication. A small group of men knelt at his feet. It was they who were making the low, rhythmic chant that was somehow haunting.

"Lady of the Snake, great goddess, mother of all that is!" Zarnan called out the words and they cried them out so loudly that they rang across the waters. "Bless our voyage and safe return, lady!"

Lia looked beyond to the piled clouds now touched with pink and crimson. The sea was already dark and mysterious as it rolled to meet them. Behind their ship the other two Cretan vessels hung on the horizon as though painted there. Lights flashed in the sky to the right and a low rumble sounded just as the cry of honor to the goddess went up again.

Suddenly a great bird came from nowhere, poised above them as if watching, circled and sped away toward the coming darkness. Lia felt her spine prickle. Had the great goddess come to view her worshipers? It must be so, for Zarnan was revolving slowly as he called, "She, great She! Life and Death! Great One of the Mountains, Lady of All! Look upon those of us who serve and honor you! Destroy those who do not!" Seven times he called this out and the bird hung against the clouds until he was finished. Then the chant was taken up again while he stood facing first the men before him and then the other vessels.

"She has come to us from the mountains of Crete." Naris spoke quietly at Lia's elbow. "Come, sit down quickly, and repeat the words of Minoan that I give you. We must appear to be engrossed."

"Why did you want to show me this?" She sank down as he ordered and drew part of the hood more closely over her face.

"She governs everything in Crete. Begin to learn of her, for surely she came among us this night. The ceremony is always performed when we are near our land. When the great goddess honors us in this manner, we are blessed." The rich voice rang with certainty.

The rational brain of Medo's daughter said that land was near and the bird simply foraged. A storm might be in the offing if one judged by the lights and thunder in the air. So her father had taught her to think. But Lia remembered the tales of Ourda, ritual dances, god-born children, the eager sacrifices in the dark groves of worship, the need for something beyond oneself, and she wondered. Medo had cried out for Ze on the bed of death; for him that had been enough. She, Lia, must rely on herself but she would go warily before the Cretan goddess in all her manifestations.

That night she tossed and twisted in uneasy sleep. Twice she jerked awake and came upright, heart hammering and sweat trickling down her back. She had walked down a dank pathway between walls of rock toward a great coiled shape with a flat, triangular head and a spread hood. Eyes burned through her and those eyes were those of a woman slighted, but one who held god power. Lia knew she went, not to death, but to torment beyond all knowing. She heard the laughter of Zarnan in the background.

"Only a dream." She spoke the words aloud to reassure herself, wishing as she did so that there were some god or goddess to set against this Lady of the Snake who must already feel herself profaned that she should appear so to Lia, an outlander. But there was only Saia, the dark one, from whom she had escaped long ago and who had set her seal on the family of Medo. "I go to Crete alone." She said the unbidden thought, remembering that Naris had spoken again of the goddess there on the deck in the windy dark and his belief was evident. He, too, might be her instrument. It was long before she slept and then only because she invoked her own image, Paon bending to kiss her, his face warm with tenderness as his hands cupped her face.

A clatter at the door roused her in the early morning. The ship was barely moving. The two men who entered set down basins of water, a pile of robes and cloths for washing. One said in a mixture of Minoan and the mainland language, "We come soon to Crete. Prepare yourself and call when you are done. Hurry." They looked at her curiously before they left and she wondered. Was a captive that unusual? Naris had called her "golden." This would set her apart in Crete?

There was no time for speculation. At last the pattern of the past days was to be broken. She luxuriated in the cool water though there was little enough of it, combed and polished her hair until it tumbled in a gleaming mass down her back, rubbed a cool, soothing oil that had been provided into her skin and chose the robe she would wear. It was pale green, which deepened to a darker shade at the waist and grew almost blue at the hem. A golden-threaded band of blue circled her narrow waist. The neckline was very low and she had to drape it several times before she was satisfied. She looked at the other robes for a moment—one was white, the rest pale brown and deep blue in muted shades—and knew her decision was correct. Then she braided her hair high around her head in a coronet, knowing it would frame her face and give her a serene look.

She shook out the final roll of material, soft, gauzy things to match the robes, and something clattered to the floor, causing her to jump back in surprise. It was a small, sharp dagger in a leather sheath with cords attached. How thoughtful of Naris to provide the weapon! She could not doubt that it was he who had done so and her spirits lifted. Now she looked about for sandals, saw none and decided to go up as she was. The dagger gave her a feeling of security as she girded it next to her skin and within easy reach of her hand. She was ready to face Crete. Her voice was steady as she called for them to fetch her.

The silent guard took her up to the deck, which was now lined with men. Land was close now. She saw flashing green foliage and glittering mountains set in the brilliantly blue sea that reflected back the unclouded sky. Ships were at anchor in the harbor and the roofs of the town were visible just beyond. She saw that the sails on their ship were furled. Paddlers in the golden-hued shades of the banner of the great goddess sat with ready arms. Zarnan, resplendent in golden robes and a tall jeweled headdress, stood at the prow of the barely drifting ship. There was no sign of Naris and no head turned at her coming.

There was a slap of oars as a small boat approached and Paon came on board. Zarnan went to speak to him; both men met in what seemed an equal number of paces and lifted one hand in mutual greeting. Paon wore a short tunic of deep blue with a flowing cloak of lighter material held with a clasp of blue jewels in a lily pattern. A sword and dagger were at his waist, ornamented sandals on his feet. A headband of blue leather held back his dark hair. His skin seemed all the more swarthy against the blue and his brilliant eyes gleamed as he glanced over the ship. He towered over all others, appearing a very prince with his proud stance and hawk profile. His eyes met Lia's briefly, then moved on as if nothing had ever happened between them.

The ship began to move and the guard said, "Go to stand yonder just behind the lord commander as is proper." He started to take her arm but let his hand drop when she gave him an icy look.

Lia obeyed but she kept her head high when she paused several paces away from Paon. He paid no attention to her but all her senses were alert with excitement. The ship rolled a little and she saw the muscles in his legs tense to hold his balance. Gooseflesh played over her arms and she fought back the sudden surge of desire that ran through her. Fortunate Hirath to have so bold a lover that he would dare what he had for her sake. Lia was conscious of bitter envy as she watched the wharf rise up before them.

The three ships came slowly in with a triangular pattern, the same one that they had held all those days at sea. Lia thought that surely there would be many welcomers but silence prevailed along the docks and the ships moored there. Houses, taller than she had ever seen, tumbled toward the waterfront and steep streets led away from it. When she put her hand to her eyes she could see movement far up on them. The sun was blazing hot but she felt a spreading chill begin to permeate her body.

Paon's ship touched and was made secure by his own men, who leaped out to attend to the task. He himself followed and Zarnan walked up to stand beside Lia. She was reminded of a great bird of prey and could not hide her recoil. He stretched out a bony hand and caught her wrist, making her realize again the strength in that scrawny body.

"I envy you your first look upon Crete. It will hold you as I hold you now. As will the goddess." His eyes were malevolent, but more than that, they were expectant.

Lia twisted her arm, then pulled sharply upward. The movement took him by surprise and he released her rather than press it. She took that opportunity to follow Paon's men who were now streaming after their commander. The other two ships were now gliding up as well. The eerie silence persisted and she saw the men looking apprehensively about. She was ridiculously glad to see Naris standing at the door of the cabin just then and lifted her hand to wave him down. His gaze rested briefly on her, then went on toward the silent town.

Suddenly there was the cry of an angry bull and then another. The very wharf shook with the power of them. The tramp of marching feet followed and some fifteen armed men appeared to range themselves before the returned travelers. They were shorter than Paon and much darker. Their loincloths were dark blue touched with red and they were wearing wide belts around their waists. The leader, older and dressed in the same fashion, approached Paon, who held out his arm in a gesture of greeting.

"Seesi, I am glad to see you. Where are all the people? Have we returned on a holy day?"

The newcomer did not respond to Paon's warmth. He drew himself erect and said, "Lord Commander of the Fleet, Harrier of the Pirates, Servant of Minos of Crete, hear my words. You are summoned to answer certain questions of a grave import to this land. Until these questions are answered satisfactorily your men will be detained with your woman and all the goods you carry here at the port."

"By whose authority are such orders given?" Paon's voice was very cold as he folded his arms across his chest and surveyed the leader.

"Mine, Lord Commander." Zarnan swept up beside Seesi. "Mine and the goddess who has spoken to me."

Paon ignored him. "I will speak with the king as is my right."

"No. King Minos sequesters himself in consideration of the holy mysteries and has done so this past moon. We must go, Lord Commander." Seesi drew himself up as one hand went toward his sword.

"You are right." Paon paused slightly and turned as if giving a last glance at his ships and the sea. His eyes locked with those of Lia for a moment, burning into them. "We must settle this." He strode straight ahead as the soldiers moved into step behind him.

Zarnan's triumphant laughter rose on the quiet air. Lia knew that his schemes were coming to fruition and that she could expect no mercy.

Chapter Eight

THE WAY OF GUILE

THE REASON FOR the silence of the town now became apparent. Other soldiers emerged from houses and side streets, curious people behind them craning their necks to see what was going on. A yellow litter borne by black men now advanced toward the wharf. Several bald, sturdy priests came out of the crowd and paced behind it. They wore loose golden robes and gleaming sandals; the snake emblem blazed on their chests. The soldiers kept the people back while others moved to surround Paon's crews. No opportunity for rebellion had been given. The litter was set down before Zarnan and the priests bowed with great deference. He waved one hand toward Lia, laughed again as he whispered to one of the priests, then entered and was borne away.

A soldier came toward her, others falling behind him. She drew in her breath; there was no choice but to go with them. Suddenly a small form stepped in front of her. "The woman does not go." Naris spoke with such authority that the soldier stopped in midstride.

"There are orders from Zarnan." The man, burly and sweating, was clearly unnerved by the hunchback. "I ask you to step aside."

"And there is this." The tone was quiet and deadly, unlike any Lia had ever heard from Naris. He held out his hand for the man to see. It held the tiny carved image of a snake, mouth open, in the act of devouring another snake. The exquisite

55

thing was of ivory and set with emeralds; a minuscule crown of gold rose from the head and the eyes were onyx.

The soldier paled and he glanced up at his fellows who had come closer. He forced his words slowly. "It is as you say. Will you wish escort?"

"Fetch a large litter. Hasten." Naris turned his back on them all and drew Lia apart. "All this is strange to you, I know. Do as you are told and all will be well."

She looked into the deformed face, the dark eyes, and then down at the little image he still held. "Who are you, Naris?"

He laughed. "There are many factions in the court, my dear. Let that knowledge content you for now."

"What of Paon? Will he be held captive? To whom must he answer if your ruler is not available? What does all this mean?" The questions burned in her brain and found voice before she could stop to think that it might be unwise to question too far.

Running feet caused them both to look up. A dark-curtained litter carried by several blacks approached and was halted a discreet distance away. Paon's crews had been herded off and soldiers still held the townspeople back. Ships moved gently in the blue water and far-off clouds met the horizon. Heat shimmered up from the stones at their feet and a large fish plopped just off the wharf.

"Did I not suggest that it were better you forget the lord commander, Lia? You must believe the things I tell you." His voice was almost caressing. "I daresay he will come to no danger. I have known him a long time and he has always been kind in an absentminded sort of way. Kind!" The last word was bitten off sharply and his jaw pulled to the side so that he was even more fearful to look upon than he had been at her first glimpse.

Lia went tense as she clenched her hands together in the blowing folds of the gown. She had almost gone too far. But how to retrace her steps? Naris was watching her closely and she sensed that he was enjoying her confusion. Friend he was not and never had been. Surely Paon knew his enemy. The emphasis on that one word, "kind," told her more than any previous action of Naris's. He played with her for what reason she could not yet fathom but there was hatred for Paon.

"Did you think I would not be concerned for him, Naris? He

took me as you pointed out. He is handsome and bold. I can see that the women of the court would find him desirable. I have been strictly reared although life on the mainland is . . . different." She looked down at her hands for a long moment and then lifted her eyes, still not meeting his gaze. One as learned as he would have some idea of the rituals of that area. Let him think what he would as long as it gave her breathing space. "But I say concern and that only. You have shown me that there are other possibilities in Crete. I would know of them, Naris. But Zarnan frightens me. I do not wish to fall victim to him." She let her voice tremble just a little and then grow stronger as she finally looked straight at him.

"How do I make you feel, Lia of Pandos?" She was reminded of the snake's hiss in the cabin and wondered if she blamed Zarnan unjustly.

"I am intrigued, Naris, but I fear you, too." She could speak the truth this once.

As she had suspected, he took it for the sincerest flattery. "We may yet understand each other. Go now in the litter." He beckoned and the bearers came closer.

When they set the litter down, Lia entered and leaned back against the pillows there. There was a rich fragrance about them that made her long for the fresh sea air about to be closed off from her. Intuition told her that she must dissemble if she ever expected to find the end of this coil but the savage part of her wanted to pull out the dagger and sink it deep into the heart of the man she thought had been her friend.

He touched her arm and smiled again. "Lia, I will come to you soon and we will discuss important matters. I trust that I will find you as agreeable then as you appear to be now."

Her tongue was dry in her mouth but she managed to say, "I am certain that you are most clever."

"Wise woman to admit it! Now, because you have been reasonable, I will tell you that Paon will appear before the Council of Four and representatives of the goddess, they who rule nominally while Minos retreats, there to answer charges made against him. The chief charge will amuse you once you cease to think of his skill as a lover." The knowing eyes raked her. "It concerns collusion with the pirates and impiety."

It took little effort to allow the tears to glisten in her eyes and for her mouth to tremble. Let him see her weak and fearful,

awed by his power and grateful for his protection. Let him
boast! Her time would come; meanwhile, defiance would gain
her nothing. She put her hand up to her forehead. "I am
exhausted. I cannot think; I do not want to think of anything.
Naris, let it be for now."

He did not answer and she did not dare raise her head to look
at him. He called something to the bearers in Minoan and the
litter moved smoothly off. She was not to be given the
opportunity to see anything of her surroundings for the heavy
hangings were drawn together quickly, leaving her in half-
light. Then the pace of her bearers increased so that she was
taken swiftly into the unknown.

Strain her ears as she might, Lia could hear no crowd
sounds, no cries of greeting or curiosity. She deemed it best to
be considered distraught; who knew what tales would be
carried back to Naris? She let out several sobs, waited and
released more. The slap of bare feet came to her ears and
someone spoke sharply but there was no other indication that
her supposed misery had any effect. She lay back and sighed.
She could only wait for now.

It seemed much later when the litter was set down and she
helped out by a stout, older woman dressed in red. "I am
Milte. You will rest here." She spoke in the mingling of
Minoan and the mainland language that seemed to serve these
people well. "Safe. You understand?"

Lia stood in the dusty courtyard and looked around her. The
house was several stories high, painted a curious combination
of red and white with touches of yellow. Halls branched off at
intervals and several small trees in pots stood about. Some
climbing vines covered one wall and made a cool arbor against
the heavy heat. She could hear a fountain trickling not far
away.

Milte was staring at her, a strange expression in the black
eyes. The bearers awaited their dismissal. Lia decided there
could be no better time to set her course. Better to be thought a
brainless fool and so allay their suspicions—certainly Naris
would know better—than to bring whatever fate they planned
upon her the sooner. She put her head in her hands, thought of
Medo and Ourda as well as impossible feeling she had begun to
feel for Paon, and wailed aloud.

"I remember my loved ones who walk in the netherworld!"

Over and over she repeated this while the golden hair fell forward over her face, then back as she swayed in her grief that did not lack too much of being real. "My home! Ah, the dead!" Once more she saw that gloating, almost envious look on Milte's face and wondered. Would they leave her to wail here until she was exhausted?

Milte put her arm around Lia just then and led her into the interior of the house. Behind her own pose, Lia had time to notice that it was well appointed with statues and paintings of the goddess, river and sea scenes, made comfortable with cushions, a fountain and bathing area, even a small room filled with scrolls and clay tablets. The chamber to which she was taken was spacious and airy. The sleeping area was raised and spread with brilliant cloths. Water for washing was close at hand. Chests lined the walls and she could see that they were filled with all sorts of garments, ornaments and paint for the face and body.

Milte said, "Rest. You are safe." She stared deeply into the eyes which Lia deliberately made uncomprehending and exhaled sharply. She made washing and sleeping motions, waved Lia back and went out.

Lia began to make weeping sounds as she edged close to the door. Her caution was rewarded for she heard the woman speak to someone else in Minoan.

"She weeps as the others did. Best to let her calm down or there will be much to pay."

The female voice replied, "She will be happy enough in her duties to the great one." Both laughed and went away.

Lia puzzled over the words. Had she misunderstood the use of "great one"? Minos the king or the goddess? Perhaps they meant for her to overhear. She was grateful once again for the languages Medo had taught her, especially Minoan, which was returning now through hearing it again. Her vocabulary had never been large but she could understand more than she could speak. Memory turned back for her now and she remembered the long afternoon under the breeze-tossed vines there on the craggy mountain of Pandos when her father interspersed learning with fabulous tales and so doubly taught her. She went to lie on the bed; her mind must remain in the present and she must be ready to face whatever came.

The next few days were peaceful enough. Her appetite was

tempted with various kinds of fish, olives, sweet wines, fruits and cakes. Her woman's vanity was lured by the strange, flounced skirts, bare jackets that left the breasts exposed, gauzy gowns to show the entire body, flowing thin robes and short tunics that covered little. There were exotic jewels mounted in strange patterns and ornaments of all types for the hair, neck and arms. She sifted through them while Milte and several of the slaves—all older women, very plain—watched. She would smile faintly and stare into space while her fingers moved aimlessly. Then she would go to lie down, seemingly interested in nothing.

A thin, dark young man came several times to try and teach her Minoan. One of the slaves remained with them at all times. Lia would try but her tongue slid off the syllables while her forehead creased and the dull look came. She absorbed all the words and intonations, trying them out later in the privacy of her room while she whispered. The tablets he used were placed where she might see and use them in her turn but she was careful not to give away her interest in them.

Lia knew that her time was limited. She would not be able to keep up this pretense when Naris came for her or when Zarnan exerted his power. She had no idea what she could do if ever she won free of them but at least the peril would be different. She was sick of drooping and being vague; her strong body cried out for exercise and fresh air. The move to escape must be made soon.

She had wandered around the house in an apparently aimless way and had learned that everyone rested after the noon meal. Even the guards at the gate of the courtyard nodded over their spears. Slaves and servants yawned and rested in their own cool corners. An old man, perhaps someone's relative, slept before the back stairs with his jug of wine. It appeared to be a casual household, an unremarkable one, but she had not missed the sharp eyes on her before the pose was set. Soon Naris would hear and come. Whatever the dangers of the port city, she knew she feared them less than the society that had turned on Paon who served it.

One noon, just after the hottest part of the day had been reached, Lia slipped into the sun-bleached robe she had found at the bottom of one of the chests, fastened the dagger around her waist and bound some of the white cloth torn from the skirt over her hair so that she should not stand out. So far all the Cretans she had seen were dark. Was this part of the fascination she had for them? She spared a moment to consider this and decided that it did not matter. Freedom, however perilous, was the only thing now.

Lia paused to look about. She was as ready as she would ever be. She felt the blood pound in her temples at the prospect of action. She passed one of the statues on her way to the door. The knowing, almost malevolent face of the goddess as she held her snakes aloft and the bare body in the revealing skirt both lured and repelled Lia. Perhaps she was being summoned to her service after all. And perhaps she was simply yielding to her surroundings, said the voice of Medo's rationality.

In the end it was simple beyond belief. She tied a few of the hair ornaments in a corner of the robe thinking they might be worth something in the streets. Then she slipped along the remembered corridor, down the narrow stair, across the courtyard and paused at the corner where the old man snored, his body obscuring the final few paces to the back stairs and the narrow street. He shifted position as she watched and curled closer to the wall. It must be done. He snorted and muttered as she came closer but did not wake as she stepped over him and into the shadows.

The stairs gave onto a narrow corridor and that opened narrowly into a stand of bushes that bore a fruit she did not know. The street was just beyond. It was a dusty track with a few leaning houses and several brightly colored places that were either inns or taverns; the sounds of revelry were very apparent. Several poles bearing carved bull's horns were set at intervals along the way. The odor of kicked-up dirt and the distant smell of the sea mingled with another odor that was vaguely familiar and brought a sense of longing to Lia. Then she banished it sternly and strode boldly out, a servant with a few hours all her own in which to idle about.

She felt eyes at her back, expected any moment to feel strong hands jerking her into captivity once more, heard voices calling out that the escaped prisoner must recaptured. She folded her arms across her chest and set her face in the vacant stare that had made Milte shiver and glance toward the statue of the goddess. Perhaps it would repel any who sought to come near her.

She passed several groups of men who stood talking and gesticulating but none paid the slightest attention to her. Three young women leaned on each other and laughed as a dark young man strode by, his waist nearly as narrow as their own. They were heavily painted, their full breasts covered by the thinnest of materials, rouged nipples shining in the brilliant light. Children ran past, shouting at each other, and a merchant, nearly knocked down by them as he tried to see over the high piled wares in his arms, shouted in his turn. The street grew steeper as they turned the corner and Lia went rapidly after them. The crowd was thicker here and she wondered what was happening. Where had all these people been the other day when her litter went so silently along?

A hand jerked at her arm so hard that she almost fell down. Her hand went to the dagger as she pulled backward in alarm. This time she would fight if she had to do so and regardless of what the consequences might be.

Chapter Nine

IT IS WRITTEN

"LET ME HOLD on a moment, there's a good girl. The latch of my sandal is loose." The old woman held Lia tightly while shrewd black eyes set in the wrecked face viewed her with curiosity and a certain amusement. "Always in a hurry, you young . . . no respect. I can remember . . ."

Lia wanted to laugh with relief but even more she wanted to get as far away from this area as she could. "Fix it quickly, then I must go." The crowds were buffeting them as they stood together and several sharp remarks that she could not understand were directed their way.

The old woman peered at her and shook herself as if to settle her rolls of fat into place. The dirty red gown she wore gave off a pungent odor that made Lia want to sneeze. "Help me over to the Street of the Horn. I know you are going there. Everyone is." She leaned on Lia while she jerked at the offending sandal.

"I have no time." Lia fought for the right words but her mainland accent came out strongly. A public gathering was the last thing she wanted.

"Of course you do." She put her face close to Lia's and the black hairs twitched on her chin. "You ran off from your duties this afternoon, did you not? Came to see the bulls and those handsome young men. Or is it that girls are more to your liking? In my time I've had both!" Her voice rose to a cackle as several people turned to watch them. "Do not worry. Your

63

master or mistress will be out to watch the nobility come down from Knossos. Likely you will not be beaten."

Lia opened her mouth to stem the flood of words. Apparently she was taken to be a slave or servant and that was all to the good. The woman had slipped into the mixture of Minoan and mainland speech that must be common use in the port. Before she could speak, there was the sound of cheering, blaring instruments, a high gonging thump that rose and fell and a heady lilting melody with an undercurrent of sadness.

"Make way! Make way! Do them honor on the holy path! Stand back! Back!"

The old woman caught Lia around the waist as the people surged forward, carrying them along. She felt the dagger before Lia could try to wrench away and her grasp was all the harder. Neither could turn away now and Lia sensed that it would be unwise to try. This must be some religious ceremony to judge from the cries of delight and homage that were rising just ahead. They were taken around the corner, across a smaller street and into a wider one that led to distant fields. Now they were jammed so tightly together that movement was impossible and the martial music was very close.

"What is it? Who comes?" Lia half whispered the words to the old woman for her curiosity was outweighing her caution.

A tall man wedged in beside them answered before her words were quite out. "What outland are you from, girl, that you do not know the bull leapers, they who are sacred to Minos? They dance with the bulls in the ceremony that honors our great goddess who is both life and death. They are specially selected for grace and agility. None but the king holds sway over them and even the power of the high priestess herself may not touch them."

He would have continued but a roar of sound drowned out his voice and the old woman pushed Lia forward with her bulk so that they could both see. Lia tried again to pull away but her grip was so strong that it was impossible. She could not have gone anywhere in this crush of people so she resigned herself to waiting for the moment.

Drumbeats began now and the high triumphal song was louder. Several slender young men in loincloths and young bare-breasted girls walked behind a huge black bull that wore a golden diadem on its head. A boy led it on a golden chain. An older man walked ahead of him carrying a tall double ax that gleamed both silver and gold as the sun struck it.

"Look! They bring a new bull!" the crowd called over the drumbeats, then cried homage to the grave-eyed young people who looked far ahead of them, as if they walked in other places. Now Lia saw the bull, fully as big as the first, his black hide shiny and his horns powerful. His head swung back and forth as he gave an angry bawl. Another appeared just behind him. This one was a mixture of black and gray with short wide horns and a hump on its back. A tether hung loose around its neck and a tall man bobbed up and down as he tried to reach for the end.

Lia saw the litters on the far sides of the crowd where some richly robed people stood together. Undoubtedly these were the wealthy from Knossus. She shifted her position as an elbow dug into her back. The old woman snapped out a sharp comment as the intruder pushed on. Her grip on Lia's waist slipped and she took the opportunity to jerk away, twisting between several others. She came up on the very front of the first row of people and paused to adjust the cloth concealing her hair. As she did so, she stared straight at Milte. The woman was searching, her eyes poised well over Lia's head but another motion would bring them into full contact.

Lia ducked down just as the humped bull made a partial dash for the people on the sidelines. They jumped back, some of the women screaming. This irritated the bull and he pawed at the ground, head twisting back and forth. His nostrils spread out as he released a bellow of rage. The smell of excited animal and sweat rose in the street. The man who had tried to get the tether waved at some others behind him and they moved up, prods at the ready. One of them, younger than the others, came too quickly. He slipped and fell prone in the dust. His cry of terror brought the bull's head up and the animal took a step toward him.

The people fell slowly back as women reached for their children, men for their wives. The bull leapers were far ahead as was the docile bull. The drums were silent but the song could still be heard. A woman shrieked close by and another gabbled out prayers. Lia stood as still as she could; this danger was greater than that of Milte at the moment.

The bull would charge at any instant and the toll he would

take of human life was certain to be more than that one boy now sprawled in terror as he tried not to move. Lia's mind fled back to Pandos as she remembered the several bulls and cows there, wild in her youth but domesticated at one time before their tamers had moved on. She had played at charging them, diving under them from sides, front and back, swinging on their horns, and trying to outrun them. Medo had soundly whipped her the few times he saw the games. "You fancy yourself a Cretan?" The remark had passed her by then but now she recalled it.

"The bull leapers are protected by Minos himself." The words of the man who thought her an outlander rang in her head. There was something else about the bulls and dying in front of them. Something to do with Paon. Paon. His face rose up before her and she invoked him silently.

Time bent forward suddenly as the bull took another step toward the boy. Lia threw herself forward, straight at the animal, both hands reaching for the nearest horn. She caught it and pulled downward with all the strength of her athletic body. The bull tried to toss its head and could not. Her hands started to perspire but she clung all the harder. She heard nothing, felt nothing, knew nothing except that her life depended on this next move. She was hampered by the flapping robe around her legs but it served to distract the bull as she swung under the massive head and reached for the other horn as it came down. Both hands took it, held and dropped away as she came to stand by the side of the now-enraged animal. It went by her quickly, whirled and came back for the charge.

Lia twisted backward, caught the dangling tether and threw it out. It was stronger than it looked and several of the bull tenders grasped at the end to pull it taut. The bull, checked, bellowed in frustration as other lines settled over its head. Men rushed to hold them and the crowd cried acclaim. The boy who had been saved was crying in the arms of a woman nearby.

Lia stood upright, wet with sweat, fighting to catch her breath and shaking with reaction. The sharp hooves and pointed horns had very nearly driven her into the dust. A long scratch on her arm appeared to be her only blemish but her robe was ripped so that bare flesh gleamed through. She had bound the cloth so tightly on her head that her hair was still covered and even the dagger was still in place. Her mouth was coated with dust and she longed for cooling wine.

The crowd was quiet again as it formed a circle around her and stared. She felt the curiosity and the leashed excitement that could help or hinder her. They were in awe for now but she remembered how quickly that could turn. She had wanted to be free of both Zarnan and Naris so she had risked her life on a bit of information gleaned from the tablets and a remark taken in the streets. Let the fortune that had saved her be with her now!

She scanned those close by and saw the old woman who had held her so determinedly gaping now. The thick figure of Milte was not far away and Lia saw anger on her face. A flash of gold in the sunlight told her that some of the watchers from Knossos were approaching. There was no time to lose; indeed, what did she have to lose except her life and that now seemed all the more precious.

Lia ripped the covering from her head and let the golden hair spill free over her shoulders and down her back to cover her with radiance as she shook it out. Then she raised her arms to the sky, swayed back and forth and called out in her deepest, most carrying voice, a voice that she had used in the echoes of the crags on Pandos.

"Bull leapers are sacred to King Minos! So it is written. I have done that act this day and I claim the privilege. I ask his protection. So has the goddess herself bidden me!"

She lowered her arms and stood very still. Had she protected herself sufficiently? Thoughts flamed into her mind as she stood there among the silent, staring people who backed slowly away as if in awe. Did I invoke the right thing, the wrong thing? What if they try to tear me to pieces? If I knew any other gods or goddesses I would cry out to them also. Paon, will Minos, your friend, save you?

"Lady. Lady." The high-pitched voice that addressed her in clear Minoan had apparently been doing so for some few moments. The flood of language was too rapid for her even now when she tried to concentrate on the man before her. He was thin and dark, dressed in thin robe of red and black that was emblazoned with the sign of the double ax. A headband shone with red jewels. He was obviously a person of importance and now was growing exasperated with her.

Lia held up her hand. "I can understand very little of what

you say. Would you speak more slowly?'' Let them hear the language of the mainland from her; it would be useful to conceal her knowledge of Minoan at this stage.

The personage in front of her was now being joined by several other men dressed as he was although in a lesser degree of finery. He said, ''I am Rar, once a bull leaper, now chief of the representatives between them and great Minos. You are not of them, you have the sound of an outlander and may not know that only the pure blood of Crete can serve in such a manner. Where do you come from and how did you learn even the rudiments of the skill?''

Lia's head went up. ''I do know that the foremost servant of King Minos, the Lord Commander of the Fleet of Crete, Royal Friend, the Lord Paon himself, faced the bulls in sport and for his life. He is not wholly Cretan. It was he who brought me to Crete. Together we had much to offer the king but my lord was taken away and I forced to claim of protection of King Minos.'' She spoke as loudly as she could, mingling the languages, and heard the people begin to mutter as they pressed closer. ''It is the law of Crete, Lord Rar, and has been so written. Those who risk their lives in the bull leaps and claim the privilege as I have done must be protected and heard. It is written!''

Never in her life had Lia been so thankful for her studies, both in youth and now, and for Naris's remarks. From them had come the knowledge that might give both Paon and herself the chance they needed. The bull leapers of Crete had stirred her imagination; now they seemed likely to save her life.

''Indeed, it is so written.'' A scholarly man spoke close by and his neighbor nodded emphatically.

''But few can make such a claim and be justified. I would dispute . . .'' Another voice rose in argument.

''I have known of that all my life!'' The crowd parted before the strident voice and pushings of the fat old woman in red who came up to Lia's side. ''We all know that what she says of the lord commander is true. Has he not defended Crete many times, drunk in our taverns, sought our daughters and come among us as our own for all that he is the king's own friend? Accept the girl, Rar!''

''Accept her! Accept her!'' The cry rose up and carried. Lia joined her voice to theirs. ''I claim the privilege as is my right!'' The wind caught her hair and tossed it about. She put both hands on her belt, spreading her legs wide, and looked challengingly at the official whose dark face was clouded with anger.

Rar reached out then and put both hands on her shoulders. He spoke softly and every word carried to those who waited. "Lady, you have done the feat and been protected by the goddess of life. Accept now the personal patronage of Minos, King of Crete, Favored of the Gods, Adored of the Goddess. So let it be done."

It seemed to Lia that she had been standing in this place for an eternity. Now she had won the first part of her battle and the sense of victory rose up in her intoxicatingly. She did not wish to thank the official for what was clearly her right but neither did she wish to offend him. She smiled dazzlingly at him first and then at the crowd. She saw that Milte had vanished, gone no doubt to relay the news to Naris.

"I thank you." It was obvious to them all just whom she meant and the cheers rose. Intermixed with them were cries for the lord commander and Rar put a hand under her arm.

"Come, and your woman with you. You must rest and be properly attired. I must hear your story." Those words were for the people. Under his breath he said, "It is not wise to inflame them as you have done. I suggest that you be silent."

Lia smiled. "I spoke only the truth. Should they not hear that?" He must not think her dangerous. "I did not think they understood the mainland language."

He surveyed her narrowly. "Remember what I have said. That language is common here." He waved his arm to someone in the distance and called out words she did not understand. Then he addressed the old woman. "You are her servant, I assume? Your name?"

Lia looked into the wise old eyes that were carefully blank. It was for the woman herself to say whether she went into this great adventure alone or not. She hesitated only slightly. Had she not first turned the crowd to sympathy for Lia and caused them to remember Paon? She lowered one eyelid and let the corners of her mouth turn up.

"I am Yanit, great lord. And I beg to go with my lady wherever she goes." She cast her eyes down and gave a little bow that caused the odors rising from her to reach Rar's nose.

He backed away. "Yes, of course. But you shall be instructed in cleanliness."

Yanit looked vacantly at him. "Cleanliness, lord?"

Lia wanted to laugh but did not dare. Her meeting with Yanit was likely to prove a bit of good fortune. Her spirits bounded up as she saw a laden man running toward them with another quick on his heels.

"Where do we go now, Lord Rar?"

"Do not call me that. My name will suffice." He snapped out the words, then sighed. "I really do not know what will come of all this. We go to Knossos, stronghold of Crete, seat of great Minos."

Chapter Ten

KNOSSOS

LIA SAT BACK in the litter chair, which was large enough to conceal her from sight and had gauzy curtains, firmly drawn by Rar, across the front. Weariness was taking its toll now and she was glad to relax as she sipped the tart wine and nibbled on the sweet cake she had been given. She rubbed a finger tentatively over the smooth finish of the enveloping red cloak Rar's servant had placed around her shoulders. It was far finer than anything she had ever owned, finer even than the clothes at the house where Naris had left her. She smiled to herself at the horror with which Rar had said, "Keep this around you; your appearance is really most improper." How should one look after encountering an angry bull? He had looked at Yanit with real disgust and summoned several other bearers for her chair. Lia laughed to herself at the expression on his face and wondered how long it had been since anything had been amusing.

She parted the curtains slightly and peered out. The houses of the port city had given way to open country, a smooth climbing road and trees set in ordered patterns. She saw olive groves in the distance, a wide plain of brilliant green and mountains beyond it. Far ahead of them was the last of the procession of bull leapers and music makers. The cloudless sky seemed to reflect against the shimmering earth and back to the faint mass of white, red and blue that appeared when Lia stared without blinking.

She leaned back again and tried to review her plan, such as it was. She apparently was safe from the factions represented by Zarnan and Naris and also from the bed of the Cretan ruler since bull leapers were held in such esteem. She had no desire to join their ranks but, since the stylized movements of which she had read would doubtless take a long time to learn and must be perfect for the honor of the goddess, she was likely safe enough in the training. If ever she came before Minos, with Paon or alone, to tell the concocted tale of the western waters and the far cold lands, then she would face that as well. She thought of that brilliant blue gaze, the warm knowing hands on her body, the intimacy of that last glance that they had exchanged and his almost unwilling tenderness before he had become once again the lord commander. She hoped that she had helped his cause. Perhaps she might even see him soon. Her flesh grew warm at the thought and of the high adventure on which she was now entering.

She felt the pace of the bearers quicken and this time she parted the curtains to look boldly out. They were nearing the city now, a vast one of many-storied houses that seemed to tumble over one another. She saw flat roofs, outside stairways, terraces, bright dwellings and some that might have been colored by the very sun, columns, flowering shrubs, trees and expanses of streets. People stood watching as they passed and she saw that they were generally slender and dark, dressed in glowing, bright colors, laughing and gesticulating to each other.

Beyond the people, the city and the fertile fields that surrounded it, Lia felt her gaze pulled upward to the highest rooftops of blazing color and grandeur. Surely this must be the palace of Minos. She saw the whole spill of brilliance surmounted by the huge horns shimmering white as they reached into the sky, a fitting balance for the mountain in its frame. She stared at this symbol of mighty Crete and was awed. Did the goddess and the bull rule jointly here?

She started to sink back into her cushions, wanting only to think of the pleasures of relaxation when they reached the end of the journey but she was conscious of eyes stabbing at her. She searched those lining the side of the roadway and felt the thrust again. Then she saw the tall figure in blue standing a little apart, two black men behind her. Their eyes met and locked.

The woman was slender and well formed even in the enveloping robe. Her long white neck supported a proud head of high coiled blue-black hair in which blue feathers were twined. Her posture was commanding, her chin and nose regal. The visible skin of her body was so white that it seemed lit from within. The dark brows were arching slashes over eyes that Lia was almost certain were black. "The goddess has touched her." She almost spoke the words aloud. The woman had a pure white streak as wide as a man's hand in the springing hair just off her forehead and the curls at her ears were just as white.

Lia let her eyes drift upward again to the great bullhorns; she could not continue to meet that merciless, assessing stare. Who could she be? One of the great noblewomen of Knossos out with her attendants to view the last of the procession? But that was no idle scrutiny she had given Lia.

They were turning aside now and entering a short line of trees that gave way to a tall house of gray stone still overshadowed by the mass of the palace. There were no watchers here although she saw what must be guards in the distance almost concealed by flowering plants. The litter was set down and Rar advanced toward her, smiling.

"Welcome to this outpost of the palace of our king. You will refresh yourself, rest, and one will come to talk with you. You need not be afraid."

Lia thought that his eyes flickered uneasily as he said the last sentence but she took the words at their value. "I am not. Those who have the protection of King Minos as the bull leapers do have no reason to fear."

"No, lady. That is true of the bull leapers." Again his eyes flickered and he waved toward several servants who were approaching. "These will serve you and your woman."

It seemed to Lia afterward that time and colors and relief meshed together for her so that no real detail of that evening and night stood out more than any other. She was separated from Yanit, taken to a cool room that seemed filled with a soft light where she was bathed, given a heady wine that seemed to sap at her senses and then her whole body was massaged and anointed with warm oils. She lay on soft cushions, drifting toward sleep while a low voice crooned songs in an unknown language. Paon's face bent over hers and his lips murmured endearments even as her arms strained toward him. Medo and Ourda walked in her dreams, whole and well as they once had been.

"You will sleep through yet another afternoon?"

The rasping voice pulled Lia upward, vaguely irritating her. She heard liquid pouring, the rattle of cup against cup, and moistened her lips. It made her realize how thirsty she was. She turned over on her back, opened her eyes and looked into the depths of the sea. Amazement brought her upright.

"Drink, lady. It is only water but it will freshen you." Yanit, larger than ever in a brilliant blue robe, grinned at Lia over the rim of her own cup, which apparently did not contain water.

Lia smiled faintly in return and let her gaze roam around the iridescent green walls and ceiling where dolphins sported, maidens swam and sea creatures moved on the tides. Everything was of the sea and its colors with the exception of a great bull painted in such lifelike colors that he seemed to be charging at them.

"I am glad you are here, Yanit. Can you remain or do you have family to which you must return?" Lia stretched, noticing for the first time that she had been dressed in a loose green garment that barely covered her breasts and thighs.

The old woman rose and waddled swiftly across the room to pour more liquid in her cup. Her movements were rapid and sure; her weight was no hindrance. "I've lived long by my wits and expect to continue doing so. People tended not to notice a poor hobbling creature who struggled from one corner to another. Later they wondered where their valuables went." She fixed Lia with a saucy eye. "And bits of dropped information! Always a good market for that."

Lia laughed aloud. "Have you found information here?" The question was a light one but she saw Yanit freeze.

"You're an outlander, lady, that much I know, and cannot understand how dangerous bull leaping is. To fail at it is an affront to the bull god and even the goddess." Her face was growing pale under the painted cheeks. "You will have heard, of course, that fair women are being discreetly found for our king that his loins may fertilize them. This way is not safe; you could be killed!" She put her cup down on the polished floor and came to take Lia's hand. "Go back to your lover while you still can!"

Lia's blood chilled. "Lover?"

"You called his name in your sleep. The lord commander. Did he take you briefly, many moons ago, before he sailed or did you lure him later?" Yanit sighed. "I heard what you told the crowd and that made me decide to come with you if I could. It was clever; he is popular with them but not so much at the court. Be warned, though. He does not return once he has sampled a woman. Seek him while you choose your next lover and amuse all. But forego this bull leaping, I beg you!"

Lia wanted to laugh and cry at this jumble of information and pleading. She longed to know how Paon fared but she could not afford to give herself away. "My course is set, Yanit. I have vowed it. Now, are there any clothes in those chests yonder?"

They looked at each other in mutual recognition, two women who knew the meaning of survival.

The next few days fell into a routine, which, for Lia, was vastly pleasant after the perils she had endured. There was Yanit to laugh and gossip with as they wandered over the lovely house or in the garden next to it; there was the deferential young slave who helped with her rapidly progressing Minoan and encouraged her by bringing new tablets daily for them to read; there was good food, heady wine, robes and jewels, servants to be commanded. But the point toward which time revolved was that in the midafternoon when a short, wiry man who spoke only in monosyllables arrived to teach her the rudiments of bull leaping.

Part of the garden was secluded by thick trees and shrubs while watchful guards paced nearby. Here Lia twisted, turned, tossed and was thrown endlessly by her tutor, who would accept no movement unless it were perfect. Her life would depend on how well she learned, this she knew, and her agility served as a goad in the tumbling lessons, the careful balancing, and the sprints that were demanded. Several times the padded wooden shape of a bull was brought out by the slaves and her tutor would show her how to place her hands on the horns and how to land gracefully. He vaulted back and forth in positions that seemed impossible, then watched her attempt them. She always fell.

She sat on the grass and rubbed her back from which the muscles seemed torn loose after one such collapse. He eyed her expressionlessly and she wanted to cry out that she felt as if alien viewers were assessing her, that danger was near. Lia knew she would not; even Yanit was not to know her speculations that something was building to a climax.

Her tutor had never told her his name or asked hers. Now he said the longest sentence he was ever to speak to her. "You will learn quickly in the bullring or you will die, for the next festival is within nine days."

She was startled into swift speech. "But surely I will not be expected to participate?" In all that she had learned of the bull leapers and their art from all the accounts, she knew that they worked in pairs of threes but never alone. Before her training reached that stage she had hoped to reach Minos or find an opportunity for escape, perhaps even reach Paon and join with him in his struggle. Time and delay were on her side—or so she had thought. "I am not ready!"

He shrugged. "Work, then."

She could gain no more information from him. It was as though he had never spoken. Her body grew stiff, her hands sweaty. She could not make even the easiest tumble and soon he stalked away in disgust. Lia stood in the warm sunlight with the blowing shade trees making patterns on her skin as she breathed in the scent of flowers and felt that she stood in the dark night. She heard the angry bawl of the bull as he rushed toward her and knew again the fear that the heavy horns would toss her. How could she face it again? She remembered her sense of danger, of being watched. But who was powerful enough to tamper with the chosen of Minos?

Later she asked Yanit if she knew anything about the festival. She would not speak of what she had been told or voice her own fears and thereby make them real.

The fat woman said, "There are many festivals in Crete, Lia. The great goddess has many faces and we honor them all. Now that you mention it, I believe there is one for the harvest just begun. Do you think we will be permitted to go? Whatever shall you wear? Something dignified, which reveals your beauty, of course." She struggled up from the cushion on which she had been reclining and came toward Lia, eyes assessing. "Two husbands and all the lovers I ever had time for, even another woman now and then, and I never had half your looks. That golden hair, those sea eyes, those long legs and slender waist!" Yanit looked back in envy on a time long gone.

Lia had seen herself in the polished metals placed around the rooms and she often watched herself as she practiced the stances, leaps and tumbles a bull leaper should know, for wide expanses of it were set up in another area. Paon's eyes and mouth and hands had told her that he found her fair; sometimes she thought so too. Yanit's words made her uncomfortable and the next ones were even more bothersome.

"You shall be beautiful that day if we do go. Lovers will flock to you—the goddess adores the fruitful. You can be both safe and blessed and I with you."

Lia had never told Yanit the truth of her coming to Crete nor of her plans. It was something she held within and now she was glad that she had. She spoke lightly. "As you wish, but now make sure that no one comes here for I must practice. The tutor thinks me slow."

Yanit sniffed and departed. Her opinion of the bull-leaping lessons had not improved; there were other ways for a woman to achieve what she wanted and so she told Lia often.

Lia saw bull shapes in her night dreams, felt herself trampled and torn apart, pulled muscles and bruised herself by day, followed the commands and actions of the tutor as she drove her mind and body, studied the tablets that told of the art and walked up and down before the miniature frescoes of bull leapers that adorned her antechamber, thinking again how impossible such feats seemed. But her body grew lighter and her touch more deft. She could not somersault, flip over and over, nor tumble sideways and backwards to land on her feet behind even a stationary object, but she was swift and compact, a high leaper and filled with endurance. If she were tested, it must be enough.

She asked her tutor once again about the festival but he would not reply. The dark eyes told her that she had improved and that must be the only answer expected.

She went for her lesson on the afternoon of the eighth day and he was not there. Stomach knotting with anticipation, she ran back to the house where Yanit was just turning from speaking with a slave who was backing respectfully away.

"Lia, lady! It is true. We are bidden to the festival on the

morrow and shall sit with the honored ones while the bull
leapers perform for the honor and glory of the goddess. Are
you not excited?''

No mention of participation. Was she safe after all? Lia said,
"I am delighted that we are allowed to attend such an
occasion." She looked at the slave and saw the faint grin slide
across his face before he bent low before her. She knew that it
was meant to be seen. Her head went up. "We shall be ready."

And the bellow of the bull rang in her ears.

Chapter Eleven

FESTIVAL

"HOMAGE TO THE GODDESS! Hail to the Great One! Honor to the Lady, the Giver of All Bounty! Honor! Homage! Hail!"

The white-robed priestesses and the golden-clad priests slowly circled the walled arena as they merged into intricate patterns, then came out in one long line while they repeated their litanies. Once the bull cry came and they sank to their knees in one fluid collective movement until it ceased. After each third completed circling they paused before the tall image of the goddess that stood at one end of the arena. She was bare-breasted and enigmatic with her sacred serpents coiled over her arms and her crested diadem blazing with jewels that caught the brilliant light of day and threw it upward. The dove and the owl sat on her shoulders and the fruits of the first harvest were at her feet. After they saluted her, they turned toward the mighty stone bull at the opposite end and bent gravely forward. It was hung with wreaths and garlanded with flowering branches. A pair of huge white horns was set before it and the silver double ax between them shone with a gleaming beauty.

Now they began to dance in a stately rhythm that held a hint of joy tamped down. One priestess called a ritual response and another answered. Musicians began to play on drum, pipes, lyre and castanets. A deep-toned voice rose over it all and the assembled crowd, silent until now, gave a moan of anticipation and excitement. Lia, sitting with Yanit on one of the lower

benches and secluded from view by several watchful slaves,
turned her head toward the royal pavilion.

It was empty as yet and while they waited she surveyed the
scene and the people. The walls of the arena, now filled with
what seemed hundreds of Cretans, were white and graven with
the sign of the double ax along with the bull horns. The men
were nearly all dark, dressed in tunics and loincloths of
brilliant colors, weaponless, sparkling with jewels. Many of
the women were bare-breasted just as the goddess was and
wore full cascading skirts in red, blue and gold that were
encrusted with gems. Other folk were more plainly dressed in
duller hues. All seemed breathless with eagerness.

Lia herself wore a white robe that covered her shoulders and
came down to midcalf. A gauzy blue cloak floated from her
shoulders and her sandals were the same color. Pearls had been
plaited in her hair, which was coiled high and secured with
golden pins. She had chosen the clothes herself, refusing the
bare-breasted fashion offered her by the servants, and had
dressed alone. They had seated her here by prearrangement and
she had seen several curious looks directed her way as the
opening ceremonies began. She felt her heart begin to hammer.
Would she live to see the night come again?

"He comes!" Yanit whispered the words in her ear and
squeezed Lia's arm so hard that she felt the bones crunch.

Others took up the cry as the priests and priestesses
separated to stand before the goddess and the bull in equal
numbers. The richly dressed men and women who sat in the
vicinity of the gold and black pavilion far to Lia's left rose to
their feet, inclining their heads before the tall approaching
figure. Now the entire crowd came upright and the silence was
almost total.

Lia glanced upward, forgot herself and frankly stared. The
heavy golden mask of the bull was crowned with iridescent
feathers and jewels of all colors. The magnificent white horns
crowned its head. But this was no king; it was borne aloft on
three golden poles that took four men to carry it, they staggered
the while. The mask was set on the high back of the raised
chair so that it seemed to dominate the watchers. Now another
personage advanced to stand directly behind the mask for a
long moment before sinking down to a seat, a signal for all the
others to sit likewise. Lia recognized the purely cut features,

the shimmering hair with its distinctive white streak, and the proud stance. It was the woman who had stared at her as they approached the palace of Knossos.

"Our king secludes himself still; it has been a long time. He wrestles with the gods and speaks with the great goddess herself." Yanit spoke reverently in Lia's ear. "He will watch over us through his symbols of power."

"Who is the woman?" Lia's skin was prickling with warning and she felt faintly chilled in the hot sun.

"Who does not know Hirath, favored priestess of the goddess, beloved of the lord Paon? Gossip has it that her family has stirred this latest charge against him—they hate him for his power and what they call his inferior blood—and that only the direct intervention of Minos himself can save his commander." Yanit pulled back and looked at Lia's face. "Nothing for you there, little one, believe me."

There was a loud cry from below and a spotted bull dashed into the arena. His head was lowered as he tossed it menacingly; light shone on the polished horns and glittered off the smooth hide. He ran from side to side as if looking for something to gore, then paused before the image of the goddess and loosed a bellow.

"They come! The honored of Minos!" The cry rose from a dozen throats and the crowd came to its feet in order to acclaim the fourteen young men and women who came out single file, turned their backs to the bull and saluted the bull mask on the royal stand.

Lia caught her breath. She might soon stand where these bull leapers stood and the enormity of what she risked confronted her at this moment.

The bull leapers were all slender and wiry, dressed in wrapped, short loincloths, hair bound firmly back. The women's breasts, were tightly confined. Their heads were high and proud, their carriage bold and free. They stood before the people, accepting their homage but not acknowledging it. The bull was quiet behind them, surely a sign of the favor of the goddess.

A single drum note sounded and four of the bull leapers formed a square. The people sank back into their seats and the bull stirred uneasily. The remaining leapers retreated from sight. Lia leaned forward to see better as one of the girl leapers danced out lightly in front of the now pawing beast. It came slowly toward her, she retreated, swayed forward, retreated again. The bull snorted and charged. One of the young men ran lightly across its line of vision and stopped. The girl came very close to the animal as it stood, readying itself for another charge. Her arm went out to take the pointed horn. The other young man stood at the back of the bull and all were motionless. Then the second bull leaper, the young girl, appeared from the side, rose over the horns as if in flight, touched the back and came down in the arms of the waiting man. The bull whirled and charged at them, head down. One of male leapers flashed at him, caught the horns in both hands, flipped up and onto the back, slid down it and came up to challenge the angry animal again.

The arena shook with cheers. Lia heard her own voice crying out in admiration for these young ones who risked death for the glory of the moment and in a true act of worship. I could never do that. Never. All that she had read and heard about the Cretan bull leapers was as nothing to seeing it in the reality. Her own attempts seemed an idle game to her now before this skill.

Bulls came now in threes, two by two, and alone. The bull leapers were everywhere, challenging, daring, tumbling, vaulting. Their actions were poetry and dance, no movement was ungraceful. The goddess was truly honored this day. Lia's fears began to fade and the spectacle excited her in a new way. Blood pounded in her temples and she was aware of her pulsating flesh, of the very marrow of her bones. She wanted physical contact with her lover, to feel him hard in her, to share the glory of life renewed and made whole again. She wanted to vault him and ride to the explosion of passion.

"You would be a bull leaper? Then come!"

Her attention jerked back at the sound of the well-pitched, trained voice which was almost directly in front of her. One of the male bull leapers was standing there, hands on his hips, a light sheen of perspiration on his skin, his dark eyes bold on her face. Two others stood at the far side of the arena, near one of the doors that led inside. The crowd was craning and beginning to murmur. Lia cast a swift glance toward the royal pavilion and saw the flash of blue plumes.

"Come! We have all begun so. Come to meet the bull." His

voice went slightly higher with just the edge of laughter in it. "Does the outlander repent of her ambition? And yet the bull is safe."

"Go! Go! The goddess will be angered!" The chant was beginning to rise.

"Lady! Do not! Faint. Say she has spoken to you. Anything!" Yanit's words came in short gasps.

Lia fought back the urge to take Yanit's advice. After all, she had known this was coming in some form. Better to face it now and be done; if she failed, she failed. Visions of stamping hooves and bloody faces swung before her and she looked wildly out beyond the thin, amused face of the bull leaper, up to the snake-bedecked image of the great goddess. The world faded into the brilliant blue eyes of Paon as they smiled down at her. He was so real that she felt her own still lips begin to form a smile in return.

Then she was on her feet, arms at her sides, back in the arena and speaking in what seemed to her to be a normal manner. "I will come for the honor of the great goddess." She waited until one of the guards cleared a way for her and walked calmly behind him while the whispers of the crowd rose up. Her legs were shaking and her mouth was dry but the deadly, draining fear was gone. Another voice rang in her ears. "I came to the bulls and I was afraid but I conquered and great Minos accepted my homage." So had Paon spoken as they lay together in that time of sweetness. He, the lord commander of the Cretan force, had admitted fear, not to his captive, but to his equal, Lia of Pandos. Let his example be hers and let him hear of it in his prison.

"I am ready." She was standing on the packed earth of the arena floor without really knowing how she had come to be there and yet the retreating figure of the guard told her that he had escorted her there. She felt the fascination of the people and their hunger for more excitement. Had she not felt the same just moments ago?

The bull leaper stretched out his hand to her and she took it, feeling the dry warm clasp of the powerful fingers. He smiled at her. "This is simply an introduction to the bull. It is something for which one cannot really prepare."

It was burning hot in the arena and Lia felt the thin cloth of her robe stick to her skin. "I am not really trained at all." He was piloting her around in a little circle now as they acknowledged the calls of the people. "Why did you challenge me so?"

The black eyes burned down into her, seeming hot as the sun. "We of the bull leapers glory in challenge. It becomes our very food and drink." His wiry body seemed to pulsate with passion as he spoke.

Lia saw his hand go up and come down again before he spun her away from him. She followed the direction of his motion instinctively, noticing that the two men who had been standing by the doorway into the wall had vanished. Curious, she turned back to him only to see that he had retreated also and was standing close to the entrance where she had come. His arms were folded across his chest and he was looking down as if in meditation.

The bellow of an angry bull made Lia swing around suddenly. Bearing down on her was a huge brown animal with curving pointed horns from which fragments of cloth hung. Red glinted from one of them. He was moving so rapidly, head lowered to toss, that there was no time to do anything other than jump to one side. She hit on the side of her foot and it twisted under her. The bull changed his course and headed for her again, bellowing as he came. She tried to rise but she was off balance. She rolled and the brightly painted hooves missed her head by the width of a finger.

He thundered by, whirled and made ready to come again. Lia shrieked and managed to rise this time. She had time for a brief look around—surely someone would come to help for her plight was obvious! But no. The people were watching avidly and the bull leaper was leaning forward, his face grave. Could he not come to distract the beast? And then the knowledge burst upon her. She had read in the tablets the origin of her predicament here. "The bull leapers come to face a bull alone; each individual worships the great goddess with his courage then and none may intervene lest she be angered." Lia's mistake was in accepting the summons; now she might pay for it in death, which would be accepted as simply the will of the goddess.

Lia plucked at the cord that held her robe. She had discarded the cloak earlier since it was only ornamental. Thank whatever gods watched over her that she had had the warning from the tutor. It had given her the chance to prepare.

The bull roared down upon her, zigzagged slightly and came again. She waited until he was almost upon her, then pulled the robe loose and flung it directly over the lowered horns as she threw herself flat and went into the rolling tumble that she had been practicing for these past days. The bull kept going toward the distant wall, shaking his head and bellowing. Lia came upright and turned to look at him as he managed to dislodge one corner of the filmy thing and made ready to pound toward her again.

The wrapped loincloth and tight breast confiner that the women bull leapers wore afforded her great freedom of movement. She had thrust into one side of the belt the dagger that had come with the clothes left for her when she arrived in Crete. It would likely make very little difference on so large an animal as this bull but it might deflect him if everything else failed. Her bruised skin burned from impact with the ground of the arena and she was conscious of her breath coming in short spurts. Did she have to fight until her death? Anger swept her, restoring and releasing. She bent her knees slightly, flexed them and waited. She was conscious of nothing but the battle for survival.

He was at her again and this time she ducked under the shrouded horn, pulled on the cloth which gave a ripping sound and checked his pace. In that instant Lia pulled out the dagger and drove it into the smooth neck with all her considerable strength. The bull staggered, twisted and turned away. With a flamboyance she did not know she possessed, Lia thrust her hands out from her sides, tilted her body backward and flipped over twice in swift succession to bring herself upright and several long strides away from the bull, which was now moving slowly toward the opposite wall as it shook its head back and forth.

"She has slain the bull! The outlander has slain the bull of King Minos!"

"The sacrifice for the honor of the goddess!"

The cries surrounded Lia and rang in her ears. Some were of shock and some of adulation but they resounded in the arena and overwhelmed her. A drumbeat began somewhere high above as the bull leaper who had challenged her and several guards came toward her now, smiles lighting their faces.

Her ordeal had ended and she still lived. She raised her head proudly and waited to greet them. None should know that her stomach churned and her head hammered. She was a survivor.

Chapter Twelve

GIFT OF THE BRIGHT ONES

SOMETHING WAS SQUEEZING her shoulder, pulling at her head, whispering urgent words that had no meaning except in tone. Lia felt herself pulled up from the warm darkness of sleep even as she tried to retreat still farther from the pounding realities that had haunted her earlier dreams. She flung her hand out to push whatever it was back and away but found that she could not move the arm. It was caught in a hard grip that was almost painful.

"Have you taken something that you cannot rouse?" The exasperated voice spoke the mainland language into her ear.

"What is it? Who are you?" The shrouding sleep was leaving her, and as she spoke the words memory returned in a flash of images. She saw the bull court, the charging beast, her own knife thrust, then the guards escorting her out of the arena to the excited cries of the people, the sun glinting off the bull mask in the royal pavilion, Yanit's praise and delight in her, then the warm bath, sweet wine and blessed sleep that was both collapse and forgetfulness. "Leave me alone."

"Come." The voice was resonant, deep-toned, male.

Lia sat up, fully roused at last. She stared into the face of the bull mask and both hands flew to her mouth. Was this still nightmare? The faint light in her chamber showed the kneeling figure beside her to be tall, his hand that gripped her arm was wide and flat, the cloak that enveloped him was golden and rich, the mask over his face was of the same hue, the topping horns of ivory.

"Put the cloak around you and pull the hood close. You are summoned and time is short." He pulled a thick golden robe toward her. "If you think to scream, do not. The fat woman and the slaves sleep deeply as does the guard."

"Who summons me?" Lia was proud that her voice did not shake as she drew the cloak over her shoulders. He had dropped her arm but the big hands were very close to her throat. "Are you the representative of the bull god?"

"You might say that." He touched a dagger in the folds he wore. "No noise, now. You will regret it if you do not obey."

Lia rose, pushed back the tumbling hair and adjusted the cloak so that nothing showed. She was surprised at how rested she felt and that her mind was alert. This was the time of accounting, then. She was called to the bed of the priest-king, who, even in his seclusion, had heard of the events in the bullring. Her future, if any, would hang on the way she conducted herself in the next few hours.

She spoke as she had in the bullring. "I am ready."

The man took her arm in his hand and they went through silent corridors to a door set low in the wall and out into the freshness of a barely graying dawn.

They walked rapidly toward the palace, which seemed to be brooding over land and city alike, its colors washed pale at this hour, the brilliant flowers and twining vines a mere tracery on the heights. Lia wondered that no one was in sight just as she had once marveled at her father's brief description of the Cretan cities. "The sea is their wall." Her mind went ahead to the coming confrontation. What would Minos be like? Old? Cruel? Bearable? She only hoped that she could spin a good tale and endure his touch when he summoned her to his couch. She thought briefly of Zarnan who had wanted to kill her and Naris who sought to use her. She had won her chance by struggle and battle and conquered fear—let her keep the victory.

She and her guide stood now in a lane of fragrant trees. A narrow staircase opened up as her guide brushed aside some low bushes with his free hand. When she would have spoken, the bull mask turned on her and she saw silver eyes shining through it. The head shook as he thrust her forward. The passage into which they came was low and roughly cut. They bent low in it as he released her to go ahead of him. Several turns were negotiated, another staircase led down and then they walked up a slanting pathway into a hall filled with sweet odors and diffused light. Frescoes in brilliant colors graced the walls and brought the feeling of undersea into this underground place. There was an ornamented door at the far end, surmounted by a huge pair of horns, the double ax and a stone bull with its head raised.

"I leave you here, Lia of Pandos. Enter and obey." The silver eyes shone as if in warning. He waved toward the door with one hand.

Lia remembered the crumpled short tunic under the robe, her bare feet and tumbling hair. This was a strange way to go to a king. She thought of the way Hirath had looked at her and a new fear came. It was likely that she was summoned to her death in this place of stone. Then her resolve came back; she walked with unfaltering steps toward the door and pushed it open.

She stared at the lush chamber, lit with massed candles set high, rendered fresh with white flowers, elegant with piled cushions and frescoes of sea creatures about the great goddess who smiled upon them. Cakes and fruit along with wine were placed on a low table. A woven chest was open and gauzy cloths spilled out. A lyre lay beside one of the cushions as if tossed there just recently. Several scrolls lay unwound on top of a stone bench. Two doors opened off to the sides and she could hear the splashing of water coming from inside one of them.

Lia stood waiting but no one emerged. Uncertain of what to do, she knew that she did not intend to venture toward those doors. It was warm in the chamber and she loosened the cloak while throwing back the hood. She might as well sit down, she thought, and crossed to the cushion to let her fingers drift idly across the lyre as she sank into the softness.

It had been Medo's favorite instrument; she had often played when they sat under the purple flowers at their home on twilight evenings. One of the songs came back to her now as she waited for the unknown to become visible. She played the first part of the melody and sang very softly.

"Over the sea foam, out of the golden dawn, my love came riding the waves, to me, to me. I will go with him to halls of shell, under the wide sea. . . ."

There was the smallest movement behind her and Lia broke off the song to rise and turn. This could be no worse than the bull. The figure standing in the doorway was very tall and clad in a black cloak that covered him from head to toe. His arms were folded across his chest. He seemed to have risen up out of the shadows, perhaps from the underworld itself.

Lia did not know if one knelt, bowed one's head or abased oneself in the dust. The wrong motion might give offense; then, too, this might not be the king but simply another minion. Possibly the proper thing to do would have been to be trembling in fright on the floor. She could still collapse in awe, of course.

She did not. She stared straight at him and said, "I am Lia of Pandos. May I know to whom I speak?"

He was silent and her voice seemed to ring around the chamber, louder and sharper than she had intended. She did not move but kept her hands at her sides, willing herself to remain calm, holding her face impassive. This might be considered insolence. Dared she speak again?

One of the shrouded arms was lifting, going to the hood and pulling it back. Lia half expected to see the face of a bull confront her, for who knew what form a ruler in whom the gods reposed their trust might take? She must not turn away, no matter how hideous the visage. The last fold fell away and she looked upon the man she had been brought to see.

"Are you struck dumb, Lia of Pandos? I had not thought you capable of such silence." The warm, intimate laughter belied the sense of the words as he strode toward her.

"Paon! Paon!" Her mouth shaped the words. Her eyes took in the lithe muscular body in the brief blue loincloth, the tumbled dark curls, the arching bars of his black brows over the brilliant eyes. "I thought you captive, even dead, your life certainly in jeopardy." Perhaps she dreamed but the hard hands that closed on her bare shoulders as he tossed the cloak away were more than memory.

"It is a long tale and you are at least partially correct." His face was grave as he looked down into her eyes. "I heard of the golden outlander, her pride and her courage before the bull. I saw that again when she faced an unknown fate now." His voice was brushed with tenderness and his fingers rose to touch her lips.

"What has happened to you, Paon?" Perhaps Hirath had taught him warmth. The unkind thought drifted across the edges of her mind. That was not true; he had been all gentleness and leashed passion when he taught her of love. She knew that she was jealous of that beautiful woman.

"We will talk later. I ask you, Lia, as I did once before, if you will have me now. For this little time that can be ours."

His breath was soft on her cheek and pulse hammered in his temple. He held her lightly with no hint of coercion. The decision was hers to make. One corner of his mouth moved upward slightly in that gesture that was habitual with him.

"For this little time." She almost whispered the words. What mattered other than that in the very shadow of death she had once more found the man who lifted her to the heights, whom she could perhaps love if things were otherwise? She recoiled from that idea; her mother and father had suffered because of passionate love. It was not a thing their daughter wanted to experience. "I will have you, my dear lord commander." This was a time apart.

She lifted her arms to him and he caught her in an embrace so powerful that she thought it would crush her ribs. Then his mouth was on hers and she was opening to him with all the denied passion of her days.

They slipped down onto the cushions and stripped their clothes from each other with frantic hands. Lia was aware of a savage hunger rising in her. Her breasts burned and her thighs ached. She felt the moist spreading between her legs as her blood seemed to flood under her skin. She heard moaning and realized that it came from her own lips. Little disjointed phrases formed themselves into a sentence.

"I cannot wait. Paon, now!"

His mouth moved over her neck, down to her nipples and on toward her mound. His hands were caressing her shoulders, sliding up and down over her breasts as his mouth left them. She saw his powerful shaft as it touched her legs and moved with a pulsing life of its own. His face was twisted with the effort to restrain himself as he drew her upward for a long deep kiss that ended only when breathing became nearly impossible.

"Now, little Lia. Now!" He breathed the words into her ear, sending shudders over her flesh.

She rose to meet him as he plunged deep into her waiting cleft. They locked tightly together, their bodies drenched with sweat as they tossed and plunged. He withdrew slightly and she caught him back again. They looked at each other as the flame rose higher and higher. Then he was thrusting and she clinging. He came down over her and took her mouth with his tongue holding hers so that they seemed fused. The storm and the burning joined in Lia and she felt that she would die if it did not cease, if it did not continue. She was out of herself, cresting in fire and falling. Then the mist took her and she arched under Paon, calling his name just as he, too, fell back from her in completion and exhaustion.

Lia woke first and stretched luxuriously. She felt relaxed and supple, deeply peaceful. She looked down at him, then touched the dark curling hair. He was lying on his side with his head pillowed on his arm, the naked brown flesh of his body glowing in the subdued light. She ran her fingers lightly down his back. He flipped over and lay, face upward, still sleeping. The long lashes curved downward on his face; the calmness of sleep made him seem younger than he was.

She reached over and let her fingers brush his maleness. It moved a little and he shifted his position. Lia smiled as she touched him more lingeringly. Greatly daring, she bent to kiss him there and the hard flesh bloomed under her mouth. Paon twisted about as the stern contours of his own mouth lifted. He murmured something she could not understand and she drew back. If he spoke Hirath's name, she did not want to hear it. This time was theirs alone; this would be her memory to carry with her all the days.

Her hand reached out to him again and this time she let her fingers stray downward to cup him. He was hard and full now. She felt her own desire coming to fruition, a heavy yearning that made her nipples rise and throb as her breath came heavily. She looked at Paon, apparently still sound asleep. Suspicion assailed her and she released him slowly, then started to turn toward her pile of cushions.

Strong hands caught her and pulled backward so that she collapsed on his chest. He pulled her down beside him and laughed into her face. Lia laughed with him as they pressed close together. He spoke in her ear.

"Why did you stop?"

"I did not want to spoil your sleep. You looked so peaceful and remote." She let her hand stray downward toward his shaft.

"I was neither. I thought of you."

"Continue to do so." She held him firmly but delicately, her fingers moving up and down. "Are you thinking of me now?"

Paon leaned back a little, the laughter still shining in his eyes. "It is just possible that I am."

Lia put her free hand on his chest and pushed him back so that he lay prone on the cushions. Then she released him, paying no attention to his moan, and rose to stretch. His gaze followed her as she came to kneel beside him. Her fingers trailed over his face, neck, stomach and to his shaft again. She circled it with thumb and forefinger and continued down his long legs.

"You drive me mad with anticipation!" He reached for her but she drew back.

"As you have taught me, Paon." She put both hands into the nest of dark hair and saw his manhood rise to her as if it had a life apart. She touched her lips to it and felt the convulsive thrust. She began to burn in her turn. His hand touched her head and she heard his gasp when she moved slowly along him, circling with her mouth just as her hands had done. She felt the hot lubrication of her readiness but wanted to prolong this moment until the last bearable instant.

"Come." Paon lifted her up and settled her over him, holding her effortlessly. She took his hands, slipping into position so that he went deeply into her as she sat above him. They sat silent, poised, until the motion began to grow, soft at first and then harder. Lia was being penetrated; she was drawing him up into her, draining him and filling herself so that she might return to him. They were one in the glowing tide that carried them high and threw them down into the swells.

Then they were drowning into each other. She lay on top of him while he was still inside her. His arms were wrapped around her while she clung to him. His lips touched her ear and she could barely hear the whispered words.

"Lia, Lia, Lia."

Then the tide carried them to shore and drained away into peace.

Chapter Thirteen

A TIME OF CHOICES MADE

LIA AND PAON sat cross-legged on the floor before one of the low tables and ate hungrily of the figs, olives, cheese and wine he brought from one of the back rooms. Now and then their eyes would meet with an impact that set Lia's blood to moving more swiftly. They had slept, roused, made love again and waked to savage hunger. In all that time only jesting words or those of passion had crossed their lips. Lia wanted him to speak but at the same time she dreaded the end of this time of glory.

Paon put down his cup and looked at her gravely. His face grew stern as the laughter that had touched it in their carefree time now faded. Lia drew in her breath and waited. They had lain together in passion but she knew almost nothing of this man who held himself aloof as if he feared closeness.

"There is no easy way to say this, Lia. You have every reason to hate me for taking you from Pandos and exposing you to such danger here but I could not have done otherwise. I had sworn my oath to Minos; you were spoils of battle. I cannot expect you to understand."

Lia knew that this was the closest proud Paon would ever come to any sort of justification for the way she had been treated. Although that phrase "spoils of battle" angered her, she knew that she must not dwell in the past. It was enough that he cared how she felt.

"It is done, Paon. Let there be no more talk of it." Boldly

she leaned across the table and put her hand on his bronzed arm, which tightened at her touch. "Tell me, instead, how it is that you, who were taken away as a prisoner, have this freedom now?" She tried to speak lightly and could not. Emotion trembled in her voice. "I feared for you in the face of Zarnan's treachery and Naris's betrayal."

Paon's brows came together in a scowl. "And did you not fear for yourself? Had you no thought for Lia of Pandos?" He lifted her fingers from his arm and regarded her intently. "You should know that jewels and wealth buy Naris. I would say that he is safely my friend again. Zarnan is old and a fanatic. My betrothed, Hirath, priestess of the Lady of the Snake, is powerful and honored by all factions. It was her intervention, together with others of my friends, which enables me to go free, discreetly, until such time as King Minos emerges from his sacred solitude. At that time all will be set aright. I can wait."

Lia did not miss the proud way he spoke of his betrothed and her heart twisted. Did Hirath love him? Surely she did. What woman would not? She herself would ever after judge all men by this hard and tender, contradictory bold Cretan. That was the beginning of love as she well knew and she began to be afraid.

"I was told that I would ornament the bed of your king, that he sought heirs. Naris spoke so. He said also that Hirath was in this plot to throw you down and have more power through Minos." Paying no attention to his growing fury, Lia told him all that Naris had said as well as the gossip Yanit had been so eager to give out.

"Lies! You are jealous!" Paon rose and strode about, his thin white robe whirling behind him. "Naris would not dare speak to me in such a manner about my betrothed! I would kill him! She is already powerful; why would she seek more? But why do I listen to this?" He came back to her and leaned over. "Lia, we will not speak of this again. I forbid it. Tell me what has happened to you since you escaped from the house of Naris. You were safe there once I managed to buy him again. He loves intrigue, you see." He was forcing calm into his voice but his face was rock hard.

"I only wanted to warn you, Paon. I find it strange that you trust one whom you can buy, as you put it." She stood up to face him, folding her arms in front of her as if for protection. Had they lain and laughed together only a short time ago? It seemed a thing out of dreams.

Cynicism was suddenly ugly on the carved features as he gave a mirthless sound. "That is the way of this world and I will not be questioned by an outlander, I, who well know the way of survival in Crete. Will you answer as I asked or must I proceed with the very good fortune that I have arranged for you?"

Something in the glitter of his eyes told Lia that she would not like the fate he mentioned. She walked over to one of the stone benches, put a cushion behind her back and, watching him sharply, launched into the tale, reliving it all again. She did not tell him that she had expected to be summoned to the king or that she had been ready to buy her life and future with her flesh and knowledge. The glory of their passion was still upon her and she could not really think he had had her brought here simply to hear her tale, much of which he must already know, and to renew the fire that had burned between them from the beginning. She dared to hope that it might be some measure of caring.

Her voice trailed away and silence lay heavy in the room. Paon's eyes searched her face but she could read no emotion on his. She felt as if he were stripping her naked, seeing her feeling for him, knowing of her quickened pulses. Was the flesh so little bond? A flush began to mount to her cheeks and she resisted the impulse to snap at him angrily. Then his words were wrapping around her and she could barely take them in for the flaming in her head.

"You are a brave woman, Lia. I know of none braver. No, not even Hirath. But foolish, too, to think that you could face the bulls and live for very long. Even those trained to it die quickly and they are often in the learning process for years." His voice sharpened. "No, this is what I have decided. When I speak to King Minos and straighten my own situation out, I shall tell him your tale, perhaps even have you come as we planned, speak of the cold lands and what lies there. When he is acquainted with your history and hears of your courage, he will release you from the bull leapers and because of our friendship I am confident that he will give you in honorable marriage to a citizen of Crete. You could ask no more fortunate fate, Lia."

Lia cried out, "But what of my own feelings, Paon? I do not wish marriage. I want to be free and it is you who deprived me of that freedom by bringing me to this island. No! No! I will not accept your disposition of me!"

"A woman must be wed. Unless you would be a celibate priestess in one of the more obscure cults of our great goddess? I do not think that you would like that. Have you not proved that you enjoy the dalliance?" He was smiling that hard smile but the brilliant eyes wore the look of passion as he moved closer to her.

Lia hated herself for the swooning senses that would not refuse his lure. "Why have you interested yourself at all, Paon? I did not choose to come here, you know?" The words sounded high and far off in her ears.

He put one warm hand on her shoulder and looked down at her. Suddenly he was no longer the lord commander but Paon, her lover. "I have been haunted by sea eyes and golden hair, a bold and beautiful woman who can fight and love in equal measure. I tried to remove your face from my heart and I could not. I had to see you again, Lia of Pandos, once again."

She tilted her head back. "Why, Paon?" Would he say it? He was a strange man, a mixture of harshness and warmth and melting tenderness even when he fought with his emotions.

"I will wed Hirath as soon as I have met with the king. My people tell me that he will soon emerge and I must be first to him so that my name is cleared. That, of course, is a formality, only. Hirath will leave the active service of the goddess and we will live here in Knossos, servants of Minos and high in his favor. She and I have been long betrothed." He spoke flatly but Lia could hear the pride when he mentioned Hirath.

"Do you love her?" Lia, too, had her pride and she did not falter. She had expected nothing else, she told herself.

"Her face has been before me for many seasons. She is the pride and prize of Knossos, honored of the great goddess; when her family refused to welcome me to their ranks, she fought them, saying she would have no other."

Ruthlessly Lia pressed him. "But you have not answered my question, Paon."

"I wanted to see you again and feel your touch. I wanted

you to know that I have ever thought of you. It was I who left the dagger in the clothes for you that day on the ship and it was I who bribed your tutor to warn you." At her look of amazement, he smiled. "I knew much of what you told me just now, I confess it. I wanted to see how you would speak of it— boastfully or in pride. You were surprisingly matter-of-fact. My king will be pleased. Hirath and I are pledged and I do truly care for her as she for me. Let that answer you."

"I am answered." Lia felt the great hammering of delight in her heart and tried to fight it back. He had thought of her and cared; his hand had been over her all the while.

"We cannot meet except in the company of others and for very good reason from this time on, Lia. Your husband will be carefully chosen; he will not expect a virgin since you are an outlander. Crete is the most enchanting and fascinating of all places to live. We have a great civilization here and you will be welcomed, I promise that." The blue eyes looked at her and this time she saw the passion there as it mixed with longing. "Will you have me once more, Lia?"

Unashamed tears came to her eyes and she did not try to hide them. "For the last time, Paon?"

"For the last time. It cannot be otherwise and I was perhaps selfish to summon you here in this manner, but there was little danger. Lia, will you come to me?" He asked the question again even though he saw the answer written in her face.

"I am here, Lord Commander." She lifted up her arms and went to him. He pulled her close as she murmured his name.

Later Paon slept, head pillowed on both arms, the long curve of his body smooth in the flickering light, the line of his face and jaw appearing newly sculpted. Lia lay awake, cherishing these last few hours together. She wanted to weep but knew that it would do no good; the facts could not be altered. There was no place for her in Paon's life and she must accept it. She could not deny that he cared for Hirath; had not he spoken the words? And still he could not keep her, Lia, from his mind. She tried to think of herself, wed and living in this land, but mind and heart rebelled. She wanted to direct her own destiny, choose her own path. Yet if Paon had offered marriage, she knew that she would have accepted but, even for love's sake, could she endure the domination of another? The choice was not hers to make, she thought bitterly. He would see to her

future as best he could but what if his own were still in
jeopardy? Suppose Hirath did truly fall in with the scheme that
Naris had told her about? Lia tormented herself with such
thoughts as she lay beside Paon and tried to envision a future
without his touch. Reason told her that they knew little of each
other beyond the fusion of the flesh but the future, whatever it
might hold, seemed barren without Paon as she now knew him.

"For the last time." She whispered the words to herself as if
to take the gall from them. He had said it and so it would be; if
she lured him to her once or twice more as she well knew that
she could, it would be his decision that would stand between
them. Let it be otherwise! Let it be done in laughter and free
choice and in the light of day! That would not make it bearable
but a little less unendurable. "Madness," said her mind, but
she who had faced the bull on impulse now sought memories
against the long darkness.

"I must go." Paon had risen up and was looking at her, his
eyes unreadable. "You will be conducted back to your
chambers when it grows dark. You have been recovering from
the ordeal of the bull and none will have missed you. Your
serving woman, Yanit, was well bought. There is nothing to
fear." He spoke coolly. He had retreated into himself and there
was no self-doubt in him now.

Lia looked around, wondering what time of day it was and
how he could tell it. "It is early then?"

"Yes, a new day has come. We are not wholly in the dark of
underground here. You may look at the scrolls or——"

"I want to go out. I want to walk in the streets of Knossos as
other people do. I want to look at the sights and breathe fresh
air, not to watch every corner and shadow, to be myself for a
short while!" She watched his eyes grow incredulous at her
daring and spoke more quickly. "We could disguise ourselves,
could we not? You have said it is easy enough to go about
discreetly. What could be simpler? I am tired of being a
prisoner!"

"You can walk in the gardens of the palace if you are safely
robed and attended." He rose and began to walk about. "I
must be seen to be in my private rooms. You talk as if this
might be a child's outing."

"Why not?" Lia let her laugh ripple out, glad that she could
disguise the pain ripping at her. He could not go from her so

easily. This was all they would ever have. All her instincts told
that they could not make love again. He had withdrawn into his
own world and she would not follow him against Hirath. "Two
peasants come to gape at the mighty city of Knossos! After all,
when again shall I be able to do such a thing? Suppose you
choose a husband for me who dislikes a woman to think of
things outside the house and the children?" She spoke lightly
but the lash flicked him and he whirled to her.

"Devil! I do not have the choice of him. That is the king's
will. I have tried to make you understand. Lia, by all the
powers of the great goddess, do not try me more in this. We
must do as ordained."

"Very well, I will go alone." She realized that she meant
what she said. She had tired to intrigue and struggle; it was
time to be a girl for the short time that this might be possible.

"You seek to use a woman's wiles. I have seen too much of
that. I prefer you the other way." He was girding up his
loincloth and reaching down for a dark cloak. "We should
never have met, Lia."

"You had the way of that, Lord Commander." She faced
him, smiling boldly, head tilted high. Even now she wanted
him and could tell that he knew it. This time, however, he
seemed unaffected. "Paon, is it not possible to have me set
free? I told you once before that I wanted to go to Egypt,
perhaps the lands beyond. I am learned and could pass as a
scribe, a seer, a dealer in the ills of the flesh—"

"You belong to Minos of Crete. None of your pleas can alter
that. And can you imagine what would happen to that fair body
of yours if you tried such mad schemes?" He fastened the
cloak and pulled the hood well over his head, then leaned
forward as if to begin a shuffle. "Do not speak to me of
freedom; there is more of that in Crete than anywhere else. You
shall see Knossos, Lia. That I promise you!"

He whirled, pressed a stone in the wall and moved behind it
in one quick moment. Then he was gone and Lia knew it for a
foretaste of the future.

Chapter Fourteen

TYRANNY OF THE FEATHERED ONE

"AND THE BULL GOD tossed his head several times that day so that the cities shook with his anger. Word went out to summon the bull leapers so that he and the great goddess might be propitiated, for all Crete was in danger. There was among them a young lad. . . ." The storyteller paused, palms up and waited for coins or offerings before continuing his tale. He was old and scrawny, his voice a thin singsong. There were few takers but he rattled on, staring at several peasants who at least seemed a fascinated audience.

"He has been on this corner for years and the tale never changes. Come on." The annoyed whisper burned through the folds of Lia's turban as Paon half leaned on her. "If you must gape, there are tumblers just down the way."

She turned bemused eyes on him and saw the laughter on the dark face which was nearly concealed in the hood that many wore in this time of day against the heat of the sun.

"I am anxious to gape." She hissed the words at him and felt her pulses jump as he urged her along. Peasants in the city for a day and eager to see the sights would surely act no differently. He gave a low laugh and this time she joined him. It was going to be all right, after all.

The brilliant sunlight hammered down on them and reflected off the baked walls of the buildings and bright clothes of the crowds that moved in the streets of Knossos. Merchants haggled in little groups or showed off for potential customers. Ladies clad in saffron and silver rode by in litter chairs carried by slaves who glanced neither right nor left. A yellow-garbed priest rushed past, followed by several small boys. A seller of cakes was doing a rousing business at the junction of a wide street with a smaller street. The tumblers Paon had mentioned were building a human tower in the center of a circle of admirers and their slender, oiled bodies gleamed as they twisted themselves into impossible positions and yet supported each other.

Lia sighed with satisfaction as she bit into the cake Paon handed her and tasted its crumbling sweetness. They had been easy comrades since leaving the apartment by a secret passage and emerging into a narrow street only hours ago. The concealing robes, thick and of coarse weave, their bare dirty feet and smeared faces, along with the waddling gait both affected, made it impossible for any to connect them with the graceful courtiers. They had watched some impromptu wrestling that turned into a fight, a foot race among girls and boys alike, visited a shop that sold bull images made of gold, silver and precious stones, drunk milk and honey at a flower-hung food shop on one of the terraces that looked out toward the palace, followed a herd of goats being driven through the city, paused to watch a potter at work while his wife painted his wares in delicate colors and wandered through a shaded area planted with vines where they heard a singer giving out a ribald song to the delight of his listeners.

Lia was fascinated by the contrast in the people: proud ladies with low bodices or frankly bare breasts and full rippling skirts, others in flowing gauzy robes that showed their bodies, still others in concealing garments even as she was, men in loincloths, belts and dangling necklaces or wearing longer skirts cut high with the encircling tightly cinched belt sparkling with gems of all types, and the sober wrapped robes of some of the older people. Soldiers, the wealthy, the poor, scholars calling out their abilities, proud servants of the goddess in peacock plumes, all seemed to be in the streets of Knossos this day.

Paon talked in low tones, explaining this and commenting on that, asking her pleasure or teasing now and then, laughing when she gave him back in kind. Lia thought that now there was acceptance between them, an understanding that would do much to comfort her in time to come. She heard the laughter and gossip of the people, realized that she could understand almost everything she heard and answer it as well if she chose. Amusement and gaiety had had very little part in her life these past moons. Now she gave herself up to it, laughing, commenting, admiring much that she saw.

When they moved away from the tumblers, who were now holding their pose as though they had been sculpted there, Paon turned her into a less crowded area and smiled down at her.

"You are fair when you are happy, Lia. I am glad we came." His eyes took on the smoky blue haze of passion and the arrogant nostrils flared slightly. "We must return soon. Will you be ready?"

It seemed to her that he asked quite another thing. Would she take all that had been between them and accept what must be? "I will be ready, Paon."

The steady fire flowed between them, not to be ignited, as he said, "Some cool wine would refresh us both. Shall we head for yonder shop?"

When they came out into the street a short while later, the sound of drums, pipes, cymbals and castanets was mingling with the calls of people to each other as they rushed to watch. A high chanting mixed with low notes was deeply compelling against the rumble of heavy wheels.

Lia stood on tiptoe as she tried to see over the heads of those wine-shop customers who wanted to know what was going on yet did not wish to leave their drink. "What is it, I wonder?"

"Just another procession, probably of no great importance." Paon spoke indifferently as he peered at the angle of the sun and turned to avoid several men returning inside, evidently having reached the same conclusion as he.

The music lured and compelled. Lia cried, "Let's at least just go and watch them pass! Then we can go on our way."

"Child! You love the processions." The warm, intimate tone of his voice made them suddenly seem alone. "Just a quick look, then." His hand went out and took hers, pressing it gently.

Lia felt tears smart in her eyes at the tenderness of the gesture and she squeezed his fingers in return. She could never say anything of what she felt, that here in the hot sun in front of a public wine shop surrounded by people, she knew without equivocation that she loved this man and would do so all her days. Flesh and mind and independence melded into one passion so intense that she shook with it and felt her hand grow cold in his. He must not know; he must never know. Her pride, at least, must remain inviolate. She gave him a quick, flashing smile.

"Hurry, we will miss it!" Lia released his hand and started toward the procession, which was now fully visible as it moved slowly along the next street. She heard his sharp intake of breath and his quick tread behind her. It seemed that he started to say her name but stopped in time. She could not look on his face. How was it that this sudden realization had come now? What might she have said if they had been alone with each other? She hurried on, thankful for this diversion.

The press of people was greater now and she was suddenly knocked off balance by a hurrying man, swarthy and heavy set, who caught her arm to steady her. The sheltering hood slipped back a little and he looked into her face. She was thankful for the turban that hid her hair and for the concealing film of dust that masked her features as well as for the folds of cloth around her neck that hid her still more. The man said nothing but the look in his eyes was one of lewd interest. Then he gazed past her, grinned and moved rapidly away. Lia, assuming that he had seen Paon approaching, pushed on up until she stood deep amid those who waited for the goddess to arrive.

It was none other than the great goddess herself who stood poised high on the wheeled platform as it moved slowly along. She flashed with gold and ivory, emeralds and rubies, her tall headdress catching the light and splintering it into a thousands shades of flame, her breasts full, the bare nipples rosy pearls, her skirt spangled with the jewels of seawater and foam, her arms and shoulders wreathed with snakes. Her eyes were alive and watching, seeming to turn as the sun poured over her face. Her mouth was set and stern but one hand was lifted as if to bless; the other held the double ax that was wreathed with lilies.

A low enclosed pavilion shrouded with white and gold cloth was behind her and two beautiful bare-breasted girls knelt beside it. Priests and priestesses, all young and fair to look upon, walked before and after the platform as did the musicians. The double axes were lifted high at the beginning and end of the procession. Several dancing girls, clad only in the thinnest of loincloths, danced to the lilting pipes and the low throb of the drums. Behind all these came wagons laden with fruit, cloth, boxes and grain.

"She goes to the palace, to her dwelling there. Praise be to the goddess."

A young woman beside Lia spoke the words reverently and they were taken up by those close around. Lia herself said nothing but stared at the great image, fully as tall as two tall men placed feet to head. The turning eyes rested on her up-turned face and she felt an intelligence there. The feeling was so strong that she shut her own eyes, fearful of this goddess who was none of hers.

When she opened them an instant later, the platform had almost ground to a stop and the dancing girls were whirling about rapidly to the delight of the crowd. The image was slightly past her just then and she shook off the feeling of apprehension. It was well enough to doubt the gods of her youth, for she had seen the death and horror they could bring by way of their worshipers. This goddess was quite another thing. "I meant no disrespect." She spoke under her breath and turned to look for Paon.

He was back in the crowd, which was swaying back and forth with the music and blocking his passage. She saw him move past an old woman and nearly stumble over several children who were climbing up on each other in order to see. He glanced up, saw her watching him and waved at her to join him. She shook her head; they could go nowhere until the crush of people thinned out and that was unlikely to happen until the procession moved on.

There was a shriek in front of her and Lia whirled around. The curtains on the small pavilion were shaking with each long drawn note of the music, which had now changed. It was luring, tantalizing and shivered on the still air. Lia cast a swift look at the face of the goddess and thought that a cloud drifted across it. The golden skin had a hue less rich than formerly but the huge eyes were moving again, flashing when the sun gleamed in them. The music went very low, held and started an upward rise.

The curtains parted and the head of a snake appeared. It was flat, black, triangular, with tiny eyes that almost glittered in the light. The body poured out now in a rush of darkness that was incredible to Lia. The thing was enormous; there was no end to it!

"She is here! The living goddess!" The cry came from a dozen throats and the people threw themselves to the ground in fear or adoration.

Lia was immobile for a long breath before she did likewise. She could not take her gaze from the snake, which was now rearing up toward the figure of the goddess as if it wished to commune with her. Then the dark body twisted over the golden one even as the coils continued to pour from the pavilion. From her place on the ground Lia still looked up and saw the slender figure of a woman emerge from the same area. She wore a dark hood and gown in simulation of the snake and she was very tall. Her arms rose up and she held them in front of her while the snake moved out from the goddess and thrust its head forward.

"Get up! Behold your goddess!" The woman's voice was sibilant, arresting, poised on a high note of excitement that was very much like that of the music which was now reaching a crescendo.

The people rose, Lia with them. She twisted back to look for Paon but could only see his dark-clad shoulder. A grinning man stood in front of him; it was the swarthy man who had made her stumble earlier. She had but one desire now and that was to get away. But how? Any attempt at departure now would seem impious, a deadly affront. She shuddered at the thought of the great snake so close to her and pulled the flaps of the turban down as she looked ahead once again.

This time the scream of mortal terror was her own. The massive head, the flickering, darting tongue, the poised coils, had reached out past the first in line and now were pointed straight in her direction! She jerked back and it followed her, dropped a little, then withdrew, streamed to the ground and started for her. There was no mistake. The people tumbled over themselves in their eagerness to get back. Lia moved with all the swiftness of desperation but there were hands on her back thrusting her forward.

"You are wanted. Be still." Several voices called out to her, the shakiness of fear and relief apparent in each syllable.

"Woman. Stay as you are." The authoritative voice of the dark-clad woman on the platform reached Lia in a haze of blind fear. "The goddess commands it."

Lia looked down at the great snake, which was now within easy striking distance of her as it reared up. She felt the sense of intelligence that she had felt earlier and wondered if this were truly a nightmare in the afternoon sun. Did the great goddess of Crete confront her in this awful guise? She had seen few snakes in her life and feared them greatly but knew that they were considered holy by many peoples. She moved and the head came closer, stopping at the very instant that she did. She stood very still, tasting her own fear and wondering where Paon was.

The music rose to a high shrillness that made her want to put her hands over her ears. The head of the snake shot past her and came around again without touching her but holding effectively in a wide coil; the little eyes seemed to meet hers and she would have sworn there was triumph there. Was she going mad?

"You have seen. The goddess has selected this woman. How greatly is she blessed!" The priestess spoke first to the crowd, which murmured in awe, and then she addressed Lia. "Chosen and favored of the great goddess, enter now into her service forever!"

The silence fell across them all and Lia knew they waited for her to speak. She moistened her dry lips and willed the saving words to come.

"I am honored beyond the knowing. But I am a bull leaper, vowed to the service of King Minos." She loosened the robe enough so that all could see the taut firmness of her legs and the smooth arms. Surely the bull leapers must venture out now and then. Only let them believe her and she would never again seek the forefront of a procession! What if they discovered Paon when he was supposed to be in seclusion if not prison?

The dark woman spoke again and the words slammed into Lia's brain, draining all hope from her. "True enough. But when the goddess personally selects who shall serve her, not even those vowed to that service, no, not even the highest in all Crete, may turn back. From this moment on until the day you die and beyond you are in the service of the great goddess!" The last sounds were those of triumph and victory.

Chapter Fifteen

LADY OF THE SNAKE

THE SILENCE STRETCHED long around Lia as she met the bold gaze of the priestess. She knew that she dared not challenge this pronouncement; there was literally nothing she could say. The faces of the people, those in the procession, even the enigmatic eyes of the statue, swam before her eyes. There was a rippling motion at her feet as the dark coils drew closer in.

"She is overcome."

"A blessed one in all truth!"

"What fortune!"

The voices spoke almost as one while people craned to see her and she caught the note of real envy in them. Passionately she wished that they could trade places with her. She had been given an idea, however, and in that might be her salvation. She let herself sway, moistened her lips again and lifted one hand to her mouth. "I am fearful. . . ." The words trailed away. "I am not worthy." Her head went from side to side as she turned around so that the folds of the turban flapped against her face.

Disturbed by the motion, the great snake gave a hiss and the head began to rise. Lia stood very still. She had seen what she needed to see, and in spite of the desperate situation for herself, her heart was a little comforted. Paon was still blocked by the dark man and ringed in by several others. He was prevented from coming to her; he would not willingly abandon her to this taking. She could not see his face but the dark figure

110

bulked large, waiting only an opportunity. She was caught in any event; let the diversion work if it could.

"I must not give way. It will only be for a short time." The words rang in her head even as she spread her arms wide and let her scream split the hot air. She spiraled down toward the snake and felt her hands touch the cold skin, saw it arch upward toward her and the forked tongue flicked almost in her very face. The terror was more real than any nightmare. She thought that any moment would bring true oblivion.

"Fetch her!" She heard the snarl in the priestess's voice. "Hurry! She cannot be defiled!"

Then there were cries in the crowd, sounds of scuffling and a distant voice howled, "My pouch!" The drums began to beat and strong arms were pulling Lia up from the writhing folds of the snake. She opened her eyes just as a large brown palm came down over her mouth, nearly stifling her.

"Thief! Get him!"

"They work in pairs! Yonder! Run!"

The cries merged in Lia's head along with the hammer of the drums and the lilt of the pipes. Her arms and legs seemed to become warm mush; her eyes grew foggy, then cleared. She willed herself to move against the grip of the man who carried her but she could not. He wore the golden garb of the goddess and the tip of his dark beard brushed her face as he placed her on the platform, just at the feet of the goddess and near the dark-clad priestess. She lay where he left her; there was no motion or feeling in all her body, only her mind was clear.

"The goddess has taken her own! You are fortunate to have seen so great a happening! Let your minds leave the petty and ponder this thing!" The priestess was swaying now as she called out the words, her supple limbs moving under the clinging robes, her voice at once authoritative and luring.

The procession began to move very slowly. The great snake slithered up and over Lia, the coils seeming to go on endlessly, until it was back in the pavilion once more. She wanted to scream again at the horror of that touch but even her throat muscles would not work. She did not even have the consolation of knowing if Paon had taken advantage of the interlude when all eyes must have been focused on her. Had the cry of "thief" been meant for him as he escaped? Would she ever know?

Color swam and blurred before her now as the procession gathered speed and the music grew louder. She saw brilliant robes, houses, a green garden, flowers spilling over the ground and white columns wider around than she herself. Then all noise faded and they went into partial darkness before coming into what appeared to be a courtyard walled with stones set upon each other. In one sense it seemed to Lia that they had just left the crowded street and then that a long time had passed. The bare feet of the priestess had been just beyond her and the curtains of the pavilion had been swaying with the motion of the platform. When had the music ceased and the procession halted? She could see only blue sky above her and the massed stones of what must be her prison.

Lia felt prickles in her arms and legs; her mouth was beginning to draw and burn. Her tongue was less of a lump and her head began to ache slightly. She was at first thankful that apparently she was not to be left in this condition for long and then grew apprehensive because she still could not move. She concentrated on trying to turn to the side but it was no use. All was silence around her and the lowering sun was beginning to strike her skin with a burning sensation. She would not burn for she was very brown but that told her something about the length of time she had been here. What sort of potion was so strong that it could do this when simply put on the palm of a hand?

Suddenly a noise made her even more tense than she was. Footsteps came close and a sandaled foot nudged her side. Then long fingers went across her face, reached up and jerked the turban away from her head so that her hair fell free. Then a face bent over her and Lia saw her enemy.

Blue-black hair touched with white at the ears and in the center of her head, a pure oval face in which black brows arched over strangely purple-black eyes—the woman who had watched her enter Knossos an eternity ago. Just now the loveliness of her was burned with triumph and the full red mouth was twisted with laughter. She put her hand to Lia's face again and Lia felt the cut of her long nails as she deliberately dug them into the skin. Her relief that she could begin to feel again was overshadowed as the mocking words began to make their own demented sense to her.

"The little bull leaper is afraid of the snake! I find that

fascinating. You will serve the Lady of the Snake in the depths of her sacred cave, and when you have time to think, you will wish that the hooves of the bull had claimed you that when you were summoned forth to meet him. Did you wonder how that came about? Know that the hand of Hirath reaches everywhere that I wish it to! Know that I am the very shadow of the great goddess on this earth!''

So the contorted face above her belonged to Hirath, betrothed of Paon. Lia knew that she had known all along who the watcher was. But why such hatred of a captive? She let her eyes show their contempt and fury. It was a mistake. The other hand, loaded with rings made in the snake emblem, slammed across her mouth. The beautiful eyes began to blaze with the hunger of passion and she raised her hand again.

Hirath was one who took pleasure in cruelty and the use of power. How was such a thing to be combatted? Lia's mind seemed to stand apart even as she waited for the blow to come. She was held in the vise that would never let go. The woman could kill her here and who would know or care? Did Paon know of this facet of his lady and, if so, did he care?

Hirath snapped out her words as she held her hand poised, relishing the time of anticipated pain. "How dared you lift your eyes to the lord commander? He is useful to me, to us, and you have dared to tamper with that! Dared! You, an outlander! And they have cried your bravery in these very streets!''

"Abuse her and you destroy the property of the goddess whom you serve. Hold your hand, Hirath. Remember who and what you are." The cold voice that had the power to send chills icing over Lia's spine now reached out to the priestess and made her lift her head.

"Zarnan, you order me. Me?" Hirath sat back on her heels, the flush of anger deepening to rose on the translucent skin. "I, the very shadow of the great—''

"I know who you are." He strode close and peered down at Lia, his cadaverous face and sunken eyes still filled with malignancy. "But remember what we plan. There will be ample time to indulge your tastes later.''

They looked at Lia then, the beautiful woman and the fearful man, both servants of some awesome power unknown to her. If the snake came out now, the trio would be complete. In the moment of her fear and helplessness, the very sense of incongruity struck Lia. Why all this interest in one girl of no great consequence? And had Hirath not said they cried her bravery? Pride warmed Lia and she felt her lips curve in a smile not of her conscious effort.

"Smile, Lia of Pandos, while you can. You will have need of courage before the great one to whom you belong and whom you have gravely affronted in your foolish attempts to escape. You and the lord commander and all those who work against us shall pay. I, Zarnan, have sworn it." Zarnan might have been speaking of the weather or any casual topic but death shone in his face.

Lia tried to speak but she could not. Hirath's laughter was gay and amused now. The fury had left her as suddenly as it had come.

"Take her. Restore her and see that she begins to learn her duties. We shall meet soon, outlander, that I promise."

She threw the dark turban down on Lia's face with such force that her breath was taken away for an instant. Then she was speaking in another language with Zarnan and the pleasure in their voices was evident. Hard hands gathered Lia up and bore her into a cool darkness that was balm itself after the sun's heat.

At first Lia remained passive and limp in the arms that bore her as though she were an inanimate bundle. She was only too glad to be free of the fury that had bloomed in Hirath's face. She did not know if the woman truly had the power that she claimed but it was certain that she, Lia, stood now in even greater danger than before. Her whole body began to tingle just then and she had an overpowering urge to yawn and stretch.

She was lowered to a cold floor with surprising gentleness and a voice spoke over her. "Move about. Your strength will come back as you do." The cloth over her face was pulled back and a container of liquid was held to her mouth. "Drink. We have a way yet to go and I do not relish carrying you." She saw dimness and massive stones seeming to whirl.

Lia obeyed, then sputtered as the potion bit deep in her vitals, restoring life and fire to her mind. The man who bent over her and peered into her face was very tall, black and muscular. Black hair stood out over his head; he wore a short black skirt and cloak. The bullhorns hung around his neck and a serpent bracelet decorated one strong arm.

"Where are you taking me and why?" She could speak slowly now and her legs were responding to her attempts to stand. He reached out a hand to steady her; his grip was not unfriendly as his eyes measured her carefully. "Who are you?"

"My name does not matter. We all serve the goddess. You are going to the great cave sanctuary, passing under the palace and rising up through underground passages known only to the initiates, coming at last to the holy place where you will be inducted into her service by the holy rites." He urged her forward slowly into the stone passage, barely lit by torches placed at distant intervals. A cool stream of air moved about their ankles and drifted upward.

She did not miss the reverence in his words. There would be no help from this quarter. Might there not be information if she forced her brain to acquire it? "I do not understand. What rites? I am a bull leaper with all that that implies."

She saw the flash of his teeth in the darkness of his face. "You will not see the sunlight again, bull leaper or not. The Lady of the Snake has selected you and none can turn back from that. Even great Minos, sequestered in his deepest cave, cannot take you." He began to walk more briskly, keeping his hand on her arm as they went further into the passages that now began to branch off.

"The king of Crete in a cave?" She had to say something or she would begin to scream at the thought of what he had implied.

The dark man inclined his head to the left where three small passages ran together in darkness. "He meditates yonder, hidden from all who would disturb him. Only the faithful know this; they know that he speaks to the goddess in all her manifestations for the salvation of us all." His voice took on the deep-toned ritual note that Lia knew from the ceremonies of the mainland. "But Minos has nothing to do with you, girl. We must hasten." He spoke sharply now and rushed her along.

Lia tried to get him to speak further but he would not and seemed to regret that he had engaged her in conversation at all. They were nearly running now and she found it hard to keep up with him at first, but as her blood began to race and the cramps to leave her body she found the movement a release from fear and anticipation.

They went through cleared and lit stone passages, into ones so narrow and dark that they were forced to bend low, scrambling over debris, before rising to hunch over so that the damp roof did not touch them. Once they waded through an underground stream, walked along a narrow precipice, then forced themselves through a tiny hole at the bottom of a wall of rock. Several times they paused to sample the contents of the flask and catch their breaths.

Lia asked once, "Why this rush? What rites did you mean?"

The somber eyes looked into hers. "We must not speak. It is forbidden now that we are close." He would say no more as they went steadily down as if into the very bottom of the earth.

Lia thought wildly that if they continued this way they would come to the very bull upon which the island of Crete was said to be poised and he would vent his anger upon one who had used his service for her own safety. She knew the tale for nonsense in her rational mind but nothing that had happened lately was rational.

They stopped before a wall of dark rock that was faintly illuminated by a torch set high above it. Her escort reached up and touched a smooth surface. A tiny section of the rock moved back with a grating sound. He pointed to it.

"You go alone from here."

"To what?" Lia was close to the opening and could hear a faint rustling inside.

"Enter the place of snakes. May the Lady of the Snake be with you to preserve you." His hand was hard on her back as she pitched forward into darkness and hisses and the door slammed shut behind her.

Chapter Sixteen

ORDEAL OF THE SERPENTS

IT WAS LIA'S outspread hands that saved her from pitching downward into the black writhing pit below. The push carried her near to the narrow edge of stone that separated the door from the abyss but she caught a projecting corner and clung to it with all the strength of her athletic body. She lay on her stomach, head forward, her feet twisted behind her, and looked into nightmare more fearful than any she had ever had.

She was high above a pit filled with squirming, writhing snakes of various sizes and shapes. Several torches burned high in the roof of the cave and she guessed that they were easily accessible to those who came to tend them, possibly through doors such as the one through which she had been thrust. By their diffused light she could tell that the place was enormous; huge rocks stood everywhere and snakes twined over them, some rising up just as the snake on the platform had done. The flat heads and flickering tongues, the heavy sliding coils and endless activity made Lia remember the feel of the snake on her flesh and reality blurred for an instant. She shut her eyes, then opened them quickly at an ominous crack under her. She shifted a little and it was repeated. The ledge was about to give way.

There was a blurred motion below her and she looked again, although the sight made her shudder. A pillar of rock reached up toward the distant ceiling and, coiled around it, was the largest snake Lia had yet seen. It was black in places and curiously mottled in others. Its head was wide and a dark hood was spread wide. It swayed and reared and coiled as if it were conducting a dance ritual. Lia wondered madly if the goddess herself had come in this form to view her victim. Her gaze shifted and went to the area just below her high perch. There she saw that bowls of milk and honey had been set out just as the ritual of which she had read indicated they should be. But these snakes had recently gorged on something far larger. They lay, black and congested, their prey, possibly small animals brought here for the purpose, still alive within them.

Lia wrenched her mind away and did not allow herself to look again. She had to get to a safer place or soon she would be down in that vile pit with them. Her fingers had gone stiff and numb with the force of her clutch on the corner rock; surely there must be another handhold somewhere. She saw that the ledge, or at least portions of it, appeared to extend for a short distance to her right before that section of the wall vanished into darkness. Some of the tall rocks were very close there and appeared jagged even from here. But far worse to Lia at that moment were the writhing black shapes on them. Another cracking sound warned her that she must move immediately; there was no time to give way to the shuddering horror that threatened to engulf her. Yet her mind would not cease to torment her; if she had not begged and demanded that Paon go out with her, they might both be safe at this time. Life and safety seemed the most important things to her now.

Lia put her legs straight out and kept one hand on the projecting rock as she slid back on the ledge. Her skin was scraped through the short thin robe that they had left on her after bringing her up onto the platform when the snake had selected her. It had barely concealed her nudity and now the cloth from the remnants of the turban was bunched up under her breasts and twisted loosely around her neck. It was hot and damp here; she wanted to throw the encumbering clothes away and gave a bitter smile at her own foolishness. She forced herself to let go her safety and turned to cling to the ridges in the wall. The small portion of the ledge to which she now hung was not wide enough to hold her body. She must stand erect and risk it.

Lia was never sure how she managed to rise. She only knew that all life had come down to this cave and that wall that was pocked and ridged as if with giant fingernails. She set one foot in front of the other three times and then the portion of the ledge on which she had been lying cracked one final time. It gave way and fell to the cave floor. Instantly the snakes were swarming over it, their bodies totally obscuring the surface. The hissing increased and the huge snake with the hood swayed even more widely from the center rock.

"I will not think about them or anything else. Only the next footstep. Only that." Lia said the words out loud and reached for the next tiny handhold. She was not the first who had been here. Someone had carved these projections that her fingers instinctively found. Whatever their fate, hers and Paon's or the unknown before, she would struggle on. She could not think what might lie beyond that curve in the wall. The ledge might end or another snake might wait. She must only get there.

She might have been in the cave for hours, days, forever. Everything narrowed down to where she might best put her foot next or place her hand so as to drew herself along. Her eyes ached from squinting in the dimness and she was always conscious that one misstep would throw her down, not only to death on the rocks but also to the snakes, many of which were almost certainly poisonous. There might have been no life other than this careful reaching, the peering ahead, the constant testing of each step.

Lia put out her foot to take another step and then realized that there was no other to be taken. The ledge did not so much end as vanish into the wall of rock that rose to the roof of the cave where other jagged formations reached down. It was sheer, with no handholds or projections. There was no way around or over it. When she looked back at the relatively short way she had come, Lia saw that since the ledge was broken off as it was she could not go beyond the place where she had entered. She seemed trapped in this den of serpents.

She sank down on her knees, careful to lean in against the wall so that she would not lose her balance. Was this the end after all the struggle? Now she let herself look down into the pit and saw that the snakes continued to writhe there; it seemed they were never still. The hooded snake yet twined over the huge rock and now she was quite ready to concede that this was the affronted goddess who waited for the final tribute of Lia's death.

It was madness, she knew that, but she shook her fist at the great snake and let her shaky laughter ring out in the only defiance it was possible to make. "Wait there for me to die! You offer me a choice and I should be grateful, is that it? Throw myself on the rocks and hope one pierces me instantly? Stay up here and starve? Try to avoid crushing myself down there and let the lesser ones below strike me? I do not like your choices, great goddess, and I did not choose to serve you! Why have you done this to me?"

The sound of her voice was repeated in her ears and with her mention of starvation she realized how hungry and thirsty she was. That, of course, was part of the punishment as seen by Hirath. But she had not thought that the priestess intended her death by any swift means. Starvation on a ledge in a dark cave did not seem to have quite the imagination one might expect of one so strange as she perceived Hirath to be. "I am going mad in truth to think and speak this way." Lia said the words in her normal voice, surprised to find that she could still speak so. How long would it take before she was driven to make a decision as to the manner of her death?

She looked over at the snake and saw that the head inclined toward her much as the first one's head had done when she was chosen. Certainly she had attracted its attention, calling out in that way. Could it reach up this far? Probably, the goddess was all-powerful. It swayed back and forth, going higher and higher as Lia watched. She drew back against the damp wall although the snake was far from her.

She heard a hiss close by and then another. Glancing upward she saw such horror as to eclipse all else. In the darkness beyond the reach of the torches she saw a pouring river of snakes coming from the top of the cave. There was no question but that they would reach the ledge and reach her very soon. She looked wildly across the pit and saw that others were entering on the opposite wall in the same manner. When she looked downward one of those just below her was in the act of swallowing a rat which fought fiercely for life. The rat was enormous and so was the snake. It took no imagination for Lia to see her own fate there.

The hooded snake was reared up so high now that the reflections of light from the dimming torches shone off the spread hood and glistened on the thick body. It dominated this

place of horror and massed death—the very goddess triumphant. It swayed slowly, so slowly that Lia felt her senses
swing with it. She leaned toward the edge again and then a
snake fell past her face. Another landed on the ledge beside her
and she kicked frantically at it only to have another take its
place. One fell on her shoulders.

This time Lia felt that she would truly go mad. It did not
matter that the snakes did not appear to want to attack her or
that they seemed as afraid of her as she was of them. It was the
feel of their cold bodies, the writhing and coiling horror of
them on her skin, the pushing heads and tiny evil eyes.
Scarcely knowing what she did, Lia ripped the remnants of the
turban from around her neck, tied them together in one knot
and slapped at the snakes with the cloth. One swing nearly
tilted her over and she drew back with a shriek only to give
another as her bare foot hit a snake just slithering up to her.
This one, larger than the others and having a strange mottled
color of skin, drew back and struck at her in a motion so swift
that there was no time to dodge. She felt the impact and knew
herself bitten.

She flung her arm out instinctively, cloth and snake went
tumbling into the void while the hooded snake seemed to grow
larger still. Lia trembled against the wall and waited to die.
Then it came to her as she looked at her arm that the snake had
struck there, just above the wrist, but the balled cloth had been
resting there and the fangs had caught it. That had saved her—
that alone.

What matter? Another would come and she would have no
defense. She looked up at the great watcher and then at the wall
just above her head. Snakes were still coming but they seemed
to flow around the outcropping of rock and the sheer wall
expanse at her side. It might have been the shifting light or the
angle at which she sat but Lia saw then what she had not seen
before. There were black indentations in the rock that led up to
a larger, darker one near the top of the cave and well away from
the one by which the snakes entered. Toeholds. Handholds.
Maybe large enough to grip if she could ever get up there and
over the swelling of rock that had prevented her from seeing
them before. It might be hopeless but she had to try.

She rose carefully, kicked out at another snake that landed
beside her and then edged over to look upward. The abject fear

of the snakes was fading a little before this puzzle that might give her a little more fighting time. The great shadow swayed far behind her and as it moved Lia saw a curve in the rock, a slight depressing that might support agile toes and fingers while the others above were investigated. Once again Lia had reason to be grateful that she had once climbed all the crags on Pandos Island and risked her life in what seemed sport at the time. In those days, she recalled, she had wanted an eagle of the skies; now she wanted her life or even a few more minutes of it.

Once again she shut her mind to anything else but the task in front of her. She stretched upward and confirmed with her fingers what her sight had told her. The hold was there but it was almost impossible to see unless you knew what you were looking for. If she had not been nearly bitten by the fierce snake and slumped down in just that way, she would not have seen the holds in the uncertain light. Lia shook her head and tested her whole weight on the strength of her fingers. The hold was true. Several more snakes wound down the wall, still avoiding this section, and came onto the ledge. One headed for her foot, another made as if to rear up and still another, black-mottled and longer than most, aimed toward her ankle. Lia knew that the more savage ones were ready for attack. Now or die!

She put both hands on the stone, balanced one foot against the wall and pushed herself upward with the other. She was clear of the ledge just as the black-mottled snake struck with such force that she could hear the smacking sound the head made on the rock. Her hands were slippery with sweat; she was hot and cold by turns and her fingers felt bruised as she held on to the rock face by force matched with determination. Her hand reached up again for the next hold and her toes rose to claim this one. She was literally splayed against the wall, clinging there precariously. She forced her way upward gradually, checking the tiny projections and declivities in the living rock visually at first, then feeling with her fingers and finally hoisting herself to the next position.

Lia looked down only once and that sent her into such fear that she could only cling to the wall and shake. The ledge was piled with snakes and more were arriving speedily. All it would take would be one coming in this direction and she would fall to the cave floor. The snakes on the ledge were beginning to coil upward and it seemed likely that they could come up in the same way she had.

She was over the out-curving rock now and going up into the darkness. The ceiling was perhaps two lengths of her body away and there was no sign of any artificial opening where it joined the cave wall. She reached up again, determined to play this out to the very end, and this time her hand touched a smooth surface just beyond the rough hold. It might be one of the pathways by which the snakes entered but Lie knew there was no other choice but to continue.

She pulled herself up to the place and saw a narrow tunnel, the mouth of which was barely large enough to admit her shoulders, stretching into blackness. She hesitated for an instant, then looked back over her shoulder at the cave of the serpents. The torches were very low now and she guessed that someone would come along to replace them soon. Would they find the snakes feeding on her dead body? The hooded snake still poised, head toward Lia, and she wondered how it could remain so for this long. All Medo's rational thought had deserted Lia since she had been in Crete and she thought now that the goddess would claim her victim any moment. Had she not dared the great one?

If she fitted herself into this tunnel and found it filled with snakes that would bite her and cause her to swell and die in agony and torment, would the goddess be satisfied? But if she stayed here, Lia knew that her fate was certain.

She went headfirst into the tunnel.

Chapter Seventeen

THE BULL INCARNATE

THE TUNNEL WENT upward as Lia pushed along. She had managed to get one arm over her head and could feel ahead with it but this would be no help if even one snake were encountered. She could see nothing and this blackness was almost more terrifying than the cave of the serpents. The purpose of such a tunnel was a thought she tried to keep out of her mind. She was slender and strong and wiry; only another such as she or young boys could even fit in here. "Or even larger snakes," murmured her mind. It could all come to a dead end or it could lead to the lair of some terrible animal. Was there not, after all, the legend of a great labyrinth on Crete where the accursed of the gods dwelt?

The tunnel floor was still smooth, almost polished, and the sides were the same. When she reached up to the roof, only a finger breadth above her head, Lia found that it was slightly rough. Was the passage this way because of some creature's slitherings through it? When it curved and she was forced to bend her body around, she thought that she could not go on. Fear of the tight place exploded in her again and nausea crowded in her throat. One of her feet brushed against the other, and when she jerked in fright, she was nearly wedged in crossways. Tears began to trickle down her dusty face as she struggled on.

There was no end to it. Everything was darkness, closeness and the deadly stench of fear, the fear of the unknown coupled with the knowledge of what was behind her. Reality was scrambling hands, thrusting feet and fighting body. Reality was the determination to live until the very last instant, no matter what. Lia knew herself for a fighter, a survivor, even though death might have been the easier choice. Perhaps she should have courted the bullhorn in the free light of day or opened her veins with a dagger point. Given the chance, even now, she knew that she would not have taken it. Paon's face came before her eyes and the brilliant excitement that had shone in it when they made love was once again hers for a brief instant. Then it faded and she was once again in darkness.

Tiny pinwheels of light began to whirl in front of Lia and the weakness in her arms and legs began to tell. She could not go on much longer. Her tongue was tight in her mouth and her lips were already cracking. Visions of springs, waterfalls, the vast salt ocean, the clean rain, danced in her head. She looked at her hand stretched out in front of her and wondered that the skin was not drawn dry. Looked at her hand and saw it! Not the darkness but a plea light at the far end of the tunnel.

Caution left Lia then and she covered the distance with a speed that would have been impossible earlier. She dragged herself to the very end and drank in the blessed light and fresh air before peering out into whatever new nightmare awaited. At least she was not to die in that tight place of darkness and menace.

She saw familiar colors: sea green, blue, the yellow of harvest and the gold of sunlight, the foam-tipped ocean and growing crops, pink, red and purple flowers. There were no people in these frescoes, only land and sea, the dolphin and octopus, delicate sea horses and painted coral, the curving S symbols that adorned so many of these scenes and always the living, divine sea that protected Crete. The frescoes covered the walls as far as she could see and the floor just below her was painted a soft blue. Light was everywhere but there were no torches. She had the impression of sunlight on warm summer fields and could almost hear the trickling of the stream that must be close by.

Lia swung herself down to the floor and sat there to recover herself before looking for a place to hide. Her legs were trembling, she was black with dirt and grime, her face wet with tears. She was alive and in the light. That was enough for now.

She looked up at the hole from which she had emerged and saw that it was part of a harvest fresco. The fields stood ready with grain and fruit; the forest was cool and green in the background and a rain cloud hovered just beyond. Her hole was part cloud and part forest, almost invisible unless you knew where to look. Peering at it now, Lia thought that her struggle there must have been impossible.

The trickle of water was driving her mad. She looked around the room or cave, whatever it was, and saw that another painted passage led off to the right. She went into the golden light of it and saw the bubbling stream moving between three tall white columns, which gave onto so realistic a forest that the birds on the tree limbs appeared ready to sing. But Lia had eyes for nothing but the water. She threw herself down beside it and gulped frantically, burying her face, drinking, lifting her nose to breathe and then gulping again. This was salvation and delight; this was restoration and recovery.

The hard voice spoke just behind her and the note of fury was so strong in it that, exhausted as she was, Lia jumped to her feet in one swift movement and came around to face the personage who stood beside one of the columns. He was very tall with a wide chest and long legs. He wore a white loincloth belted in gold. His feet were bare, his skin bronzed. But it was his face that held her attention. It bore the marks of many scars that shone white in the light. These were not disfiguring but rather compelling. His hair was the color of ripe wheat, as were his brows, and his eyes were the chill gray of the winter sea. He might have been in his middle years, for there were lines under his eyes and across the scarred forehead, and his mouth was a straight, disciplined line. He was speaking again in that same tone of voice and this time his hand made a cutting gesture. The long white scars running the length of them both seamed the flesh and riveted Lia's eyes to them.

"I do not understand your language, sir. If I intrude, I am sorry but there was no help for it." She thought if she had to stand much longer she would fall at his feet. He must be one of the priests of the goddess and doubtless had snakes ready to hand. He might even try to send her back. Her jaw tensed and she stiffened to resist.

He saw the motion and the gray eyes noted her exhaustion.

He spoke in Minoan as she had. "This is a holy place, girl, and you defile it. You must go. How did you come here?"

"I will be glad to go. Will you point the way? These passages confuse me and I have taken the wrong turn." Foolish to think she could fool those watching eyes. Even the commonest laborer of the city would not venture out looking as she did.

"You are shaking. Come, I will give you wine and you shall tell me how you came to this place and how you dared to disturb me." He strode closer and placed a hand on her bare arm.

Lia saw that the anger had faded and now curiosity shone on his face. Food and wine. If he had wine, surely he would offer food as well. She could not go on without rest. He was looking at her hair and there was a strange quality in his gaze that she could not identify. It made her uneasy but was nothing beside what she had endured. She inclined her head obediently and let him lead her toward an inner room.

Lia had an impression of cool white walls and floors, serenity and light as her escort led her toward a low table where fish, cakes, figs and dates as well as several types of wine were placed. An arrangement of white cushions was along one side. He gestured for her to sit. She hesitated only briefly and, when he snapped his fingers impatiently, sank down into the softness.

"Eat. Drink. Take your time."

She obeyed, glancing up at him just in time to see that odd gaze cross the dark face. "I am grateful for your hospitality." He stretched his mouth in what might have been a smile and began to pace up and down, arms folded in front of him.

Food and wine had never been so good. Lia ate as though she never expected to do so again but she was careful with the wine. She must keep her senses about her. The man or priest seemed kind enough in a detached sort of way but very little about Crete was safe or as one might expect it to be.

He was speaking again in a thin, distant voice. "How did you come here? It is the order. I am never to be disturbed. It is worth life itself to disobey that."

Lia lifted her head to speak and thought it odd that he suddenly appeared so far off. "I came through the snakes. But who are you? I want only to be free, you see . . ." Her words trailed off and lassitude pervaded her body. "What was in the

wine? I have fought this far and I did not . . ." She tried to
rise but her legs would not work.

He bent over her and the gray eyes pierced through her. It
was as if the crystal gaze of the great goddess had suddenly
been transmuted into this single person. "The wine is subtle
and it has affected you because of the great weariness you
have. You shall not be harmed; I promise it. Rest and we will
speak again when you are recovered." He smiled—the sun
briefly splitting the clouds on a dark day. "I am not without
influence in this place."

Lia did not believe him but she could not fight against her
body. The clouds closed in again and she leaned back on the
cushions, accepting the fate that could not be altered. Before
her senses faded utterly, she felt the long scarred hands on her
hair and saw the secret smile that did not touch the rain-swept
eyes.

Lia dreamed. She walked in sea foam, entered into an
undersea world of blue and green, was dressed in flowing
draperies of the same color and sat on a soft golden couch
where someone unseen touched her face, kissed her brow,
lowered her bound up hair and spread it over her shoulders.
Then she was taken in tender lovemaking by one whose face
she never saw and whose body she did not recognize. She tried
to call him Paon but he silenced her mouth with kisses. She
knew it was a dream and one did not question dreams,
especially such delightful ones. He went behind, kissed her
neck, trailed soft kisses down her backbone and onto the
softness of her buttocks, then ran his fingers through her
tumbling hair and vanished. She walked through the sea foam
calling "Paon, Paon" but there was no answer as she began to
rise through the mist that was suddenly cold to her love-
touched skin.

Lia awoke in the sense that she was aware of different
surroundings. She lay on the white cushions in the white room
but now one wall was bared to reveal the fresco of a charging
bull, a great red-brown one with white polished horns and
flaring nostrils. The great bullhorns that adorned the entrance
to the palace of Knossos shone pictured above him. She tried
to move and found that she could not. Her arms were bound
behind her and anchored to something that held her immobile.
Her legs were spread wide and bound to golden rings set deep

in the floor. She was naked and perfumed; her hair tumbled over her shoulders and she could smell the cleanliness of it.

The bull man came out from the very body of the charging bull and stood over her. He wore golden gloves on hands and feet that were made to appear those of the bull. The white horns were painted on his dark chest and the symbol of the double ax shone golden on his arms and legs. His lifted member, long and hard, stood out from his strong body. The bull mask was golden, ornamented with jewels, and the eyes were set with crystal. It covered all his head and fitted closely to his neck.

Lia wanted to twist away, to struggle, to cry out, but she found that she could not. It was as though she still dreamed and was but half awake. The crystal eyes fixed on hers and he came nearer. All desire for battle left her as he nodded once. Her own head moved up and down and she relaxed completely.

It was as well for her that she did so. He straddled her, came down on her in one swift movement and thrust so deeply into her womanhood that she felt impaled. He drew himself out and came down again, the crystal gaze never leaving her. Some portion of Lia withdrew into the sea mist. She watched him move up and down once more on her lower body in an act that was almost ritual. He was deep and hard in her and once she felt the faint stirrings of a strange desire. It faded as he put one of the gloved hands on her breast and flicked the nipple, then hammered down on her for one final time.

He remained inside her, sitting erect on her and looking at the captive she had become. Lia felt him and knew the utter strangeness of that scrutiny without feeling either resistance or anger. So he might have used a vessel for eating or drinking; this action seemed to have no more meaning than that. She lay and returned his look, woman by god possessed.

White horns and golden signs mingled together as Lia's spread body began to tingle. The creature above her faded out and she saw Paon's face, the brilliant blue eyes lit with passion and laughter. She felt his hands on her breasts and lifted her own to cup his chin. Their mouths met and fused. He disappeared and she rode in the sails of a great ship that sped over a far sea. The horns of the bull became the eyes of the great goddess and once again the hooded snake of the pits looked at Lia.

Her scream split the air and she jerked upward, her heart
hammering in terror. She lay on a yellow couch in another
small white room. Food and drink waited on a table just at her
hand. A pile of gauzy gowns, hair ornaments, water for
washing, a golden comb and some bright yellow flowers had
been placed on another small table at the end of her couch. She
was naked but covered with a soft white robe that smelled of
sunlight and air. Draperies in white and gold hung over the
doorway and from somewhere just outside she heard the
plaintive notes of a single lyre.

Incredulously Lia held her wrists up. There was no sign of
them having been bound; the skin was unmarked there, though
bruised in other areas from her struggles in the tunnel and pit.
She pulled the coverlet away and examined her ankles. No
markings and her lower body seemed untouched. She shifted
about experimentally. Some tenderness was present all over but
surely if she had been bound and ravished by a bull creature,
there would be some visible sign of it. She had simply had a
vivid dream. As for her present state of cleanliness, doubtless
the priest—surely the blond man was that—had ordered his
servants to clean her up as she slept.

She thought that she must have rested long for she was
nearly fully restored, although content to lie here for a while
longer. If he were connected with the worship of the snake, he
might give her back to Hirath but Lia did not think the priest
would give her up so summarily. There had been an air about
him that would demand an accounting from both sides. She
must begin to plan her tale.

She turned over on her side to think and the coverlet rasped
the end of her breast. Her hand touched the nipple and found it
tender, a bit red. The bull creature had touched her there but
only lightly. Had she hurt it in the dream? Yet Paon had
touched and fondled her breasts with no hurt coming to them.
His teeth had caressed them; his mouth had drawn on them.
Strange. She brushed the thought aside and started to toy with
ideas but her mind would not focus.

Then a familiar voice spoke just outside. "The slave may
have dared to come here. She has stolen a most precious object
and must be apprehended at once." It was Zarnan.

Chapter Eighteen

ABYSS OF CRYSTAL

LIA LOOKED AROUND for a weapon to defend herself. She had not endured so much simply to be taken again. One of the hair ornaments had a sharp silver point that glittered in the light. She picked it up and held it while she pulled on the nearest gown, a thin lavender one that left her only scantily clad. She belted it with the matching cord, thrust the pin of the ornament into it, emptied one of the heavy bowls of fruit and carried the bowl with her to the corner nearest the door. It was little enough but she could fight with what she had.

". . . slave. The eye of the great goddess has been taken and she was the last there in the sanctuary! The great one is already angry with our land; the earth has moved more frequently of late. Only let us check the foremost apartments." Zarnan had evidently been talking for some time and his voice was growing angry.

A calm male voice said, "He cannot be disturbed and the high priest should know better than to suggest such sacrilege. Even though the kingdom were falling and the bull shaking himself loose from the land, still the mighty one remains in retreat. You shall not enter, not even the lady Hirath who speaks with the goddess herself."

Lia clutched the bowl more firmly, waiting for the moment when they would brush aside the objections and simply come in. Was the speaker her priest-protector? Factions in temples and among the gods were common things; at least Crete was no different in that respect. That might save her yet.

The silvery voice of Hirath held the ring of prophecy. "The slave has done dishonor to the goddess and must be found. That is but an omen, however. Convey this information to your lord. There are those who dispute his power, saying that he has ruled too long and unwisely. The seas roil about us and the land shakes. Others seek his place and the fires of sacrifice rise. The goddess demands his return and I, her priestess, am ordered to remain such. The seed must be set. Tell him! I speak with her voice in this!" Her words rang deep-toned in the silence that seemed to go on and on.

Zarnan said, "It is all our lives and fortunes. Tell him and let us seek the slave."

"No. Go from this place. If the holy soldiers must be summoned to remove you, you of the highest in this land, I need not tell you the penalty." The voice of her protector was matter-of-fact, even casual. "I do not think the slave is the primary reason you have come here and lies do not become this place."

Suddenly the bull roar, angry and warning of readiness to charge, shook the floor beneath them. It sounded twice more and stopped.

"You are answered. Go."

It was Hirath who spoke. "For now. Come, Zarnan. Your lord has been warned."

Lia expelled her breath slowly and lowered the bowl as she heard the stone door beyond swing into place with a heavy grating. She was saved again and now she was in possession of valuable knowledge. Only one person in Crete was in seclusion. Only one person was so honored and protected, King Minos of Crete. And she, Lia of Pandos, stood in the anteroom of his stronghold.

She heard the scuffling movement of sandaled feet approaching and jumped quickly onto the couch, jerking the cover up to her shoulders. When the same voice spoke from the doorway she allowed her lids to flutter upward and droop drowsily. Her whole body was tense with the enormity of the scheme that had come to her.

"You are awake? You will not leave this room. There is nothing to fear and you will be questioned later. Do you understand me?" The speaker was of medium height, wearing a white tunic and white headband. His nose was beaky, his eyes black and sharp.

Lia yawned once and then again. "So sleepy. I don't have to get up yet, do I?"

"No, of course not. Sleep all you wish. I regret disturbing you."

Lia feigned sleep once more but he stood watching and it was all she could do to keep her breathing regular. Finally he moved softly away but she lay still and counted the waves in the ocean, an old device of hers to lure calmness or sleep.

It was impossible to tell day or night in this place of light but Lia believed that she must have slept for what passed for a night before the coming of Hirath and Zarnan. She could not imagine how they knew that she had escaped from the place of snakes but there could be no doubt of her fate if they found her now. The blond priest might be her best hope and if she found him it might be well to tell as much of the truth as was feasible, but those who lived by the favor of factions might well die by them. She was an outlander, surely not yet subject to the laws of Crete, and she was a bull leaper in a sense. The god had visited her in a dream; the snake goddess had inclined toward her. Further, she knew the tales of the cold sea and of the loyalty of the lord commander. Might these things not entitle her to an audience with great Minos? If it were death to disturb him, then it was surely death to remain as she now was, hounded and endangered. She would take the chance. Her spirits swung upward and she smiled behind her hand. If ever she won free of Crete and its mysteries and came to the land of Egypt, she would purchase a few props and set up as a prophetess-healer of small maladies. Certainly Crete was offering her lessons by way of Zarnan and Hirath. "If I live . . ." She breathed the words as if they were a talisman and rededicated herself to that credo.

Shortly afterward Lia rose and slipped out into the white room she remembered, beyond to the hall of frescoes and into a still wider passage painted red and white. There was no sign of any person, no sign of any human habitation. She slipped along, moving behind columns or dodging back against the walls as the passage went now up, now down. There seemed little need for such caution but she was wary. Was she wrong in her speculations? Perhaps the blond man kept a solitary shrine and the others sought simply to harass him. She went on; by now she preferred action to useless thought.

The way was now lit by torches set high in the walls. The floor was red and white, the main passage zigzagged strangely and the ceiling sparkled golden in the flickering light. Lia felt something move under her bare foot suddenly and, remembering the snakes, leaped aside and backward. Something fell in front of her and clattered. A black object ran toward her at the same time. Light flamed along the knife blade that would have embedded itself in her heart had she not made that double movement. The giant black spider moving toward her was one of the deadliest kind known; one bite meant an agonizing death.

There was time only to react. Lia snatched the bright hair ornament from her waistband and threw it to the side in one swift motion of her hand. It made a pinging sound and bounced. The spider went toward it and settled there. Lia picked up the knife and ran for her life, staying in the very center of the passage and moving on tiptoes, well aware that intruders might be expected to skulk to the sides and thus release other traps. Once she stumbled over an exposed rock and saw part of the ceiling begin to tremble as some stones rained down. It took no imagination to guess the landslide that would have occurred if she had hit it harder. Now she knew why no guards patrolled this area.

There was, as always, nothing to do but go on. She walked cautiously, moving as lightly as she could, one hand on the knife. In one sharp corner turn, she saw a shimmering ruby set in the stone of the wall. It could easily be taken if one were in search of such things. As she stared at it Lia saw the movement just above and noticed the flat head of the great snake there. Part of the wall would come away the moment the jewel was touched and the snake would be upon the thief.

She backed away and went deeper into the reddening passage. That color covered walls, ceiling and floor. It made her think of blood, perhaps hers soon to be shed. She gripped the knife in both hands now and went into a half-crouching position as she crept along. Her heart was banging and her ears rang. Something was about to happen; all her senses told her that.

There was a faint clicking above her head just then and she looked upward to see a mass of glittering pointed knives sweeping downward. She sank instinctively to the floor and it fell away around her. There was a booming sound and she cried out as the world seemed to turn about itself. She sat on a small section of stone which was barely large enough to take two small steps on. The rest of the floor had turned downward into a pit, which was set with tall spikes ending in glittering knives that sparkled in the far torchlight. The ceiling was so low that she could touch it and crystal spikes interspersed with knives hung from it also. Small dark spiders crawled in the pit and on the ceiling. Lia could see that they were very like the large one she had avoided earlier but they were no less poisonous.

She could neither go ahead nor retreat from this place which was so cleverly planned to shield a king. Luck or chance had been with her up until now, but no longer. She balanced on her perch there in the red glow and knew the bitterness of defeat, the fear of a dreadful death, and the angry tears burned in her eyes. Then she tossed back her hair and lifted her face in a gesture of defiance that could have no hope of success. She would brush spiders away; she would hack at them until there was nothing else to do. Easier, perhaps, to use the sharp knife on her wrists but she had not yet come to that.

"Is it you?" The incredulous voice floated at her across the abyss. "Lia?"

She thought it only part of her imaginings but looked across at the far wall which was shadowed and dim. A figure stood there, tall, cloaked, well blended in darkness. But she knew that voice, for it rang in her dreams and whispered in her thoughts by day. Wonder of wonders that he was here! It might be a trick, although she did not know what purpose would be served.

"Paon." His name came from the depths of her throat once and then again. "Paon."

"It is I. By the goddess, what are you doing in this place? There is no time to lose. Obey me exactly and you have a chance. One touch on any of those spikes or knives and you will die in terrible agony. The spiders will be upon you very shortly; they respond to motion. Will you do as I say?" He came out from the wall and stood looking at her.

"Yes." She could say no more but it was enough. Those trapped in this place would pay the full penalty. His description chilled her blood and she could not doubt the ordeal that was to follow.

Paon reached behind him and drew out a long pole that folded into two sections. He unfastened this and extended it toward Lia's perch, being careful to make sure that it did not touch the spikes. She watched the fragile-appearing thing weave toward her and knew with a certainty what was expected.

The end of the pole landed at her feet and made a metallic sound as it did so. Paon was standing on the far end, testing the balance with one foot. The pole was bigger around than her arm but it seemed to be a thin dark thread stretching across the deadly chasm. The distance to the wall was not that great but to Lia it was endless.

"It will hold. The ends are so made that they will adhere to the rock. Walk it, Lia. Do it now." He spoke calmly; they might have been going out for a stroll together.

"I am afraid."

"You have been afraid before. Come." He snapped his fingers impatiently. "I cannot come to take you to safety, you know."

Lia knew. He sought to rouse her spirit and stir her to response. He could not know how hammered down that spirit was by all the experiences of the recent past. She hesitated, staring down at the thin expanse of the pole. Could she do it? She remembered heights scaled, branches swung on, canyons crossed by means of vines and limbs. But that had been Pandos.

"Lia." Paon raised his voice a little. Urgency trembled in it.

She half turned and saw that the spiders were beginning to drop from the ceiling. Time had run out.

"I am coming." As good as any words to die by. She would not be alone; she would take his face before her into the darkness.

Lia set one foot on the pole, which gave slightly under her weight. It was not wood at all but some supple metal that seemed to catch at her skin. She put the other foot out and stretched out her arms to balance herself. Paon was murmuring soothing words as if they were a litany and his hands were moving, encouraging her to come. Step, step and step again. There was no reality, no dream. She was in a void where she must remain erect and balanced. The robe slipped from her shoulders and was hanging over her spread arms, leaving her breasts bare. She felt the soft touch and involuntarily looked down.

She had not come even half of the distance and the spikes shone red in the light. The spiders scuttled among them; more must have come in, for the floor was black with them. The air was growing stale and her feet were suddenly slippery with sweat. She felt herself tilt. One arm waved; her legs began to tremble with the strain placed on them.

"Come, Lia. Love, my love, come." Over and over Paon was speaking the words that might have no meaning other than this moment but she could see his dark face now, worried and tormented, the high cheekbones standing out more than ever.

The shift in thought took her mind away from fear long enough for her agile body to respond to life's demand and she was steady again. She set her eyes on his and walked once more, slowly, carefully, into his waiting arms.

They clung together, arms wrapped tightly around each other, his lips on her hair. Then she lifted her face to his and their mouths fused. He kissed the tears from her eyes, caught her in his arms again and hugged her so hard she thought her ribs would crack. She put her arms around his neck and they stared at each other in mutual wonder.

"You saved my life, Paon. I am forever grateful." She was almost formal in her politeness, she thought, but their embraces had said so much.

He smiled at her and the warmth of it sent delight coursing through her veins. Then he leaned forward to kiss her throat and she was conscious of the hanging robe, her bare breasts and near nudity. Color began to rise in her face as she reached down to pull the cloth to herself.

An iron hand caught hers and another brushed the robe back. Paon lifted her breast in fingers that were no longer gentle. Lia stared at his face, which was now harsh and older in the space of an instant. His scornful gaze held hers and dropped again to her breast.

"His seal is upon you, lady. You have not wasted your time, I see."

"I do not understand." Lia looked at her breast and saw, just above the rosy nipple, the golden sign of the double ax.

Chapter Nineteen

HALL OF JUDGMENT

"IT IS THE SEAL and will not come off, as you well know."
Paon watched Lia run her fingers over the golden mark that
was set into her flesh. "Why did you come to this place of
danger? Did you seek to lure me or others?"

The harshness in his voice beat at her as she pulled the
remains of the robe back over herself and let her hair come
forward so that it hid her bosom. She could not think what the
mark meant but she remembered again the bull creature of her
dream and how her breast had tingled. The only thing that
mattered right now was the loss of Paon's warmth and joy in
their reunion and safety.

"You make no sense, Paon. Of what are you accusing me?"
She had started to placate him but those angry blue eyes were a
challenge and she rapped out the words in response. "I see the
mark but I have no idea who placed it there or what it means.
Perhaps you will tell me."

"You belong to another. One far greater than I. I seek him
and you go before me." He put his hand on the dagger at his
waist; the silver handle gleamed under the edges of the dark
cloak. "Willingly or unwillingly, it does not matter."

Lia gave him look for look. "Then let us go. I am eager to
get out of here." She stepped forward to where light gleamed
from a corridor just ahead.

His short bark of laughter held no amusement. "You will

never leave it, Lia of Pandos, or do you pretend to be ingnorant of the fate of those who service the great bull?"

She stared at him in horror as he caught her wrist in that hard grip and pulled her so that she stood in front of him. He was waiting for her to beg and question. She jerked back so hard that his fingers dropped away and her head went high.

"I thought you were anxious to leave here, Lord Commander."

He was beside her in one swift stride but he did not touch her again. "That title is no longer mine, lady. Perhaps you know why."

Lia said no more but paced beside his tall, grim figure as they went out into the narrow, well-lit corridor that zigzagged back and forth in a strange manner but offered no more traps such as she had recently endured.

Once Paon pulled her back from an innocent-looking section of floor. "Trapdoor." The one word conveyed her thoughts back to the pit of snakes and she thought it not unlikely that another such existed beneath them now. They walked single file through sharpened spikes set in the cave walls and came to an open expanse where a great stone stood high, ready to tumble down and crush those unwary enough to be heading for the golden door just beyond.

"Do you wish to come further?" Paon was almost taunting as he turned to look at her. "You can wait until he summons you and be safe."

"I will come." Lia had decided that nothing she could say or any avowals would make any difference to him in this mood.

He gave that mirthless laugh again. "Of course you will. I never meant to let you out of my sight." He held up his hand before the fury on her face. "There is no time for that. Move as I do and stay low. Out there we can both die."

He tossed his cloak aside and stood revealed in near nudity, his powerful body gleaming, his profile perfectly cut and sharp. Lia tensed for yet another test. Still, when he began to run in the zigzagging pattern of the corridors, she did not at first think of danger as she followed at his heels. She heard the rumbling as if a landslide were about to begin and then saw four great boulders coming at them from four directions. Someone was calling out in the distance and it seemed that they were about to be crushed. Then they were only a short away from the door and safety. Paon threw himself to the side one last time and Lia did the same. The boulders thundered together with a crash that must surely be heard in the port city. Then Lia and Paon were gasping for breath as they pressed against the wall. Four soldiers armed with flashing swords confronted them a moment later and they were speaking in that language that Lia did not understand. Paon waved toward her and spoke in it also.

One of the soldiers put his blade to Paon's throat and the expressions on the faces of his men were filled with fear. Lia moved closer to Paon but he motioned her back and one of the men took her by the shoulder. Paon spoke sharply and the man pulled the robe away from her breast. The golden ax shone in the reflected light. He released her so quickly that she fell to the floor. The one holding the sword to Paon moved and Paon pushed him backward. Then he was at the great door, rapping four times in succession. A hollow booming began and over it his voice rang out.

"Minos, Lord King, I invoke you! Come!"

The door seemed to shiver inward and the guards fell back before the explosion of light that engulfed them. Out of this came a softer booming and Lia saw that the pathway was open into the brilliant white room ahead. Paon strode boldly in; she came behind him although it was apparent that he had forgotten her existence.

A tall man dressed in flowing white robes stood before the fresco of a charging bull and a mighty serpent with spread hood that was rising from the green sea. His arms were folded across his chest; eyes of a piercing gray regarded them with detachment but his mouth was both set and stern. It was the blond man whom Lia had met earlier. Even then she did not realize as she looked at him with surprise and recognition. Paon's sharp intake of breath made her think how he must view this and she turned toward him.

He sank to one knee before the blond man. "My lord, I would not have sought you out in this manner had the case not been desperate and involved more than myself. Will you hear me out?"

"You jeopardize all our lives, Lord Commander. The king is not above this law." His voice was cold, commanding, and his eyes raked Lia and Paon. "You know the penalty."

"I know." Paon was unflinching.

Lia gasped and went to both knees before Minos, King of Crete, Priest of the Bull, Servant of the Great Goddess. She was appalled that she had not known—but how could she? Remembering the remoteness of those eyes and the icy bearing, she wondered that she had ever thought to amuse him with a tale. As well to think of approaching the crystal-eyed Lady of the Snake.

"Get up. I do not require that my people prostrate themselves before me. Speak, Paon. The time is short."

Paon rose as bidden and his eyes went to Lia. She came up from her knees to stand waiting. She could read nothing in his or the king's face.

"I would speak privately with you, my lord."

The cold voice said, "The woman came with you, did she not? Speak before her, then."

"As you command." Paon was no longer hesitant. He was now the bold commander Lia had first known, a man sure of himself, determined and ready for the struggle whatever form it might take. "There is a plot to take you from the throne and send you to the death of ritual. It is felt that you have too much power consolidated in your hands and do not use it to put forth the greatness of Crete. We rule the seas; it is time to venture out by force of arms and these people would do so. Crete could go into decline, they say, because of your policies and your known interests in peaceful trade, peaceful colonization and expeditions. There is no son of your loins to hold them back. It would be easy to supplant you, especially since you linger long in sacred meditation each season and do not come forth to rule."

He paused for breath and Minos said, "Be specific. Or can you?" Warning rang in his voice.

"The high priest Zarnan has used his influence with the servant of the Lady of the Snake and those of the court faction who favor a policy of aggressive measures against Egypt. They have moved against me, held me captive until your return to the world, tried to work against others of your friends—two died suddenly of a fever that was no fever—and have caused the people to speak against you in the streets, crying out that a strong and powerful ruler is needed lest Crete lose her supremacy. They say that I have consorted with the pirates and have failed in my commission. There will be an attempt on your life within the next day or two in these very sacred walls and it will be undertaken by the high priest himself, who seeks to name the next Minos."

"How do you know all this, Paon?"

"My betrothed is the lady Hirath who serves the Lady of the Snake and who has lent herself to the plot that she might learn of it and so let you be informed. It was she who helped me to get free and who urged me to come here if I could." Sweat was standing out on Paon's brow now and he spoke earnestly. "Lord Minos, move to destroy these plotters! You have been my friend and ruler since I first arrived in Crete; it was you who lifted me up despite my outlander blood that some others found demeaning. Rise and come out, I ask you! The plotters are many but they can be dealth with."

Minos nodded gravely, putting a hand to his chin. "And the woman who is with you?"

Paon started visibly. "The outlander bears your mark, Lord Minos. I assumed that you had her fetched to you."

Lia said, "I am Lia of Pandos, King Minos. I was captured by the lord commander, stolen away when he was taken for treason against you and I was imprisoned by one he thought friend. I thought to save myself by joining your bull leapers and did so for a time but that same Hirath of whom he speaks had me taken and placed in the pit of snakes. I had just come from there when I met you in the white room. She and Zarnan came to seek me and to warn you; I fled and came here in my attempts to find a way out." She looked straight into the gray eyes and hoped that he knew pure truth when he heard it. "That one who imprisoned me said that the lady Hirath would seek to remain a priestess, for power is there, that she would attempt to lure you to her bed, Lord King, and so have a chance for the heir. Failing that, the plot to destroy you would be joined. She is cruel and dangerous!"

Minos looked toward Paon. "She speaks of your betrothed. What do you say to that?"

"Nothing to her, Minos, my friend and my king. She is yours and the words of her mouth are yours to deal with as you see fit. I am to wed the lady Hirath and the contract was made years ago. Her family has ever hated me. It was she who protected me this time and who learned of the plot. But for her I might have been dead, slain by those who wield daggers in the night. You offered Hirath to me in marriage at the time of her cessation as priestess. Your will is law to me and I have found her both fair and brave." Paon faced his ruler boldly now. "Will you not return to the palace and claim that which is yours?"

"Lia of Pandos is also fair and brave. She has undergone many ordeals and survived them all. She is a worthy carrier of my seed." The scarred hands went out suddenly and the fierce eyes looked into the distance. "She was no virgin. Did you despoil a virgin destined for me, Lord Commander?"

Paon opened his mouth to speak; red spots burned high on his cheekbones as he turned toward Lia. She felt her own face flame with shock. It had been no dream. Minos had come to her in the guise of the bull and taken her those times. Taken her as though she were a vessel waiting to be filled.

"We lay together twice, Lord Minos. He is handsome and I hungered for him. My father wed me when I was quite young to a young man who was slain in battle a few moons later. I fought against the marriage but later I grew to love him. I wanted no other. Later we went into exile on Pandos and I tended my father until his death." Lia lied boldly and hoped that he would believe her.

"There was no child nor hope of one?" Minos spoke very softly but there was something else behind his calmness.

"No, lord, there was not. My mother only bore the one and that after great travail." She caught her breath and continued. "It was I who sought the lord commander and he did yield unwillingly."

Paon would have spoken but Minos held up his hand. The brilliant light shone on the scars and sent a chill down Lia's back. "You came in good faith, Paon, but it is still death to disturb the king at meditation. Death for you and the woman. I have ever rested my faith in the great goddess and she whom I serve will protect me." He waved toward the bull rampant. "I am his priest-king and he speaks through me. His voice has been in the earth and I am to reign long. What are court factions to me beside the very words of the gods themselves?"

Paon shrugged. "What then is your will?"

"The great ones are affronted. I shall have to ascertain their will and inform you of it."

"Every word he speaks is truth! Only beware of the lady Hirath!" Lia cried out knowing it was hopeless.

There was movement in the room then, a swift coiling motion similar to that of snakes. When Lia looked around she saw that three of the guards had entered behind Hirath, Zarnan and a fat, balding man with a savage face. All bent the knee reverently before Minos, who commanded them to rise in a tone that was almost absentminded.

Zarnan said, "We were close by, Lord Minos, and hoping to speak with you if you deemed it time to emerge from your holy seclusion. One of the guards told us what was happening and we came at once." His voice rose high in what appeared to be anguish. "Intercede for us all that the gods do not strike us down before they can be propitiated!"

Hirath picked up the same note and her cry seemed to encircle them all. "Perhaps the great ones are not angered, Zarnan. Did not the king speak long with these interlopers? It appears that they came before him by his own will despite the holy oath of seclusion that was taken. If that is true, this goes beyond the anger of the gods to their righteous destruction!"

Zarnan was very like the hovering, brooding snake of the pits as he stood there with the light blazing on his bald head and cadaverous body in the loose robe. In his measured response to Hirath, Lia heard the echo of rehearsal. "For the gods destroy those who do not serve and obey them and rightfully so! Priest, king, ordinary person—none are above it. Guards! Seize this man and woman! Take them away for judgment!" He waved an imperious arm and the guards advanced hesitantly. He turned back to Minos. "Lord Minos, the king of Crete, I must speak in the name of those I serve. Did these people gain admittance to you through your will before you had undergone purification and signaled your readiness to return to the world? If so, you, too, must answer to the great ones."

The fat man spoke for the first time. "We know that he did not. Minos of Crete, prepare yourself!"

Lia glanced at Hirath and saw that the woman was literally glistening with triumph. The beautiful face, the silver-streaked hair and lithe body were suddenly ripe with the nearness of ambition fulfilled. Now that she knew the ways of the body, Lia did not miss the barely hidden lust as Hirath watched

Paon. Did he believe now in the perfidy of his betrothed, she wondered? Then she thought that it did not matter at all; a power that could harry the ruler of Crete and perhaps destroy him could also stamp out such a one as herself. Life was measured in hours for Lia of Pandos.

Minos folded his arms again and let his gray eyes rest on those before him. The guards moved back slightly; the others were still before the power of this man. He said very softly, "The bull god shall answer for me." His face was rock still as his lips pressed into a thin line.

And the roar of the angry, charging bull rang in his temple.

Chapter Twenty

THE QUEST

THE BULL CRY came three times in succession, resounding from the ceiling, the walls, and seeming to shake the very floor under their feet. Then the concentration of sound faded to an angry snort as Minos held out both arms in an imperious gesture, his scarred palms thrust toward the group and his head tilted slightly back as though he listened to something they could not hear. There was another roar just then and it was accompanied by a banging sound as if an angry bull sought to break out of confinement. Minos spoke in an unintelligible string of sounds which might have been an answer. There was a final burst of sound that came from all around and total silence fell.

The king of Crete faced them again and this time priests and guards alike moved back. Even Hirath was pale, her breath coming in little shuddering gasps. Paon went to his knees and Lia followed. She fixed her eyes on the stern face that seemed to merge with the bull and serpent of the frescoes against which he stood.

"He has spoken to me and laid out his commands." Minos spoke clearly, authority in every syllable of his voice. His arms came down slowly and one hand touched the stone behind him. His words rose in the quiet. "Summon the watchers, guards! A mighty thing has happened here!"

Lia heard them rush to obey, eager to get out of this fearful presence. There was a stir behind and Hirath moved forward.

The woman had courage, Lia thought, but surely this was not the time to challenge Minos further.

"Lord Minos, I would ask . . ." The low controlled voice faltered to a stop at the sight that confronted them all.

The great hooded snake that came from behind Minos wound around his feet, twisted up his torso to his neck and rose up over his head. The heavy coils should have bent Minos down but, wrapped in the darkness of the snake with his blond hair and powerful features, he was the ruler of upper and lower worlds in Lia's sight.

"The great goddess is among us." Minos now nearly whispered but all could hear him. "I and I alone in Crete am the recipient of their combined commands, the bull and the snake."

The silence was almost savage as Hirath sank to her knees, head still unbowed. Lia sensed her fury and knew that the balance could shift. With daring she never thought to have, she lifted her voice up.

"Hail to Lord Minos! The gods have spoken this day!"

Paon took up her cry and added, "The voice of the great ones! Minos, our king!"

There was a clatter at the door just then and a hubbub of voices responded with cries of adulation. Lia turned her head carefully and saw brilliantly robed men and women, golden-attired priests and white clad men swarming in. Color flashed on jewels and fabrics; the room was alive with light and motion. Only Minos, snake-crowned and golden, was unmoving and stern before them all.

They made to kneel and he waved one hand. "Rise up. I will speak with the voice of the gods, they who this day have been affronted." A murmur ran over the room but it was quickly silenced. "Fetch the mask."

Someone ran to obey. Lia rose and drew back to avoid contact with Hirath, who now stood between herself and Paon. Zarnan, face expressionless, was just to the left of them. Minos dominated the gathering and she knew that the balance of power had, for the moment, turned. Blood pounded in her head and she felt the trickle of sweat on her back. So much had happened in so short a time that she could not sort it all out. She could only stand and await the next move in this impossible game of power.

Two young men in white robes returned carrying a wrapped object. They approached Minos very cautiously at his imperious gesture. He reached out, took it, shook the cloth loose and held the golden, white-horned mask in front of his face. The eyes were of glowing crystal and the nostrils shone dark. Red, green and blue stones encrusted the edges. Light poured onto the horns, which seemed almost translucent in its glow. A guard advanced to the side of the king and stood, legs widespread, as he held aloft the double ax. The snake was unmoving, dark body ominous against the gold.

The bull voice, loud and menacing, boomed out again. Lia clenched her fingers in her palms and felt the nails cut the flesh. Paon's dark profile was sharply etched as she darted a glance at him. Then the words and their meaning took her. Her stomach knotted up as she listened.

"Mortals have attempted to influence the gods and restitution shall be made at once or this land shall suffer! The king has been challenged by those who say that the sacred rituals of seclusion and return to the world have not been observed. His role as representative of the great ones—all of them—is therefore in jeopardy and his voice is blunted. Not so! The king rules and those who challenge him challenge the gods! They seek power, forgetting by whose command they live!"

The snake leaned forward to hiss and the bull mask shook with the force of the voice issuing from it. The silence in the room was acute. Lia did not dare breathe and she could hear her heartbeats.

"Punishment is meted out. Those who have challenged Minos shall retire to their respective temples where they shall do the work of the lowliest servants of the gods. Thereby they learn the fruit of ambition. Those set low formerly shall be high over them. Such is my will.

"The male offender who first sought out the king is banished until a sacred quest into the cold lands shall be fulfilled. He leads and others go with him. The nature of the quest I will reveal to the king this night. The female who has been both bull leaper and the honored recipient of the king's seed shall be set apart to serve at his court. Such is my will. Obey it!"

The voice ceased. Minos lowered the mask and looked at the people who murmured in awe. Lia caught Paon's savage gaze.

The pulse in his temple was hammering although he was outwardly still. They stared at each other until a movement beside Lia made her turn away.

"Come, lady." The girl was small and young, dressed in delicate white draperies that flowed over her slender figure. "You must rest now."

Lia was suddenly exhausted in mind and body. She was only too willing to obey. Hirath's gaze raked her as she passed and the people parted, staring in their turn. As she went out the door Lia saw priests clustered around Minos. They remained a respectful distance away but the great snake was slowly coiling down his body.

The girl took Lia through a maze of passages that went ever upward and conducted her finally into a yellow room hung with pale green cloth. Food and wine stood ready beside a couch. Lia sank down on it, thinking that she ought to question the girl as to what would happen next but she was too weary.

"You are the protected of Minos. Rest."

The soft voice drifted into Lia's ears as she lay back and let the whirlwind take her. This time there were no dreams.

Lia could not have said how long she slept; since she had been a prisoner all sense of time had departed. She was wide awake and looking into dark eyes in a pale face bent anxiously over her. It was the same girl but her calm was gone as she put white fingers on Lia's arm.

"You are summoned. Bathe and we will dress you. Hurry!"

Even as she spoke other women entered with vats of water, robes and chests of gems. Lia did ask questions as they removed the tattered garment she had been wearing but no one would answer. She gave herself up to their ministrations, relieved that she felt her old self once more and ready to discover what new struggle would present itself.

They dressed her in the full flounced skirt, sparkling with jewels and tightly belted around her narrow waist. It was brilliant blue as were the sandals fitted to her slender feet. Her breasts were lifted high by golden straps that supported them and crossed over her shoulders. Blue jewels ornamented the straps and shone in transparent gauze which was arranged to lie casually over her bosom. The mark of the king shone clearly through it. Her hair was lifted high over a coronet of blue and allowed to flow freely down her back. One woman worked over her face, touching it with strange substances, and then held up a polished square for her to look.

Lia saw a stranger there—a woman with a oval face and slanting dark brows, red lips and darkened lids. Her high forehead was smooth and serene but her large eyes shone with excitement. The coronet gave her a regal air and the golden hair seemed to shimmer. It was a proud face, no longer that of the young girl, who, not so long ago, had climbed trees and run free on Pandos while she thought how to cajole Ourda.

The woman took the square from her and brought a cup of wine which Lia drank quickly. She was beginning to think that nothing good could come from this summons. Perhaps she would see Paon again and he would think her fair. Her blood stirred, warming her cheeks. What quest would he be sent on? She might never see him again and his betrothed hated her.

"Come. We must hurry." The young girl was beside her again and this time fear shone over her face so that it was beaded with perspiration. She walked ahead of Lia who was followed by several others. As they walked up the passage they were joined by four guards in golden loincloths. Their pace was swift. All of them avoided Lia's eyes.

They went through a maze of rooms and connecting halls that led first to one direction and then the other in a pattern that Lia found totally confusing. Soon they entered a long hall hung with shields embossed with the double ax. The bull and the snake faced each other at opposite ends in magnificent frescoes. Pictured Cretans brought tribute to both while dolphins swam in the eternal sea and maidens danced before them. Courtiers stood whispering as their procession passed and Lia saw the curious expression in the eyes of many.

From the hall they went into a smaller one, turned and entered an ornate room. The floor shimmered with fragments of gold and crystal laid down on the stone. The air was scented with flowers and perfumes. Stone benches extended along the far walls and they, too, glittered with gems. The entire chamber was frescoed with peaceful scenes of rivers, birds, animals and fish. A throne stood at the end; it was draped in gold and blue. Minos, wearing a white garment and crowned with the snake and horns, sat upon it. On either side of him two pairs of fierce dragons, painted green and blue, forever snarled at each other. The king sat between the beasts, ruler of them all. A stone path of steps led downward to what appeared to be a sacrificial place.

Lia looked at those who waited on the benches. Hirath was there and several of her priestesses. Zarnan was with the fat, savage-looking priest who had challenged Minos. Other priests and some red-clad courtiers stood apart. All seemed poised as if for attack. The face of the king was as hard as the rock behind his throne.

Lia's escort fell away and she stood before the throne and its occupant who stared at a point just beyond her head. She thought that perhaps she should bow her head before him but that was not her nature; she looked boldly at him and heard the low hum as the spectators took note of her action.

Minos spoke in a level voice. "Lia of Pandos, hear me. The Snake Goddess did take you for her own in the street on a day not long done. She did protect you in the pit of serpents and now she claims you again. She is affronted by your actions and demands restitution. The man who was once my lord commander, Paon, goes into the cold lands to find a supply of a precious metal vital to Cretan expansion. You are to accompany him. In that land the stones walk and fabulous jewels are their living eyes. You shall bring back two such that the goddess may be graced. She has laid her commands thus: two rubies the size of your fist and the very stone from which they came."

Lia was startled at the wave of joy that swept over her and fought to conceal it. The company of Paon and freedom! What else could there be to give life richness? She whispered, "I, Lord King? How is this to be done?"

"The soldiers of Crete go with you and with Paon. The will of the great ones must be carried out or their curse will follow you both to a painful death and beyond into the netherworld. Their priest goes with you to watch and mete out justice should you think to shirk this quest."

He paused and Lia dared to ask, "And if I carry the child of the king?"

"Rather say that you carry any man's spawn! By your own admission there have been others and a woman must come virgin to him! So has the goddess spoken!" Hirath was standing straight and tall, her vivid face alight with satisfaction as her voice cut across Lia's.

"Silence!" Minos was standing now, his figure seeming to merge with those of the snarling dragons, the tall crown glowing with an unearthly light. "Your family's power will not protect you forever, Hirath! Be warned!"

The woman sank back down on the bench, her head bent. Lia watched Minos carefully and saw the fascination there before the heavy lids came down. She knew then who meant to drive her from Crete. Surely Hirath knew that the prospect of a voyage with Paon would delight Lia! Or did Hirath simply wish to rid herself of a rival?

"The voyage begins in ten days. You are to return to Knossos in two full turnings of the seasons. Then you will face the great ones again and learn if your offense is mitigated. At that time I, myself, will speak to them in my own behalf. All is held in abeyance until that time."

He came down the steps of his throne and paced slowly by, looking neither to the right nor to the left. The company was silent, bending before him as he went. The young woman who had tended Lia came up to her and touched her arm, nodding toward a passage that was bright with light.

"Wait." The hard voice spoke behind them and Lia whirled around. Paon stood there, his sardonic face burning with an anger that was barely suppressed. He wore the blue that was the color of his eyes and court jewels flamed at his neck and wrists. Heedless of any listening ears, he said, "I do not know what you hope to accomplish by forcing yourself on this voyage! You, the eye of the goddess! You who lay eagerly with our king! I cannot prevent it since it is his will but you shall wish that you had remained in Knossos rather than seeking for power on a mission such as this. Guard yourself, lady!"

"You cannot think that I forced this, Paon!" Incredulity rang in Lia's voice as she faced him. She heard someone laugh beyond them and felt a flush come over her. "How could I? And there is no reason."

"I know you to be a schemer and full of wiles. Heed my warning!" Paon turned away from her and held out his hand to the woman who approached. "Hirath, we must hurry or the king will be kept waiting."

Hirath gave Lia a look of pure triumph mixed with hatred as she moved away with Paon. Their shared laughter burned in Lia as she followed the beckoning young girl out of the sight of the courtiers.

The days of waiting had begun.

Chapter Twenty-One

INTO THE SEA FOAM

THE SILENT MAIDSERVANTS arrayed Lia in the color of the goddess, the golden skirt that was flounced and full, a golden short jacket that displayed her breasts and a thin robe of tissue of gauze that covered all. A golden diadem was set in her hair and sandals of the same hue were on her feet. They held the polished mirror for her solemnly and she saw the new hollows in her cheeks, the accentuated bones and the faint shadows under her eyes. One girl came up with wine and as she took it Lia noticed the slight tremble in her own hand. She waved the girl back and took a restorative sip. How long could it take them to bring a litter from the palace?

Lia stood there under their eyes and thought of the past days. She had been taken from the court and lodged in a small stone dwelling on the far grounds. It had two rooms and a little flower garden where she was permitted to walk under guard for a few short minutes at varying times of each day. The rest of the time guards surrounded the house and silent servants watched her. There were no scrolls, no tablets, no work to be done, nothing to relieve the pressure of the thoughts that crowded in on her. She could do nothing but pace up and down and think. She had tried to maintain the condition of her body with the bull-leaping exercises and tumbling procedures but one of the watching servants had informed her that this was not permitted, that if it continued she would be restrained. After that Lia lay on the too-soft couch, forcing her mind to return to the happy days on Pandos, recalling the lessons with Medo and alternately tightening and releasing her muscles simply that she might have something to do. She recalled all the tales of the cold lands—few enough—that he had told her and tried to remember the lines of the coasts as he had traced them for her so long ago. At first thoughts of her plight and Paon's strange rejection occupied her daily and emerged in her dreams in the little time that she could sleep. Over and over she relived their brief passion and sharing. Over and over she fought the love that had been planted in her unwilling heart. Slowly she began to find some mastery over the inertia and fear of the unknown as she retreated into the past when she roamed her island, learned what her father had to teach and loved Ourda. In that recalled simplicity Lia found the strength to endure this time that stretched endlessly out.

When she was first brought here, the young priestess who escorted her had said, "You are under restraint of word and body in holy deference to the great goddess. None will speak to you except in the most serious of circumstances and if you speak you will not be answered." That command had been followed by those who attended her. She had spoken to them at first but had been ignored and finally she ceased to bother.

In the long days and nights Lia had come to be grateful for the watch that was kept over her, for she suspected that Hirath or Zarnan might yet try to dispose of her. Nightmares of the pit of serpents still haunted her and Hirath's triumphant eyes followed her. What was the woman's influence over the ruler of Crete and who had ordered Lia's own seclusion? Questions rang in her head and made it ache so that she appeared drawn and pale in the mornings.

Then this dawn she was roused and dressed in the total silence to which she was becoming used. A guard had entered to say, "The litter will soon be here. Have her ready." Lia shuddered at the impersonal tone. She might have been of no more interest to these people than one of the stones at her feet.

There was the sound of running feet and a swiftly silenced question just then. The servant took the golden cup from Lia's hand and jerked her head toward the door. They went out to the gold-and-black-draped litter that bore the combined symbols of the double ax, bullhorns and the coiled snake. One of the black bearers held the curtains back for Lia and she entered without a

backward glance. Action was doubly welcome after the days of
enforced silence and the rapid movements as they bore her
along were all the more exciting.

Once she thought to peer out but the muffling curtains were
wrapped so securely that she was unable to do so. The journey
seemed to last an eternity. She could hear nothing except the
slap of the bearers' feet on the road. She had never realized
how much the sounds of normal life mattered until she was cut
off from them. The days of silence and watching combined
with this quick, hushed trip made her wonder as she often had
if she were meant only to go on the way to death. Her
excitement was replaced by a feeling of foreboding that grew
stronger as the moments went by.

The litter was set down suddenly and the curtains pulled
away. One of the bearers reached in to help her out and another
dropped a flowing gauzy cloth over her head as she came erect.
It tumbled to her feet and made her view the world in what
seemed a pouring of sunlight. She stood on the same quay
where they had landed before. Hordes of silent people stood
watching, unmoving. The sky was brilliantly blue overhead
and the warm breeze blew back her draperies. It was the light
and feeling of life, not the dark cave to which Lia felt she was
being conveyed. Ever after, she thought, she would hate caves
and the loss of light.

A group of priests, distinctive in gold, white and black, were
boarding a large ship hung in those colors; the sail bore the
combined symbols of bull and goddess with the snake rampant.
A smaller ship was behind her. Lia saw the glint of weapons
and the movement of many men. Its sail was dull white and the
body was dark brown. Paddlers on both ships held their oars
ready for instructions. But it was the ship toward which the
bearers were now guiding her that held Lia's attention. It, too,
was large, only slightly smaller than that of the priests and the
high prow bore the image of the goddess carved in gleaming
dark wood. There were decks and at least two cabins that she
could see. A white sail flapped in the freshening wind, a man
strode forward to speak with another and both turned to look at
the crowds on shore. The man was Paon. The one with whom
he spoke was Naris.

Lia almost stumbled and would have fallen had it not been
for the dark hand under her arm. A cry went up from the

watchers, a doleful sound that was nearly a wail. Above her on the ship the banner of the great goddess was broken out and the paddlers took their positions. An ornamented walk stretched from the quay to the deck where she saw a dark-clad figure waiting for her.

She set her foot on the walk, hesitated and then went resolutely along it, holding to the rope that served as banister. She looked into the face of the person who was to receive her and started with shock. The woman was perhaps twice Lia's age and the remnants of great beauty still clung to her face and body, but she had red scars and lumpy flesh as if she had been trampled by an animal. One hand was deformed and several of the fingers gone. She leaned to the side as though twisted that way. Her forehead was high and white; her eyes gray blue. She beckoned to Lia and gave a grimace that was an attempt at a smile.

Lia smiled back, stepped onto the deck and extended her hand. The woman backed away and waved upward toward one of the visible cabins. She tapped her mouth and shook her head. Lia took this for more silence and nodded. She would obey the dictum for this time.

The ship swayed and then the people on shore began to wave as they called out the requests for the blessings of the gods on this quest. Musicians played, banners waved and some few in the crowd began to weep. Majestically the ship began to move toward the sea, the others behind it. The cries from the bank followed them.

"May she keep and guard you!"

"Return! Return for the honor of the goddess!"

"Bring her back from the cold lands!"

The words mingled and floated on the warm, sea-scented air as the ships slid away from Crete bearing the commands of Minos, her king and priest.

"Tell me your name?" Lia spoke cajolingly to the woman who now stood with her before the small cabin and indicated that she should go inside. "Surely we can speak now?"

"You waste your breath, Lia of Pandos. She committed an impiety against the goddess and her tongue was torn out for it. She was specially chosen to accompany you as your slave. You see, she failed at the bull leaping many years ago. I would say that you both have something in common, is it not so?" The smooth voice of Naris insinuated itself between them. He had come up on noiseless feet and now stood, immaculately clad in red linen, looking at Lia and smiling that terrible, deadly smile. "We are met again, though not exactly in the same circumstances as previously. Are you not pleased to see me?"

"Should I be?" Lia felt her skin chill as she looked at the woman beside her and then at this betrayer. She was flung back to the first days of her captivity when she had trusted him. "Why are you on this trip, Naris? Does the lord commander so trust you?"

He laughed in real amusement. "He is not the lord commander, Lia. The charges against him were not disproved, you know. He must be tried when and if he returns. Impiety can be performed against the person of the king as well as the gods; it covers much. He also had no say over who came with him, as I imagine you know. He fought against your presence very strongly yet here you are." He turned to the slave wo nan. "Conduct your mistress inside and see that she is ready. Do not linger or you will be whipped!"

The woman made gagging sounds and bobbed her head as if in fear. Her eyes entreated Lia to come and a dark flush mounted on her mottled skin.

"Do not speak that way to her! She is a person and shall be treated as such. If she is indeed my slave, I and I alone shall command her! Tell me her name that I may call her." Lia moved close to the woman and touched the shrinking shoulder. It was incredible that she should ever have faced the bulls and had the courage to survive what must have happened in the arena as well as what happened later.

"Bold as ever! I would have thought that you learned caution in the course of your adventures." Naris spoke in a manner that was almost friendly. "Call her Walan. She will answer to it. Now, you are doubtless eager to know why I am here."

"Yes." She knew it was foolish to antagonize him.

There was malice in the dark eyes as he said, "Paon will come to your bed when the light dies. You are to be obedient and pliable. He is not in a good mood."

She gasped. "Why does he send you to tell me that? Suppose I do not wish it? In fact, I will tell him myself. . . ." She looked down in wonder. Naris reached out a strong hand

and closed it on her arm, holding it so hard that the bones ground together.

"It is ritual and you will obey. Beyond that I do not intend to speak." He grinned and it was as though the teeth of sharks ground on their prey.

Red flame swept over Lia. All that she had endured and suffered at the behest of the worshipers of one god, goddess or revered animal both in her childhood and on Crete, the pain inflicted because of religion and faith, the using of her as though she were symbol rather than human, suddenly melted together in one whole of hatred. She pulled free from Naris and listened to the voice that was crying out. Her own.

"Sick of it! Sick of it, do you hear? They wear your faces, these gods you serve and you worship yourselves, Cretans, mainlanders, whoever! You try to use and manipulate others for your own ends. It is all useless, pointless, cruel! Your goddess is yourself, Naris! Your god, yourself! Just as all the others. Ugly, evil, destructive! Do you think for one instant that I believe in this holy quest? Your king bought time for himself, rid himself of potentially dangerous factions, stopped others for a while and used religion to do it! I know how, too! I saw how when he stood there—"

An arm caught her from behind and slung her down to the deck, bending her head forward so that she choked on the words. Above her a familiar voice, filled with shock and outrage, was saying, "Raving, certainly, but blasphemy? That cannot be permitted! Trial by the priests who follow us and punishment is the accepted thing. You heard it! The whole ship did!"

Naris wanted her dead. That realization held Lia still as she realized just how easily she had fallen victim to his baiting. But why? That question seemed to have no answer. Then strong arms were gathering her up and holding her. Lia had the presence of mind to lie limp against Paon as if she had fainted.

"That is true but she is an outlander who lacks the proper education. I will instruct her in the proper uses of a woman and she will be silent before her betters; that I can promise you." Paon's voice was harsh and his grip on Lia's body was so hard as to be nearly bruising.

"But you heard what she said!"

"I did and she will say no more. Let it be for now and we will talk later. All is well, my friend."

Then Paon walked a few steps with Lia, entered the cabin and tossed her down on some piled cushions. She opened her eyes and looked into his brilliant ones which were dark with anger. The slave hovered near the door which was screened with woven materials and latticework. Paon waved his hand at her and she vanished with a little gasp of fright.

"Whatever possessed you to speak that way to Naris? Have you quite taken leave of your senses?" He spoke with such irritation that the pulses in his neck began to jump.

Lia was furious all over again. She sat up and glared at him. "I am so utterly weary of being regarded as a tool and used as one. He told me that you would come to my bed and bade me be obedient. You know, Paon, that I am no slave but a free woman who was not taught so. Perhaps women are slaves in Crete but I am not one of them and you shall not regard me so!"

He gave a smile that did not reach his eyes. "You belong to Minos and the goddess; surely that fact has been made clear to you long ago. You draw breath this very day because of the king of Crete and for no other reason. You will not speak of him again as you did out there. Is that quite clear?"

"I would like to be alone, Paon." She lifted her head and looked haughtily beyond him at the expanse of the cabin, which though small was equipped with chests of clothing, one open and filled with scrolls, jewel boxes, paint for the face, sandals and the comfortable cushions on which she sat. There was even a window now covered with brown cloth. "I am very tired."

He rose and began to unfasten the belt and loincloth which were all he wore under the loose gauzy jacket stamped with the double ax. That unreal smile was still on his lips.

"You serve the goddess on this mission and I am, nominally at least, the leader of it. As such I represent both the king and the male counterpart of the goddess and the very bull himself. We are expected to lie together; this will induce their favor of the great ones."

"I do not wish it, Paon." Lia spoke with simple dignity. She did not want him in this cold, determined manner.

"Take that gown off or I will tear it from you." His tone was conversational but his eyes flamed. "It does not matter what you want. Every action will be reported to those powerful ones who sail behind us. Your foolish words a short time ago may well cost us our lives. Now come here!"

He pulled her to him and she did not resist as he began to loosen her clothing. This would be the pattern of their lives from now on.

Chapter Twenty-Two

TIME'S CAPTIVE

PAON PUSHED LIA back, spread her legs and thrust into her body quickly as if determined to finish and depart. He hammered down on her until she was nearly in pain, his hands holding her arms down and his eyes half closed in his impassive face. She lay still, knowing that she was only the receptacle to him and that he fought his own battle. Once this would have been all delight to her, for some caring would have been present; now it was nothing.

He jerked free of her and lay on his back beside her, body streaming with sweat, his excitement already fading from the unwilling force of his demand. Lia turned her eyes away from him. If only he would go and leave her alone. What demon twisted in Paon that he could be both loving and tender, then remote and hard as he was now?

"I have to stay. They will wonder if I emerge too soon." He folded his arms under his head and yawned. His eyelids drooped as his breathing steadied. Moments later he appeared to sleep.

Lia shifted uneasily, trying to reach at least part of her discarded clothes without disturbing him. She felt that she was naked before a stranger and a vague shame brushed at her. Her glance went down her body and she saw with surprise that the golden mark was fading from her breast. She touched the place, finding that the tenderness was gone. What would happen if she should be carrying a child? Ourda had told her that Ze, her mother, was pregnant only the one time and others in her family had been the same. There seemed little chance but Lia knew she dreaded the possibility. Her own danger would increase; that chance of her having been impregnated by Minos was one of the reasons she was being sent with Paon. Hirath's doing, she thought.

"Inspecting the wares? Small market here, I fear." Paon, leaning on one elbow, reached out with his free hand to cup the perfectly formed breast. His dark face bore the beginnings of a sneer. "Just think, Lia, if you had remained in Knossos you could have lured the king again. Slaves have little interest for him, however, and that is all you are."

"Why do you speak that way, Paon? Surely you, of all people, should understand my circumstances and know that I willed none of this." Her puzzlement and hurt rang in her voice.

He gave an unpleasant grin. "Let us see if you will this." He set both hands to her breasts and began to rub the nipples with a slow, sustained movement that made them rise. Still rubbing, he bent forward and put his mouth on hers, his tongue probing deep.

Lia's breasts felt inflamed and her loins began to ache. She tried to draw back but he seemed to seal her to him. His tongue moved and drove into hers. She moaned and opened her eyes to see the triumph in his. It was too late in any event. Almost unwillingly her body rose toward his and her tongue twisted in his hot, eager mouth. Her arms went out to pull him close as they lay together in the cushions, legs entwined, in the hungry seeking that could only end with their fusion. Lia ceased to care in those moments about motive or domination; all she wanted was to feel his stalk rise and bloom inside her, to feel his mouth and hands as they drove her into a frenzy of passion.

Now Paon thrust hard inside her as he held her to him. His eyes were blazing blue and his whole face suffused with desire. Lia clasped his bare body and knew the hard strength of it while he withdrew and entered her the more deeply. Suddenly part of her mind stood apart and she was able to hold back the surging power inside her. She wanted to experiment and know him in a different way.

She twisted a little to the side, dislodging him, even as she reached out. "Come, lie down. Hurry. Let me." He stared at her for an instant but in the haze of passion that surrounded them both, nothing but gratification mattered. He stretched out and allowed her to mount him. She took the throbbing tip and inserted it slowly, delicately, into her own wetness and moved up and down just as he had done. Paon's face writhed and his entire body moved convulsively. He called out but Lia held him, drawing out the time.

She moved harder now and let his shaft come deeply inside her, once and twice and yet again. She caught his outspread hands, settled down on him and rode with the instinctive motions of the flesh. He rose up partly; she leaned to him and he drew long on her nipples with his hungry mouth. When she made to rise again, he held her and their eyes met in challenge as the savage burning of the loins began. They went faster and faster in the heat swirl, locked in a clasp that could only end with mutual release.

Lia felt that she was being torn apart. She was poised on the edge of a sword that drew back and forth across her senses. She was on the side of a mountain that was threatening to fall on her. She was the pivot that drove the man under her into a longing as instantly intense as her own. He called her name and she answered, then there was only the crackle of the rising fires and the quaking of the earth as they were tossed to the heights.

She lay on top of Paon, who was still inside her. Her face was buried in his sweating shoulder and his arms were crossed over her back, holding her to him. Her fingers touched his crisp dark hair and she inhaled the scent of sandalwood that clung to it. She felt at peace. All her very self seemed to have been drained out in that time of mutual satiation and delight. Sleep drifted very near; she felt herself floating on the sea-green waves and the sun touched her face as it had done so many times before.

"You can sleep later. I want you to listen now."

The sun was Paon's fingers pushing at her to rouse. His voice was cool and even as he moved her aside and found his loincloth. Lia stared up at him, wondering how he had regained his senses so quickly. She wanted to lie beside him, be touched now and then, laugh and whisper tender words. She wanted to hold him and run her fingers over the smooth brown skin and rippling muscles, to trace the arching dark brows and trail kisses down his long back. She wanted him again in the slow rousing of their bodies to blazing ecstasy.

"You will remain in this cabin except for very brief nightly walks with your slave. There will be no speech with anyone and certainly not with Naris, who will be told that you commune with your ancestors, the goddess or sea spirits— anything he is likely to believe. I will come to you daily; it is expected but you need have no fear that my attentions will be prolonged."

"How long do you expect to keep me prisoner? Paon, I am so utterly weary of secrets and prisons!" In spite of all her intentions Lia felt her voice quaver.

He turned that cold look on her. "Lady, it is not my doing. I have observed that you have a keen interest in self-preservation. If you wish to live, you will seem to obey as I have told you until the priestly ships turn back. Then you may do as you wish."

"Be free, you mean?" The prospect sent a wash of delight over her, which receded quickly as she realized once more how bonded she felt to this enigmatic man.

"Have I not said it?" He fastened his belt and strode away, pausing at the door to say, "You will obey?"

"I will." There was nothing more to say. Once again the gates were closed between them.

In the days that followed, the ships of Crete went before strong and favorable winds. Lia walked in the section of the deck permitted her, seeing no other person except Walan. She sat facing into the wind, which carried the scents of salt and freshness, thought of that first voyage that had brought her to Crete and of all that had happened since that time. She watched the moon in these nights and saw that the distant darkness on the horizon must be land; they were never out of sight of it but she knew from the maps that soon they must enter the open sea. She was never disturbed in these nightly vigils for all that Paon had said her walks must be short. The nights gave her peace and she slept by day, waking to try on some of the gowns stored in the chests and peruse some of the scrolls and tablets packed in others. Walan guarded her door and saw to her needs; the devotion on the slave's face never altered. Apparently she considered that Lia had fought well for her. Lia was grateful for the caring.

Paon had returned once to her but he was in a dark mood and would say nothing. They sat sullenly silent until he decided it was time to go. The next afternoon her flux had begun. There would be no child and Lia was blessedly thankful even as she wondered what Paon's son might look like. After that she did not see him again and knew that Walan had indicated her condition to him. When it was done, there was no resumption of his visits. She tried to tell herself that it did not matter; their bodies might have true sharing but there was no communion of mind and heart. Her flesh longed for him, however, and she fought it back, knowing that this time of comparative peace must be used for what lay ahead.

The moon waxed and waned as the winds thrust them onward. The ships stopped once during the day at what appeared to be an island and took on provisions. Lia heard angry voices and tramping feet but a guard stood before her door and that day her window was partially secured. When she was released for the nightly walk, all was as it had been.

It was not long after this that she woke to stillness and heat. Walan stood beside her pillows with a cup of tart wine and urged her to rise and dress. The gown put out for her was white and gold, loose all the way to her bare feet, and completely covered her. The golden hair was fastened at her neck in a roll held only with a simple clasp. The slave held up a section of polished metal for Lia to see herself and she saw that her face was pale, her eyes faintly shadowed and her cheekbones clearly defined.

The brilliance of the day nearly blinded her when she came out onto the deck. The wind blew her gown against her body and tossed curling strands of hair against her cheeks. She breathed deeply as she looked out at the other two ships, which were very close to their own. The others had their sails furled, and on the deck of the ship that bore the priests, she saw a group who appeared to be arguing. Paon was one of them. There seemed to be few men left on their ship. Evidently it was time for the others to turn back. She could see no sign of land but there was a faint blue smudge far to the right, so they were not yet into the far sea.

A faint call came from behind her and she turned to see a man lying under a canopy a short distance away. When she came closer she saw that it was Naris, very pale and shaky as he clutched a wet cloth. Two white-clad men sat close to him and viewed her with impassive eyes.

"Naris! What has happened to you?" She knew him to be an enemy; he was so fearfully ugly in health that illness only seemed to make him a thing of nightmare.

"I have been poisoned." He seemed to have little strength but his voice had a viper's venom. "I only pray that the gods will let me live to return to Crete."

"Poisoned!" Lia remembered Paon's watchfulness, his insistence on caution around this man. She recalled, too, the anger Naris had shown in the face of her own. "Surely not! Have you been this way long?"

Naris mopped his forehead and signaled to one of the men who came to hold his head and offer wine. "This is Paon's doing. I would have dealt with you both, questioned you, determined the extent of your perfidy, but I was struck down and remained this way, better some days and worse others."

Lia heard the cracking of a sail as it filled with wind and men called to each other. The ship moved under them and the first draining heat was fading. The slave girl was suddenly at her side, pointing and gesticulating. She said, "I do not understand you, Naris. Paon considers you friend. As for me, I recall words of bitterness, delivered in the heat of what must have been a fever. Perhaps a forerunner of you own sickness." She stood up and glanced ahead to where several people, just arrived from the other ship, were clustered together.

"Lord, it is time to go aboard." The man who had given him wine now approached.

Naris gave a hiss. "So correct, the both of you. So punctilious! The flux is on her. The night sweats have come. She wrestles with the goddess. Oh, there were many excuses why I might not pursue my inquiries! Your lord commander is devious but he shall not return in honor from this quest." He gave a weak giggle. "He may not return at all and you, you, are to be devoured by the goddess."

Chills poured over Lia there in the sunlight and she rubbed her arms with stiff fingers. Naris's servant gathered him up and carried him toward the others, the sound of his giggles rising in the stillness. The other man followed, inclining his head briefly at her before heading to the place where a rope ladder hung. Lia felt piercing relief that Naris was leaving this ship; she did not want to think about what his last comment could mean. Now it was as if the air were being cleansed with his departure. Paon had protected her. He had dealt with Naris whom he half held to be friend. Had it been for her sake or his own?

As if she had conjured him up, Paon came toward her, shedding the loose white cloak and revealing his bronzed body in a dark loincloth. The harsh look had left his face, which now wore a look of relaxed gravity. A bearded man walked behind him. He was in the middle years with strands of white in his hair and very black eyes. He was followed by a boy of about ten who looked about with great curiosity.

Paon said, "This is the Lady of the Snake's very representation on this voyage, Lia of Pandos and Crete. Lia, these are Chalc and his son, Elg, priests of the bull god who will accompany us on the quest." He waved one hand and a yellow-robed young man of about Lia's age stepped forward. "Mardos comes from the goddess who favors youth and courage shown in the bullring. Welcome to our ranks and welcome to our ship, the *Lily Flame*."

Lia murmured a greeting, as seemed expected of her, and returned their stares with a look of composure. Other men were coming on board now and still others were leaving. It was as if the entire company of the ship was changing. *Lily Flame*. A strange name for a ship, she thought, and her lips curved upward. The young man, Mardos, caught her eye and smiled in return. Her heart lifted and then she saw Paon's baleful glare.

"Safe journey! Prosperous voyage! The blessings of the great goddess upon you forever!" The half chants, half calls of farewell came from the three ships as they drifted away from each other, the great sails billowing out. "Return to Crete in safety, servants of the goddess!" The final cry came as the other two turned about and began their passage, seeming to skim over the waves as if eager to depart.

The wind blew hard suddenly as the *Lily Flame* set about and began the journey into the great sea in the service of the great goddess of Crete.

Chapter Twenty-Three

THAT WE MAY LIVE TO SING OF IT

"TELL ME MORE about the mainland and Pandos Island. You just ran around as you liked, doing what you wanted with only a few lessons now and then? How marvelous!" Young Elg settled his feet more securely under him and fixed serious brown eyes on Lia's face. "And the secret caves and the pirates. I want to know all about them, too!"

Lia smiled at him. "But I have told you several times already, Elg. You will be bored in the long days over the cold seas. I will strike a bargain with you. Tell me about a young priest's life in Knossos and we will trade tales. How is that?"

"Well, all right. But you go first." He laughed at his success and waited for her to begin.

Lia began the familiar story, surprised that some of the pain was lessening. She could speak of Medo and Ourda, their squabbles and laughter and teachings, her escapades and exploits with all the fondness of memory that a child become adult knows. As she talked Lia was conscious of the changes that had come about in just the very few days since they sailed on their own. Land was still visible at scattered times but now and then the sea took on a colder, bluer note, appearing to melt into the sky. Seabirds were not seen as often and sometimes they saw great fish rolling far ahead of the ship. Paon spent much time in his own cabin or alone on the high deck. She saw him only in passing and his manner was remote, much as it was with the men. The thing that mattered to her most, however, was that she was now allowed to come and go freely both day and night. Elg was instantly her friend, plying her with a hundred questions that demanded instant answers. His father, Chalc, was grave and deferential, his eyes unreadable. Mardos was almost openly admiring; often he would sit a little way from them as she and Elg talked and would volunteer a question or comment of his own. She was carefully noncommital; danger made her watchful.

"Lia! Lia! What about the pirates?" The urgent young voice rang in her ears as Elg came closer. "Why have you stopped?"

"What? I suppose I was dreaming." Lia was not aware that she had ceased telling the story. Knowing Paon's hatred of the pirates and his suspicions of her involvement with them, she was careful to tell only the rudiments of that tale along with some of those that had been old when Medo told them to her in earliest youth.

A step sounded beside them and they looked up at Chalc, whose bearded face bore a half smile. "It is good of you to amuse my son, lady. I must take him away now and give you time to yourself. He must not miss his lessons in ritual and history."

Elg frowned at his father, whose eyes grew stern. Lia intervened, "Sir, I have the honor to represent the goddess on this journey, but as I am newly come to Crete, I know little of her other gods. Might you not instruct me, also?"

Chalc looked her up and down. "It is true that the goddess chose you; I heard that story and know that you, an outlander, were greatly favored, and if this quest is successful that you and the lord commander will stand high in the councils of Minos. Knowledge is ever useful. Yes, lady, join us. It will be good for Elg to repeat his lessons. You will understand that the sacred rituals cannot be revealed to a woman, but other than that, you shall have the benefit of my wisdom."

He spoke so pompously that Lia wanted to smile but she had schooled herself to impassivity. "I am grateful."

So, in deference to her expressed need for fresh air and sunlight, the lessons were conducted on the deck within earshot of sailors, paddlers and the special contingent of Cretan soldiers sent with them. Chalc unbent more and more toward Lia and she sensed that his grudging approval was being given.

Lia knew that the great goddess, of whom the Lady of the

Snake was one facet, was the giver of life and death, ruler of harvest and weather, embodied herself in chosen women to take the seed of Minos and provide the next ruler and was sovereign of sky, earth and the netherworld. She was eternal female, the personification of sensual joy, destroyer and maker. If she, Lia, has been touched by the goddess in one manifestation, destruction could as easily come from another side of the great one.

The bull god was male power and strength, the shaker of the earth. The priest-king served him even as he served the great goddess. The great bull roared through Crete; the horns of consecration and the double ax were his symbols and his power was expressed through Minos, chosen of the great ones.

Lia now saw more clearly the struggle for power of which Hirath must be the center and thought, as the other woman must have, that it was entirely reasonable for a woman to rule in the very stronghold of the great goddess. The powers of bull and snake might be linked temporarily, but one must fall.

Elg came to her one morning as she looked out over the dancing waves and the cloudless sky. Sea foam spurted up before them and the ship seemed to bound along. "There will be no lessons today, Lia. Know why?" Without waiting for her to shake her head, he went on. "My father and the others will invoke the great ones in a secret ritual that I am considered too young to see. We have passed the last land before the open sea. He says that now we enter the dangerous part of our journey and must be protected.

"Just think, Lia, in time to come other boys will listen to tales of this quest and the holy things we brought back from the cold lands, the exciting things that happened and how we won through! All our names will be recited in the litany to the gods!" Elg's eyes were shining with eagerness. "But you would not know how a man feels about adventure since you are a woman."

She smiled at him. "I understand quite well. On my island I, too, hungered for excitement and meant to have it." And because of that, Ourda lay dead, her grave untended. The guilt for that had not touched Lia for a long time. Strange that it should do so now.

Whenever Lia glanced upward in the next three days, and sometimes in the nights as well, she saw Paon keeping watch.

Sometimes others stood with him and she noted that they worked over the ship constantly, tying down anything that might move, packing and repacking oars, ropes and weapons. The wind faded little by little from the sails of the *Lily Flame* and the sky became overcast.

The sea was gray in cast with small slapping waves growing to larger ones at times. The air was heavy and hard to breathe. Sometimes light flamed in the skies ahead of them and great boulders rattled down stone alleys without ever falling on them. Lia had seen enough storms build to know that this would be a powerful one. She had watched them rise to intensity and fade across Pandos but then she and her family were safe in the cave to which they retreated in time of danger. Here there was only the trackless ocean.

Just before night of the third day of such weather, Paon spoke to them from his deck. He had become browner in the sun and his dark hair was longer. His teeth flashed brilliantly white against his tanned face and his voice was full of confidence. Lia knew that he spoke primarily to the priests and the soldiers who had spent most of that day staring at the sky and waves. His own sailors must be veterans at this kind of survival.

"You all know that a storm is coming. We are prepared for it and there is nothing to fear. Find yourselves a place, settle into it and make sure that you do not wander about. The *Lily Flame* is made for weather such as this and journeys such as this. We will emerge unscathed."

He started to turn away but Chalc called out, "Commander, we must offer a sacrifice to the goddess that the storm will not be long or dangerous. The ship must be stopped, the sail furled and the cleansing ritual begun. Give your orders that this be done."

Paon put his hands on his hips and viewed Chalc with a look almost of scorn. "There is no time. We still have much to do and many calculations to make. I cannot halt them."

"She will be offended! You dare not!" Chalc's voice rose in intensity on the hot air, which felt threatening. "We will all be punished!"

"Look at those clouds yonder. Gales, blazing light, and rain are coming with them and the wind will soon rise. Go, priest, and pray. I must see to my ship." He beckoned a man to him and began to give low-voiced orders.

"I warn you, Paon!" Two of his priests came to stand beside him. The three bulked large in the fading light.

"The goddess has given us wit and intelligence and knowledge to be used by each person in his own special way, Lord Chalc. The commander does this now and I think that she will understand if you go to the prayers that we all must surely need." Lia spoke clearly, wondering what sort of a fool Chalc was that he would argue with an experienced man at such a time.

All heads turned toward her and Mardos said, "Well pronounced, lady. I agree as we all should."

"Do you speak for yourself or the goddess?" The sharp query caused a murmur to arise as Chalc stared at her.

"Common sense. You could say that she gave it to me and I use it." She knew that she should have been more tactful but these religion-maddened men stirred her anger.

Paon's bark of laughter caught them all unawares. "Truly said! Get to your duties now and be quick about it!" Lia's eyes met his for an instant and the camaraderie between them made everything worthwhile.

They dispersed rapidly as the wind began to rise and the first heavy drops of rain spattered on deck. Chalc stood with his priests and called out to the goddess but the ship began to pitch and several sailors ran toward them to take them inside. There was a tremendous roar and the sky seemed to split with noise and light. Everyone scuttled for safety as the roar came again. Lia was not the only one to think of the bull cry or see his anger in the growing intensity of the storm.

"All are angered! They cry to us from the very sky!" Chalc's robes filled out with wind and his deep-toned voice rang with certainty before he was abruptly taken to shelter. His priests followed, chanting entreaties to every god they knew.

When Lia reached her cabin, she found that everything loose was fastened down securely and Walan was waiting. With her were Elg and Mardos as well as one of the young sailors she had seen standing with Paon. Two of the Cretan soldiers sat impassively in a corner.

The sailor said, "I am Qeno, lady. These are Dua and Sard. The commander bids me say that we must all remain together, watching out for one another and making sure that none interfere with the running of the ship while the storm goes on." He looked at Elg and smiled warmly. "You would want to be with your father, lad, but he has other duties. You will understand."

"Of course, the women must be protected." Elg waved an expansive hand to include Walan and the slave's eyes filled with tears. "I will tend to matters here."

"All is well here." Mardos spoke to Qeno but his eyes, dark and hungry, were on Lia.

She resisted the impulse to check her gown and stared past him out the door. The bursts of light were more frequent now and the ship was beginning to bounce about alarmingly. Why think of a man's desire when she might very well soon die? Her fear was growing rapidly.

Qeno went to the door and bawled something to another sailor who went dashing away. Then he came and settled himself beside Mardos so that the younger man's view of Lia was blocked. When Mardos made as if to shift around him, Qeno moved again and his gaze was steady.

"The wind is rising even more. We will ride before it as is best. This may be a long night. Who will give us a merry tale?" He grinned at Elg.

The boy cried, "I will! I will! Once there was a pirate chief who . . ."

The young voice lifted over the boulders of heaven, the splitting light and the wind's howl. The *Lily Flame* rose and fell in the waves with a cracking of timber. Mardos folded both hands across his middle and his face grew white. The two soldiers leaned forward as if fascinated by the tale and Lia permitted herself an inward smile despite her clammy palms and roiling stomach. The tale Elg told was one she had recounted earlier to him but the twists were his own. He would make a fine priest, she thought.

The ship spun in the maelstrom and the gods spoke from the clouds. Death hovered around them while the danger grew with each passing moment.

Chapter Twenty-Four

THE SHATTERED BLADE

TIME WAS DARK and endless. There was no reality but the roaring wind and rain, the waves that swept back and forth over the *Lily Flame* and the ones that pitched her to their tops, then let her fall into troughs of water far below. The company in the cabin had long since ceased to tell tales or even exchange comments. They clung to the floor or to ropes that had been attached to the walls for that purpose and to each other. Lia and Walan wrapped their arms around themselves and huddled into little balls. Lia wanted to include Elg but he tossed his head, vowing to remain with the men.

Everything was wet now, for the waves were growing higher. The blazing spitting light continued to be accompanied by the rumbles and roars from the sky. At times the ship leaned so far to one side that it appeared she would capsize and then she would be flung back in the other direction. Lia felt that it was only a matter of time until she would be torn to pieces by the beating she was enduring.

Once there was a cracking noise that sounded over the wind and the desperate cries of men in pain. Qeno edged to the door on hands and knees—no one could stand upright in this—and peered out. He tried to smother his exclamation but could not. Lia called to him, as did one of the soldiers and his face was ravaged as he turned to them.

"The mast is down, shattered by that last burst of light!

176

Some of the men were directly under it. One bank of oars has been swept away."

The soldiers rose but he held up one hand. "We stay here. That was the command of Paon and it has to be obeyed." They sank back down, one expelling a sigh of what might have been relief. "We protect each other. Come now, let us clasp hands and hold together."

There was nothing more to be said. They tried to draw comfort from their closeness but were so flung about that it was all they could do to maintain even a sitting balance. Mardos was growing green and white by turns but managed to hold on to the contents of his stomach. Lia was thankful that she had eaten only a little that day but found herself longing for wine.

The cabin grew lighter but the storm did not abate. They were bruised, cold and exhausted but nothing mattered except survival as the ship went down into the pits and up again. Once she poised on a wave so high that she was turned end to end and a wall of water came into the cabin, smashing them back against the floor and causing Lia to cough and gag while she clung to the hands of Walan and Qeno.

"Another like that will destroy us. Chalc was right! The goddess is angered! Propitiate her!" Mardos was struggling to his knees, howling over the wind.

"Sit down, fool! If we break apart you will need all your strength for swimming or paddling." Qeno was dashing a flood of water from his nose and hair. Slightly shorter than the soldiers, he was solidly built and had compelling gray-green eyes. His face carried the marks of knife wounds and Lia suspected he had seen many a battle though he was only a few years older than she.

"Blood will satisfy her! One life for all!" Mardos called out so piercingly that Lia turned her head from the sound.

Another wave, only slightly less large than the first, swept over the ship, which now rocked back and forth before starting straight downward on the power of it. It seemed to Lia that they were headed straight for the bottom and she screamed with the others.

"He is right. Get Chalc." The soldier spoke to his companion as the *Lily Flame*, impossibly, righted herself for what might be the last time.

"Stay here." Qeno rose up before the man who brushed him

aside as though he were a child and made for the door, Mardos behind him still calling out for blood to satisfy the goddess. "Fools."

"He is right and you know it." The remaining soldier's eyes flashed as he pulled himself to a sitting position.

"Sard, the commander cannot be disobeyed. Dua will answer for this." Qeno threw himself at the rope as another wave innundated them.

Lia clutched Walan and felt the woman's body shake. Now Elg crawled over to them and burrowed in. Lia put her hand on his head and he lifted terrified eyes to her.

"We are going to die. I know it."

She tried to think of something comforting to say but there was nothing. Her own eyes filled with tears and they clung more closely together as the cracking, splitting sounds came again from the body of the *Lily Flame* while the waves beat unmercifully at her and the cabin grew dark once more.

It seemed an eternity and an instant before the thin, watery light appeared again and this time there were men in the doorway. Wet, frightened men with the determination for self-preservation in their faces. How they maintained their balance was a mystery to Lia but they did so and advanced purposefully inside. Chalc, white robe clinging to him, forehead bleeding from a wide cut, eyes wild and rolling, approached Qeno. Four of his priests were behind him; one of them was Mardos. All of them stared at Lia and a terror stronger than fear of depths of the cold ocean began to build in her.

"What do you want here? Return to the places you were sent by the commander." Qeno rose and balanced himself on legs that wavered with the pitch of the ship.

"We have come for the woman." Chalc's voice was hard with purpose. "She represents the goddess; she shall go to her and plead our safety." He lifted one hand and they saw the huge ceremonial knife gleaming there.

The other intruders leaned against the door for support and Lia read her death in their expressions. She cried out, "No, if you must have blood, take one of yourselves!"

"Get out!" Qeno had no weapons but he tried to advance on them. The ship fell into another trough and he went down. The priests pulled him outside and the sound of Mardos's hysterical laughter rang through the storm.

Chalc advanced on Lia. "Come, girl. This very day you shall sit beside the goddess you serve. Your blood shall give us life." He lifted the knife.

"Sacrifice yourself then, if you are so eager. Think how much that will be welcomed by gods and the goddess herself." Lia gathered her legs under her and tried to plan how to dodge him and thus give herself another bit of life.

"I am chief priest here." Fury flamed out his eyes and blossomed in his face. "What you suggest is blasphemy!" Heedless of the twisting ship and the pouring rain that was blowing in the door, he raised the knife higher and threw himself directly at Lia. "Accept this and save us, great goddess, Great One of the Bulls, save us!"

Lia pulled back and the blade whistled past her head. She started to twist around and was flung to her knees by the ship's movement. Then a young body rushed in front of her and a voice was crying out.

"Do not do this! It is not right! Father, you cannot . . ."

Elg's call died in a gurgle and a choked scream as the heavy knife slammed down into him. Blood spurted up in a drenching geyser that exploded in Lia's face and ran over her body as she bent over him, heedless of the danger that still threatened. Even as she looked, he gasped and ceased to breathe.

She went mad then. With a power she did not know she had, Lia jerked the knife from Elg's flesh, held it in both hands and lunged at the horrified Chalc, who was gaping at what he had done. Lia had no eyes or caring for anything else but revenge. She drove the knife into his stomach with a force that sent him reeling backward. She fell on top of him and drove the knife even deeper. His blood mingled with that of his son and his cries became moans.

Lia tried to regain her balance but the ship was in one of her thrusting downward motions and she could not. She screamed at the man beneath her. "Murderer, foul murderer, murderer! Blood! Is that enough of it? Do you have quite enough? Murderer!" Then she was gasping and crying, flailing out at the hands that pulled her upward.

Chalc was not dead. His moans filled the cabin. The other priests stared at Lia in awe and horror but none of them moved. Walan held her in strong arms and was making unintelligible sounds. Then suddenly there was a wave greater than all the others and a veritable hammer of water poured over them all. The *Lily Flame* went over on her side and stayed there. Living and dead alike piled onto one another as the next wave came.

The wild desire to live drove everything else from Lia's mind and she fought upward with clawing hands and feet that kicked out. Foam and salt water entered her mouth, the wave hit and pushed her down again and her breath was going rapidly. She saw Walan going down and reached out for her with desperate fingers. She caught the neck of the woman's brown garment and fought upward. Strength came to her from some unknowable place and she came to the surface with Walan.

At that same time the ship was thrown upright with a hard slapping sound and this time she remained there. Lia and Walan sat on the floor and swayed back and forth. Elg's body was in a corner and Chalc's had been swept half out the door. There was no sign of the priests and Mardos was just struggling to rise. The remaining soldier was groaning in a low voice while clutching his head.

Mardos stared at Lia and his white face was lit by a look of awe and horror. "They are dead and you live. What manner of woman are you? Are you truly the goddess?" His laughter grew mad and then he began to vomit. "Kill me, too. I profaned you." His shaking was all over his body and the laughter rose again.

"I have to get out of here, storm or no storm. Come or not as you wish, Walan." Lia rose and made it to the door by clinging to the walls and fighting for control. Let the sea sweep her away. She did not care. Once again death had come in the name of the faithful and she had done blood murder. She would do it again. The boy had died to save her and she had avenged him. That was enough and more.

Once outside, she saw the wreck that the once proud *Lily Flame* had become. The mast was only raised stubble and the sail seemed to have vanished. The upper cabin looked pounded in and the bank of oars on one side was not only demolished but looked as though it had never been. The prow seemed twisted around and the head of the goddess, once visible to all, was wrenched off. "All the better." She said the words out loud and relished them. Several shattered bodies were visible, but as she watched, a wave swept across the deck and they were gone.

It was then that Lia noticed the waves were not as strong and that the wind no longer had that eerie howl to it. The ship still rose and fell in a manner that would once have terrified her but now seemed almost natural. The clouds were low and heavy; rain poured straight down, but the fearful blazes of light and noise were gone.

"You got your blood! That is what you wanted after all! Are you pleased?" She shook her fist at the lowering sky and screamed out the words. "Are you? Murderer, too!" Lia sank down at the door and let the rain stream over her. She no longer felt capable of life or death, only hatred for those who demanded blood and those who took it. And yet she must count herself among that number. Ourda, Chalc, Elg. Chalc had deserved it but the others had not.

Then strong fingers were pulling her hair and slapping at her face. A determined voice was saying, "What has happened? Qeno had some wild tale . . . gods, are you all right? What happened? Answer me!"

"Paon!" Lia lifted her face and looked into his anxious one. It was bruised and exhausted; there were circles under his eyes and new lines beside his mouth but the brilliant blue eyes still blazed into hers with a look that once she would have given much to kindle. "Who is navigating?" She could not say anything else, no other words would come.

His hand went down her face, touched the part of her robe that was still soaked in blood, pushed and came away. "Are you hurt? Nod your head if you are all right. Qeno tends the ship or what is left of her. Lia, damn it, talk to me!"

"I killed . . . I did. I killed." Then the words were spewing out of her mouth in an uncontrollable stream. She clutched at his arms and willed him to understand.

Paon pulled her against him and rocked her back and forth in the same way that she had done with Walan. He might have been soothing a frightened child. "Qeno told me some of what was going on. They threw him out, you know, and nearly broke his back in addition to almost sending him overboard. We will weep for young Elg, Lia, together, and we will erect a monument for him. Do not weep for Chalc; he sent many to their deaths in his time. He was once the official executioner of the willing sacrifices—yes, Crete has them, too. I vow that he enjoyed it. Stop wailing now. You have been braver than I could be. Hush, now."

Lia leaned into his arms and felt his mouth brush against her sodden hair. The rain was less heavy on her back and the ship even more steady. Paon was right. They lived and that had to be the important thing. His hands tightened on her body and she squirmed closer as the agony of the past time lessened slightly.

"The storm did not lessen even a little until blood was shed, Paon. Were they right, after all?"

"Who knows the will of the great ones? We must do as seems best to us and leave the rest to them. I have not presumed to speak with the gods and I rather question those who do. I have no answers, Lia." He spoke softly but very firmly.

"Your answer is enough for you, is it not?" She sighed with weariness. If only they could remain this way forever with no movement or demands; she burned with exhaustion and the aftermath of terror.

"Paon! Commander, come!" It was one of the sailors who came rushing from the upper deck.

"What is it?" He stood but continued to hold Lia close to him.

"Land is just yonder. The coast looks clear. Maybe we can land if there are no reefs."

Light shone on Paon's face and he grinned at the sailor who allowed his face to relax in answer. "I am coming." Then he said to Lia, "You cannot go back in that place. Your woman shall be fetched and you can go to a little shelter we have made of the sail. I do not know where we are but we have been preserved and that is all that matters for now."

Lia turned her face up to his and forced a watery smile to her lips. "That is all that matters, Paon."

Then before the watching sailor and any others about, Paon took her in his arms and they embraced in the glory of life restored.

Chapter Twenty-Five

IN LOYALTY IS MY SWEARING

WHEN LIA LOOKED at the rain-shrouded coast ahead of them and saw the jutting rocks where the surf beat, it seemed to her that a landing would be impossible. The wind blew them straight ahead and the oarsmen who were left struggled to guide the wounded *Lily Flame*. She saw Paon rowing with the others as he called encouragement to them. She wished that there were something she and Walan could do but he had bidden them remain in the hastily rigged shelter behind her old cabin.

Lia felt chilled and cramped; if they had to swim in the event the ship were broken on the rocks, she did not think that she could make the first struggle against drowning. Her head rang with exhaustion and her very bones ached. All that had happened recently took on the aspect of a dream and she thought to see Elg coming toward her to ask again for a story. She would weep for him if she lived. She would weep for herself and the fact that she had taken human life but at the same time she would rejoice because Paon cared and showed it.

The ship tilted, shifted, swayed for long moments to one side and back again before settling. Lia saw the rocks rise like huge hungry teeth waiting to engulf them. There was a ripping sound matched by scraping paddles and the shouts of the men. Then suddenly the ship floated free in a small natural harbor between the rock walls. The water here was only mildly ruffled, although now they could hear the booming of the surf as it hammered to get in.

The *Lily Flame* was propelled closer to shore, which was a long strip of sand with a dense row of greenery behind it and tall trees that bent before the wind. The Cretans rose and stood looking at each other in amazement that they had survived. Walan reached out to take Lia's hand and they exchanged sighs of relief. The wind was lessening in force here in this protected place and the rain even felt warm to their skins. Several men were already overboard, swimming and checking to see where the ship might be moored so that they could disembark gradually.

"Let us give thanks to the great goddess and the holy ones of Crete who have preserved us!" The strong vibrant voice of Paon rose and the men began to cheer, their voices husky with emotion. "Our quest is favored; let none doubt it, for we live to continue it and the dissension is quelled!"

Lia's mouth went dry. She could not, would not, take part in such mockery. Several of the sailors looked toward her but she stared straight into the distance and firmed her lips. Out of the corner of her eye, she saw Paon glance her way but his face was inscrutable. Once again she wondered at the changes of emotion that could render him gentle at one time and remote, even indifferent, at others.

"Post a guard on the beach and several of you maintain a watch here. The rest of you take your ease while you can, for tomorrow we must try to find out where we are and start repairing the ship to sail on." Paon scrutinized the skies and then leaned toward one of the younger men who was speaking clearly.

"But, Lord Commander, how can we continue to the far lands with our ship in this condition and so many lost? Should we not turn back to Crete and Knossos? Perhaps the storm was sent to warn us that the quest is not to be attempted."

Lia saw several others nod agreement. If they knew of the carnage in her cabin, what would they think? Or perhaps Qeno had already told them. She felt her legs shake and knew that she must rest or fall down there before them all.

"What does the priestess of the goddess say?" It was the same man who had questioned Paon.

He roared at them now. "Go and do as I have bidden you.

Look yonder at her! She is nearly collapsing from exhaustion. I command here by order of King Minos; remember that. I will speak with the priestess on the morrow but for now I command obedience. Go and give thanks for our survival!"

Then the world spun around Lia and she was barely conscious of Walan's leading her back to the shelter and placing a reasonably dry cloak over her. She was bludgeoned down by sleep and there were no dreams.

It was the late afternoon of the next day before she woke to a heavy exhaustion that seemed to weigh her down. The rain still fell but the fury of the storm was diminishing. Men were already at work clearing the *Lily Flame* of her wreckage, cutting down trees, hunting for food in the forest, building crude shelters for themselves. Walan took her to the place that had been set aside for them, a naturally protected area in the rocks that thrust out above the beach. Woven mats of branches on one side secluded them and cloaks dried over the fires set just inside were placed over more branches for their comfort. After eating wine and cheese, Lia managed to stir herself from her lethargy to ask after Paon but Walan waved toward the work that went relentlessly on and shrugged her shoulders.

"Will he go on or turn back?" She spoke aloud but the woman spread her hands and shook her head. Lia sighed; she could not bring herself to care what happened. All she wanted was forgetfulness. After Walan left she drank more wine but the visions it brought were filled with blood, bull cries and snakes.

Her sleep that night was haunted. The branches pierced her skin and the sandy floor was even more uncomfortable. Her mind fled ahead and went back as she tossed. Walan slept beside the door, clearly exhausted from whatever she had been doing. Lia did not want to pace and waken her but she knew that she could not stay in this place and fight the dual burdens of reality and dreams.

She slipped into one of the short tunics that had been brought and bound her hair back with a cord, then slipped silently out into the wet world. It was still night and raining but there was a freshness that told her that morning could not be far. She supposed that guards were posted but did not really care if they saw her or not. Ever since the death of Elg she had felt that she hated Crete and all that it stood for. Even Paon's face dimmed before the intensity of that feeling.

Lia slipped along the beach until the camp was out of sight and then began to run as hard as she could. She was soaked, her hair was loose over her shoulders and blowing in her mouth, her foot came down painfully on a sharp rock but she was oblivious to everything except the physical need to run. At some point her side began to hurt and it grew painful to breathe but this was only right, it appeared to her mind, and she ran even faster. The beach twisted back and forth, bordered always by forest and the huge rocks that would threaten any ship. The part of her mind that could still think wondered how Paon and Qeno had known just where to land the ship, or had that been a lucky thing? Perhaps the goddess guided them. That struck her as funny and she began to laugh. It was so funny that she sat down the better to enjoy the joke.

The rain was only a gray mist now and the darkness had lifted. The east had a faint pink tinge and some gulls hovered over Lia's head as she sat there on the wet sand and indulged in what she thought was laughter. It was not. The sobs rose up and engulfed her, sticking in her throat so that she could not make a sound. All sorrows, past, present and still to come, were hers at this moment in time. She wanted to weep for herself and Paon and the love that might have been theirs had they met in some other way but all that she could see was Elg's face. Bitterness, guilt and horror rolled over her. It was too much to be borne. She tried to scream out at the mindless fate that had brought her to this time in her life. How had it been that she had once gloried in the thought of this quest and the adventure promised? What was she but a pawn of gods—if they existed— and men who were but beasts? Her face went into her hands and she began to weep. She was nearly silent at first and then the strangling wails came until she poured herself out on the sand, beating it and sobbing in the release of emotion too long held back.

When Lia at last lifted her head and breathed deeply of the salt air, she was so tired that movement seemed an impossibility, yet she wanted to wash in the cold sea and be cleansed. More than want, it was need. She looked around but saw nothing except forest and beach and rocks. It was full morning now and the clouds hung low. The air was warmer than it had been and seemed to penetrate her as she drew deep breaths. The heat of Crete was far distant and she wondered if they were indeed in the northern lands.

She stood up and pulled off her tunic, then plunged into the icy water which immediately sucked at her in a powerful undertow that threatened to bring her up under the rocks. Here was a fight she could understand and all her senses took joy in it. She swam strongly, fully conscious that the innocent-looking beach plunged off deeply into unknown depths. She went first toward the rocks and then backward, pulled downward and spewed back up to the surface. All her body fought the treacherous pull and a wave slammed her forehead, whirled her around, then, with the aid of her quick moving arms and legs, deposited her on the sand again. A gull cried over head as she lay there in exhaustion and a curious pride welled up in her. Life was still good in spite of all that had happened and what else might come.

"Are you quite mad?" The sardonic voice spoke just beyond her. "Are you trying to destroy yourself?"

Lia rolled over on her back and looked up into Paon's face. There were shadows under the blue eyes and grim lines around his mouth. The muscular body seemed more powerful than it had been and she saw bruises sustained in the storm on his arms and chest. He wore a white loincloth and a dagger was strapped to one side.

"Why did you follow me?" She heard her voice, husky from tears and weariness, rise up from the great void that suddenly was between them.

"Why?" He repeated the word as he stared down at her naked body that she made no effort to cover. "I wished counsel with the chosen of the goddess; so did I tell my men. Why? I worried about you, Lia. Is that not enough?"

Another woman spoke the next words. Lia simply listened. "No, Paon. It is not enough. I want nothing to do with you. Nothing to do with Crete. Nothing. Nothing." She sat up and pulled her hair over her shoulders.

His expression did not change as he said, "Lia, do not turn from me now." He put out a hand to her.

"You want me to praise the goddess in front of your men and to say that she had spoken to me, her chosen representative! You seek to use me, Paon, and well I know it." The bitterness rose and foamed out of her. It was a blessed relief to say it to him. "I saw your king Minos imitate the bull voice and bring the sound all around us—a cheap trick. I know that your betrothed is in his bed and that this quest is but a ruse to buy time for his throne which is likely toppling! If I, the outlander and prisoner, know this, do you not think that all Crete knows? What do I care? Leave me here. I will have no part any longer!"

Paon caught her shoulder and his eyes were chips of frozen ice, his voice no harder than the rocks just beyond them. "I have never explained myself to any woman, Lia of Pandos, and I do not do it now. Suffice it to say that I have sworn an oath to Minos, king of Crete and my friend. I will keep it so long as there is breath in us both."

She laughed in his face. "Then more fool you! Do you really think you were meant to return to Crete, lord commander of the fleet that was? Blind and foolish, I call you again and to your face!" She wanted to hurt him, to wound him deeply, but he just looked at her with that cold composure nothing could alter.

Suddenly Lia sprang past him and began to run again, wanting only to escape him and all that he represented. Tears ran down her cheeks and she tasted salt in her mouth. She remembered how he had held her in the moment of their safety from the storm and his gentleness when she needed it most. When she tried to think of how he had taken her from Pandos, she felt only the great emptiness that her life now was. She ran on, faster and faster. She had not taken into consideration her exhausted body and chilled state. A piece of rock caught her foot and she fell downward with a thump that took her breath away.

Once more Paon was beside her and this time he scooped her up in his arms, held her there so tightly that she could not struggle and carried her to the edge of the forest. He put her down on a bed of moss and knelt down, his cold blue eyes fixed on her. The time of reckoning had come.

Chapter Twenty-Six

THE BONDING

"You must stop now." His voice was conversational, as calm as though they sat together at table and were friends. "You will rend yourself apart behaving this way."

Lia looked up at him and shivered. Her head spun and whirled with all that she might say but there was nothing that might impress him. She said slowly, "You promised me that I might be free. Release me, Paon. I mean it."

"In a strange land? No, Lia, I cannot and will not. When we return to Crete, I promise to intercede for you if I have any influence." He moved his hands up and down her arms, forcing the blood to run more warmly in her. "I would get your tunic but I think you might run away."

"No. No. I am cold. Bring it to me." She thought with longing of the cool green woodland, flowing rivers, high cliffs and peace. If this land were like that, she would be content. But it was strange, she decided, that she felt so unreal, so removed, and yet her tongue spewed out words once barely considered. "Or does the lord commander think only of Crete and never of the individuals who make it up? Friendship? Loyalty? These are bare concepts. There is no reality to them."

His face was almost as weary as she felt. "Come." He picked her up again and walked deeper into the wood, pausing under a canopy of young trees and low bushes. Leaves and moss made a soft bed that was barely damp. They were screened from the outside world as Paon sank down and set his mouth on hers, holding her firmly but tenderly so that she could not escape.

Lia was his prisoner, struggle as she might. His eyes burned deep into hers with a power that was beyond passion, a determination that she meant to resist lest she lose all that was truly herself. But as his tongue sought hers and teased it and lured it into response, Lia's flesh bent to Paon. She went soft and pliant under the thrust of his stalk, which entered her and pinned her steady. When she rose, twisting and lifting to him, there was no longer any question of escape. His hands no longer held her arms but now roved over her nipples and smooth bare sides, played in the long swirls of golden hair and tantalized her skin.

They joined in love's battle, rolling and tossing in a mutual hunger that was near to desperation. Lia clutched him as he lifted her high and rained kisses on the smoothness of her slender legs, then drove at her again, found her ready and lifted her to the height of anticipation. Then they lay side by side, legs and flesh joined, mouths drinking deep as the time drew out. The earth shook and the storm poured down again. Lia was in the center of a darkness that opened to light. She shut her eyes and rode with the fury until it deposited her, limp and exhausted, into peace.

Paon pulled her close to him once more but this time the gesture was one of warmth and closeness. Passion's fires were banked for the moment and she was both drowsy and content. Thought had no conscious power; she was emptied out. As she relaxed against him Lia wondered briefly about their safety here in an alien land and started to mention it. The words could not come, for she was too tried to say them. His fingers moved in her hair and his voice drifted over her, soft as petals on the summer wind.

"Sleep, Lia. I will watch. There is nothing to fear and you will not dream."

She did, however, and knew it for that. Paon and she floated on a gossamer sea in a small ship. Others chattered behind them and flames rose in the distance, a destruction that could not reach them. They were safe and all was well, but she felt the presence of the great brooding snake of the pit. Sunlight caressed their bodies, warming them and giving life. "Only a dream." The voice spoke in reality as they floated. She felt tears sliding down her cheeks until she looked up into Paon's brilliant eyes and knew that she need weep no more.

The warmth made her want to stretch and turn so that every part of her body caught and held the light. Had she been underwater for so long then? Why was she damp and chill? Her hands rose and encountered solid flesh. She opened her eyes and saw Paon bending over her, obscuring the sunlight that shone directly onto her skin.

At first it seemed a dream within a dream, that tall figure outlined by radiance, the black head crowned with brilliance, profile carved and clear, and from somewhere around them a single bird was pouring out joy. She had gone to sleep in a dun world, heavy with rain, and roused to the sun, which had been so long vanished that it now was the greatest of gifts. There had been pain and loss and hurt but these, though sharp, were dimmed for the moment.

"Will you walk with me, Lia? The time has come to speak." Paon, as always after their lovemaking, was reserved and distant, but this time his eyes were wary. He held out her tunic, now nearly dry, and then drew her to her feet, turning away as she slipped into it. "How do you feel?"

Lia shook her hair back and drew a deep breath. The fuzziness was gone from her mind and the unreasoning fury from her heart. She no longer wanted to hurt him, to tear him apart. Freedom she did want but in a place and a way of her own choosing, although she had cried out truly to him only a short while before. Cretan politics still filled her with loathing, but until that freedom could be attained, they must be endured. Paon had reached through the fog and the hatred to touch that which bound them together, the lasting passion, and so had restored her to her own humanity from the abyss of rage and loss. How to say it?

"Much better. I am somewhat restored." The nearly formal words dropped between them and he turned to look into her eyes. Their glances held and there was no need for words.

Paon took her in his arms and held her. Lia sheltered there for an instant and then put her arms around the broad shoulders, touching her fingers to the curls clustering at the nape of his neck. They stood there in the sunlight, listening to the hammering of their hearts and the crash of the ocean.

Passion was in abeyance; this was warmth, comfort, friendship and safe harbor after storm.

Shortly afterward they were walking slowly down the beach, moving almost aimlessly, as Paon sought for words. Lia knew that he would speak in his own time and could not be hurried. She knew, too, that what he said would affect her whole life. She was spent from struggle and content now to drift; it was enough that he walked beside her.

"You know that this journey must be completed." His voice was as tired as Lia felt but there was determination in it. "All the things you have said about Minos and the reasons for the quest are basically true—I will not dispute them with you. Had we remained in Crete we would have been destroyed one way or another. Factions seek to dislodge Minos and I am plotted against because I am his friend. A quest so directly laid out is holy and sacred; no hand may be raised upon it and the plotter live. He bought himself time and gave us safety."

"Paon, listen to me. Why go back? I know that Hirath and Zarnan are behind many of the plots and counterplots." His blue eyes were points in the dark tan of his face but she rushed on, heedless of his response. "We could go to Egypt; we would survive well and we would be free! If you did not wish to remain with me, there would be no demands. Think of it, Paon!"

She would have said more but he clamped his hard fingers on her mouth and fairly spat the words out. "I have tried to explain to you and you have not heard a word. Can you not understand the simplest rudiments of loyalty? And I will hear no more accusations against Hirath. The mission goes on. What do you want for your willing help? The flesh? For a certainty I can oblige you there. You are a good partner. Freedon on our return to Crete? If it is in my power and I believe that it is, I will petition Minos to send you to Egypt since you seem to long for the place. Jewels? You shall have them." Mockery twisted his face. "Did I ever think you were a different breed, Lia? Not really."

She looked into the implacable eyes and fought for control. "What manner of man are you, Paon? I do not wish to serve your cruel goddess. Have I not made that clear?"

"Abundantly. But you shall, and the reward is to be as I have stated. Either that or spend the voyage and our time in the cold lands a prisoner in the very small confines of your cabin. The choice is yours. As to the kind of man I am, a woman asked me that long ago in another land and in another life. Her hair was red-gold and her eyes blue as the pale sea. She was my kin and she died by my hand. Now make your choice and be quick about it! When I return in a few minutes, be ready!"

Lia watched him stride down the beach, the world whirling around her again at the revelations he had made. Did he see that other woman when he looked into her face. Was that why the gentleness and the very understanding that he sometimes exhibited would so swiftly transform themselves into cruelty? She knew she feared these changes of his. A murderer? She did not think he lied. Murder had shown in his eyes just then.

"Commander! Commander! Are you and the lady all right?" The cry came from the distance as five men, arms at the ready, dashed toward them. "Commander!"

Paon turned around and began to walk back. The men clustered around Lia. She thought them vaguely familiar but could not think of any names to put to them. They bore the marks of past days, for they were gaunt and bruised, their eyes flickering everywhere.

"We are quite all right. What is it?" She heard her voice come steady and sure, not at all as if she had passed through several emotional storms just recently.

"The commander and you were gone so long. Qeno sent us to look for you and report back. He said . . ." The speaker grew silent as Paon walked up and fixed a compelling look on him.

"I bade you work until I returned. Do you obey me or Qeno? Time is valuable, for we must sail soon."

"The graves are dug, lord. The dead await and the sun is high. We thought the time right." The man, tall and brawny, was yet nervous before that hard blue gaze. "The lady priestess will chant the holy dirges and we will give them to the gods in the blessed light. So did Qeno say and we thought the words were of you both."

Lia and Paon locked glances across the men, who drew back slightly. Lia remembered her passionate protestations and avowals, her determination to reject Crete publicly and forever no matter what happened, but she knew herself to be grounded in reality. She was one who meant to survive and she had her life, her well-being, to protect. Decision taken, she drew in her breath and said slowly, "We will bury them in the faith of the great ones, as is proper, but we are in a strange land and know nothing of the power of their gods. Let us, therefore, go quietly and respectfully before those whose names we do not know lest the shades of those we bury suffer in the worlds beyond. Those we serve will understand."

"But the sacred ceremonies must be done!" The speaker was aghast and the others moved closer to him.

Lia felt the trickle of sweat down her back. She could only hope that this mild stance of hers would be enough for both self-respect and to satisfy Paon, who stood, face inscrutable and arms folded, before them.

"Perhaps she is right. I distinctly heard strange wailings in the night. Those were none of ours." One of the men fingered his dagger as he looked about.

"We have discussed it. She is right. All know that the gods war among themselves. Respect must be given. That is my word and I shall be obeyed." Paon gestured that they walk before him to begin the return. "Further, I intend to speak with you all when our mourning is done. We continue to the cold lands."

Lia sensed the opposition in the men but somehow she knew they would obey. He had upheld her as well and with that she must be content. In the war that was to continue between them she knew that Paon was this time the winner.

Chapter Twenty-Seven

BEYOND THE KNOWN WORLD

THE BODIES WERE shrouded in cloth and lay together in a communal grave deep in the woodland just as Paon had commanded. Walls of rich dark earth reared up, the air was heavy with the scent of flowers and salt sea and the sun was warm with golden light. Little clouds drifted in the benign blue sky and scudded before the errant breezes. Several of the men remained behind to guard the *Lily Flame* but the rest of them stood listening to Paon speak the rites for the dead and looking at Lia, who was at his far left. Mardos, the other young priest, still suffered from injuries affecting his mind and was not present. Two others, in the early stages of their training and sent on the journey for experience, were with him, as was their duty.

Lia gazed at the grave and wondered which body was that of Elg. She tried to tell herself that he likely walked bold in the netherworld, regaling the gods with tales of mighty exploits but she could not believe it. They all were dead meat, rotting into the ground and in the next seasons the vegetation would be far greener here. All that was important was this moment of life itself, the breath in one's body, the feel of the air and the touch of warmth, the tenderness of human love if one were fortunate enough to possess it, the taking and the giving of the ordinary pleasures that were so fleeting. Paon and his empty words! What had he gained from all that he professed? And she? Those she loved, dead on a distant island, and she herself in captivity with freedom so far away as perhaps never to be realized. But honesty made her think of the passion she and Paon had shared and would again, the tenderness she had felt for Elg and the silent camaraderie that was between herself and Walan. The world was still fair and she was young. So her mercurial emotions swung back and forth while the tears gleamed in her eyes.

Paon was making it easy for her after all. He lifted his arms in an all-encompassing gesture, bent before the grave, then rose and turned to Lia as he said, "As the goddess is life, even so is she death and renewal. Our men are dead but they survive in her. Is it not so, lady?"

Lia was not sure what was expected of her but she imagined that if she did act immediately, Paon would make good his threat of earlier. She could tell nothing from his impassive face and eyes. "It is as you say, Lord Commander. As they believed in her power, so are they blessed. I, too, say this."

They all stood silent for an instant and a huge butterfly, purple and blue with gold-striped wings, flew out to settle on one of the piles of earth beside the grave. Immediately it was joined by four others. All sat waving their wings gently, oblivious to the people so close.

Lia felt the easy tears of sorrow come to her again and it seemed that this beauty was indeed a gift, a reminder of the transience of life. Then she recalled that the butterfly was thought to be the symbol of the returned dead in some phases of Cretan belief. She said quickly, "And the symbol of that blessing is yonder." The men sighed collectively and she saw the gleam in Paon's eyes. The wind blew back her hair and one of the butterflies came to investigate, landing on her arm for a brief instant before whirling away, the others behind it.

"We are answered." Paon's voice shook a little as he added, "Fill in the grave. Our duty now is to the living."

Later that night as the fires blazed up and they ate of the fish and rabbit obtained by hunters earlier, Paon rose to speak to his men. Shadows ran together with the light on his lean body and arrogant face. He stood easily, one of them yet set higher, a man touched by king and gods alike. He spoke of the duty a man owed to these and to his country, of the command and the quest. "It is not that we go into truly unknown territory. Men of Crete have gone before us and we carry their records; this was long ago but Cretans endure. They will sing of us one day in Knossos and in the cold lands."

They were divided and rebellious, needing only a spark to ignite mutiny. Lia felt the undercurrents and heard Paon speak to those also. He was beyond the man she loved and feared; he was sorcerer, lurer, enchanter. Even though she knew his methods she could not help but be affected by them.

He spoke of families and children, women to love and women to dally with, fortunes to be won and fame to be found. There was adventure, adversity, possible death and drowning—this was to be expected. "And who among you would sit beside his grapevine and his olive grove in his age, knowing that such an opportunity was lost? His shade would wander disconsolate forever. Storms come to mariners on the sea in all times. Men go mad with fear and slay each other. These happened to us and we found safe harbor. The ship can be repaired easily enough. We bear the blessings and commands of king and gods. Would you forsake all that lies before us because of nameless fears? Shame would be our lot in Knossos. One does not fail Minos so lightly."

He paused and one of the men called out, "Easy enough for you, Lord Commander. You are his friend and he would spare you." An assenting growl rose from his listeners.

Lia leaned forward, fully conscious of the fire's gold on her hair and body in the loose tunic. Whether she willed it or not, the shadow of the goddess was still over her. "The lord commander and I would be the first to pay for that failure, both if the quest is unsuccessful and if we return now. So has Minos declared before the goddess." Actually, that was very likely true, she thought.

"I will have no dissidents. Vote and the majority will carry. The woman speaks the truth." Paon faced them, hands outspread, waiting.

There was silence as the men looked at each other and then at him. Lia saw that their ranks were decimated greatly. Soldiers, sailors and priests of whatever degree had numbered over ninety when the other ships turned back. Now they were about fifty or less. No wonder they feared when such a catastrophe happened at the beginning of a journey of this magnitude. Slowly, Lia rose and stood in the same pose as Paon. The fire lit them both with a glory that set them apart. The wind lifted her hair in the same way it had that afternoon. The booming of the sea could be clearly heard in the shuddering quiet that bound them all.

"On with the commander!"

"I hold with the lord commander!"

"To adventure! To glory!"

"The commander! The lord commander!"

The cries rang around the circle and suddenly men were leaping about in an excess of exuberance, shouting, capering, giving bawdy howls, slapping each other on the backs and waving their arms at the laughing Paon. He came down from his normal reserve with them and joined in the celebration, lifting a jug that was making the rounds, saluting it boldly before handing it back. Lia had sometimes spied on the pirates at Pandos when they acted this way and understood the release it gave. Their dead comrades would be pleased to know that they were well mourned and now remembered.

She withdrew to her shelter and the company of Walan but their shouts and the sounds of hammering as the work on the *Lily Flame* went on with renwed vigor kept her awake until long in the night. When she slept she dreamed of the butterflies and the enigmatic eyes of Paon as he told her that he was a murderer.

The next few days moved by rapidly as the men worked on the *Lily Flame* in shifts. Lia and Walan sewed on the sails as well as doing repairs on all types of garments, evaluated and checked the stores, cooked and dried meats from the various quarry brought in by the hunters, roamed the near woods looking for edible roots and berries, bringing water from the fresh stream they had encountered and storing it for the voyage. Paon worked with his men by day and retired by night to peruse his tablets and scrolls. His eyes were everywhere, sharp, demanding, assessing.

The days of sun held and when, one morning, Lia encountered him returning from the beach, she saw that he was burned even darker by his recent exposure. His cool nod, the absence of interest in the blue eyes and his obvious preoccupation stirred her unwilling senses and she drew back from him in anger at herself. He interpreted it another way.

"You are quite safe, I assure you. Your behavior since our talk has convinced me that you will give at least lip service to the continuance of the quest. I thank you for your assistance. It was a wise decision." He was already looking past her up toward the *Lily Flame* and the men who swarmed over her.

"I assure the lord commander that I do not fear him and that I will hold him to his promises when, and if, we return to Crete." She also could be cool and tart.

Little points of flame danced in his eyes. "I do not wish to hear negative statements even in supposition. Remember that. The men are with me now; we are welded into one whole and I intend it to remain so." He might never have touched her in passion and tenderness, never cried out the pain of his long-gone past that yet walked with him. He was the commander of the expedition, not Paon the man. "I must go. They are watching."

"I do not delay you. Go." Her blood rushed up into her face and she felt her cheeks bloom. More than ever she felt the need for the quiet walk before their regular work began. "They have surely seen you speak with me before."

"I have taken a vow before them all. It is customary, as you know, for the commander or chief to visit the representative of the goddess on such an expedition as ours. In view of all that has happened, I have vowed not to touch you until we reach the shores we seek and are safely begun on our mission there. It has won them to me all the more." He stepped around her.

"And to me as well." She snapped out the words before she could think of a calmer response to this male arrogance. His shoulders quivered once but he did not turn back.

"Excellent. Then we are in agreement." He raised a hand to those working and they shouted a greeting.

Lia stood for a moment, resisting the urge to scream after him, knowing that in the future her very life might depend on the esteem in which she was held by the other voyagers. It was hard to admit to herself that she wanted Paon more in this time of rejection than at any other since their confrontation on the sands of this unknown beach.

Five days later the *Lily Flame* put to sea. She was no longer the lovely ship dancing proudly on the waves with the triumphant goddess leading her forward on the prow. Now she was scarred in places, new in others and well patched in still more. The decks and masts were repaired, the oars set in readiness, stores packed and loaded.

Lia stood with Walan at the door of their cabin, which had been carefully cleansed and rearranged. There was no way to avoid the horror of what had taken place there but flowering branches had been put out and cloaks hung over the dark walls. The window was left open and the salt scent of the sea came to them with every breath. She knew that it would be bearable.

Paon stood on his deck in the pose that was habitual with him, legs spread wide and arms folded, hair tossing in the wind. The sails of the *Lily Flame* bellied out and the coast that had sheltered them began to fade from view. One of the men began a song and it was taken up by the others so that the chant rose to lift spirits already high with anticipation and excitement. Lia could not distinguish the words but Paon's pleasure was evident. She smiled a little to herself for all this was infectious and, when she glanced up at him, saw that he was scowling at her. She gave him an even brighter smile and was amused when he turned his back to look out over the sea. Indifferent he could never be; perhaps it was her own curse that the same was true of herself.

Now they entered a period of calm and tranquillity when the *Lily Flame* sped unchecked before the winds and all the days were sunlit, the nights clear and starry, the sea smooth and deeply green. The stars guided them and Paon spent much time studying them. Lia would lie before her door in the darkness before the dawn and wonder about the sea paths, speculating on these same stars and of all the times mariners counted on them. Had she and Paon been able to talk to each other she would have asked him to teach her more about them but he would greet her coolly, she would respond politely, and there would be no more between them.

The nights were colder but the days continued warm as Lia spent much of her time pacing the deck, watching the sea and sky as she had always loved to do on Pandos. Here the old feeling of peace returned to her; between her contemplation of stars, sea and horizon she was but an infinitesimal speck in the vast impersonal scheme that continued on forever. So were they all, she felt, and how much could their struggles matter after all? Here the gods and their battles, men and their search for power, her own twisted, longing relationship with Paon, all melted back in the vastness. She watched, looked and was comforted in a way that she had never been since leaving Pandos.

Sometimes she talked with Qeno, who was always pleasant if diffident. Three of those under his direct orders, Edon, Kra and Nes, brothers who had been seamen all their lives, became friendly with Lia in a cautious, awed manner and told her fantastic tales of mountains and cities under the sea, huge fish with benign natures, which were larger than their ship, far battles in strange lands. She knew much of this fantasy but welcomed the diversion, wondering if this was how Elg had felt.

One day Lia was standing on her deck, face lifted to the early freshness of sea and air, a woven shawl around her shoulders, when she saw movement on the horizon, the motion of many bodies and water spewing up against the fading clouds. She gazed in wonder as they drew nearer and then shifted off, well away from the ship. There were flat heads, huge sleek bodies that turned effortlessly in the waves, enormous tails that flipped and rolled; it did not seem that these could be fish. And she had laughed at the brothers' tales!

Now the spouts rose higher and the great heads were more distinguishable. She tried to count and reached ten before they shifted and moved so quickly that it was impossible to tell their numbers. It did not seem that they were in any danger from these giants and no alarm had been raised. When Lia looked about, she saw that the men watched with as much fascination as she did. Paon was talking with Qeno, an urgent discussion by the sound of it although no actual words could be heard.

"The great fish travel together. Some say this is an omen. Others are apprehensive." It was Kra, dark and small-boned, shorter than Lia, who suddenly appeared at her side. "We are not very far from the cold land."

"It is a beautiful sight." She watched them cavort and roll, the rising sun striking light on their backs. Then recognition of what he said came to her. "How far? What is it called? Where?"

Kra shrugged, "It is the talk. The secret land, lady, where there are such riches as men kill for; the land unnamed, the dangerous place where the stones walk. Not far. I can say no more." He moved away in his peculiar, half-rolling stride that spoke of a lifetime on the sea.

Lia felt excitement and the beginnings of fear. The tranquil interlude was over. A new challenge awaited.

Chapter Twenty-Eight

LAND OF MYSTERY

FEW OF THOSE who traveled on the *Lily Flame* slept in the next few days and nights as the signs of land became more obvious. Birds circled over them and mingled with the gulls that followed in their world. Fresh woodsy odors came over the water at night and sometimes they saw branches washing in the waves. It was much colder now and Lia found herself searching the chests for warmer clothing. The sea was more gray than green or blue and melted into the clouds. Several times they heard strange howls over the distance and questioned each other as to their meaning. Walan put her hands over her ears and backed away into the corner of the cabin, eyes wide and fearful. As before, Lia found it hard to believe that she had once been brave before the bulls and the maiming she had undergone. Once just at twilight Lia looked far ahead of them and saw the distinct movement of a sail on the horizon. The lights of the sunset, pink, purple and gold, had faded to a mild tinge and she thought at first that she had been mistaken but then it came again, a sharp flash and billowing above a dark hull that drifted into the coming dark.

Others had seen it also. Sound traveled swiftly over water so there were no calls to prepare but the men came to alertness, catching up their weapons, making sure that others were in readiness and maintaining themselves in watchful ranks. Paon walked among them, whispering, and she saw once more the renewed respect in which he was held.

Lia knew that it would be useless to try to find out what was going on or what was expected. She did not think that they would do battle; certainly their ranks were too decimated for that. In these quiet days of thought and contemplation a suspicion had begun to grow on her and only Paon could satisfy it.

As night came on and the *Lily Flame* swept forward, Lia relaxed and listened to the soft snores Walan made. She reviewed facts, tales and suppositions in her mind as well as the actions of Minos and the richness of Crete that she had glimpsed. She thought of the Cretan mastery of the seas about that island and beyond, a race of sailors with the capital city unwalled, the near decadence of the society and the sharp honing manner of the bull leapers. The urge to seek out Paon gnawed at her again. As she restlessly sought sleep she had cause once more to be grateful for the learning she had received from her father and had pursued herself, however abortively, in Knossos and on this voyage. Sea routes, history and battles swam together in her brain. When she turned on her side for yet another time, Lia found herself curiously content for the first time in a long while. This was not the passive acceptance of the days on the open sea nor yet the endurance of what must be.

Two days after she sighted the sail, Lia awoke to see land but a land with such coasts as might repel an army. Jagged rocks with great waves crashing against them, dark cliffs, rearing boulders, sheets of stone rising into mist and behind them green forests lifting upward, all showed this to be a dangerous and inhospitable place—certainly the cold land of legend.

The *Lily Flame* stayed far out to sea, the sailors watchful and cautious, the oarsmen ready to propel her back and away from the swirling pools, tides and boulders that waited to snare her. Paon, a map ready in his hand, guided them on. Qeno stood to receive his orders and bawled them out in a powerful voice. Once the ship was sucked forward by a whirlpool and thrown to the side, narrowly missing a black wall of rock just below the waterline. The currents pulled remorselessly at the ship, reminding Lia of the storm that had been so disastrous to them all.

"Back, back and to the left! To the north!" Helmsman and

steersman obeyed the order as best they could. "Watch for the shallows!" Back and forth flashed the oars and those working with the sails adjusted them as the wind helped. Soon it was as though the danger had never been. The sea was smooth and serene once more but the dark coast remained ominous for all that the brilliant morning sun poured down on it.

When they were running before the wind again, Lia went to her cabin to search for clothes suitable for this land. She had an idea that Paon might intend to leave her on board and she determined to give him no excuse. Sturdy sandals, several tunics reinforced with thicker cloth, durable cloaks, two sharp daggers to thrust into her wide belt, a smaller one for her sleeve; she was well prepared. Walan put both hands on the pile and shook her head, grimacing with her need to speak. She pulled out one of the daggers and pantomimed what Lia supposed to be a sacrificial offering, pointed one hand at her mistress and cowered in a gesture of fear that was not for herself.

Lia smiled. "Thank you for your concern, Walan, but I shall go with them when they go ashore and nothing shall prevent me, especially not you, nor even the lord commander himself. Rest yourself; my decision is made."

The woman sank down and began to weep. Lia put her hands on the shaking shoulders but Walan was not to be comforted. What did she see or know? Could she foretell the future or had the courage she had once known simply departed completely? Wearily Lia ceased speculation and went up to watch the horizon again.

All that day they passed around the jutting crags and green-crowned cliffs, sometimes venturing close and moving out to sea once more. Now and then Lia, looking upward, would see the thin thread of a waterfall in the green and catch the sunlight flaming on it. The men were silent before the coast and the prospect of the land beyond. None of the brothers came to talk to her as they usually did and she wondered if they had been warned away for some reason. All her instincts warned her to be ready and she heeded them.

That night before she lay down to sleep, she braided her hair around her head in a coronet, put on the green tunic that ended well above her knees, placed her other things where she might reach them at an instant's notice and finally dozed to the familiar swaying of the *Lily Flame* as she breasted the seas far from shore.

It was well that Lia was prepared, for when she heard the shuffle of feet and the muffled whispers, the light was barely gray in the cabin. The ship was still and calm after all the many days of movement. Walan slept in her corner, a cloak obscuring her face.

Lia wasted no time in speculation. Hastily she sponged her face in the tepid water kept for that purpose, threw on the rest of her clothes with special attention to the weapons, drew the cloak around her and peered out around the mat that hung over the door. She saw men climbing down the rope ladder attached to one side of the ship and others, apparently those left to guard her, standing by and murmuring as they looked up at the rearing cliffs, the near-dary sky and back at the gray sea. The *Lily Flame* stood well off shore and close to a long thrust of rock that partially protected her while the sea crashed against the jagged ones back behind her. Men were already walking up to the sands at the end of the rock and Lia saw the small canoe returning for others. She had thought to slip ashore but now there would be no chance. She must brazen it out.

Boldly she pushed the mat aside and walked out over the deck to the ladder. Then the waiting men watched her come and one smiled in tentative fashion. The smile left his face when he saw Qeno come walking toward her, his face as stern as Paon's ever was. The morning wind, cool and fresh, tossed his hair over his forehead and he lifted an impatient hand to brush it back.

"You should be resting in your cabin instead of coming out to watch us go." He spoke softly but there was firmness in his tone.

"I did not come to watch." Lia lifted herself to the ladder and settled herself on it, trying not to think how far down it was to the dark, cold water. "I go with you."

"Your pardon, lady. You do not. This is no journey for a woman. The lord commander has ordered that you remain."

"And where is the lord commander?" Qeno came closer and Lia edged down the ladder a little as it jumped under the weight of those just climbing off.

"Yonder on the sands. Lia, come back!"

She went down the ladder as rapidly as she could, heedless of his orders to return. Others were coming down above her, and just below, another small boat, almost a raft, was taking on another man. For an instant she hung suspended in a dark abyss of wind and water, clinging to a tiny mass of woven threads. Then, as she fought back fear hands reached up to take her and a voice was laughing in her ear.

"Bravely done, lady! Let him yell. We are glad to have you with us."

He was only a brawny shape in the gloom but the welcome in his voice was beyond question. She breathed out her thanks and settled in the tiny space allotted her and the paddlers struck out for land. She heard the mutter of prayers and thought that if she professed any faith, now might be the time to pray, for Paon's wrath was certain.

He loomed over her as they landed and the man who had assisted her vanished as did the others. Lia stood with one foot in the water and the other on the sands of this inhospitable land as she faced him.

"There is no use telling me no, Paon. I meant to come and I have. You would not like it if we fought here in front of your assembled men. Furthermore, I wish to talk to you at the very earliest opportunity on a matter of the gravest importance. I go with this party!" She had tried out diplomatic speeches in the night. She had been serious and earnest. Now she had blurted out words that the gentlest man might take offense at and her voice, pitched higher than she intended, reached to the men who had withdrawn from them.

Paon stood back, looked her up and down, scowled, then burst into laughter. He wore a dark tunic and loose cloak. A sword and dagger hung at his belt and a headband held back the curls from his forehead. The carved profile was clear in the dawning light.

"Will the lord commander explain what so amuses him?" How dared he laugh at her!

"You are ready to do battle before it is even necessary! How well is our goddess represented in you, Lia! I wanted to leave you for your own protection." He waved at the weapons she carried and laughed again. "Come if you must. You have earned the right." At his words the men gave a low cheer and he stepped forward to take her hand. Only she could hear the next words. "Foolish that you are! Your fate be on your own head. I cannot risk a quarrel now."

"I thank you." She gave him look for look and saw his eyes change from barely veiled anger to another expression that held both sadness and the beginning of passion. It had been long for them both and Lia felt herself swept by longing. But her mind rebelled; she would not yield so easily.

Now the morning sun was lancing down around them and the scent of flowers came to her. The black cliffs shone and the green of the woods blazed by contrast. The men clustered together but, at Paon's dark look, fingered their weapons and went with him to welcome the next contingent arriving from the *Lily Flame*, which swayed serenely in her harbor beyond the roaring waves. Lia saw that two of the brothers, her friends Kra and Edon, were in the ranks now forming up and she was glad. The remaining priests had not come; perhaps they needed to tend young Mardos, still not recovered from his shock and from bruises suffered during the storm.

"We must go now. If any among you is in any doubt or wishes to return to the ship, you have my leave, indeed, my command, to go back." Paon swept his gaze over Lia's resolute face and those of his men. No one stirred. "Good. Remember that you stand with me for Crete and our king!"

They gave a soft cheer, then fell in behind Paon as he walked briskly over the wide sands and toward the waiting woods. He half turned and called to Lia. "Walk with me."

It was an order and she came, obedient to the command. The suggestion of a smile on the mobile lips, the way his dark brows arched above the long-lashed eyes and the long, firm fingers that touched the hilt of his sword, moving on it as smoothly as ever they once caressed her body, stirred her blood. She fought back the sensations he aroused and walked beside him as they entered the wood and began the slow upward ascent.

"Where are we, Paon? What is this land?"

"You have studied the maps even as I. You heard the charge of Minos. Can you not guess?" There was a challenge in his words but no anger. They might have been strolling on the streets of Knossos as they had done so long ago.

"Tell me." They were speaking so softly that the first two men behind them could not hear.

"It has many names. The cold land. Land where the stones walk. Anglia. Britain." He hesitated. "Island of tin."

Lia felt the cold start down her back. "We are not here to search for gold and precious jewels, are we? The quest is not for the 'living eyes of the walking stones' as the king stated, is it? The goddess gave no commands for such a stone through his mouth. You have known all along where we were going and what we will do, have you not?"

"Is that so unusual for the leader of an expedition? And keep your voice down!" Paon was nearly whispering. "Have you speculated about this with those who linger about you? Talked to your woman? Been indiscreet? By the goddess, if you have you shall pay for it!" He caught her arm and pulled her deeper into the wood. Even in his alarm he did not forget to look cautiously about and up at the cliff face which rose above them and which they must soon climb. "Is that what you wanted to talk to me about?"

"It is. Did you think otherwise?" His face went hard and still but she knew that he had thought she meant to lure him. Pride burned in her and she tossed her head. "I have speculated with no one and you know it. Did you set them about me for that purpose?"

"We talk at cross-purposes. What do you really know, Lia? Will you tell me for the sake of us all, forgetting any anger that you feel toward me and toward Crete itself? Can you do that?"

She was quiet as they walked along and he allowed her time. In the distance the great waves crashed, a bird sang in the branches over their heads and the warm wind brushed her hair, loosening little curls to dangle on her cheeks. She pushed at them with one hand as she tried to formulate the words.

"I have only thought and put things together, Paon. I have no secret fountain of knowledge, only tales and legends and my father's travels. King Minos spoke of a precious metal necessary to Cretan expansion. I thought precious stones. You said island of tin. Tin is necessary for the making of weapons—some combination with another metal, I think, to make yet another. It is here in quantity, is it not?"

"Mixed with copper to produce bronze. Who controls the

source of supply controls power. Crete is in ferment." He faced her, his face dark with urgency. "There are spies set among us, Lia, and they endanger us all."

At that very moment the bushes rustled slightly and the point of a sword began to emerge from them.

Chapter Twenty-Nine

DARK FORGOTTEN PATHS

PAON SWEPT LIA behind him with one quick motion and his sword seemed to leap into his hand. She caught up the largest dagger, holding it ready. There was no time for fear, only the recognition that she stood with him against whatever danger might present itself.

"Who are you? Come out of there immediately!" Paon spoke the first words in Minoan, the last ones in a language that appeared a collection of several. Lia could understand most of it and wondered wildly if the inhabitants of this land spoke the language of her own mainland.

The bushes shook and the sword point fell. Kra came out, dark eyes blinking rapidly, his face worried as he gazed at Lia. "You were so far ahead of us. I wanted to make sure both of you were all right."

Paon laughed shortly, "You were listening, of course. What did you overhear?"

"Nothing, Lord Commander. I just thought that Lia . . ." His face flamed red as he averted his eyes from Paon's.

"She is safe with me." Paon's voice went gentle but his eyes were assessing. "We speak of building a shrine to the goddess when we reach the uplands. Go now and return to your fellows."

"Yes, yes." He backed into the bushes and they could hear him pushing through them at a rapid pace.

When the sounds had faded away, Paon said, "Either he is

quite loyal to you or else he is a clumsy spy. We will talk later."
He motioned to her to follow him as they walked back to rejoin
the men. "There is much to be said."

The pace that Paon set the rest of that morning and afternoon
was one that might have exhausted Lia had she not been as fit
and supple as she was. Even some of the men were panting and
blowing as the day grew warmer. They went into the cliff itself,
up dark winding trails composed of rock and hard earth,
through wind-twisted trees and vines that made structures of
their own, down over boulder-strewn tracks, beside inland
sands and marshes and more woodlands, coming at last to a
smooth river beside which they made camp in the last moments
of twilight. Guards were posted and the others were cautioned
to rest while they could. After eating some of the dried food
they carried with them, most were glad enough to obey.

Lia waited for Paon to summon her but he did not. He took
one man with him and went off to inspect the river as he called
to them. The moon was a slivered edge in the sky when she
saw the man return alone. He sank down quietly, with no hint
of concern, but she, mindful of what Paon had told her, thought
that it would be easy to slay him and return with a tale of
innocence. Paon might be lying in the woods even now.

She rose and drifted slowly toward the trees. When the
guard looked at her inquiringly, she gestured toward a spot
close by as if she meant to go there to relieve herself and gave a
slow yawn. The man who had been with Paon was even now
snoring as if he had never moved.

Once out of the guard's view, she ran in the direction Paon
had taken. Undergrowth impeded her passage and she tried to
be silent, but something skittered away from her with a
flapping of wings and an angry cawing, a vine wrapped around
her ankle and nearly sent her sprawling. Regaining her balance
and forcing herself to calmness, Lia went more slowly and
emerged near a gentle curve of the river where stones thrust out
in the form of a seat.

The land was reasonably flat here before rising to hills and
massed woodlands that were dark against the fading moonlight. In the far distance she saw a glow in the sky as though a
fire had been lit on one of the hills. It rose, lifted, dropped back
to a dull pink and disappeared. The sight might have come out
of her imagination, so swiftly had it come and gone. Her

feelings of disquiet grew stronger and she clenched her fingers around the dagger she had not known she held.

The dark figure sat, bent over with its head in its hands, feet in the water, unmoving. It could have been a rock, a shaping as old as the river itself, a very fresco of despondency. Lia knew Paon instantly, knew that he lived and breathed, and the joy that shot through her made her want to laugh and sing and scold him all in one breath. Once again the very depth of her feeling for him shook her.

"Paon! Are you injured? Can I help?" She wanted to warn him of her presence; it was unlike him to be so oblivious.

He lifted his head but did not look her way. His voice was that of an old, old man past all hope and expectation. "Go back to the camp, Lia. You should not be here."

Never had Paon sounded so. He had pride, arrogance, tenderness, warmth and passion in plenty; defeat was no part of him. She came up to kneel beside him. "Are you wounded? Let me see."

"I am not hurt. Will you please go?"

"No, I will not. I stay here and you will tell me what is wrong." She put both hands on his shoulders and forced him to look at her. The lines that cut his face were harsh and the dark curls were tossed. Then he was staring over her shoulder and the bitterness on his face deepened.

Lia turned to see what he was so strongly affected by but she saw only the high clouds racing over the dark sky as the sliver of moon glowed faintly. Then the strange fire gleamed in the distance and faded once more.

"Tell me." If he would dispute with her, touch her, stride away, do anything besides sit there in blind acceptance of something that she could not recognize.

"Tell you? Why not? Crete has long traded with many countries in many different ways and for many products. From here we get tin and copper to make bronze, not only for weapons but for many of our tools. Supplies of tin have dwindled drastically in the past seasons and our traders had no reason for it. Two recent expeditions were lost. I was to find out the reason for the loss of trade."

"And this evening you met some of those who have dealt with Crete in the past . . ." She let the words trail away encouragingly.

"This country is in the midst of an invasion of foreign tribes. Every stranger is suspect. Trade with outlanders is doubly so, an offense against the gods and all that. I had directions to the person most likely to tell me about the situation here. His family had mined the tin and grown wealthy and civilized trading with the Cretan ships. We found them slain, their homes trampled, fired and piled with rock. There is no reason to doubt that others have suffered the same fate. The warning fires are on the hills; our ship has been spotted and the hordes will be looking for us. The mission is lost."

Lia relaxed a little. Fearsome as such happenings were, they did not touch her directly. They were close enough to the coast so that they could return quickly to the *Lily Flame*.

"Then the spies on board will have nothing to gain." Paon could not be blamed for war in this far land.

"They will come into the open now, and the men will follow them. Had I been able to reestablish the trade, they would have had me slain and gone back with the good news to their credit." He rose and went to the bank where he began to pace back and forth. Lia walked beside him, conscious that although he called her by name and addressed her, he was in another world of battles and doom.

"You speak so easily of your death, of our defeat, by the men who have sworn to follow you or by the tribes. Surely you do not believe that?" She kept her voice light and speculative.

"No commander could truly think so," he admitted, "but it is always best to know the worst that can happen. I would slay you with my own hand before allowing you to fall into the clutches of some of these people. If we go down to death in the sea or here in this land or survive to return to battle in Crete sometimes seems to matter very little. And yet there is another who does not deserve the fate that will come if we do not return and return victorious."

He was silent and Lia, looking up at his face which was so dark and cold, thought that he spoke of Hirath. Of a certainty that woman would deserve all that befell her! This resigned and despondent Paon frightened her. She had tried to shake him with the revelation of some of her feelings and had only roused him to speak of war. It was still unreal to her that this lovely country, unwelcoming though it appeared, could be so fearsome and still she believed he told the truth.

"Hirath did not impress me as one who could not attend to herself." For her life she could not resist the remark, even though he had been angered every time she tried to discuss the other woman and forbidden her to even mention the priestess.

"Commander? Is that you?" The soft whisper came just as the wind rose to rattle the leaves near them. Qeno and a burly man Lia had seen at a distance emerged cautiously from the trees and came toward them.

Paon gave a low laugh. "I trust you have reason for this interruption? We discuss the affairs of the goddess." His warm hand came down on Lia's shoulder and drifted downward in a casual gesture.

"Forgive me. But there is talk. We have seen the fires and the men wonder at their meaning."

Now that Qeno was closer, Lia could see the glitter of his eyes and the stiffness of his posture. She wanted to jerk away from Paon, angered that this man should think they dallied in the wood and had no thought for anything else. Why did his gaze run over her suddenly with that practiced ease when previously he had been both friendly and respectful?

"You know their meaning, Qeno." Paon's other hand fondled the curls at Lia's ear and his voice was lazy.

"Yes. But what do you intend to do?"

"Do? There is war here and the tin cannot be obtained. I found that out this evening. Any attempt at trade is hopeless. We must leave this island immediately." He blew idly at her neck, then glanced up at Qeno. "Tell the men we leave at dawn."

"But there is a circle of standing stones hereabouts and reports of treasure. We cannot return empty-handed to Crete!"

"True, but the sea is wide and the *Lily Flame* a sound ship. There are ways to get treasure if you take my meaning." Paon shrugged. "Go, do as I have bidden you. We will return shortly. Go!"

Qeno smiled, suddenly amiable. "As you order, Lord Commander. I am certain that you know best."

Lia felt the iron pull of Paon's fingers and the force that controlled him. She had to help. Her body went pliant against his. "Do come, Paon. You can confer in the morning. Have we not waited long enough?" She was smooth, a little pouty, woman denied to the breaking point. "Paon!"

He pulled her to him and kissed her roughly, waving the others away with one hand while he drew her toward the soft grass at the riverbank. The words he muttered were those of passion and hunger but interspersed among them were, "Now the spies will show themselves."

His longing for her might be that of pretense at this particular time but Lia felt her senses respond all the same. That would forever be her link with Paon, no matter what else might transpire between them. But now in this rude playacting, with the danger fires burning on the hills in a land of menace, she felt united with him in a bond beyond passion. And though another woman haunted his heart, Lia knew that her caring for Paon was not wholly unreturned. If ever there were another man for her, she would know by whom to measure him.

Chapter Thirty

MARCH TO DEATH

LIA LAY STIFFLY in the folds of her cloak. Kra sat beside her and, a little beyond them, Qeno walked with the guards. It was deep dark and just before dawn. All around them the others slept, a few snores breaking the silence. Now and then a bird gave an experimental chirp and subsided. An animal would rustle the bushes and those standing watch would swing about, ready for action.

"That is the tale, Kra. I cannot tell you how frightened I am. Surely the goddess and the great ones are with us but this land harbors strange forces. The lord commander and I have done our duty this night but I am very uneasy. We must go from this place at dawn. He says the tribes will not attack until their scouts are certain of our numbers. By that time we can be on the ship and away. Do you not think that is a good plan?" She spoke little above a whisper, knowing that the silence would carry her words.

"I am glad that you have told me, Lia. You are a true servant of the goddess. I will fetch wine for you. You must rest while you can." He squeezed her arm and looked down at her with friendly eyes. "Yes, rest."

When he came back with the wine, she sipped a small amount and professed exhaustion. "But wake me with the dawn. I have no wish to linger here one moment longer than I must. Thank the great ones that the lord commander is a

217

reasonable man and knows when to retreat." She yawned deeply and watched him.

"He is most reasonable." Kra smiled at her and drifted away toward his own spread cloak.

She was conscious thereafter of conversations with that man or this with words such as "tribes," "war" and "treasure" figuring largely. Some roused others or sank back to sleep again. Soon the entire camp was in a state of ferment. Qeno leaned against a tree and yawned as if in weariness but his eyes held that same glitter. As she feigned sleep and looked through near-closed lids Lia began to believe that she was right in thinking that some potion had been put in her wine.

"Where is the lord commander?" It was Adib, one of the older sailors, who kept much to himself, approaching Qeno.

"He labored long last night and rests beside the river." There was the faintest hint of a snicker in Qeno's voice. "The woman, too, is weary. You have heard the tale she brought? And which I heard him speak with my own ears?"

"Yes, but I would speak with him as would most of the others. Hear him tell us of the situation here and the possibility of treasure. He talks of piracy? There is none who hates the practice more! I will go and find him!"

"The lord commander. Find him! Let him speak!" Other voices picked up the words.

"There are great riches here. Who comes with us to seek them?" It was Kra, coming to stand beside Qeno. "Was the quest not honorably laid upon us by the king? That talk of tribes is foolishness. We of Crete can best any who challenge us. Who comes?"

"Who has harmed Lia?" Edon spoke up in his gruff voice. "You speak of treason here."

Qeno said, "She is simply drugged for her own protection. Who is with us?"

"I!"

"And I."

"No, bring the lord commander!"

Other voices rose in disagreement and then a strong petulant cry rose up as someone strode forward, men walking behind him. "Stand with us, men of Crete! We will bring back all the treasure of trade and jewels. The commander has misled you.

Help follows behind us and together we can quell anything!
The fortunes of the goddess are with us!''

Lia dared turn her head slightly and saw that it was Mardos
with the young priests, several of the men from the *Lily Flame*
and two dark men whom she did not recognize. Mardos looked
older, more fit, and the timid, vague manner had dropped from
him completely.

"Let us take him and the girl and hold them securely. His is a
vanishing cause. You know the turmoil in our land. These men
and their ship have come across the great sea for prizes here.
Seldom have we been out of their sight and they will work with
us. Who is for us?" Qeno, Kra and Mardos stood together,
waiting. Footsteps rustled in the grass as some men came to
join them.

Then there was a total silence. Lia tensed herself, dagger in
hand. The time had come. In one swift motion she threw the
covers aside, screamed as loudly as she could and tossed the
dagger so that it quivered at the very feet of Mardos. Then she
was standing erect and calling, "Paon! Lord Commander,
come!"

A rain of arrows seemed to fall around the conspirators as
they grappled for their swords. Qeno made for Lia but she
stepped back and reached for the other dagger close at her
waist. An arrow sang through the fresh morning air and
slammed into his shoulder so that he fell at her feet.

"Stand still or the next will be for you, Mardos. Perhaps
you, Kra, or the gentlemen behind." Paon had his bow at the
ready, the arrow aimed at Mardos. He was smiling, lips curled
back over his white teeth and blue eyes alight. Twelve men
stood behind him, one or two of those who had come inland
with the party and the others strangers, all dark and thin and
wiry as if they belonged to one family. Their weapons were
also aimed. "Come here, Lia." He lifted the bow so the arrow
was aimed at Mardos's eye and the other men did not stir.

Lia walked slowly to his side, careful not to get in the way of
the bows. With her movement the men began to separate so
that in a matter of moments Kra and Mardos, along with the
two dark men from the other ship and four of the original party
stood together. Qeno groaned from the ground as his blood
poured out. Lia felt pity for his pain, for she remembered that
he had been kind to her, although for his own purposes.

"Bind them and take them back where they cannot hear us. Two of you stand guard and the rest return to our counsel." Paon lowered his weapon as the order was obeyed.

"We are too many. You cannot escape justice, Paon. Who do you think engaged us to begin with and who sanctioned all that we have done? You have powerful enemies, you who call yourself lord commander of nothing! Zarnan is affronted and Hirath walks beside the king—"

"One more word and you shall be gagged, Mardos! In fact you have said enough as it is. See to him!" Paon spoke calmly and the man next to him rushed to comply. The prisoners were hustled away. Then Paon put his bow aside and took Lia's hand in a firm grip. Those around him waited for him to speak but she was first.

"You gave me that tale to tell them! You lied to me so that I would be convincing in it and so spur the conspirators to reveal themselves. And I thought that you were cast down, dispirited!" She thought of what she had told him and her cheeks stung with the rising blood. "I am not the tool of the lord commander!"

One of the dark young men said something in a liquid language that sounded as if the sea crashed on the rocks of the coast. Another laughed as Paon answered him in the same language.

He held her hand in that grip that she could not break without jerking away. "Later I will tell you what you must know." He raised his voice and spoke to his men. "The tribes are at war with each other and this land runs with blood. The traders of tin are civilized and wish no part of it; many have been put to death and the mines ravaged. These men with me are traders who have gone into hiding but are willing to enter into contracts with Crete if they are kept secret. The tide of battle will turn, they believe, and so a limited output can be arranged. We can meet with them and arrange details. There will be no plunder here. These people may one day unite and be our allies. Is that understood?"

There was muffled assent among them all and one, bolder than the others, called out, "But what of the other ship they mentioned? How did you find these people?"

Paon said, "I have traveled much in the service of Minos of Crete, my friend and my king." He emphasized the last words as he looked meaningfully at them. "Twice I have come here. There are signals we used to contact the traders in those days and now as well. They still work. You need know no more than that. As for the other ship, I can only assume that the spies bought the services of those in her. I took precautions before we left. Those who guard our ship now can be trusted. That same tale you heard here was passed about and caused the spies to come here. The *Lily Flame* now stands out to sea."

Adib asked, "Give me the privilege of being one of their questioners, Commander? I know how to wring the truth free. We will soon know all there is to know about the other ship."

Paon's mouth grew hard. "Do so. Take two others with you and use any means you must but make sure that they are not so tormented that the truth cannot be known."

Lia gave a gasp at his harshness before them all but she knew that it had to be. No mercy would have been offered by those who strove for power. She thought again that she greatly admired Paon for his control in the matter of Hirath. Mardos had hinted of the relationship with Minos. Friend and betrothed—it must be a bitter thing. She was beginning to learn how he had risen to the position of power that he once held in Crete. He was devious and clever but honorable for all that.

Adib beckoned to those beside him and was gone. Then Edon said, "It was my brother who was so against you and I did not know. I will avow my loyalty to you, Lord Commander, if you will believe me."

Other voices murmured of loyalty while some looked sheepish and tried to avoid Paon's searching gaze. He said, "I have asked for your pledges of loyalty on several occasions. I will not ask it again. We will live or die together on this island and must trust each other. There are no more tests."

A thin scream drifted on the cool wind just then and the sun-dappled leaves above them stirred. The sounds of the serene river and the plaintive call of a wild animal mingled as they stood together. There was a flash of blue wings as a bird settled on a flowering branch near Lia's head. She tried to shut out the next scream from her consciousness and concentrated on the black, gold and blue butterfly that lifted from the flowers just as the bird landed.

The symbol of the goddess! For once Lia was glad that she had so many. She lifted her hand and pointed to the butterfly.

The men watched as it rose high in the sky and vanished over the bushes and into the trees. Then she spoke softly, "Her hand is over us. Who can doubt that she walks beside the lord commander?" She hated to compromise her own lack of belief but it was necessary.

"The goddess! The lord commander!" The chant came slowly from Lia's lips and was taken up by the men, growing in intensity as the light and shadow played over his face while he stood, a bronzed carving, in front of them.

"I thank you. Now we must march inland and turn again toward the sea. Adib and the rest can join us later in the day." Paon issued his orders and turned to the dark men, speaking swiftly in their own language.

They nodded and faded back into the trees, keeping a distance but still remaining in sight. Paon called to Lia to walk with him as they had done earlier and soon all were underway. There was silence in the ranks and the men continued to look about nervously. Lia felt as if eyes were directed at her back; she was compelled to glance downward many times for she thought her foot might encounter a snake. Chills came and went on her arms despite the warmth of the day. It was all that she had been through, she told herself sternly, and also the lack of sleep. But she could not convince herself. She gave a soft sigh of exasperation.

"Lia. Lia, forgive me that I led you on as I did. I had to. Can you understand?" Paon was so close to her that she could feel his warm breath on her cheek, and when he took her arm, the betraying flesh jumped in answering urgency. "I am grateful for your help."

"You are the commander. You do as you must."

The gentleness left his voice as his fingers dropped away. "You are quite correct. I have to carry out some part of my mission and I have to get us out of here alive. I have to bring enough back to Crete so that Minos can rule and consolidate himself. And there are personal reasons." He moved a little ahead of her, his broad back and muscled shoulders seeming more powerful in the shady wood where they now moved. "I am responsible."

"Of course. I understand perfectly." Lia felt that she would almost rather not talk to him than exchange these same statements that led them nowhere. The sense of doom

quickened in her and she longed for something else between
them, some closeness that could be taken into the darkness if
that were to come. How would she feel, she wondered, if he
were far away and in possible danger? He and Hirath had been
long betrothed and he must love her. Did not she, Lia of
Pandos, know that one could not choose where one would
love? "Paon, do not agonize for her, for Hirath. When Mardos
said that about her . . . it must mean that she is all right."

"I am certain that she is." His voice was made of ice and he
strode on ahead, leaving her to walk behind.

Once more Lia felt that she was rebuffed. She did not try to
speak to him again. The gulf yawned between them; the pain of
it was becoming increasingly familiar.

Paon kept their pace slow but steady. The sun was high in the
sky in the full brilliance of day when they paused beside a little
stream to refresh themselves. It was there that one of the men
who had gone with Adib to question the spies found them and
spoke in low urgent tones to Paon. He, in turn, bade his men
draw around. Lia came to stand at his elbow.

He said, "Qeno is dead. Before he died he told them that
Mardos, as we knew, represents one of the struggling factions
that seek to discredit our king. He was supplied with money
and jewels to buy support. That support includes the worst of
the pirates who eluded us. They occupy the ship that followed
us and are in full fighting trim since they lost none during the
storm that decimated our ranks. Their numbers are double our
own and they are fully able to fight on land. He boasted of our
defeat before he succumbed. I wanted you to know this. There
are no secrets between us now."

One of the men gave a harsh laugh. "Well, Lord Commander, I still think any man of Crete is better than any six pirates
and we have proved this in times past. No change, I would
say!"

Some of the others spoke agreement and Paon smiled a little
bitterly.

"More information will be forthcoming. We will go on
toward our goal until that time. Then we must plan further
strategy."

They walked on into the golden afternoon over fields where
flowering bushes rose up and the scent of the sea was ever with
them. The dread that had been with Lia that morning increased

and she almost wished that whatever was to happen would do so. She looked to the far horizon and saw a hill that appeared to be topped with standing figures. Her low exclamation reached Paon, who turned and followed her gaze.

"Oh, those. They are on many of the hills hereabouts and sometimes in other places. There is a mighty circle of them on a plain inland. Some of the tribes worship at them. They might have been built by giants." His tone was musing. "In themselves they are nothing to fear. Even if they live as some men say, humans are far more evil and dangerous."

"Where did you learn such bitterness, Paon?" She had sworn to say no more about anything that might touch on the personal but behind the sternness in his face she saw something of her own dread.

"Much of it at the hands of women, my dear." He was walking beside her and speaking softly so that the men could not hear. "You have wanted to know, now you may as well. Curiosity belongs to your sex. You thought I worried about Hirath?"

Lia said, "There is no need for you to say anything that you do not wish."

"But I wish it. Poison must be let out. I loathe the woman. The day does not dawn that I do not wish her dead."

Their silence drew long and deep as his words burned between them.

Chapter Thirty-One

THE MANY NAMES OF LOVE

"IT IS SIMPLY said, after all. How very easily we are trapped by our own emotions! I looked on Hirath long ago and found her the fairest woman I had ever seen. She knew of the world, was experienced in the ways of the court, her family is one of the most powerful in Knossos and Crete itself. I was favored by Minos and he agreed to our betrothal against the wishes of her family, who wanted her to wed a great official whom she professed to loathe. It was due to them that she was chosen to be priestess of the Lady of the Snake with a time limit on her release. Not even Minos could set that aside and he bade us wait. Long before that, however, I knew that Hirath was dangerous, scheming and cruel; we were drugged with each other, feeding on heightened hungers and demands. We conducted our relationship in secret, for all believed her virgin and she would have suffered the death could it have been proven otherwise, but there were many whispers which her people silenced with gold and cruelty. She went into retreat before she was taken for the goddess and there she bore my child, my son. How could she be large with child and it not known? Flowing gowns, seclusion, gold—easily enough. Even then she plotted and flirted with power, knowing the regard in which the king held me." Paon wiped one wet hand across his brow, which was also wet. The lines in the dark face were burned deep but his eyes were brighter than Lia had seen them when he looked at her. It was as if some of the baffled anger in him were draining away a little at a time.

"Your son? How old is he?" She had to say something, for the burden of glory in her was almost too much to bear. The beautiful and glorious woman held no corner of Paon's heart! He knew her for what she was and had always done so. But, said another part of her own heart, still he had taken her in passion and it had not mattered.

"He has five summers. His name is Hir-Pa." The words were flat on the air.

"And you hate his mother?" Lia wanted to demand the information from him.

"She would have had him killed at birth if it had not meant exposure for her. Later she used my caring for him as a rein and rule over me. She is very powerful now and means to remain the priestess, taking lovers as she will and even coming to the bed of Minos. He does not know of the child and she may bear one for him and Crete. They who serve the gods are inviolate. She could kill Hir-Pa and only I would suffer. If I do not obey her, it will be done."

Paon stopped walking and caught her arms in his grip. The sun burned down into their faces and time seemed to stop. Lia looked into the face of his agony, feeling all her hurt in his.

"He is small for his years. His right arm that should hold a spear and a knife, that should touch the faces of his parents, is but a nub on his shoulder. His left leg is shorter than the other. Lia, by all the gods, how can I say it? Why did I start this?" His strained whisper struck her ears. "He has no mind, nothing. There is only voice and motion and sometimes a smile. He is secreted away and tended by those paid by Hirath but I would swear that he knows me at times. Fool that I am, he is my son and I do love him! For that I have endured her demands, so that he may live."

He began to walk faster than ever, pulling her along with him, oblivious to their surroundings and careless of where he put his feet. Dimly, Lia could hear the men behind them but she would not have cared if they had suddenly been overtaken by all the forces on this island. She saw into Paon's heart and mind and ached for him as never for any other.

"She could easily kill him with her own hands and care nothing for it. She no longer wants our marriage but she wishes me to be hers whenever she commands it. I roamed the seas, had my own command and thought of her only when I had to. Yet there is that about her which can lure and hold men. Even I, knowing what she is, still desire her often. Hirath wants to be the uncrowned ruler of Crete and may even aspire to the throne of Minos himself. I acted the part of her cohort when I accused you of forcing yourself into this expedition—it was needful."

The slow, bitter words stopped and he tramped along. Lia could think of nothing that might comfort him and there was no way to express what she felt for this tormented man who had endured so much.

"Thank you for telling me, Paon. I understand."

"I think that you cannot. You will understand, though, that I can have no interest in you when we return to Knossos. I well know that Hirath plots with Zarnan against Minos, but if our mission is even partly successful, he can hold his own against them. I have endured Naris and his plots because he hates her and has many contacts. He thinks she has a hold over me but does not know what it is. I use him. You wonder that I continue to do so. One day I shall take my son from her and she will be no more. But her power is strong and she is feared. She may feel that I hate her but I have tried to make her think otherwise. She is cautious, maintaining holds over those who can be of use to her."

"So much intrigue! It sounds unbearable." Once Lia would have wondered at a man who could hate a woman and yet be hungry for her flesh. Now she could comprehend that fact and begin to understand. She felt pity for Paon even as she wondered what her own future would be like without him.

"I tell you that if Minos were not my friend and I pledged to him and if it were not for my son, I would long since have resumed my travels. Or at least I often think so. Then I remember Crete herself and how I have fought, sailed and participated in the life there, been a part of it. I belong there and doubtless will end my life there. Who can say?" He shrugged his shoulders and played with the sword at his waist. "Battle is far simpler. Now you know, Lia, what no one else knows and I marvel that I could tell you." There was a faint edge of incredulity in his tone.

"I would hope that you feel secure in the telling." She

paused briefly and he turned to look at her. "All that you have said is safe with me, Paon."

The golden sun poured down around them and the breeze blew softly as it brought the scent of flowers. They stood together for only an instant but nothing in Lia's past experience with Paon had prepared her for the intensity of that shared time. Their eyes locked, clinging with a power that shook them both. Lia saw beyond the barriers that Paon had, of necessity, erected into the soul of the youth who had come to Crete, survived and learned to fight. She saw the nature of his trap and knew, with a thrill of horror, that only the death of Hirath could ever free him. Somehow, in the feeling that their closeness gave her, Lia believed he, too, saw how it had been for the young girl of Pandos island and the overwhelming changes that had altered her innocence. He held himself accountable for this as well and that was his added pain.

Something flashed in her mind and she looked back to their first interlude when he took her prisoner. He had spoken of a woman he had loved and of his flight from Egypt and across the sea to another land of rivers. There had been little enough in his comments and later Naris embellished them but she sensed that this had much to do with his divided emotions where she was concerned. So much to know and to wonder! Would they survive to speculate?

"Commander! Commander!" The cry was indistinct but the desperation in it jerked Lia and Paon aware.

Paon swung around to see his men gathered together, several of them supporting one other who was bleeding profusely. He hurried toward them, Lia following. She saw that the man was one of those who had gone with Adib to question the spies. There was an open, gaping cut across his cheek and another on his throat. His chest had been hacked and ribbons of flesh dangled down as though they had been pulled there by eager hands. He was gasping for breath and attempting to speak through his own blood.

"They came . . . many. Killed. I only . . ." The words trailed away as they laid him flat on the ground and Paon knelt beside him. He looked up into the ring of faces around him, coughed and shuddered. Then the faint sounds began again. "Not pirates or any we know of . . . attacked us and prisoners. Took Mardos. Another, too. Cannot see!" The wail lifted and subsided.

Paon said urgently, "The natives attacked you and took Mardos as well as several others away. Is that it? Are you the only one alive? What did they look like? Were they like the traders? Thin and dark? Try to tell me, man. We will tend you. It will be all right!"

Lia sank to her knees beside them and touched the man's forehead. Light as her fingers were, he winced. Then he looked her in the eye and his anger seemed to gather for his face contorted. "No!" She drew back when Paon waved impatiently. He produced a small leather flask of wine, touching it to the pale lips.

The man coughed again and whispered, "Hairy and blue. Blue! She? She? No!" Blood spurted up and out over his face. He gasped, shuddered and died.

"What did he see?"

"She? What did he mean?"

The babble of questions rose as they looked cautiously around, each man fingering his weapons, knowing that they were well exposed on these sunny slopes in the clear light of day. Lia glanced toward the distant hills and fancied that she saw figures moving on them. The old dread returned and she wanted to run before it. But her world was here, in this fight, and there was to be no turning from its demands.

Paon straightened up and surveyed them all. Under that sharp gaze the murmurs and questions ceased as men grinned a little with embarrassment, shuffled their feet or looked down at their fallen fellow with the shock of loss. The call of a bird came suddenly and was as rapidly answered. Then there was only the silence of the countryside around them.

"I want you to scatter, each man going his own way. Cover as much ground as you can, double back, circle, confuse any who may pursue you. You are responsible for yourselves. We will meet at the beach, at the great pointed rock, in five days' time." His face was stern as he held up one hand to forestall their protests. "I order it. There is no other way that we can survive and have even some hope of fulfilling our mission."

"But, Lord Commander, how can we run before these natives? What of the honor of Crete?" The young man was snapping his fingers against his sword, his eyes angry. Others muttered but grew quiet before Paon's glare.

"You speak foolish words, Speo. We honor her by staying alive and doing what we came to do. You and one other shall take Lia with you. Guard her person as you would the living flesh of the goddess. I will have your word on that."

Lia cried out but her voice was lost in those of the others as they demanded. "What of you, Lord Commander? Where do you go? What plan to save the mission do you have?"

He said, "We waste time talking. There is little enough time left to us as it is. I am familiar to some of the traders and I am fluent in the language. The natives who are with us now will not protect us or engage in any battles for our sakes but they will lead me to those powerful enough to negotiate a contract for what tin they can mine and we can get. They can then guide me back to the rest of you. I will take one man with me." He looked over them all in the hush that fell after his words. "You, Morb. Will you join me?"

The short, spry man, weathered with years of sun on land and sea, his bright brown eyes only slightly darker than his skin, strode forward and smiled through blackened teeth. "Gladly. Eagerly."

"I shall come also." Lia stepped up to Morb's side and fixed Paon with her most determined look. "It is my right as a full member of this expedition."

"I am the commander and I say it is too dangerous. The men follow my orders and you are not exempt." Paon shaded his eyes and surveyed the horizon before letting his gaze come back to Lia. "You see what fate our comrade has suffered. That and more could happen to you. Do not waste our time with foolish demands."

"I am supposed to be safer running about the woods and hills with the others? They will have the chance to run and hide if need be; you have the difficult task of persuasion with the very real possibility of failure. Should the goddess depart from us, the danger could be even worse. I have the honor to represent her; she rules earth and sky, might she not be more sympathetic to us as we walk boldly among these people who do not know her? It is her place and I demand it in her right!"

She held him with her eyes but she heard the stir behind her and knew that at least some of the hearers agreed. Paon had once used that argument on her, even ordering her to invoke the name of the goddess, and she had refused; now she used it shamelessly for her own ends and recognized that fact. She did not mean to be separated from him in the little time that remained to them. If that was foolish or selfish then let it be so—she meant only to have something to remember in the barren years. And, another part of her brain informed her coldly, this would be good practice for the role she meant to assume in Egypt when she arrived there from Crete, mistress of enough goods to ensure the setting up of herself as minor healer, prophetess, seer and dealer in love potions. There were many gods in Egypt; she would select a lesser one and move under that guise. One thing was certain. She could not stay in Crete, love Paon and watch the destruction that must surely come.

Paon's lips quirked, and in one of those mood changes that never failed to surprise her, he said, "You are bold, Lia. But I understand that your concern is for the goddess. Naturally. I honor you for it." The barb was theirs alone.

"Then I come with your consent?"

"Or without it. But if there is trouble, as there is certain to be, I will have no woman's tears. You know the odds." His eyes were steady on hers and once again the world seemed to narrow down to the two of them.

"I know and accept them."

As she spoke there was a murmur of approval, and when she turned, the collective faces of the men regarded her with a kind of awe. Her action was fitting in their eyes if not in Paon's. The man called Speo was now glancing worriedly about, although the silence of earth and sky was undisturbed.

"The natives who were with you, Commander? Where are they?"

Paon shrugged. "They have gone their way. I told you, they will not become involved in our struggles. They are traders and cautious but they will assist me alone, I believe, just as they did with the spies." He bent down again to the fallen man and brushed his hand across the wounds. "We will bury him, Morb and I. Lia shall invoke the great goddess. The rest of you scatter. Hurry! When we meet at the beach the *Lily Flame* will be close. I sent a message by one of the natives who journeys that way."

Speo said, "Be careful, Lord Commander." He wanted to say more but his throat closed up and he could only put out a hand toward Paon, who reached up and took it for an instant. "Hasten, men! Obey our commander!"

Momemts later they were melting into the bushes, slipping back toward the woods and sliding into thickets with all the practiced ease of those who had done this many times before. Then Lia, Morb and Paon were alone with the body of their comrade as the soft wind chased clouds over a brilliant sky and birds called to each other, oblivious to the hunted who moved among them.

"Take him down by the thicket where that big bush overhangs. The earth should be soft there." Paon bent to his own orders and as he did so his hand brushed Lia's. He jerked it back while Morb stared curiously.

Lia saw the set bleakness of his face and knew that he, too, felt the strange dread of the unknown she had experienced. Paon, lord commander of Crete and leader of this expedition, did not believe that they would emerge alive from this land.

Chapter Thirty-Two

PASSION'S BATTLEGROUND

THE SMELL OF damp earth mingled with that of the distant sea with a faintly bitter odor of crushed herbs. The wind pulled at their garments, whirled overhead and carried the far-off hint of rain. Lia heard the cry of a night bird and the answer of another. A wolf howled, then was joined by several more. Something crashed in the brush near them and then moved rapidly away. The hand closed more firmly around her arm and the voice of her escort spoke in that liquid language so like the sea and the crags. She could not understand but only hoped that it was meant to be reassuring. The blindfold was bound securely over her eyes and men walked on either side of her. The journey seemed to be taking forever; the sense of her own helplessness increased with every step she made.

After leaving the others that afternoon, she, Paon and Morb had moved carefully over the barely discernible trails, through glens, over marshes and rock beds, always careful to avoid the open spaces. They had watched for signs of pursuit but there were none. Paon walked with his hand on his dagger, cautioning Lia to do the same. Morb had his out and his eyes flicked everywhere. The sun vanished behind walls of cloud as a mist began to rise from the ground, obscuring much of their vision.

The dark-haired men had seemed to rise from the mist, their own weapons ready, faces menacing as they came around the Cretans. Paon spoke swiftly, motioning to the others for silence and allowing them to take his weapon. Lia saw them nod and look at each other; there were at least five of them and more waited beyond the nearest scrubby tree, before one advanced to her, gesturing that she should give him her weapon.

"It is all right. Let him blindfold you. The way is secret. We will come to no harm." Paon murmured the words in the language of the mainland. His gaze was compelling on Lia and Morb.

She smiled slightly at him and allowed the man to adjust the thick cloth over her eyes. Morb gave a muffled curse but obeyed. Her daggers were taken from her and hands took her arms. She wanted to shake free of the damp fingers pressing into her skin but dared not show any sign of distaste. Morb grumbled again as one of the men spoke to Paon sharply.

"Do as they wish, Morb. Stay here with the guards and give no trouble. Our lives on it." Again the softly slurred mainland language from Paon and the muttered snarl from Morb, who was obviously struggling to control himself.

Then the endless walking had begun. No more words were exchanged and Lia felt that they walked in an eternity of darkness mingled with chill. She wanted to speak to Paon but did not dare jeopardize his dealings with these people. Her legs were stiff, her mouth dry. She thought it would not matter if all the tribes of this land were after them if only she might have something to eat and drink first. Memories of warmth and comfort seeped into her mind and she tried to concentrate on them as her feet followed along with the escort.

The roughness underneath her sandals gave way to smoothness quite suddenly. The air lay warm against her chilled body and she began to shiver. The hands dropped away as the men said something in a low voice. She heard them walk away just before she lifted uncertain fingers to the blindfold. She felt someone close to her and spoke softly.

"Paon? Paon!" There was no answer as she said his name more loudly. She ripped the cloth away and stared into the eyes of a young woman only slightly older than herself who was standing directly in front of her.

The woman had long loose dark hair and green eyes framed by sooty lashes. A short green garment covered breasts and hips while a golden dagger gleamed at her waist. Her lips were red and soft as she smiled at Lia and held out one hand. She said something in the rippling language.

Lia said in very low Minoan, "Where is Paon?" As she spoke she looked about in surprise. They were in the center of a small wooden hut with earthen floors covered with flowers and leaves. A type of candle glimmered in three corners of the area, illuminating a raised area covered with cloaks. Food and drink waited on a rudely built table which stood in the center of some massed branches. A low fire blazed in a trench close to her feet and the smoke was wafted upward to a hole in the ceiling.

"Back soon." The young woman spoke in halting Minoan, the words so flattened as to be almost unrecognizable. She touched her chest. "Aelth. I." With another brilliant smile she waved at the table and made gestures of eating. Then she turned her back slowly and walked over to it.

The intention was plain enough and Lia knew blessed relief. She joined the other girl and made the same identifying motion as they sat down together. Over cold meat, a strange sort of bread that had an oddly sweet flavor and a tangy beverage that made her nose tingle, Lia pointed to objects, saying their names in Minoan and trying to repeat the sounds her companion made. At one point she rose and brought a thick woolen cloak to Lia, then pointed toward a stone container of water. Lia shuddered; the thought of a bath was not appealing at this moment. Aelth laughed, and in a moment Lia joined in. They sat together over cups of the heady liquid as the language lessons resumed. Lia felt her unease slip away and drowsiness crept in.

Soon Lia was able to wash in the cool water and enjoy the touch of it on her skin. Aelth gave her a gown similar to her own and fastened it with a belt of gold with a curious clasp, a large stone encircled by two snakes over a butterfly. The symbols of the goddess! She looked up at the girl in surprise but Aelth shook her head and poured Lia another cup of the liquid. This time she sipped, loosened her hair and shook it free, combing it with the stout comb she had been given and enjoying the relaxation she felt. She did not know when Aelth slipped away or when she knew that she must sleep for only a short time or tumble over where she was. The instant that she rose to go to the spread pallet, she realized how potent the drink had been. The world spun as she put her head down and welcomed the oblivion.

Rivulets of warmth spread over her neck and back, burned slightly at her nipples, caressed her stomach and rose again to the corners of her lips. Lia moaned and stretched, vaguely conscious that she wanted that touch to go lower, much lower. She drifted on the sea, felt it cradle her body and rise about her in an all-embracing gentleness. She raised her arms, turned slightly to seek the depths, as she had so often done in the past, and touched solidity.

"Will you wake to me, Lia?" The voice was so soft that she barely heard it. "Lia. You are dreaming and smiling all at the same time."

She opened her eyes, which seemed to have weights on the lids, and saw that Paon lay beside her. He had pushed aside her gown as he touched her with slow fingers that called up delights she knew well. Now he propped his head on one elbow and hand while he leaned close to her, his breath stirring her hair as he spoke softly in her ear. One finger of the spread hand moved very slowly over her erect nipple and she felt her legs move convulsively. Already the lubricating moisture was between them. Her skin was beginning to prickle as the slow, sweet burning rose.

"Paon. Where have you been?" How long had she lain thus while he touched and roused her? The drink had made her lethargic. She wondered suddenly if that was the purpose. Then she did not care, for he was here, making her want him, caring that she did and smiling that enigmatic, carved smile that banished all other thoughts.

"No. No thoughts for now. Only feeling." He sat up, cuppled both hands around her face and kissed first her lips, her neck and throat, then drew her closer and thrust his tongue deeply into her mouth while his hands sought her breasts. She yielded eagerly, drawn by his power and knowing somehow that this first demand must be his.

It seemed to Lia that his mouth would take and mold her own, so deeply did they fuse. She put her hands downward to his stalk, finding it pulsating and hard. Paon moved back, slipping downward and taking her with him so that she released him lingeringly. She was under his body now, covered by that powerful length even as his hands caressed her urgently and his mouth never lifted from hers. She pulled as close as she could and yet it was not enough. She wanted him inside her but she also yearned to preserve this moment, the time when they were truly one body.

He was drawing out the approaching time of culmination, for he began to kiss her eyelids, chin, the side of her neck and shoulders. His hand cupped her right breast for an instant before he lowered his mouth to the nipple, which went from a heavy, swollen thing to a long throbbing flame of pleasure as he played at it with tongue and teeth. Lia put her fingers behind his head when her body arched upward and the moans began. He paused just when the hunger became a tangible reality and touched his lips to the other breast. When Lia tried to reach for him, he withdrew very slightly, beginning to invoke the fire again in her.

She lay back again at his urging while he continued his path down her body. The nearly spent flames in the trench just beyond them would leap up every now and then to illumine his long muscular body or to cast his shadow on the walls. The sweet smell of crushed herbs was in the air and the covers beneath them had been dried in the sunlight. They two existed in a world that was their own; nothing else mattered for this time and this place.

Paon came to the edge of her golden mat, pausing to let his hand explore lightly as he looked up at her. His eyes were a deep, smoky blue, his mouth a sensual curve in his tanned face. She drank in the sight of his lean, hard form, the erect shaft, the broad shoulders and tumbling dark hair. He surely thought only of her at this time but still she wondered what went on in the confines of his mind. Did he think of Hirath, whose body he had said he still desired at times? Her ardor shifted and his touch seemed to intrude.

He caught her withdrawal and said, "Now is not the time, Lia. Let me give you pleasure." He waited for her nod before sliding his fingers into her moistness, spreading them wide and starting to work on her mound with his thumb in gentle, tantalizing strokes that made her begin to shake.

Was this the way he felt with Hirath? Caring for nothing but the continuing motions and movements that reduced her to shivering delight? His mouth was now where his fingers had been and the darting tongue, coupled with those drawing, pulling sensations, kindled the building fires, made them rise and drove all conscious thought from Lia. She arched, rose and melted into softness that seemed to swing her back into the very arms of the sea. She lay with legs spread wide, his head pillowed on her thigh, and let her herself drift in the momentary peace.

When his fingers began to slide down her smooth legs and his face turned inquiringly toward hers, Lia felt the forerunners of passion touch her once more. She smiled at him and bent forward to kiss the dark curve of his left eyebrow. He caught her to him, allowing her to feel the erectness of himself and his hands conveyed his own readiness. She touched him twice and felt the quiver that moved over his entire body. He had held himself back and now he was barely able to contain it.

She pushed her body back as he had done, then put one hand on his chest. "Let me, Paon." She half crouched over him so that the light could play on her golden skin and the soft globules of her breasts. Her shimmering hair fell down her back to crown her with light as her passion shone out of her eyes. Lia knew how she looked to him; it blazed from his eyes and pulsed in the stalk which she now held with a gentle touch at first, then moved the skin up and down so that he grimaced with pleasure.

She let go, rose and stood above him, her pelvis turned toward his face for a quick moment before she swayed from side to side, his eyes following her every motion, bent to kiss his forehead in a chaste motion and then let her hand trail down his stomach to take him up once more.

"You are witch-woman! A sea witch!" His gasped words were barely audible. "I cannot bear this."

"Shall I stop?" She touched her mouth faintly to the glistening tip which jerked, seeming to rise to her lips.

"By the goddess! No!"

"I am mortal woman. Say it."

"I will say anything. Anything!" He was spread out as she had been and was fast losing any control. His forehead was beaded with sweat and his hands moved convulsively.

Lia put her mouth to him again and drew his length into it. Her tongue went around the little ridge, caressed the tiny lip, drew and pulled and sucked at him until he moaned with the delight of it all. A faintly salt taste grew in her mouth and he swelled out there. She felt as she had when his tongue took hers; they moved together in answer and thrusting. He would explode in her, she knew, and his life power would be hers. They would join and penetrate each other. It was time; her lips worked faster and faster. He caught her hair as his whole body rose higher, thrusting him down her throat in a strangling repetitive motion that was both frightening and exciting. Her instincts had taken over; her mind no longer considered anything but only felt. Paon gave a low groan, then there was a painful tug on her hair and he twisted away from her mouth in one swift jerking movement.

Lia raised her head and stared at him as he crouched beside her, the dark brows drawn together, his stalk swollen and turgid, his eyes raking her face and body. The taste of him was still in her mouth, the mark of his hands was on her, and her flesh cried out for his but she knew in that instant that she was afraid of him. The blackness rose in him so that she could almost see it and, hating herself, she slipped back a little.

It was the wrong thing to do. He rolled toward her, placed his whole length on hers, held her hair on both sides of her face so that it was painful to move and thrust himself into her passion-heated body that was eager to receive only a short breath ago. This was no tenderness nor caring. This was man relieving the urge of the body. His face and eyes told her that as he hammered up and down, his look savage. She wanted to close her eyes but she would not. Lia gave him look for look while he held her and finished the passion they had begun.

She could not call her body traitor. She had longed for this culmination and now, as he penetrated her to the very depths in a few swift thrusts and drew her upward to fling them both down with the rapidity of a fall, she welcomed the release. Paon moved quickly away from her and she heard his heaving breaths as he tried to regain composure. She felt as though she had been beaten and her throat was beginning to ache. She did not want to look at him or think of what this might mean. Only the comfort of sleep could release her.

But the triumph or pain was not to be hers alone. Paon sat up, put his head in his hands and his shoulders twisted with a dejection that was instantly mastered. Lia forced herself up and pulled her rumpled gown over her naked flesh. She and Paon gazed at each other. His anger was hidden and the mask of the lord commander was firmly in place.

"You may sleep now. You will not be disturbed again; that much I can promise you." His tone was cool, dismissing. He was reaching for his loincloth, adjusting his cloak.

"As the commander says." Her head was high but her heart was aching with loss.

He strode out the door without a backward glance and hailed someone close by. She could not understand the words but the tone was jovial. They should have been lying together in tenderness and sharing. What had gone wrong? Lia put her head down on the pallet and wept bitter tears, sobs that none must hear, for pride alone could sustain her now in her loss.

Chapter Thirty-Three

REVELATION

LIA WOKE TO utter silence and lay for a moment remembering the night just past. The room was alight with day but there was no indication as to whether it was morning or afternoon. The fire in the trench had been replenished at some point while she slept, for it burned readily, giving a comforting warmth against the chill she felt as she rose. A cloth was spread near it with food and drink laid out; a basin of water, comb and clothes were close by. Her eyes were sticky and her hair trailed over her shoulders. She was just as glad that no one was about. Part of her wanted simply to return to the pallet and pull the covers up over her head, forgetting everything, especially the necessity of seeing Paon again soon. The rest of her mind knew that she must do what she could to herself and venture out with head high, face impassive, just as she had faced the Cretans all along.

"He shall not touch me again. I will not go to him." She said the words aloud to bolster her courage. She only hoped that she could remember the resolve if Paon came near.

The world was shrouded in mist when she emerged from the hut a short while later. She had braided her hair in a coronet around her head and her face was so well scrubbed with the cold water that it tingled. The blue shirt came well below her knees but was full and swinging when she fastened the ties around her slim waist. The short jacket was too large; still it did well enough when she tied the ends under her breasts and

241

the loose woven material was soft to her skin. Her feet were bare. She felt naked without her daggers but there had been no sign of them.

Lia looked about, wonderingly. Her ears told her that a stream or river was close by and there was a watery freshness in the air. The tips of trees thrust through the cloudy whiteness. She could see outcroppings of jagged rocks off to the left. Beside them were several dark huts that blended into the landscape. A barely recognizable path ran through the bent grasses at her feet.

After the sunlight she had seen in this land, the cloudy chill was ominous. It seemed a prelude of the future. The thought suddenly struck Lia that perhaps she had been abandoned, deserted in the night by the angry Paon and these people he knew well enough to trust. All her senses rebelled against such an idea but the very strangeness of the night and morning made her hand go instinctively to the place where she usually carried her dagger.

A voice called out something in the liquid, craggy language and she whirled around. No one was in sight. A high voice rang out again, punctuated this time by a trickle of laughter. "Who is there? Where are you?" Lia heard her words come eerily back on the calm air. She forced herself to stand very quietly as she strained all her faculties to determine who or what was near.

The laughter came again and this time there was a rushing sound with it. A child of perhaps three or four dashed past, paused, circled around her, stared and went on his way as fast as he could. His face was familiar. Lia gave a shaky laugh as she realized that it was Aelth's own. But where was she? Perhaps the child would lead her in that direction. She started after him, thinking as she went just how foolish her imaginings had been. As much as Paon had told her, after all they had endured together how could she believe him capable of deserting her?

The mist moved again and this time she was not frightened. The man who came toward her was only slightly taller than she and a little stooped. His hair was nearly white and his eyes gray but his face did not show age. He wore a white, short garment that shone against a pale skin. He was so nearly one with the mist that Lia almost failed to notice the instant greed in his eyes.

He spoke to her in the native language and touched his chest before extending long smooth fingers toward her face. She could not help it, she backed away and shook her head, indicating her lack of understanding. He smiled, the tips of pointed white teeth showing. They had been filed that way, Lia realized, and a revulsion swept over her.

"Lia! Lia?" The soft accents of her name in Aelth's own pronunciation were sweet and sane in this altered world. The white one moved back but his smile never altered and those strange eyes did not change.

"Here! I am here!"

Aelth materialized, smiling and lovely, long hair tumbling down her back, the child in her arms, both of them gazing interestedly at Lia. She turned to greet them and heard the faint crackle as the man drifted deeper into the mist.

An unfamiliar voice speaking Minoan startled Lia and then filled her with a rushing excitement. "You are the priestess of whom my friend spoke. Welcome to our land both for yourself and for his sake. I wish that you might have had a more peaceful time of it but you know that we are in turmoil. I am Eridor. My wife, Aelth, you met. This is my son, Fal." The quick dark man who strode forward was a little less tall than Paon, his body thin and muscular, his chest scarred by a long puckered gash that did not tan. The hand he extended to her was hard and very strong. His smile was friendly but the black eyes were bleak.

"I am Lia of Pandos. I do thank you and your family for the hospitality." The polite words made Lia feel as if they stood in the bright halls of Knossos, not the mist-shrouded woods of a land where every hand seemed lifted against them.

"Pandos and Crete." Eridor glanced over her head, frowned slightly and asked, "The white-haired one? You saw him?" At her nod, he stepped closer. "That is my uncle Thulf. He was touched by the gods long ago. The fire from heaven rested in the oak and both reached out for him. He speaks in strange tongues, foretells the future sometimes and wanders over the land. You should not fear him."

Lia was indignant. "I do not. I was only startled." She had seen lust in those eyes but it did not seem to matter very much right now. Here were friends, a modicum of safety, someone to talk with. "Where is Paon? Are there others here? Is this the village of the tin traders?" She felt the red rise to her cheeks at the rude spate of questions. "Forgive me, Eridor. I do not mean to demand of you."

He smiled again and this time it touched his eyes so that they were warm. The hard face was gentle and he seemed younger suddenly. Aelth came close to put her arm around his waist. Fal slipped to the ground and began to run ahead of them. Eridor began to walk slowly along and Lia came to his side. They rounded a curve of the path, went past several more huts that seemed to huddle under the dripping trees and moved deeper into the mist, which was now lifting to reveal more rocks and bushes. The sound of the river grew louder.

"I understand your need for answers but some I cannot give. Even Paon is not allowed to enter too deeply into our secrets. One of our young women has conducted him to a special place from which he will return shortly. We are one of the entryways to those of the tin workers; our village is small and we move about. You need not worry. I think that the negotiations Paon wishes can be safely carried out." Eridor smiled at her again as he spoke the soothing words but she saw that his fingers closed hard around Aelth's shoulder.

His did not appear to be a face that would smile easily; the thin lines were bracketed around his mouth and the planes of his cheeks moved together as he talked. Lia wanted to ask him just what was happening but did not want to risk the friendliness that was offered. She wondered if the rites that Paon was attending—she had no doubt that this was what was meant by "special place"—were those of purification and sensuality. She fought back the jealousy that shot through her.

Fal came rushing up to seize Aelth's hands and pull her ahead. He spoke eagerly to Eridor but his father motioned him back. He grinned up at Lia in a way that reminded her so much of Elg that she was forced to turn her face away.

The pale eyes that met hers still had lust in them but now there was calculation as well. The uncle, Thulf, was leaning against a nearby tree, watching them and rubbing his fingers slowly together as if caressing himself. He spoke to Eridor but his gaze did not leave Lia. She stared at him, wondering that he did not blink or change expression. It was as if they were engaged in a silent struggle; she could not look away from him. Eridor was answering, his voice low, with a thread of anger in it. Thulf cocked a white brow, snapped out something and vanished into the wood.

Aelth and Fal had gone on ahead. Eridor and Lia stood together in the silence of the morning; only the sound of the river broke it. She had that sense of menace again and kept herself from blurting it out only with a powerful effort of will. Now Eridor walked on a few steps and waved his hand. Lia looked down and could not keep herself from gasping.

The valley was spread out just below the river in a tangle of green wrapped in soft white. The river was a small one but fairly wide and she could see the shimmer of flat white stones as the mist was blown into tags by the breeze. The valley was small, folded into the curves of the bordering hills, and might have been almost invisible from some points. Their own place of viewing was a great flat rock above a sheer drop to some jagged ones just below. It was beautiful and isolated, changeable when the mist rose and shifted.

"It was a truly good life here once and can be again." Eridor was almost musing. He turned to her and said again, "We will feast and talk when Paon returns. We must make our arrangements."

She was rude once more but something about this situation was rendering her nervous and more so by the moment. "What did Thulf say?"

"Nothing. He speaks in riddles. This one was about gold and the mist and standing stones ready to drink."

"I see." She did not but she did not wish to pursue her concern about their host's kinsman with him. The stones on the hills and the fires beyond them came back with sharp force. She thought of the men, their comrades who had sworn to serve Paon, hiding in the grass, behind cliffs or running through the woods, perhaps even encountering drops such as the one where they now stood. "I do not think there is time for feasting, Eridor. Paon will have told you of the ship that trailed us, of the disposition of our men. . . ."

He scrutinized her face so sharply that she did not think he heard her words. "You love him." It was a statement, not a question.

"He is his own man. I know that well. I want only my

freedom." She knew how crippling love could be. Did it not make her want to forget everything and pour out her heart to Paon? Had her father not cared so passionately for Ze, her mother, that his life was blighted with her loss? Even Paon himself, torn with love for his helpless son, and she, loving Elg as she now knew she had, were torn with differing loves.

Eridor shrugged but did not try to press her further. He spoke with the voice of memory; his face was somber as he looked out over the valley where a slow rain was driven before the wind. Soon it would reach them but neither he nor Lia paid any attention. They moved in another, younger world.

"He talked of her a little in those days when I first knew him. It is hard to believe now that we were so young, both fighting in those endless wars of the land between the rivers. We drank too much and I, just a boy fleeing the demands of my family, wishing to see the world outside this island, saw a vision of what love might be like."

Here was Paon's shrouded past in front of her! Lia had to say something to encourage him but caution held her back. She murmured, "And now that vision is made reality."

"I have been fortunate. She is my second wife and both were dearly loved. The turmoil here threatens everything." Eridor sighed heavily. "It is long since I saw Paon and knew that he was betrothed to the priestess of his goddess. At first I thought you were she but her savagery is not yours. Yes, he told me of her. He is my friend and I wish him happiness. I will do what I can for him in memory of those days when we were so close. But you, Lia, of you he does not speak."

Only honesty would serve her now. "I know he loved a woman and fled Egypt because of her. Nothing more of that. He told me of Hirath."

"In all the time I have known Paon I never knew him to love a woman. Take her, dally with her, sometimes become friendly as with a man, but never in love. It is strange that I reveal his secrets to you whom I have not met before this day and yet there is that thing about you that encourages free speech. And I know of your caring for him." Eridor began to pace back and forth as he hooked his fingers in the belt from which his dagger hung.

"Tell me." She barely whispered the words.

"Her name was Kaha and they were wed when both were

very young, as was the custom in their part of Egypt. Paon's family were originally wanderers who settled in the north, kept to themselves and grew prosperous. They rarely mingled; when they did it was with the nearest neighbors only. I understand there was a great closeness between them. Kaha was an heiress and desired by others, some of whom took exception to her preference for Paon. One day, while Paon did some solitary hunting, a raid was mounted. All perished; mother, father, a younger sister and brother, Kaha and her only brother burned in the fire that destroyed houses and property as well. Paon, younger than you may be now, returned in time to see the flames dying. He knew who they were—there had been no secrets about the protests and jealousy. He sought them out one by one and killed them lingeringly; they could find no protection from his fury. It may be that he had help from some of the river outcasts who were his friends of youth, he has never said. Nine scions of the wealthy, nine of those who serve pharaoh, slain. The outcry went up and he was forced to flee for his life. No matter that he was the one sinned against. He was not a true Egyptian, they said, and his people had not served in the armies of expansion nor come to the court of great pharaoh. So they sought him to kill him. Paon learned in the course of his revenge that his sister, mother and Kaha had all been raped. Only several days before Kaha had mentioned that she might be with child, but it was too soon to tell. He loved his Kaha with a young man's first passion and adoration. The scars and the bitterness are with him still."

The low voice died away but the scenes of violence and carnage lived on in Lia's mind. She saw the young girl and Paon as they lay together, heard the shy news she whispered, felt the tenderness of their kiss, knew the warmth of his family and the gentleness of their love. Both she and Paon had been torn by the cruelty of the world; it was part of the bond between them.

But another charge remained. She whispered, "He called himself murderer and described the woman, said she was his kinswoman."

"Yes. The faithless wife of a cousin talked of Kaha's youth and innocence among a band of those who had wanted her. The talk inflamed them and she rode with them to do the deed.

Taking pleasure in it! Paon killed her and well that he did so! She was as guilty."

Avenger he might be but never murderer. Lia had not believed it and she had buried it away. Now she could feel endless pain for him. She could understand his retreat from her in moments of passion, the ready anger, his reluctance to show feeling, even his desire for Hirath and his hopeless caring for the son who would never see his father's face and recognize it.

"I thank you for telling me, Eridor. Why have you?"

The wind grew stronger as it swirled the mist up toward them, carrying the scent of wet earth and salt sea.

"Paon is my friend no matter how many seas lie between us. You care for him and it was right that you know."

Now the odor of charred wood came to them both and once again Lia thought of that other fire which had burned in Egypt.

Chapter Thirty-Four

THE BETRAYED

THE SOFT RAIN began to fall shortly afterward but Eridor showed no desire to seek shelter and Lia did not like to urge it. She watched him pace up and down on the great stone, around its edges and back again while he stared down into the valley. All the while he talked of impersonal things, and sensing his need for this, Lia interposed questions or exclamations. The air was chill and they grew soggy while time stretched out in a tight band as her uneasiness grew.

At any other time she would have welcomed the flood of information, for he spoke of the great stones that were thought to have been erected by the immortal gods themselves at some time out of the memory of man and how they were worshiped when they stood. The one at their feet might have been such and was revered as part of the lookout over the valley. He told her of the race of giants who walked this land after the gods left the stones and of those who claimed to have seen them. Legends and speculations melded into one and always Eridor watched the valley.

He spoke of the tin trade and those of distant lands who had come in the past to bargain for it, of the secrecy and caution that was practiced due to the scarcity, the watchers of the sea lanes and the battles for the precious metal, of the secluded areas where tin was worked out, washed, smelted and shaped before being brought to the coast, and of the precautions that must be even more stringent now because of the tribal wars that raged and discontent even among the traders. His words were general but Lia understood the old tales much better now and thought that the fabled riches of the cold lands they described were very likely the tin and what could be made from it even as Paon had said.

Eridor paused and said in quite a different tone, "Ah, he comes! I think, yes, yes, I am quite sure that all is well!" He swung around and smiled into Lia's questioning face.

"What is it, Eridor? What have you been waiting for?"

"You, a priestess, must ask that? Paon comes and the approval is with him."

Lia looked toward the valley and could see nothing. She turned back to Eridor with exasperation as she shivered in the cool blast of air. "I do ask." She wanted warmth, a hot drink, food and an end to speculations.

"There are . . . initiation rites . . . renewal. I can say no more than that. I must go to meet him. Wait here for us." Eridor was suddenly aloof but his face was flushed and his eyes sparkled. "He is my dear friend but had matters been adverse . . ." He moved swiftly into the trees, a high, nearly soundless whistle coming from his lips.

Lia sat down abruptly on the great stone and rubbed her fingers over her arms in an attempt to ward off the permeating chill. The rain was only a faint drizzle now and the mist still hung low. Eridor was right. She did not need to ask questions. She knew well enough that Paon had been subjected to some sort of ritual that had meant, if not life as opposed to death, a certain powerful danger to him, the mission, his men and Lia herself. That was why he, Eridor, had remained with her for so long and talked as he had. She thought of the Minoan rites with a shudder and did not want to know what they were here.

The stone seemed curiously warm but there was no reason for it to be. Glad of something to divert her mind, she glanced down at it and saw the faintest of markings in lines and whorls well faded with antiquity. She trailed her fingers over them, pushed aside some of the accumulation of moss and dirt and felt familiarity push at her mind. The sun or a snake or a crown? None of those and yet having to do with them all. The gray wet world, the danger all around, the god-haunted stone—Lia felt an interloper in this place and she rose hastily to look for Paon and Eridor.

There was no sign of them. Annoyed, she shook out her damp clothes. She did not intend to wait one moment longer. Why had Eridor said to wait here? Likely they had forgotten all about her. She tried to summon up anger at Paon for the previous night but that was a thing of the past. She understood now and, in that understanding, cared all the more.

"Hssss! Hsss!" The sound, sibilant and sharp, came at her with all the strength of a flung stone. "Sss!" The rain-wet branches flipped back and forth not far from her and a figure began to materialize from them. The hissing noise came once more and the light glittered dully on the filed teeth. It was Thulf.

He beckoned to her, his hands with their long bent nails waving as if they were separate entities. His eyes glittered with a combination of fascination, lust and strange laughter. He made the hissing noises again as he moved forward and a little back as if hesitant to approach her and yet unable to resist doing so.

Lia could not help it; she retreated, shaking her head and saying firmly, "No. No. Go away. I do not understand." She started to go around him and he was there in front of her, edging her back to the stone. Did he intend to push her off? Surely he could not have murder in mind!

She stepped onto the stone's edge and felt that strangely coursing warmth touch her foot. Inadvertently she looked down and thought that of a certainty she was losing her senses. Just at the place where the stone touched the ground and the moss ended, there was a tiny opening and coming out of that opening was a white foam mixed with bloody ooze and several long filed teeth. What beast lay below, waiting to emerge?

Her senses swam as Thulf hissed at her again and came closer. He ventured too close. Lia jerked her eyes away from the stone and curved her hand so that the edge was hard. She would aim for his neck, try to stun without hurting him for the mad must not be injured. Not for the first time she thought of the useful things she had learned in Crete, both from her reading and in the training for the bullring.

"Get away from me, Thulf!" She knew the words to be useless. He would not understand. She would not look down just as, on Pandos, she had scaled the craggy heights, always in terror of falling but knowing she must do it. Then she jumped at him and he moved backward hastily. She heard the thump of the stone behind her and then she was running down the path to the side, not the way she and Eridor had come but a way that must surely lead back toward the little village. Behind her, Lia heard the high, maniacal laughter mixed with a soft clapping.

He did not attempt to follow her and the soft rain began again. She welcomed the touch of it on her flushed face as she slowed her pace, not wanting to burst in on the others and have to explain to Eridor that his god-touched uncle had frightened her or that she had seen a huge stone move in a bloody ooze. She could not explain that to herself.

The tree under which Lia paused was a large one. Its branches swept to the ground and leaves had piled high under it, packed down with their own weight. The bole was wide enough to shelter several persons. That thought no sooner crossed her mind than a shadow seemed to melt out from behind it and start toward her. Her first thought was that it was Thulf coming after her again and she opened her mouth to scream for help, all else forgotten.

A hand slammed across the back of her neck and she fell dizzily to her knees without a sound. Then, before she could move, a cloth was fastened across her lips and drawn tight behind her head. Her arms were pulled behind her and bound firmly with cords. She was pulled over into the leaves and partially covered with them as her captors sat down in front of her.

There were three of them, all singularly alike with green-blue eyes, pale skin and darkly blond hair. Blue marks in an odd design were painted on each temple and the backs of their hands. They wore skins and carried large knives. Their feet were bare, painted with the same design in red. Grins split their faces as they viewed her and one reached out to touch her hair, laughing as she jerked backward. One drew his knife across her throat with such savage relish that she felt the tiny droplets of blood slip downward and the first tiny thrust of pain. The other now unloosed her braids, caressing them with both hands and laughing softly. Lia dared not resist but she let her eyes show the baffled rage and hatred that she felt.

There was a movement just beyond them and a hissed order. The men moved back, hunched down and sat on their haunches. Thulf slipped into the shelter of the branches and grimaced, then burst into low laughter that showed all his filed teeth. Her captors laughed as he did and spoke softly. Lia pulled at her bonds and wondered how far she would get if she just jumped up and tried to run.

"I would not be foolish. They believe that the spilling of blood is a sacred duty and honor to the gods. The shedding of yours—that of a fair woman with hair the color of the sun—would be a propitiation to those gods, far older than those of your Cretan land." He spoke in pure and faultless Minoan with a pronounciation that made some words hard to understand at first.

Lia could only stare at this man she had thought to be incapable of rational thought or speech. He stood taller now and there was only determination in those light eyes. His hands were on his hips, his legs spread wide as he looked fixedly at her. This man was far more to be feared than his other manifestation.

"The outlanders are being gathered up. The stones will have cause to bless us, their worshipers. All of you have been promised and the blue-eyed one who has profaned us previously has made his own bargain. Life will be of great fascination in the days ahead." He laughed as he spoke to his men, apparently translating his last remark for them. They rose and moved closer. "You will wonder, will you not, just why you happened to be where you were when I came to frighten you down this very path? Why did Eridor bid you remain? Why did your lover not come to seek you out on his return? Has he given you to us? Ponder on these things, woman of the sun. They will be your last thoughts before the great ones and they will trouble you on the journey. You who have come to this land and taken from us that which is ours have much to account for. Think on these things as you lie before that which you sought to pillage."

Thulf spoke faster and faster, his eyes now glittering as he thrust his face closer to Lia's. He dropped into the language of his men from time to time and they nodded appreciatively.

"And do not think that help will be coming from that other ship. Our coast is deceptive and we are quick with lights to lure. Tin you came for and gold and jewels! Your very bones shall be ground to powder at the feet of our stones!"

"Lia! Come down!"

"Lia!" Two voices, male and female wound together in a soft chorus that sounded from a distance. "Lia!"

It was raining harder now and there was a rumble in the skies overhead. Cold drops drenched them as a swift wind rattled the branches of their tree. Thulf stepped back and gave a quick gesture. Two of the men tumbled Lia backward into a small ditch and held her so tightly that she could not move. One held his dagger to her throat again. The man standing beside Thulf suddenly lifted himself up and mounted high into the tree top to lie along a great limb.

"Hsss! Hsssss!" Thulf sank low into himself, began to wave his fingers back and forth in front of his face and bounced on the balls of his feet as he disappeared up the path.

Lia's head was pushed downward so that she could see nothing except leaves and grass as she lay on her stomach, the knife held now at the edge of her neck.

"Lia! Where are you?" This voice was Eridor's. It was sharp, touched with anxiety as he called out her name again. There was a long pause, some irritated speech in the native language, the sound of Thulf's voice now high-pitched and nothing like the passionate man who had denounced her, and then her name was called over and over.

"You left her here at the stone?" Paon spoke in hurried Minoan.

Lia jerked slightly and the warning knife jabbed. Rain trickled down from her shoulders and she could not help but think that her blood might soon follow. The questions that Thulf had raised were already coming to haunt her. Had Paon struck a bargain with these people? Did her fascination with him blind her to what he might very well be?

"Just here. She seemed interested in it but could have wandered off looking for more of them. You do remember how excited you were when you first saw them all those years ago, Paon? She probably circled back and is even now on her way to Aelth. Shall we go back and see?" Eridor was smooth in his urging but his accent was flat, the words emerging roughly.

"What did your uncle say? Had he seen her?"

"He sees nothing. He has his own world." Eridor called Lia's name again several times, then seemed to move away for his voice was less distinct. "Let us go down. She would not explore in this chill and with danger all around, as you know."

"I must find her! I must!" The desperation in his cry rang out strongly.

One of Lia's captors shifted slightly and she felt the weight of his body increase on her back. They were breathing shallowly as they held themselves taut for attack or murder. In spite of the threat to her life and the terror she could not help but feel, Lia thrilled to Paon's determination to find her.

"We should get some of your people and come search these woods. She could be hurt, unconscious, even wounded and unable to cry out. If she is not with Aelth we must search."

"Of course, Paon. As you say." Then Eridor raised his voice so that it would carry clearly over the rain and penetrate the distance. "But you do remember the terms and the bargain, do you not?"

"Have I not sworn it?" Paon was angry; the familiar tones carried just as Eridor's did. Then, in a lower tone, he added, "Let us go, Eridor. There is no need to remind me further."

Lia heard them walking through the bushes and then the only sound was the rain as it sluiced down.

Her body was beginning to cramp and she was growing colder with the immobility forced upon her but that was nothing compared to the desolation of her mind and heart. She could not tell if Paon really had fallen in with what appeared to be a scheme of Eridor's or if he were part of some plot that went beyond the other man and embraced the destruction of all the Cretans, as Thulf had indicated. She could not believe Paon false but she did know that Eridor spoke for her benefit just now. The doubt planted in her mind was real, just as they had intended that it should be. And the tale he had told her about Paon's past? Strangely enough she believed it. That was altogether consistent with the little Paon himself had hinted and what Naris had said so long ago in another life.

One of her captors brushed the leaves off them and bound her legs securely. The other man slipped down out of the tree and jerked his hand in the direction of the stone. Then he bent and picked Lia up, tossing her over his shoulder with no visible strain. She thought to struggle but knew that it would prove nothing. Best to remain quiet and observe all that she could.

They slipped through the woods as easily as the mist itself, skirting open areas, sliding over the rock faces and moving downward at a swift pace. Blood ran to Lia's head and she began to ache all over. When their pace increased to a swift trot and the rain grew heavier, she thought not in terms of the fate Thulf had described but of being able to stretch out and move around or sit up.

And so Lia went into yet another captivity. This time, as she had always been, she was alone, but all the more so because for the brief time she had shared with Paon their camaraderie— aborted as it sometimes was—had shown her the measure of what she might truly want one day. Now those days were in the balance.

Chapter Thirty-Five

STALKERS OF THE SHADOW

LIA WAS FLUNG down on the stone floor so hard that her breath was taken away. She lay as she was while she tried to assimilate her surroundings, fight off any showing of fear and gather her wits together. She had been bound and carried over her captor's shoulder for so long that now the world spun and whirled. All that long, rainy day they had moved inland with no pause for rest and now at twilight had come into this wide, dark passage, which opened up into light and warmth, the sound of many voices and a ring of curious faces just beyond her vision.

Someone was speaking in a low, rhythmical voice that held the hint of a chant. She turned her head slowly in that direction and saw a white face above such a flash of jewels in the firelight as to make the features unreal. Her sight cleared a bit and her head ceased to ring as she concentrated on that figure which, as it came closer, was revealed to be a man well into age, white-haired and dark-eyed, dressed in white and ornamented with all manner of stones.

He bent down and looked at her, speaking slowly in several different languages as he did so. She shook her head slowly, then stopped as it started to ache. He jerked out a knife, brandished it briefly, and, face expressionless, aimed it first at her chest, reversed the side of the blade and slashed the bonds at feet, wrists and mouth. She sat up carefully, feeling the strength drain from her as he watched. Then a young man approached holding a white furry cloak which he dropped over her. Another came with a curiously wrought cup of blue and gold which held what appeared to be milk. She could not hold it for her hands were too numb. The jeweled man took it and gave her a compelling look before holding the rim to her lips. Lia drank because she had no choice and because she needed sustenance.

In moments she was aware that it was a very heady and powerful brew that made the world seem far away and yet very clear. She was able to reach down and pull the robe up over herself so that her flesh no longer quivered with the damp. Then she looked around at the waiting people and was able to think about her predicament without the knowledge that it was real.

It was as if another person sat here and observed the long hall lit with tamped torches, the ceiling high and partially open in places, the milling people whispering as they watched, the curiously carved stones on the floor, the shimmer of jewels from far back in the dimness and the restive motions of the man at her side. It was Lia of Pandos and yet some other individual who rose slowly and stood erect in the suddenly hushed area.

Someone gave a nervous cough and was quickly silenced. Lia turned in that direction and saw, for the first time, a thing unbelievable. The men and women, both dark and fair, seeming of a civilization above that of the tribes to which Eridor had referred, were standing beside two long, shallow ditches filled with human bones. The skulls were placed on sticks and upraised to give the impression that they were looking out over the hall. Fresh branches and flowers lay before them. When the firelight flickered, Lia saw the huge stones that were part of the walls. The carvings on them were snakelike in appearance but resolved into squat images with huge eyes and flat hands. The eyes were of blue, flashing jewels. The color of the sea and sky, of Paon's eyes.

Lia knew that if she showed horror or revulsion her doom would be upon her all the quicker. They waited for her reaction and hoped it would be adverse. The quality of the silence told her that. Just so had she felt in the area of the bulls in Knossos. The crowd was expectant and ready to be amused. But that had been in the clear light of day in a test of physical strength and agility, a test of her wits. Here was another matter.

She inclined her head respectfully at bones and images, then revolved slowly around, her face expressionless. A low murmur swept over the people; they were disappointed now but there was the promise of pleasure to come. It angered Lia and she forgot her caution. She was no plaything! She was her own inviolate self and they should know it if she died in the next breath!

"Why have I been taken from my friends and brought here? Who and what are you? I have been treated ill at your hands and I demand to know why!" She rapped out the questions in a combination of Minoan, the mainland argot and gestures that left no doubt of her meaning. Her hearers gasped at her, their eyes as wide as those of the images.

A burst of laughter sent them scattering and a sharp order rang out. One of the torches blazed upward as a couple advanced toward Lia. A servant ran forward with benches, put them hastily down and withdrew, passing so close to her that she could see the sweat on his forehead and hear the intake of his breath as his tongue passed over dry lips. Then her attention was riveted on those approaching.

The man and woman were not as tall as she but both were haughty of bearing, regal, immeasurably ancient with crumpled skin and brilliant, blazing eyes of blue that were sunk deep in their sockets. They wore white robes trimmed with blue and the woman carried a blue cane made of some shimmering material interspersed with white. Lia thought they might have come from some barbaric medal or carving, for their faces were predatory and cruel, their mouths set in ruthless lines. Was this the look of Hirath in time to come? The thought that she could even recall the woman at such a time made her lips quirk upward before she could stop them. Those around them murmured, then grew silent as the woman lifted one golden-decked finger.

"You are bold, woman of the invader. Can you not guess to what fate you go?" Her accent was like Thulf's but her Minoan was more understandable if less correct. "I cannot think Thulf would not have enlightened you." She gave a trill of laughter readily echoed by the man beside her.

"He hinted. He enjoyed that; I think it is very like the man and I barely know him. As to the fate . . ." Lia shrugged her shoulders. "I serve the great goddess of Crete and she has come to this land with us. I doubt that she will desert her followers. If she does, then let it be so."

The woman smiled as her eyes went over Lia's body. "You are for the stones. That is enough for you to know. But you are, for the moment at least, the guest of the Stone Guarders, those who watch at the gates of the underworld. There are many of us in this land. The closest thing to our names in your language is Jies for my lord husband here, Danir for myself. We rule here and it is absolute."

"You have not answered my questions." Lia raised her head and gave them both a long, calculating look. "I suppose you will not but I would like food and drink, dry clothes and a place to rest. Surely the stones are not honored by me in this garb." She touched her wet garments disdainfully. Proud and bold she certainly sounded, she thought, and yet she knew instinctively that this would come closer to saving her life for even a little longer than any show of meekness.

"I know of the goddess." Danir sank down on the bench close to her. "She must be powerful in you."

Jies cried, "Careful, lest our own be offended!" His voice was weak but resonant and his eyes were those of a young man on Lia's face.

Danir said, "You shall have what you ask. That is the right of the guest. But if you attempt to escape you will be bound again and slain as if you were a peasant offering in the spring."

Lia was mortally tired of invoking the goddess and even more of trying to outguess these people. She decided that she believed in nothing and then wondered that she challenged their gods in their own dwelling place. She believed in credulity, the willingness of people to turn others to their own beliefs by threats and murder, savagery and illusion. Any self-respecting god would strike her down for that and here she still stood, the rudiments of a scheme growing in her mind.

"In Crete I was a priestess of the goddess. All that happens happens by her will." She let her voice grow weary, dull. "It was she who took my family and my love from me and brought me to serve her in the temples of Knossos; having taken all, she gave me herself. I am here. So be it."

Danir beckoned a young girl forward and spoke briefly. Then to Lia, "She will see to your needs. You will be guarded well. While the rain continues nothing can be done, but when it ceases the time of propitiation will begin. I do not think that you will be as bold or as resigned then."

Jies said, "You are no Cretan, girl. That hair is the color of those in our own north country. You will tell us your story in the morning and there will be no lies. Is that understood?"

The young girl, perhaps twelve, hovered at Lia's side, staring up at her. Lia answered, "Shall I hope the rain continues or ceases? At the moment it is of small matter to me." She saw Jies lower his lids and dared hope that she had at least given him something to wonder about. "Now may I rest?"

They waved her back. Danir's mouth turned up in a pleased expression and the people crowded around them. Two guards came to Lia's side as the girl who was to attend her walked in front. As they came to the ditches Lia paused before the images, bent her head and spread out both hands in the gesture that the Cretans sometimes used before the goddess. A hiss of surprise or shock went up from those behind them but Lia pretended not to notice. In this battle for her life so much would depend on her manner and the skill with which she could play a role. Once again she was thankful for the experience of the bulls. She might not win but she would struggle mightily before her life was taken. It was only fitting that her weapons would be the very gods themselves. Real or not, she would use them and their worshipers. And should she lose, Lia knew that she could snatch a dagger and use it on herself. But life was so precious—that was only a last resort.

She was taken to a small room off one side of the hall. It contained skins for covers, a small stool and water for washing. A kind of meat stew and a chunk of bread along with a spicy drink were brought also. She was handed a warm robe of heavy cloth to put on in the place of her damp clothes and the girl combed out her heavy hair. Balm was put on her face, arms and ankles. Then Lia was left alone to sleep. She heard the guards tramping outside and the mutter of conversation as well as the sound of someone singing a triumphant song. Then all was blotted out in exhaustion and release.

Lia slept and knew that she slept but the reality of what she saw was emblazoned in her mind. She went before the bulls of Knossos, saw their horns and hooves come near to her face without touching it, saw the cave of snakes and the sacrifice of a young girl who did not resist and the hooded snake with its shadow rearing against the light, walked beside the pyramids of Egypt, went into the land of the two rivers and saw once more those same images that were here, and beheld the great goddess of Crete, wreathed in snakes, great crystal eyes flashing as she merged with the vision of Lia's childhood and the worshipers who would destroy life in the name of their faith. Lia stood before her and then in the same breath she was again on the warm stone with Eridor as he told her of Paon's past. All whirled before Lia. Then she was in Paon's arms and the hunger of their times together melted into one.

She woke to warmth, the fresh scent of rain and a strange sense of resolution. The dream was vivid in her mind and she recalled its details, trying to find some reason for it. All knew, of course, that dreams held messages and revelations but Medo, her father, had taught her that they were only residuals of what the mind had collected in memory just as the gods were too often the reflection of man's own cruelty. She had believed but some part of her remained aloof, credulous. So it was now. Lia knew that she had no one to depend on but herself and even if she should win free of these people by some miracle, there was little chance that she could survive alone on the land, especially if it were as much at war as she had been told. Yet somewhere in the bare outlines of the scheme that had occurred to her the night before, the instinct that had caused her to be both bold and proud before those who could slay her horribly in a breath, and the happenings of her dream, Lia felt that a chance lay.

She heard voices outside her door, then it swung back and she looked up at Jies, whose eyes were raking her face, tumbling golden hair and partially exposed bosom as she sat naked under the covers. He looked even older today than he had last night but his body was erect under the loose brown mantle and his mouth bore a calculating smile. Lia wanted to jerk the cover up to her chin but she dared not antagonize him. She shook her hair forward and shifted about, listening intently as he moved closer and spoke in a low voice.

"Do you know what will happen to you? To that body still young and soft? To that smooth face and those full breasts? Do you really know the fate to which you were brought? You were so daring last night, so fearless. We have seen none like it and now Danir says the gods will be all the more pleased because of it. I think the brew went to your head. I wanted to see you again."

Lia said, "I am honored that Lord Jies—or should I call you chief?—takes an interest." She pitched her voice low and waited. Again the overwhelming sense of the bullring came back to her. Was she about to be tossed or gored? Her touch must be delicate. "To what fate?"

Jies must have seen many winters, for his skin was yellowish and hung in folds down from his eyes, neck and arms. His neck was corded and his hands shook but the watchful eyes were only slightly faded. His fingers bore rings of silver and gold as well as one of the brilliant blue stone. On his left thumb there was a flat stone carved in the manner of the great stone above the valley where she had stood with Eridor. It bore the symbol of the snake and a great eye also.

"The ring is magnificent. I have never seen one like it." Lia reached out one finger as if to touch it and then drew back as Jies put his other hand over the ring.

"The ring is sacred to the gods, my dear. None except myself may touch or hold it." He came closer and sat down on the edge of her raised bed. He grinned and the snags of his teeth showed dark. "But you asked a question, I believe?"

Before Lia could move backward, his hand darted toward her and he caught her bare arm in a grasp very much like that of a sea crab. His touch was rasping and dry but hard. Chills ran up and down her back as she tried to pull away.

Jies laughed. "Once young maids did not act so at my touch. Do I offend you?" He put his face nearer to hers and she smelled his rancid breath. "I have sired many sons and outlived them all. And their son's sons. The favor of the gods is on me. Do you doubt it?"

Lia forced herself to stillness. She must not allow him to know the measure of her revulsion. "You were going to tell me of the reason I was taken, my lord. Naturally I am eager to know."

He grappled toward her breasts, muttering as he did so. The scent of unwashed old man drifted up and she saw the caked grime on his hands that bore the jewels. Revulsion stirred in Lia and she thrust him away at the same time as she pulled the covers tightly around her. He rose shakily and stood staring at her, venom in his gaze.

"You shall dress and come with me. I mean to show you one of the wonders of this land. The wonders that are to be your death. It really all fits together very well." He began to laugh at his own humor.

That laugh was joined by another. Danir stood in the doorway and leaned on her blue, jeweled cane. She, too, was even more ancient this morning but the white in which she was enveloped gave her dignity even as it seemed to enhance the cruelty of her expression.

"Ah, my husband! She would have none of your game, I see. You must pay the wager!"

Chapter Thirty-Six

RING OF STONES

JIES STOOD ASIDE as his wife swept into the room. Lia stared at them, thinking that both were mad. Just then two husky women entered carrying a tub of water which they set down hastily and retreated. The young girl who had escorted Lia here the evening before brought a cloak and some other materials along with a small box, gave Lia a fascinated glance and vanished as swiftly as she had come.

"I do not understand." That was a safe comment, Lia thought wryly.

Danir turned to her. "It is simple, Lia of Knossos. I rather thought that you would repent of your bravado of last night and seek to save your life by indicating an interest in my husband, who is powerful enough to intervene against the gods. He did not think so and he made a wager. I hope you have not angered him." She laughed, the sound hard in the chilly room.

Not Lia of Pandos but Lia of Knossos. Lia gave the name a brief consideration and wondered if she would ever see that beautiful place again or the man who had made life vivid for her. She said, "I have told you. All is in her hands. I am content to have it so."

"Let us see if you still think so after you have seen the stones." Jies stripped the blue ring from his finger and handed it to Danir with ill grace. "There is something dead in this woman. I do not like this situation at all."

"Only because she did not lure you!" Danir spoke swiftly to

265

the old man in their language and they both went toward the door. She turned back to Lia for an instant. "Hurry and dress. There is much to be done."

Moments later Lia was luxuriating in the warm water, scrubbing and rinsing her hair and body in the cold that remained from the night before. She did not let her mind dwell on anything but the most immediate future. It was a tactic she had learned long ago and it had saved her much agony since. It was a way to remain sane; she ignored the small voice in her brain that told her that soon she might yearn for the release of madness.

She dressed quickly in the softly woven white robe belted with blue, pulled the leather sandals, which fit surprisingly well, onto her feet, plaited her long hair into one rope and let it trail down her back. The warm white cloak covered her from neck to ankles and she drew out a length of white cloth to cover her head. Then she called out her readiness to those outside, and once again the young girl served as escort with the two somber guards pacing just behind.

The hall was empty and dim at this early hour but Lia could see its great size in a way that had been blocked last night by the milling people. The ditches and the images were still vivid reminders and she averted her eyes as they walked past. Several corridors led away from the main area on both sides. She assumed they led to more rooms, possibly better furnished than the one where she had spent the night, and wondered if this were the equivalent of a palace or court.

Now they entered a long narrow passage barely high enough to clear the two men's heads. The floor was of hard-packed dirt, the ceiling was rounded and the air smelled vaguely of incense. It was a relief to see, far ahead, the light of the rainy day. The young girl stood back and motioned to Lia to go on. One of her guards pushed her in the back as she hesitated and she whirled on him, eyes blazing and hand extended. She said nothing but there was no need. He retreated slightly and left his fellow to indicate that she should go ahead. It was a small victory but it told Lia something valuable. Why did these people alternately woo and threaten her? Yet the guard seemed to fear her. They had not done so in the woodland nor on the trip here. She would remember.

There were more guards at the entrance and several held a

canopy over her as they walked a short distance up a grassy hill to where a shelter of hides and branches stood. Jies and Danir were there, as was the priest, who still wore his jewels. His strangely mocking gaze met Lia's and then shifted abruptly. Several other men and women stood behind the royal ones, their faces interested but impassive.

But it was not the people who caught and held Lia's attention, riveting her to the spot she stood on as she gazed beyond them out into the plain, which was brushed softly with rain and lay in mist. The standing stones reached into the sky, far taller than several men standing on each other's shoulders. They were so ancient in appearance as to have been there when the gods cast the world. Their shapes were blocky and twisted or slender and spreading. She counted fourteen of them and thought that there might be more beyond. Those were in a rough type of circle and two of these were crowned with huge flat stones lying across their tops to form a roof. Off to the right was an avenue of smaller stones arranged to lead directly into the circle. They might have sprouted up out of this land of crags and cliffs, might have been a product of some strange growth within the earth. She did not know but she did know that this place was haunted by god and man. It was a place of destiny.

Lia turned slowly to one side and looked back behind them. She saw trees on top of a mound that ran east and west for a long distance. It was covered with grass and bushes as well. Some of the guards stood beside her and she realized that this was the hall where she had been taken. But underground? The thought of the work involved was staggering and yet it was logical. Defense would be easy and she did not think that many would venture near the stones in any case. When she recalled the stone flooring and the stones embedded in the walls, she knew that others had begun the building long before these people. The wide-eyed images flickered in her mind again and she felt as if she were forgetting something of vital importance.

"This is a sacred place." Lia breathed the words of absolute truth.

"Look yonder." Jies pointed to the east, lowered his hand and began to caress the ring which was the holy stone he had told Lia about. "They will go there."

Lia peered into the gray distance, thankfully drawing the

fresh, cool air into her lungs as she examined the rocky terrain filled with clumps of low bushes and spiky-looking flowers. A line of trees was visible not far away, and in the silence that was all around them, she could hear the rush of water. She looked back at them and saw their eagerness.

Jies smiled. "The stones go there to drink on the night of the great festival. It is ritual."

"I see." She did not but something had to be said. The air of suppressed amusement did not leave her watchers. "Perhaps I am foolish but I do not understand. Will you explain?"

Jies raised his eyes to Danir, who nodded. "Certain of the Cretans who came to steal and pillage have been captured and are held beside yonder river. The stones will crush them on their way to the water. It is part of the sacrifice. There are many standing stones in this land; there are many worshipers. You will have seen the great circle in the north?" Lia shook her head as he rushed on, obviously enjoying this. "Ours is the second greatest. Thulf has been one of us for a long time but before that he traveled there and watched the sacred ceremonies, then chose to live apart for reasons of his own. Our land has been defiled and we have sworn war upon those who come; our watchers are all along the coasts and he is one of them. You will make an excellent sacrifice, a propitiation to the stones."

Jies had been speaking so rapidly that his tongue tripped and twisted over his words. His face grew red with the effort and he was forced to pause and rest. Danir took the opportunity to translate for the others, her voice strong and sure, a little gloating. Lia tried to think what to say but the power of this place was rendering her mute, draining away her will.

Jies cried, "You have served your own goddess, you say. Well enough. She shall fall before our gods, who are of the wind, sun and storms. You shall offer up the fruits of the land before them and then the great stones shall press the life from you! That is the fate set aside for you!"

"The sacrifice is bound in place and the great stone is slowly lowered. It takes a considerable time. The ceremony is very holy." Danir added the final words and her old face took on the predatory look of the hawk.

Lia had known they meant to kill her. That fact was repeated often enough but this sounded as if it were a thing of torture.

The ring of faces around her was expectant, fascinated. Here was a new game to play, a new method of amusement. Lia drew in her breath very slowly as she let her gaze drift out to the gray-veiled stones and back again. Then she looked back and saw the priest beside Jies watching her avidly. It was time to make answer; the length of her life might depend on the words she chose to use now.

"I think that this is all foreordained. Last night I dreamed of far lands near rivers and I saw the faces of your gods of the hall yonder. My own goddess moved with them. It may be that she comes to this land and that she walks with her priestess. Myself. She chose me and she has taken fear from me. I have been a bull leaper in Crete and walked through the cave of snakes untouched. She took much from me but she gave much also. I have danced the sacred dances before her and seen her hands held out to me when the smoke of the blessed rose." Lia let her voice rise and throb. Use their own weapons against them, she thought. Play upon the fact that the will of their gods was so often their own made manifest. She swayed a little and let a note of ecstasy take over. "My own father walked in the land of the rivers and saw the images that are here. He came to this land and lived to return. Another, the leader of this very expedition, did the same. She reaches out for followers and comes to seek them. She honors your gods as do I but her patience is short!"

Lia stopped as the wet breeze blew over them and little gusts of rain spattered near. She turned her head as if listening, allowed a look of relief to cross her face and lifted her hands in brief supplication. Then she spoke softly into the quiet, hoping that they had all observed closely.

"The will of the goddess will happen even in this very center of your worship. She has spoken it."

They stared at her, seemingly wrapped in the spell of her words and the lack of fear she portrayed. Lia knew with all her instincts that the only thing that had preserved her this far was the fact that she was totally different from what they expected and that they were intrigued by it. Had she wept and wailed, given way before the clumsy lure of Jies, even tried to placate them, she did not doubt that she would now be more closely imprisoned or perhaps be prepared for sacrifice by the attentions of several young men. That sort of thing was

customary and it was natural that a priestess not be a virgin.
But her demands and arrogance, even her lack of concern for
her life, all attitudes which could be easily tested later, were
providing them with titillation now. Let them think her
agreeable to anything, let them think her fanatic in her
eagerness to prove the goddess victorious here, only let them
leave her free long enough to distract them and then she would
fight for her life as she had done so often in the past. That fight
would take the form of running, hiding, anything, but she
would not be taken captive again.

Danir was drawling, "You are bold, indeed, to challenge our
sacred ones at their very shrine."

Jies translated what she said and murmurs went up. Lia did
not miss the glances of speculation, the flickering anticipation,
as their eyes raked her. A thought struck her just then and she
almost reeled from its impact. What if they, too, played with
her? These people did not appear to be a simple tribe,
worshiping deities of field and stream or marveling at the
mighty stones as they brought offerings of food and drink.
They were not the blue-painted men who had slain some of the
Cretan soldiers. Their jewels, the manner of their amusement,
the images of the gods with great eyes—all were puzzling.
What manner of people were these?

There was no help for it. Lia knew that she must continue on
the path she had begun. She gave them all a bold look,
revolved slowly about so that her gaze swept the stones and
then gazed upward. The silence drew and spun outward to
encompass the landscape and the river beyond. She thought
they must know she played a role, but did not all those servants
of the gods do the same? She pushed all negation from her
mind.

"The great goddess of Crete is in this land. You hold her
priestess but she is everywhere. The great mother and the
female! All-conquering and all-knowing! I challenge your gods
in her name! Let there be rivalry between them! I will stand for
her. Who is your principal god and what is his name?"

An angry cry came from several of those assembled and the
priest stepped in front of them, hands outspread in a placating
gesture. Danir and Jies exchanged looks of what might have
been satisfaction, their faces seeming even older in the gray

light. The priest walked over and spoke earnestly to them but they shook their heads as one.

Danir gestured at Lia's guards and they moved nearer. Lia was gratified to see the awe in their eyes and the way their fingers touched their daggers nervously. Then the old woman rose and brandished her jeweled stick, first at Lia and then toward the great stones and finally at the sky. The ruined mask of her face turned toward Lia and it was as if another power used her tongue, for the Minoan phrases were guttural and choppy, hardened with another accent.

"Woman of Crete, Lia of Knossos, Priestess of the Goddess. Your challenge is taken up! This night shall be the manifestation of the power that has come with me. You shall die and your bones tossed in yonder stream. You shall not have this land nor these people! The journey has been too long; the way too hard! There can be no vestige of you here! Remember that when you lie between the stones and they take the life from you! Let your goddess remember that when next she attempts to enter this land!"

Danir's entire body was rigid and taut. Her head snapped back as the lines of her face seemed to smooth into something else, an alien thing barely under the skin and just restraining itself. Her eyes grew round, wide, and contained a glimpse of both horror and delight. The wind swirled around her feet and blew her robe out slightly. The clouds above them parted briefly and a finger of sunlight glinted off the nearest of the stones. The people moaned and huddled together at this very clear omen.

Lia was dry-mouthed with fear at what she had unleashed, although she knew that all priests and priestesses must be ready to supply direction if the gods did not. But who really knew what lay all about them? Not even Medo's rationality could hold back the idea that the challenged god of these people might very well be speaking to her from the mouth of Danir.

"Will you name yourself to me that I may know?" She heard her voice emerge in a manner that was almost calm.

"I have many names!" Still the same gutturals. Still the oddly tilted posture as Danir's delicate old body strained to encompass this being. "Try one not used for many long seasons. It is as good as any. I am Ut-Nammaru-Sed! Despoiler of cities! Taker of women! Foe of all who deny me! Death to those who challenge me!''

Lia felt the hot air of the desert, saw the blood of soldiers, fought in the armies and saw the city rise, shimmering and beautiful on the horizon, knew the bitterness as its destruction neared and heard the moans of the dying as the old gods faded before ones more kind. She shook her head to clear it, struggling to remember all the ancient tales she had read. Surely this had to be one of them.

"Death! Death! Death!" Danir's guttural cries ripped out of her and she fell heavily downward. She lay where she had fallen as the watchers gazed at Lia's stricken face.

Chapter Thirty-Seven

DANCE OF THE RECKONING

LIA INCLINED HER head, watching the reflection of the jeweled headdress in the tall sheet of burnished copper placed against one wall. The stones flamed in the torchlight of this underground place and gave her an exotic appearance but she seemed to see another face under them, a woman with skin and hair of night, a woman who had wanted to live just as much as she did. She tore the lovely thing from her hair and let it fall into the chest. Her imagination was running far ahead of her and that would be fatal on this night when all her wits must be sharp if she were to have any chance at survival. These were only jewels and precious materials, after all. Things did not bear taints; that was only for people.

She remembered her question to Jies as they brought her back to the underground hall shortly after Danir, recovering from her faint and recalling nothing she had said, was borne away to her own chamber. Lia could still see the old face, now. nearly malevolent, as it turned to hers.

"Lord, tell me, is the god whose name your wife shouted the principal one here? Is it he whom you honor always at the great stones?"

"I heard her call no name! She shouted only gibberish. She is unwell and the festival is always exhausting. You shall have cause to regret what you have unleashed here!"

He had hobbled on ahead, leaving Lia in the circle of guards. She knew he lied; no one could have mistaken all that hoarse shouting for meaningless sound. They wanted to throw her off balance but they also wanted to enjoy the fruition of their game.

She had been brought to this stone cell underground, far beneath the hall and close to the river, for one wall was very damp and the air was chill, where chests held treasure beyond the realization. There were finely woven fabrics with strange designs on them, gauzy draperies, robes loosely spun and so soft that they caressed the skin, cloaks of all colors and even the furs of animals in white, gray and black. Necklaces, headdresses, sandals, long ropes of jewels in black, pearl, green, ruby, amber and blue were massed together in a glittering confusion to delight a woman's heart. By sign language the first guard had indicated that she was to array herself in whatever she liked. Then, bringing his hands together in slow pressing motions, he had pantomimed the death that was to be hers. She had forestalled his pleasure, however, by turning away and exclaiming over the chests. She would not quail before them. The slamming of the stone door was eloquent of the fact that he had achieved no satisfaction.

Lia tried to shut away mindless terror by trying on costumes in an endless succession. But other images and unknown faces rang in her mind's eye so that she finally turned away and began to investigate the entire array of chests at random. She still had no idea what she would do when they brought her to the stones tonight; all that she had really accomplished was that she would be unbound and not be brought supine into the arena of death. That would have to be enough. Once before they had tried to slay her in Knossos before the bulls and she yet lived. Always there was hope. Paon's carved face rose before her in this time of memory and she longed once again for the touch of his hands, the caress of his mouth and was thankful that at least she had known some semblance of love.

The bottom of one of the chests yielded what appeared to be a delicate set of shackles for wrists, neck and ankles. They were made of beaten gold, ornamented with pearls set in a whirling design of black stones with droplets of rubies. A long chain of green stones connected them and the collar was wreathed in pearls. Lia put both hands on the strange thing and wondered what its origin was. Such a shackle was never meant to hold a prisoner; was it perhaps used for some game of passion, love's sweet prisoner? Or possibly some odd per-version?

Idly she turned over one of the black stones, then another and another. There was writing on them all. At first glance it appeared to be part of the design but when she took them over to the place where the highly placed torch shone brightest, Lia could tell that a master hand had crafted not only a thing of beauty but a record to be deciphered.

She ran her fingers over the symbols and tiny, convoluted forms but nothing came readily to mind. There was some curved figuring that could have been ornamental only but she doubted it. She saw the recognizable form of a lion being led by a female figure crowned with horns, a prostrate man being devoured by a sea creature and men at battle while three suns stood in the sky. The rest was carved so closely that it exhausted the eye to consider. Yet there was a strange familiarity to all this that flung Lia backward in time to the lessons with her father in the summer sunlight there in the arbor covered with purple flowers while Ourda sang at her work of preparing food.

Lia stood up abruptly and began to circle the room. She had tested the walls and floor earlier. There was no way out of here but she needed to check again for sanity's sake. Nothing anywhere. She sighed and leaned against the wall where the river smell was strongest. How could they have fashioned only one way out of their treasure storehouse? But it was so. She pulled and thrust at stones until her fingers ached; then she touched lightly, experimentally. The place that held the treasure of these people secure could also hold herself.

Finally she accepted what she must and returned to prepare herself for the ritual, whatever it was to be. She chose a loose purple tunic of gossamer thin material which clung to her breasts and came to just above midthigh. This she belted with a band of jewels in the same shade. A long rope of black and white pearls hung around her neck and descended into the cleft of her bosom. Her feet she left bare but she slipped four emerald rings on her toes so that they glittered as she moved. She loosened her golden hair, rubbed, polished and combed it until it gleamed like sunlight in the sheet of copper when she looked there. Part of it she drew back from her forehead and fastened high with jeweled pins. The rest streamed down her back to well below her buttocks. In it she wound several light necklaces of green and blue. Curving bands of gold adorned her smooth arms and gave her tanned skin a sheen. Then she drew from one of the chests a diaphanous overgrown with billowing sleeves in shades of sea green to amethyst and sewn with gems of that color. It was the garment of a queen. When she slipped it on, settled the trailing skirt and turned to look at herself, Lia could not restrain a gasp. She could not believe that she appeared so. The woman there was tall, mysterious, regal. Her eyes were the sea depths and the planes of her cheeks were so sculpted that her whole face was alluring, remote, a woman out of time.

"I wish that Paon could see me." She said the words aloud to hearten herself and then had to fight back the tears that they invoked. Hard sobs shook her. It was all she could do not to give way; if she did so she would be lost for certain. Frantically she sought for something to occupy her mind until they came for her.

She picked up the set of golden shackles again and began to pace back and forth while she looked at the glyphs there. She forced herself to concentrate, allowing no other thought to enter her mind. The woman and the lion—what was that? It had a meaning and she knew that meaning from another time. Then the soft, dry voice of Medo rang in her ears as if she had just come for her lesson.

"You will observe, my daughter, that here mortal force strives with mortal force. Human with animal, human with each other, human with nature. Their gods are separate. So it is with the Akkadians and present always in their works. A most sensible view, to wall off their ideas of the gods. Now in this writing . . ."

Akkadians in this far cold land? The people of the two rivers had come this far from their world and for what reason? She had studied little of their language, for Medo had decided that Egyptian would be a more useful language to study. She stared at the black ornaments and wondered how it had come to be here, this set of shackles that never held true prisoner.

Then, as if in answer to her questioning, she found that she could figure out a few of the symbols, those around the figure of the lion and the woman. Her tongue formed them in the language of the mainland. "Battle of the dead . . . eaten

. . . dance to destruction . . . shorn of the gods who took me . . . long journey." There was nothing more that she could understand. The words were rote and ritual, belonging to any epic or song of war. They were a puzzle to which she would never know the answer.

She heard the stone door being shifted inward and knew that they had come for her. In the brief moments before it swung wide, she carefully detached three of the flat black ornaments and slipped them into the small pouch attached to her belt. She buried the rest of the set deep in the chest and jerked the lid down. When they entered she was standing, arms folded and head up, in the center of the room, waiting.

The priest, she supposed he must be chief of them, who had been with Danir and Jies that morning, was at the head of four guards and four others dressed in white. Their stares were all the approval she needed; here was awe and surprise and male interest combined. The chief priest bent his head either in admiration or politeness and the others followed suit. Then he held out his arm and she took it, laying her fingers gracefully across his and noting that his dagger hung within easy reach should she attempt to grasp it.

Their progress was slow and stately as they went through the empty hall, down the long corridor and came into the open air of twilight. Lia filled her lungs with the freshness of earth scents and flowers. The wind was warm against her skin; all chill of the rain had completely gone. The brilliant orb of the moon was just beginning to lift and a few soft clouds drifted high above. A call of a sleepy bird came from the trees near them. The roar of the river was more pronounced now as it mingled with the howl of an animal in the distance. Far off Lia could see the flames on a hill and guessed them to be the ones of warning about which Paon had told her. That was only days ago and yet it seemed to have happened in another life.

Now they were moving again. It appeared to Lia that all her living culminated in this moment when she saw the standing stones lit by the ritual fire, which blazed higher than they were and rose to the ceiling of the great ones as if in challenge. An avenue of smaller fires led to the huge one in the center of the circle of stones. People stood all along it, holding branches and flowers. The brilliance of their clothes and jewels was revitalized by the flames. The stones glowed red and pale gray

in the light that moved across them, so that they truly did seem
real, gods with their feet solidly planted in the plain, gods who
might walk at any moment.

Danir and Jies sat on rock thrones placed to the left of the
central fire. They were so covered with gems that they blazed
in the night and, from a distance, seemed to be the epitome of
earthly beauty. A long line of girls and women were walking
among the stones, moving hands and feet in a slow, rhythmical
dance punctuated by songs with a steady beat. Movement and
song were at variance with each other in a strangely luring way.
People moved about talking, drinking from cups filled by
servants with jugs, breaking into dances, kissing and hugging
each other, pointing at the slowly rising moon and calling out
as they did so. It might have been any scene of worship and
revelry anywhere were it not for the bound captives that Lia's
sharp eyes saw just beyond one of the smaller stones.

There were about twenty men and women grouped together,
watched by guards and forced to keep their faces turned toward
the festivities at all times. They were of varying ages, some
younger than Lia or in the prime of life, others white-haired
and lined. Their skins were pale for the most part and their hair
was either pale gold or touched with it. She wondered if
perhaps they were taken all together from some tribe that
warred against her captors. As she came slowly by with her
guards she felt their despairing eyes on her and someone called
out before being silenced by the nearest guard. Lia. felt her
sympathy go out to them; she could so easily be herded there
with no chance for anything but death.

She was brought to stand beside Danir and Jies, neither of
whom paid any attention to her. A group of brilliantly clad
people, perhaps the same as those of the morning, stood to one
side, drinking and talking. The moon was higher now, a nearly
full orb floating majestically in the sky. They pointed to it,
lifted their cups and turned to watch the stones, excitement
lighting their faces.

The tempo of the music was increasing now. It was lilting,
stirring the blood, promising satisfaction and yet denying it. It
was as if one rose to the heights of passion, hesitated and fell
back, only to attempt to rise anew. Lia felt the frustration, the
hunger and the belated thrill of more to come. She saw that the
others were affected in much the same way, for the dances

became more wanton, the people wilder as they kissed, touched and thrust themselves at each other. It was nearly an orgy except that nowhere was there any form of consummation. All was provocation and delay. Danir and Jies watched, their mouths loose with anticipation.

Suddenly there was a fierce howl from many throats. Lia whirled around to see one of the captives, fighting and struggling with all his might, being bound down on one of the flat stones that rose, a high table, just off the center of the circle where they were now assembled. Another huge stone was poised in place well above him and held there by an arrangement of ropes and thick sticks. The fire shone on the stones and crackled hungrily. The people cried out and laughed at the same time. The moon lifted and the pale light seemed to join with that of the flames.

Danir turned a passion-crazed face to Lia. She had painted her skin with red and white to simulate the colors of youth but she seemed already dead, so revolting was her look. Jies was the same. Lia wondered that they were even human in shape. Now Danir cried, "They call for death and more death! Even in this way do we draw strength for the quarter of time just ahead! The moon and the sun are our lights; they absorb our blood gifts and return them to us! Watch, woman of Crete! Watch and do not turn away or you shall be bound and made to watch!"

She and Jies lifted their right hands in the same sharp gesture at the same moment. All sound died away as the people gazed first at them, then at Lia and last at the stone where the young man was spread and flattened out. His screams were increasing in intensity now. Lia was horrified to see that two of the men closest to her had bulging erections that their scant loincloths could not hide. She knew what was going to happen; she knew that they meant to disembowel the captive or cut out his heart. How she could watch and not faint was another matter. This might be the time to try to get away but how could she, guarded as she was? The crowd would tear her to pieces. Danir and Jies would take pleasure in such an action. Best to wait and feel pity for the luckless ones; soon enough she herself might be there even as they.

The silence drew out. Nothing moved. There was only the crackle of the fire and the progress of the moon. Even the howls of the victim were hushed. Lia's palms were wet but her skin crawled. She felt the breathless waiting of the people and their eagerness was a palpable thing that threatened to destroy her.

Danir screamed the words first in her own language and then in Minoan as her laughter burst out. "Drop! Drop! Kill!" She fixed her gaze on Lia's face and did not shift it.

Lia was unaware of anything but the fact that the great stone above the captive was being pulled slowly back with a creaking of pulleys. The supports were removed and then it poised for a long, slow moment, a slab as old as time itself, before it fell with a shattering thump onto the sacrificial victim whose blood spattered out from the joined stones even as his screams still hung in the air.

Lia's own screams rose with the others as the world rocked back and forth in blood smears of light and dark. Now she saw her own fate.

Chapter Thirty-Eight

DEADLY BEGUILEMENT

LIA'S SENSES COULD not bear the horror. She retreated to the place where she had so often gone for solace and pleasure—the undersea world where the water was warm and caressing on her skin and the sand glistened all the more white when touched by the distant fingers of the sun. There fish moved slowly by and she floated serene in a safe world. She saw the stone rise and fall, knew the hideous waiting and the agony of the victims as they were placed in each other's blood, watched the explosions of the people as they coupled or released themselves, saw death and torment in such detail as to haunt all her nightmares should she live to have them, and did not move or turn away. Why should she when this was but a momentary dream and the limpid green world was the reality?

Two victims remained. A man and woman in their late youth, bodies perfectly formed, stood naked together, facing their fate without an outward murmur or cry. The orgy of blood was temporarily halted as the crowd drank in this unusual thing. The music, demanding and insistent, began again and the people turned toward Lia, faces questioning. Danir and Jies conferred briefly, then Danir rose, leaning on her blue cane, and went to her.

Some old woman, voice strident, was reaching down for her, dragging her upward, pulling her into the air she did not want. The water was growing bloody; it was rising in her throat to strangle her. Now sharp nails were digging at her flesh. She tried to return to the undersea world but it was receding. The darkness of the octopus was all around and she would die in either place.

"The gods are pleased! They wait for your blood, woman of Crete! You challenged the great ones and you have watched the sacrifices die! Will you be so unmoved when your turn comes after these last two? For you the stone will come slowly, slowly and how we shall relish it! I see that your goddess has not taken you away. Did you think she would come in a mighty swoop to catch you up to safety?" Danir laughed as she translated her words for the benefits of those around them. The laughter was not in her eyes. She knew that in some mysterious way the full horror of what she had been forced to watch had not yet come to Lia. Eagerness for that realization flamed in her face and that of Jies as well.

It was Lia and yet not Lia who said, "I never asked such a thing of her. It was ever my intention to dance in her honor at a proper place in the ceremonial. That time has now arrived." Her voice, calm and full, carried out over the assembly and caused the revelers to gaze up in surprise.

Jies cried, "No! Your very presence here is challenge enough to the gods. Your goddess has not saved you. It is time for you to die!"

Lia stared out at the bloody stones and the remaining victims, then at those who waited, savage as animals were not, for the last drop of appeasing blood and show of fear. Her fog was lifting and she was afraid as she had never been before in her life, she who had faced death many times so recently and yet fought on.

"Take her. Bind her." Danir shouted in two languages and was answered by her people.

Then there came to Lia a power that she had never known. She lifted her arms high above her head, whirled and faced them all, her face twisted in the rage that this bath of death had brought to her. The name entered her words and possessed her as she cried it and others at the top of her voice.

"I shall honor the great goddess, the Lady of the Snake, the Mother of Earth and the Netherworld, Giver of Life and Death, with the dance. In the name of Ut-Nammaru-Sed, the despoiler of cities! In the name of Sigash, mighty destroyer and devourer! Hursupa, swift flame of the gods!" The names of the gods of the far lands rolled from her tongue and where she could not think of any others she made them up so that the invocation continued until she was breathless. Then with one final cry, she ended it and stood with folded arms, head inclined as if she listened. "Ut-Nammaru-Sed!"

The flame shot across the sky directly above them and fell as quickly as it had come. Another followed and another. The silence shook and then the priest, pale under his jewels, spoke to Danir in a whisper. She hesitated, then nodded. He looked at Lia expressionlessly.

"Dance, priestess of your goddess. You have won the right." He spoke in perfect Minoan. Then he waved toward the people and they moved far back, eyes hard on Lia as she started away from Danir and Jies.

Lia called to him, "Let there be music! Let it be loud and joyful!" Her mind recoiled from the fact that very soon the heavy stone would smash down upon her body, crushing it into a pulpy mass of blood and flesh. The anticipated pain and terror were made all the more vivid by the sight of those earlier deaths. Now she saw the blood eagerness in all the faces about her. Blessedly, her own anger rose up. In the little time that existed for her, Lia knew that she would hear the thump of stone on living flesh and hear the cries, shielded though she had been by her retreat into the sea world. If she could catch up a dagger and use it on herself before they took her, it would be all the mercy she could crave.

She spared no time to think about the flames launched across the sky just at the time of her utterances nor how the priest had come to speak Minoan to her. Nothing was left but the confrontation and quick death. She looked up at the moon now hanging in the crevice of the largest stone, giving brilliance anew to the firelit scene of revel and destruction. Then she put out both her arms in the compelling gestures of priestesses that she had seen elsewhere and spoke in the mainland language for what must be the last time.

"If you exist in any form, Lady of the Snake and of Crete, come to these fiends and kill them! Kill them!" Her voice rose high and mad to the sky as she shook her clenched fists. She did not expect an answer; she knew the gods.

The music began quietly at first, with low piping sounds that rose with the movements of Lia's feet as she swirled out into

the center of the circle, hands writhing and twisting over her
head in emulation of the snakes in the pit she remembered. She
stepped among them, bowed, swung back, climbed and shook
into rapid motion. The gown billowed out, catching and
reflecting the light so that she seemed bathed in it. She bent
down so that her breasts almost tumbled free, bent backward so
that her hair nearly touched the ground in a stream of molten
gold, spun round and round on one slender foot, paused and
swayed there. The music kept up with her, challenging and
threatening by turns, but always there was the note of
anticipation, the promise of culmination in blood. There was
the wailing of horns, drums were thumped and hands were
clapped. The pipes sang out high and clear and were answered
by low, throaty calls from many voices.

The part of Lia's brain that stood aside from the anger and
fury she felt now told her of the power she was beginning to
wield as she danced there in the circle of the old ones with two
lights, those of earth and heaven, on her. She was the link
between the two at this particular time and she knew it. When
she whirled closer to the people, they backed away. Once she
stretched out bare, enticing fingers and they drew back, fear in
their eyes, fear in the very stronghold of their gods, whoever
they might be. Then Lia grew bolder. She advanced to the very
area of the sacrifice, a space sheeted with blood and scraps of
flesh. They did not follow. She whirled and ran at them, crying
phrases born out of her turmoil, tossed herself back and forth
as if torn by battling gods saw the wonder on their faces as they
kept back. She risked a glance at Danir and Jies, those
glittering malevolent figures, but their faces were impassive,
their hands still. She had a little more time.

"Now, goddess! If you live!" She hurled the words to the
sky as she writhed low to the ground and rose, thrust upward as
by great hands. The music slowed, became just the thump of
drums and the slow beat of hands. Lia tore the overgown from
her body, flinging it free as she stood poised in the light with all
eyes clamped upon her. "Now!"

She held them and she knew it. This was power; this was the
reason to exist and one could grow drunk on it. This was
savage reality. Only that bare crust of power kept her from
being devoured by the beast. Lia cried out as she bent low,
wrestled to the ground by the great ones. Shamelessly she

moved her smooth body, knowing well that in another mood she invited the people to rape. For this instant, however, she was inviolate.

Now she was flat on her stomach with her hands pressed down. Her whole body was taut and straight. She had come as close to the outer ring of stones as she dared, causing it to seem as though she had been brought there by the pull of the gods and great ones who warred within her body for possession. She raised her head a trifle and saw that only a scattered few people stood between the spot where she lay and the open plain beyond the stones that led to the river. It was not far but she had no idea what the river was like nor even how deep it was. No matter; choice was no longer a thing she had.

Lia heard a howl come low and ringing over the drums. Even the animals were closing in, drawn by the scent of fresh blood. Anything was preferable to the stone. She rose a little and dropped back down, shook her head back and forth, gave a low cry of exhaustion and shivered so hard that it was readily observed. She listened to the murmurs for an instant and then, under her breath, she said, "Be with me." The words might have better been meant for the goddess but Paon's arrogant face and brilliant eyes were in her mind as she hurled herself upward in one strong movement that set her erect, her body poised and in position. She gave one long breath before flinging her head back, bracing her arms, and somersaulting sideways over and over in the movements she had learned for the bull dance in Knossos.

Her muscles had forgotten nothing and her blood surged warm and alive in her veins as she came erect once more, now on the very periphery of the great stones. She had one quick glimpse of the frozen figures as they gaped at this seeming triumph, then the hurried motion of Danir warned her that time was life. She turned and ran.

In the very moment that she did so the air was alive with howls, the snorting of the wild boar, the savage cry of the wolf, a crashing that might mean hungry bears maddened by the odors around this place. Lia did not care. Her one thought was the river. She could hold her breath underwater for a very long time and she could lie quietly in a sheltered place without moving for even greater periods. What had once been pleasure could now mean salvation. She hurled herself at the river with the speed that she had once practiced against the animals of Pandos. Enraged cries came from behind her but she forced herself not to think of what would happen if she were caught.

An arrow tore the air just at her side and she zigzagged slightly, knowing that she was an excellent target in the pouring moonlight. Her toe caught on a root and she almost went down but managed to recover herself just in time. Another arrow landed just ahead of her. She heard the cries mingled with howls and heard the crackle of fire but now nothing else mattered for she was at the river bank.

Bushes clustered along it and trees trailed branches in the swift water. She saw that it was fairly wide, with several visible curves that vanished into a wood not far away. There was no time to lose. Lia jumped just as an arrow sliced at the brief tunic she wore. Others arched over her head as she went down, touched the sandy bottom and rose, stroking as hard as she could, thankful for the assistance of the current. She hoped now that it would remain deep for a great way.

It not only remained deep but carried her over some rocks and small rapids, between several crevices and into a whirlpool before tossing her up at last onto a low bank overhung with flowering bushes. The river spread out from there into a smooth expanse of silver in the moonlight. Just beyond the bushes Lia saw a huge tree, rearing taller than any she had ever seen. The upper branches were tossing in the wind but the lower ones were curiously still.

She knew that she should get up and go back out into the water so as to put as much distance between her pursuers and herself as she could but her body was limp. It was as though she were lashed to the spot by her own exhaustion. Her breath came in ragged gasps as her heart hammered in her ears with such force that she recalled the drums of the stone circle. Perhaps if she forced herself to sit up and drink some of the cool water, it would refresh her. She dared not linger here.

Then there was a plopping noise in the thicket just beyond her and she heard the sounds of drinking. She went rigid for an instant before turning cautiously over on her stomach, thankful for the protection of the flowers and leaves overhead. A small deer stood in the shadows, head now raised as it listened. The very air seemed to stand still. Lia's mouth parted. All her breath drained away. She was frozen in place, unable even to move her fingers from where they clutched the sand.

In the shadow of the great tree and seeming to be part of it was a wide, flat stone, as tall as two large men and glowing faintly gray in the diffused light. As she stared another swam into vision just beyond. River mist swirled up and around but she would have sworn that others waited just over the rise of the bank. The standing stones, which no human lived to see as they walked, had come to drink. So did legend have it.

Lia was ready to believe anything. The death she sought to avoid had come to find her. How would it be? Would they crush her as she lay here or would they pursue and crush her as she tried to flee? She was too worn out even for anger at the fate which had allowed her to free herself and then caught her so cruelly. Truly she was hated of the goddess.

The little deer suddenly bounded out of the water, saw her, stood for a moment and then, avoiding the tree and the stones, dashed around them and rushed into the woods. A bird cried raucously and flapped out to circle before moving out over the river. Lia stared at the stones as the world faded into a chill gray light. She knew where she was and what she faced but the fear faded. She wanted to try to rise but knew that she dared not. Mist floated over her, drifted on the surface of the water and went into the tree. It enveloped the stones and hid their shapes. Lia shut her burning eyes and waited. There was a great heaviness in the air; the time of striking was near. She thought, not of Paon and the goddess, but of Pandos island and those who had loved her as she them. She would have done no differently, she thought now in what might be her last conscious action, not in all the things she had done since her father's death. It was as it was and there must rest. The silence enveloped her.

The warm wind blew on her face. Her arms cramped and a tiny fish nibbled her great toe which hung over in the water. Odors of flowers, fish and mud mingled as an owl hooted several times. She heard the river gurgle and slosh as she had not before. Cautiously she opened her eyes and shifted her position to allow the blood to move.

The stone was merged with the tree and hanging vines grew over it. It did not seem to have moved since life began here. Several others, broken and tumbled down, lay about. At one

time some sort of temple or dwelling must have stood higher
up and later fallen. It would account for much, she thought,
and still Lia knew that she had been threatened with a far
greater danger in the past few moments than the perils of her
overwrought senses. The moon was high and pale now, sliding
down the sky into repose. The far light curved over the old
stones, speaking of a time and a worship so far removed that
mind could scarcely contemplate it. The crystal eyes of the
goddess flashed in Lia's brain suddenly and she wondered if
she had been answered.

She had no time for contemplation. She must head for the
coast and the Cretan ship yet stay in hiding as well. Her legs
trembled with stiffness as she rose and waded out into the water
to begin swimming once more. Another sound from the bank,
just at the place where the deer had been drinking, caused her
to look up. An indistinct figure stood there, his weapon shining
faintly.

It was too much. Lia bent down, barely knowing that she did
so, and caught up one of the sharp rocks at her feet. She held it
and waited. If he came just a bit closer, she would hurl it
directly at his head with all the power in her strong arm. Then,
once again, for her life, she would flee.

The waiting drew out as they watched each other.

Chapter Thirty-Nine

NIGHT FIRES

"LIA? WAIT. Do not run away." The low, even voice came to her as if from another life. The words were spaced and very clear as if the person spoke to a child or one who might have difficulty understanding. "Lia. It is all right. Wait there and I will come to you."

"Who are you?" She knew whose voice she thought it was, but had he not agreed to abandon her? Had he not made a bargain with Eridor? No. She was not to be deceived. The rock was hard-edged and, properly thrown, could do a good amount of damage. "Show yourself, but come no closer."

The man stepped from the shadows, his hands held low at his sides and his movements slow. "What have they done to you, Lia? Surely you know me?"

"Paon!" The name ripped from her throat as she saw the pain on his tanned face and the weary slump of his shoulders. Caked blood showed on his left shoulder and an open cut showed on his temple. His dark hair was pushed impatiently back. He wore a wide Minoan belt that bristled with two knives, a sword, a small ax and a short dagger. "What do you have to say to me?"

His head jerked back and she saw his nostrils flare. "You are able to understand me when I speak to you?"

"Certainly. I warn you, however, if you try to prevent me from leaving here, I shall throw this rock and my aim has always been excellent." Pain knifed through her but she stood steady. "You betrayed me. Did you expect me to forget that?"

A long-drawn-out shout came from far behind them and was answered by another as a low thumping of drums began. There was a howl of agony, then all faded into silence. Paon put both hands on his hips and surveyed Lia, his face expressionless.

"If you believe that, throw your rock. I am coming to you, Lia."

"Stay back!"

He began to walk toward her. She backed away and he followed. He said, "There is no time for this. They will be after us very soon."

Lia spat, "They are your friends, remember? You gave me to them!" She hurled the rock, not at him, for not even in an extremity did she think she could hurt him, but to the side, so that it whistled past his ear.

He ignored her action, moved close to her and caught her up in his arms. Holding her so close that she could not move and could barely breathe, he set his mouth on hers, not in passion but in a tenderness and relief so great that she went limp. Her hands rose to caress his face and clasp around his neck. They stood so for only a moment before Paon released her and stepped back.

"I swear to you, Lia, that I had nothing to do with your capture and imprisonment. We must go from this place, and quickly, for they will pursue you and already valuable time has been lost. There is no time for explanations!" His face was stern but his eyes hungered for her.

"Swear? Swear by what? I am done with trust, Paon!" Lia heard her voice rise hysterically and thought that soon she must scream at the very thought of enduring anything else. The terrible wet thumping of the stones as they fell upon their victims was hammering in her ears. Nothing else seemed real. The man who faced her was but the figment of her dreams.

"By the sacred soul of my dead wife, Kaha, whom I loved! By my son, denied me! By Minos, my friend and my king. By your very self, Lia! I swear by these! Will it be enough for you to trust me until I can give you incontrovertible proof?" He looked into her paling face and nodded. "Eridor told me all that he said to you. It is better that you know." Impatience took him. "Will you come?"

Lia knew that there was really no choice open to her. Death in the wilderness or betrayal by this enigmatic man whom she once thought she loved and possibly still did? In her heart she believed that he must have an explanation and was willing to wait for it. Besides, the rising hysteria in her cried, Better to die with him than alone. A quick dagger with the man of her heart might not be so bitter a fate when she recalled what she had just witnessed.

"Yes." She held out her hand and he took it. He pulled one of the daggers from his belt and gave it to her, unsmiling. She hefted the blade and tried to smile but her lips would not curve. They looked at each other for another instant before Paon jerked his head at the woods.

"They will come down the river in boats specially made for fast travel. That offers no escape. We must go through to the crags. Can you endure a little more?"

Lia wanted to laugh wildly but could only nod her head. What did anything matter? They were doomed in the end. As she matched Paon step for step as they ran, she tried not to think but her mind ran on, fixed in the dreadful ceremonies she had so narrowly escaped. She thought again of the young girl, unmoving and steady as the stone fell, the frightened child, twisting and struggling in the last breaths, the blood spilling and staining the ground in rivers of red. Her very sight was red-tinged; it would be that way until she died. She was exhausted and still she could run forever. She was glad to see Paon and yet she wanted to scream out her anger at what she thought he had done. How could she trust him? How could she trust anyone?

Time blurred after that. The moon grew paler then and vanished in the wheeling sky which soon grew gray. Birds roused, beginning to give their morning calls. Once a dark shape loomed up at them, snarling before drawing back; yellow eyes glittered above white teeth as it stood over a smaller wolf. Lia thought then of herself and Paon. No wonder it did not challenge them. Mist hung in the glens as they sped through them, along tracks that animals used and over stream beds dried up generations ago. They never came into the open country but slipped behind trees, around crags, going up a hill and past another, pausing to listen in this covert or that, and always keeping their weapons ready. Lia's feet ached and burned, her head hammered even more and her eyes felt swollen in her head. She was a body in motion and would go on until she dropped.

It was full light when Paon put his hand on her arm, gesturing for her to look downward. She obeyed cautiously and saw that he did not miss her reluctance. They were standing at the side of a small rise that was covered thickly with bushes and clustered rocks. Several leaned together and it was into these that he vanished completely. She called to him, the sound harsh despite all her effort to be quiet. He rose up just ahead, springing from the ground. His face was lit with brilliance and the blue eyes flamed.

"They have been here. At least three of our men, traveling together. The rock is marked with the double ax and turned on its side, one of the signals I gave them when I mentioned secret places on the way to the coast. Come, we will rest here."

Lia smiled, her face stiff, unable to move back. Paon started to touch her and drew away as he pointed out where to go. The rocks hid a small rounded area where soft grass grew around some overhanging bushes that effectively concealed the place where they entered and the tiny exit. A few pink flowers shone in the first light of the sun, their petals so delicate that they seemed to float on the air. A stream had once gone through here but now only a faint trickle, enough to nourish the flowers and grass, remained. The drops fell downward with a faint pinging noise.

She sank down on the ground and put her hand to her head. Both began to shake as her whole body took up the rhythm. Paon knelt beside her, tilting her chin up. She tried to pull away but could not. He gathered her close to him but held her so that she had to look at his face. He spoke slowly, just as he had at the river.

"You are safe for now, Lia. We are no longer in the area those people travel. Few know of this place and I think I can call these that do, friends—or at least friends enough not to kill us. You may fear Thulf. Do not. He is dead by Eridor's own hand."

That stirred Lia and she relaxed a little. "I do not understand." She wanted to pose questions, to have him explain and answer, but the effort was too much. She let him guide her into the shade and close to the flowers. He sat down and pillowed her head on his lap. His fingers began to play gently in her hair as he talked of the sea, its moods, the creaming waves, the patterns of light on the surface and how they were reflected in the sky. Lia went again into her undersea world but she did not go alone. This time Paon was with her.

She woke to the hammering drums and falling stones in the blood-red light. Terror and anger blended into one. She had to escape and yet she could not move. She was bound and the stone was coming slowly down. When she tried to scream there was only silence.

Then hands were on her shoulders, turning her over, and she looked up into Paon's face. She had been lying on her stomach and now was twisted on her side, clawing at the grass. He squatted beside her as he ran his fingers up and down her arms to warm the flesh. The sun had shifted so that the place where they were was now in the full light of what must be noon.

"You must tell me about it. Every detail. Now." It was a command.

She swung her head back and forth in denial. "I want to forget it. I will! What are you, Paon, that you want to know about that obscenity?" Her voice shook with loathing. His face swam in red light and his eyes seemed to take on that color. "No!"

"Tell me!" He shook her a little. "I shall keep after you until you do, you know."

Lia tried to turn her back on him but he would not have it. Remorselessly he pulled her to face him. Her head roared and the light grew redder. Anything to make him leave her alone! She thought she screamed at him but his face did not alter. So be it then.

She started with meeting Thulf and the explanation of him that had been given to her by Eridor. The bitterness rolled out as she recounted the conversation she had heard after her capture. The pain in Paon's face made her glad. Had she not suffered all this due to him and his so-called friend? Then the flow of words went on unabated. Nothing could have checked them; the torment was relived in each horrifying detail. She told of her part and those of the others with such clarity that Paon saw it all and endured with her. The part about the sacrifices was recounted so explicitly that Lia wanted to be ill. She had not realized how the protection of the sea dream had helped at the time. Now she knew that she saw it as it had happened and that these recollections had struggled to break out so that they could be borne. Paon had been right to force her.

Now he was saying, "Finish it. End it." The dark face was close to hers and the sheen of tears was in the blue eyes. He, the arrogant and the bitter, felt her agony. But had he, too, not known much of this?

Lia heard her voice, empty now and exhausted, go on with the escape and the encounter with the stones. "Real or not, I believed it so and do now. I saw them come to drink and lived. I invoked the goddess back there and came free. Paon, I cannot think, even yet. There is so much I have to know. . . ." Her eyes clouded as tears ran down into her mouth and hung on her lashes. Then she was held against his chest, his arms around her and hers clinging to his back. The storm of weeping kept on until tears were past and the dry sobs racked her hard enough to make her chest ache.

He spoke to her in terms of endearment, made soothing little sounds, patted her head and back. It was no use, she could not stop. Finally he picked her up and carried her across to the droplets of the stream. There he bathed her forehead in cool water, made her drink some of it and stretched out with her in his arms. Against that solid bulwark, the scent of the lifting flowers in her nostrils, Lia slept once more.

When she came awake it was to his lips, the soft curve of his mouth pressed to hers, his hands on her sides, gently caressing. His face was strangely young and tender. He had washed away the marks of battle and only a faint bruise remained on it. His eyes asked a question; she moved closer in answer to it.

Their joining was of the senses but, far more, it was a union of spirit and caring. Their mouths locked together, then he explored her body with eagerness as her hand touched his shaft, lingered and rose to tickle his stomach and returned. There was no time of waiting. Neither could bear it. He parted her thighs and entered her with a long deep stroke that made her writhe in delight. She arched her buttocks, rising to meet him and drawing him all the way into her, not allowing him to pull back. With a groan he came to her mouth and breasts as he thrust. His tongue circled her rosy nipple, pulled it into his mouth and released it as the familiar, eternally new quake caught them, spinning them both into a vortex of pleasure and sweeping all before it.

Now it was Lia who held him to her bosom as she ran her fingers over the broad, muscular back and firm flesh. She kissed the black curls and played with the lobes of his ears, rubbed his neck and caressed his shoulders. When he slept, his arms around her waist and his face buried in her naked lap, Lia sat very still so as not to wake him and remembered their times of lovemaking. There had been much of it in anger, passion, heat and misunderstanding but she believed that this was true union, not only for her but for him as well. Both had sought to give and they had received in full measure.

Later the soft rain began and they took shelter under the rocks in a slight rounding of the ground where they fitted closely together as they talked, not as lovers not yet as friends, but soldiers who endured much. Lia thought that they were bare to each other, all secrets and sores laid clean. She would not speak to him of her love, nor of the nearness to it that she sensed in his responses to her. He had his own battles to fight in Knossos; Hirath would release him to no other woman and their son was the surety that would hold him.

They looked out into the soft grayness, heard the roll and clatter of the heavens, felt the wind begin to rise and drew closer still for warmth. Paon, after telling her about his friendship with Eridor and speaking again of the tin traders and their methods, gave a reluctant sigh and touched her face with the tip of one finger.

"The time has come to answer all those questions, Lia. Will it pain you to speak of them?" He who had forced her to the agony for her own good, now hesitated. "Soon we have to leave here and travel on."

She shook her head, watching his face. He was never the betrayer; surely she had known that all along.

"I will be quick then and we will not mention these things again. The rites I entered into were those of fasting and purification and the taking to my flesh of one of the young girls of the traders. Eridor, as chief, offered and all would have been offended had I not. You, as priestess of the goddess, might also have commanded a man of your choice; it is custom here. I refused for you." The quick smile lit his face and faded at her expression. "In your stead and for myself, in return for the trade if ever it can be renewed and for the honor of my friend, I swore that the goddess should not come here, that nothing of her service should ever touch those who traded here. I promised to take you, representative of all she is, away. In return, all that I asked in the name of Minos, insofar as they could give it, would be mine."

Lia expelled her breath softly. "And now?"

He shrugged. "It was a gamble. I do not think Eridor has the power to resume trade with Crete. There is a darkness on this land that may engulf it completely. It was not so in the past when I was here. I lost nothing in the promise. At any rate, Thulf was a spy for those who took you and had been all along. Others vanished from the villages of Eridor's people, taken by surprise and sacrificed in propitiation. There are many cults here but theirs is one of the most savage. Some factions of it practice the eating of human flesh. They are intelligent, learned and vicious as you have reason to know. We suspected what had happened and I was determined to seek you, no matter what, especially when I thought of the others and their fate."

Droplets of rain splintered into Lia's hand as she stretched it out and brought it to her lips. A sudden happiness rose in her. She would have done the same for him, so closely were they bound in harmony now. It could not last but in these moments when happiness must be snatched from death, she was glad beyond the telling that she had them.

"Thulf was too innocent. I made a slighting remark in front of him and he took offense. I think he was partly mad. Eridor killed him in that rage that he tries to keep tamped down; in expiation he offered to come with me in my search and several others of his clan wanted to come as well. One was Aelth's brother, who lies dead back at the stones. We tracked them, saw the ceremonies begin, thought you dead until that procession started and then fired the flaming arrows in an effort to distract them. The old ones are dead by some of those arrows. I was far enough back so that I saw you head for the river and could rush to intercept you. I nearly missed you, as you know."

Lia said, "The arrows came at the right time. They took it as a sign from their gods." The horror fought to return as she looked into the intense blue eyes so near her own.

Paon sighed. "I know that every hand will seek to destroy us now. Eridor and his few will be safe enough because of Thulf's participation but the traders and those of the tribes, probably even those who took you, will be after us. Normally they do not come this close to the coast but we must see. And our men are scattered, the *Lily Flame* is out to sea and the pirate ship waits."

"Not to mention the coming storm. Great odds." She kept her tone light.

He kissed her lips in a swift gesture. "Lia, I may never be able to say this again. You have endured much here in this land and in Crete. I have never known a woman so brave, especially at the stones when you thought yourself alone and yet won through. I honor you and I have never known a woman like you. I never shall again."

Lia knew then that he would not speak words of love; for him this was the greatest and ultimate tribute. It must be enough.

Chapter Forty

THE HAMMERING

IT WAS FAR into the afternoon of the next day before Lia and Paon reached the crags overlooking the coast. Rain soaked them, chilly winds bent trees over and snapped branches back, icy stones fell and the sky rattled. They had walked all night, hidden for some of the morning, then moved stealthily on. Lia forgot what it was to be warm and dry. Nothing mattered to her except that she was free and alive. The nightmares came when she slept but Paon's touch was ever reassuring and his voice gentle. He had told her that few would venture out in such weather; pursuers would be discouraged by their own proximity to the coast. She observed that he kept constant watch just as she did. Several times she thought she saw movement far behind them and drew his attention to it but repeated attempts to verify pursuit proved fruitless. They guarded their weapons and hurried on.

Lia had long since removed the jewels and stowed them in the pouch at her belt, but even without their added luster it was a rich ornament. The thin tunic concealed nothing of her body, and although she had bound her golden hair back in s single braid, her appearance showed plainly that she was not of this land. Paon, too, was set apart by his height and darkness. He had told her that others of her coloring were farther to the north. They had speculated idly as to where they came from and who was first here, they or the darker, smaller people of the south. Such talk held the night horors at bay for a time.

They had come through the woods and to the wide flowing river where the sands moved deceptively in and out and a ship might enter at its peril. Entering it and swimming rapidly for a time before doubling back had been one of the devices they used. Hiding in the rocks and watching from trees were others. But the sense of being watched was forever with them although they did not discuss it. Paon found no more signs of his men. Lia knew he believed them slain or captured.

Now she stood with Paon between two crags and peered out to sea. Waves crashed against the rocks, withdrew and hurled themselves upward again with a roar. Sky and sea and rain were dull gray against the darker coast. Clouds hung low, nearly obscuring some of the way they had just come. The force of the wind was so strong that Lia had to hold on to Paon in order to remain upright.

"No sign. Nothing. Yonder is the great pointed crag." He gestured to the far left, straining to see through the rain. "The beach is small, visible only at certain times of day. We shall build the signal fire there and hope our ship is safe in these waters. As for the pirate vessel and those traitors . . ." He made a quick stabbing motion, his face savage.

"Is there some place hereabouts to hide and wait until the time has elapsed for us to meet the others?" Lia knew their chances of escape were very narrow but she did not want Paon to know she doubted.

His hair was flattened by the downpour but curls still attempted to spring up and his white teeth flashed in the dimness as he said, "There are many caves along the coast. We will move about among them. Some of the men must have escaped detection. My men and I responsible! I should be with them, whatever their fate!" He started away, leaving Lia to follow as best she might.

She looked up, away from that resolute back, and saw the flash of red out of the corner of her eye. "Paon! Look!" He whirled so quickly that she knew he had seen it also.

"Hurry! The caves. They are ruled by the gods of the sea, many of these people believe, and we can only hope they will not come. A vain hope, but all we have." He gave a rueful laugh and held out his hand. "Walk with me."

She put her fingers to his and together they ran over the slippery stones.

Lia was reminded of the caves on Pandos where she had so often roamed. Paon, seeming to know every section of this forbidding and deadly coast, led her into places impossible to see even when very near and showed her openings in sheer walls that birds might have missed. His fear of pursuit showed itself in the inaccessible spots he chose to hide in and the fact that the caves he selected always had a back exit, however small.

The one selected for this night faced onto a far drop. Surf boomed hollowly underneath the cliff and the storm roared at the entrance. Rocks tumbled together at the rear of the low-roofed cave but it was possible to slip through them. They drank rainwater collected in little pools, ate a handful of berries Paon had snatched earlier as they passed a bush and tried, with little success, to ignore their snarling stomachs. Lia had thought she would never want to eat again but her healthy body demanded food.

"Tomorrow we will go to another cave. Fish are often tossed up on the beach or in the rocky pools." Paon looked over at Lia as she stood wringing the water from her thin tunic and hair. His face was sober. "Are you very cold?"

She laughed in spite of her discomfort. "Freezing! But I see the marks of chill on your skin as well. The cold land is rightly called so." She did not know if he played at games or was serious. For all that she understood of Paon, in many things he was still a mystery to her.

"I know a remedy if you are willing." He came so near that his breath stirred her hair but he did not touch her.

She tilted her face to his, knowing that the leaping passion already tinted it rose. Would he find her fair? "Willing? You might say that, Lord Commander." As soon as the words came from her mouth she knew she had made a mistake. His eyes went a cold, slate blue and his jaw grew hard. He whirled around, beginning to pace as he rubbed his hands together. "Paon, I did not mean . . ."

"You did well to remind me of who I am, Lia. How can I sport with you in this place when my friends lie dead, the mission a failure and my men scattered with a pirate ship waiting to destory what is left, if anything is left? Lord Commander, indeed! I am not worthy of that name!" He glanced at her, then away. "It is not your fault." He began to pace again.

Lia went to the cave opening and stared out at the blending of storm and sea. Why could they not comfort each other? What did he think he could do in the night? She recalled that the title of lord commander had been stripped from him on their first arrival in Crete and later restored when he was sent on this mission. To one who had endured what he had and risen so high, it must be bitterness in very truth to face ruin. His fierce pride would not let him discuss that worry with her. She gave a sigh of annoyance. Why worry about Crete when it was likely they would never leave this island? Was it not practical to take what they could while they could?

They took turns sleeping that night while the other remained on watch. There was nothing to be said between them. Lia regretted her careless words more than ever but she was wise enough to know that Paon's torment would have surfaced without much more delay. She listened to the fury of the storm, which was rising rather than abating, twisted back and forth on the cold stones and fought back the nightmares.

The new day dawned gray and dim. Paon put down his daggers for her and said, "I have to go to the beach and search. Stay here and do not go out for any reason. I will be back very soon." His hand touched hers impersonally.

"Be careful." Her lips were stiff and locked. She hated this barrier between two people who had shared and lost. She did not have the means to cross it.

Paon saw her struggle and turned from it. "Yes, of course." Then he was gone.

Lia lost track of time after that. She watched the storm and tried not to think of the *Lily Flame,* possibly torn to pieces on those very rocks below. She paced to keep warm, practiced the tumbling exercises that had helped to save her life, sat in a small huddle and sought the undersea world of dreams in vain. There was no escape from the here and now.

In an effort to divert her mind, she took the black ornaments from her pouch—those ornaments that adorned the delicate slave chains in the hall of her imprisonment—and looked at them once more. She tried to translate the language but could get the sense of no more words. Yet the odd familiarity of them plagued her even beyond the bare rudiments of the Akkadian that her father had taught her. She turned them this way and that, absorbed in the puzzle and wondering at the riddle they posed.

"Put down the holy objects. Your hand demeans them." The level voice spoke in precise Minoan

Lia dropped them with a small cry and started up but sank back quickly as she saw, just across the narrow cave at the back, the tall figure of the white-haired priest who had been at the sacrifices. He held a long sword of curious, shimmering metal with red edges. A curved dagger was at his waist and his hand rested on it. On the thumb of that hand she saw the ring that Jies had worn, the long flat stone with the strange writing twisting between a raised snake and eye. He wore a wide collar of blazing jewels in red, purple, green and blue, the centerpiece of which was a huge brilliantly red stone surrounded by smaller ones in pink shading to white. His eyes were blazing with triumph as he watched her.

"That is it. Just sit quietly." He touched the lovely red stone. "The gods themselves know nothing finer. It is from the Silver Mountains of a far land, the gift of a god to a king in that land. With it and this ring and those ornaments you hold, I am supreme in my rule."

"Then you want only these?" Lia let her fingers drift over the polished surfaces. The daggers lay on the floor near the precipice. Too far for her to leap without going over.

"No." He came nearer and she saw the bulge of his erection under the clinging white robe he wore. "I want you."

"I will kill myself before I allow you to take me back to that horrible place! Get away from me! I mean it!" She was on her feet despite the uplifted sword. She knew that she would do anything to avoid that fate and the conviction poured through her voice. "How did you find me? Get away!"

He paused and eyed her greedily. "You fail to understand. I am Varet-Sant, ruler, since the death of the old ones, of 'Dians in direct order of succession. You shall be my woman, bearer of my children, queen in all but name. In all the legends there is no woman like you! When the children of our union go to the gods, our people will prosper! You were brought here for me. I know it. You spoke in our language and you knew the name of our ancient gods."

"You are Akkadians from the land of the two rivers. How

did you come here?" Lia tried to ignore the glittering sword and the lust in his face. Doubtless his followers were close behind. He might think what he would but she did not think that he could protect her against the blood lust of his people. He would enjoy himself on her body, then give her to the stones. Better that she chose her own death! Her head went back proudly but her heart was leaden with fear. She did not want to give up any chance of life, however slim.

Varet-Sant said, "Long generations ago we lived there. A king arose who wished to unite the lands and despoil our sacred traditions. He was mighty and we could do nothing except fight. He went against the gods, thinking himself mightier than they. One of our number tried to kill him and failed but the king lay close to death. Unfortunately he recovered and went on to conquest but in the time that he feared for his life, he promised us ours. We were forced to go forth as we were in several small ships, meant to sink when just away from land. However, we survived by faith and sacrifice. The bloodiest and greatest of our gods, Ut-Nammaru-Sed and his family of great ones, went with us and protected us. He is lion and despoiler, served at the sacrifice of the stones. We came here after many trials and settled. We are not the first. The great stones were here when we came but they are the symbol of our faith."

Lia thought she heard a rustle of movement above the sounds of wind and rain. Paon returning on the tiny track of rock near the entrance? His murderers ready? Varet-Sant's men drawing closer?

"You need not look for your companions. Some are dead just down the way with the wreckage of that ship. We left lights, which glow as if they were held up to guide it in, but it was already torn apart on the under rocks. All tribes here do that. We plan to extend our power, you see, and want no outsiders. You are a woman of bravery and beauty. I will have you." He stepped so close that she could smell his hot breath and see the yellow dye in his beard. "The color of the sun of our lost land!" He put the point of the sword to her throat as he touched her hair and let his other hand slip to her breast. Then he pushed her back and pulled the ornaments from her unresisting fingers, exclaiming over them as he did so.

"What is their meaning?" Lia heard the rustling again and wanted to scream out. Distraction might be best. Her nails bit into her palms. She would rake them down the side of his face and leap to the side. That would give her time to get the dagger. If it were his men she might try to make him think she would be agreeable to his orders. She could not allow herself to think that the *Lily Flame* had been lured in so early or that Paon lay dead. But he had said "companions." Who else but the Cretans? Perhaps the pirates? Surely they knew this coast and all of its peoples.

"They are the symbols of the relationship between our god and his people. We are yoked and yet we serve with freedom. The carvings on it are the records of our going forth and the lands we touched. Elsewhere we have recorded the generations and their numbers since we left." He touched the great collar and the red stone seemed to take more color as he did so. Then his interest turned. "Come here. I will show you how fortunate you are to have my interest."

"How can I trust you? You may wish to kill me." Lia allowed a small smile to play over her lips as she shrugged so that her breasts moved against the thin fabric of her tunic.

"I will decide what is to happen to you! Your goddess may be powerful in Crete but she did not save her followers here, did she? You do not fear me yet. I am not such a fool as the old ones were! No, Lia of Knossos, there is no choice for you and I shall do with you as I please!" His eyes flamed as he lifted the sword and put it to her breast so that the skin was pricked. Her blood flowed out as he pushed harder.

Lia cried, "Surely you do not plan to take me with the sword! Put it down so that we may give each other pleasure!"

"Your escape from the stone ring was masterly but you cannot escape me." He hooked one foot behind her legs and flipped her to the floor with ease. His strength was so great that he held her there, undisturbed by her struggles and the twistings of her taut body. Then he lowered himself onto her and raised the sword again. The light from his jeweled collar matched that of his eyes and the blade hung before her face. She ceased to fight as he drew it again over the flesh just above her breasts, cutting away the tunic and causing rivulets of blood to stream downward. They stared into each other's eyes.

"What are you going to do?" Lia felt that the longer she could keep him talking, the less likely he was to continue his game of blood. She knew now that rape was not what he had in mind.

"You want a master. I am he." He moved the sword up toward her chin, his powerful arm pressing it down, and began to lick the blood from her skin in a slow, tickling motion that suggested he meant to keep it up for a very long time.

Revolted, Lia struggled and threw him slightly off balance. He rose up in a lithe movement and slammed his hand across her face, momentarily stunning her. The world spun as he bent to view his handiwork. She stiffened her fingers and drove straight for his eyes, the sword forgotten as it lay flat on her breasts.

Veret-Sant dodged instinctively, caught up the sword with both hands and aimed it at her. "You dare to fight me! After all I have offered you, you dare! Abomination!"

Lia lunged at him, a move he did not expect. The sword clanged down on the stones and they rolled together in a battle she must inevitably lose. She jerked at his collar and it came free. He hit her in the face again, his own lighting up with lust and murder, the black eyes gleaming in the whiteness of hair and beard.

Then he was on top of her and shouting in Akkadian as his hands went around her neck. The light began to fade. His weight bore her down. He jerked, shuddered, contracted and went limp in the space of a single, pausing breath.

Chapter Forty-One

ORDINANCES OF HEAVEN

HANDS PROBED at her neck and pulled up her tunic. Someone brushed her hair back and kicked at some rocks so that they rattled. A voice was cursing in a Minoan of which she could only catch scattered phrases. She opened her eyes and stared upward, wondering what new horror could confront her now. The rest of the 'Dians had arrived, she supposed. But where was Veret-Sant and what did he mean to do with her now?

"Lia? Are you all right?"

"Did he hurt you?"

"The commander will be furious! Is she rousing yet?"

Lia sat up, ignoring the cries and stared at those she had thought dead. Speo, Morb and a dozen other faces familiar to her from the *Lily Flame*. The men who had separated only a few days ago and who had arrived safely after all! Tears ran down her cheeks and into her mouth as she looked at their browned, worried faces and saw the concern in their eyes. Priestess of the Goddess, Servant of the Lady of the Snake, and Lia, her very self. For whom did they really care? It did not matter. She put out her hands in gratitude.

"The priest? Where is he?"

One of the men, little more than a youth, said with grim satisfaction, "In the sea with his foulness. His treasure is here." He held up the collar, sword and dagger as well as the ring. "I saw him over you and threw my knife. Killed him immediately, too."

"I owe you my life. I thank you all." Her gaze went from face to face as she smiled at them. "How did you come to be here? What of his followers? And Paon, where is he?"

Morb said, "The priest either came alone or his men have fled. There was no sign of anyone as we came up. We came separately to the pointed rock as the commander told us. Some have been around here since yesterday. We saw him walking on the beach this morning and went to join him. He told us to come here and fetch you."

"You were just in time." Lia put both hands to her throat, then let them slip down to her sword-torn flesh. One of them had put his battered cloak over her and now she pulled it around her as she stood up. "Let us go quickly. I cannot bear this place."

They stared at her in puzzlement as she walked over to the ledge and looked down at the boiling sea, the slanting lines of rain and the savage rocks. Her enemy was dead and she saved. Glory rose up in her when she turned back.

"What is it? I am quite able to walk."

"Lady, are you not meaning to give thanks to the great goddess who brought us safely out?" It was the youth again, watching her with large eyes.

Lia resisted the comment that they were not yet free of the this deadly island. She stretched out both hands, lifted her head to the expanse of sea and sky beyond and spoke, not in ceremonial words, but to friendship, love and honor, those intangible things which might, of themselves, be holy enough for worship.

"For the rescue and the release, for the power that has released us, for the bonds that hold us together, we are truly grateful. Guide us free of this place and bring us to Crete once more. Accept our gratitude!"

They crossed the wet stones, clutching walls of rock in the sluicing rain, moving in single file as they picked their way down. The sea boomed and roared. Great waves rolled in, showing the teeth of the dark crags underneath. It seemed to Lia that the very earth here was twisted out of shape and pulled from bindings underneath. Often on Pandos she had felt the shaking of the land; Ourda had said the gods were angry and fought over their domains. Perhaps they did so here as well. She thought of her words to the goddess and the relief the men seemed to feel when she was finished. The old weariness at such things pressed down on her—surely none was less likely than she to prove an advocate for others before the goddess and yet they gave her that special role.

The wind tried to hurl them back as it howled among the crags. Lia was grateful for its savagery just as she was grateful for the very breath she drew. She was alive and with friends when she just as well might have been dead or back in captivity among the 'Dians. Now their jewels and symbols rested in the pouch at her belt. How very strange all life was! Strange and wonderful!

The beach below the pointed crag was no more than a sliver of sand and rock at this time of day. The relentless sea struggled for mastery and flowed out again only to return. There seemed no place that a ship could land or even approach, but on a higher level of pointed rocks, Lia glimpsed some fragments of wreckage and several huddled figures. The remnants of the *Lily Flame*? If so then they were lost.

Suddenly Paon was among them as if he had emerged from nowhere. Others were climbing from the rocks around them and she recognized others from their own ship. Her eyes blurred with thankfulness and it was through that haze that she saw Paon's face twist with pain although nothing could hide the happiness of finding most of his men safe.

"Lia, what has happened to you?" The wind whipped the cloak back so that he saw the markings on her bosom, the black marks on her face and her near nudity. He gripped her arms and gazed down at her anxiously.

Morb and another man began to speak with each other and came to a swift halt. Paon held up his hand so that Lia might give the tale. She sketched it out in a few hurried sentences, hating that her voice shook but unable to control it.

"By the gods, you could have died and I not known it. But I would always know it, I believe." He pulled her into his arms before them all and kissed her cold lips, caressed her face and held her as he spoke to the men. "I thank you for her safety. If the great goddess is with us, as I believe her to be, we shall soon see the last of this cursed land." Jubilation rang in his voice, causing Lia to look up at him. He continued to hold her in his warm embrace and she was content to remain there.

"What is it, Paon, other than the restoration of the men that makes you look so?"

"You are all right?"

"Of course." She smiled and was excited by the warmth in those brilliant eyes. There was no barrier now but they might not live to taste the delights of passion again. How often she thought that! Was it a warning?

"I must show you!" He led her forward as the men came behind them. They climbed up on the rocks and he pointed. "The big man yonder, his face is toward us. Is he not familiar?"

Lia peered at the drenched body. She had seen enough in these past days so that it did not shake her. One side of the skull was dented in but there was no mistaking the purple scar down one part of the chin and into the neck. He had been bald; she remembered the shining pate in the light of many fires as she watched from the secret places on Pandos. He had also been taller than anyone else and blockily built. Her father told tales of his savagery but these were mixed with gallantry. She had not known him but he was from her past, which was now so far away.

"Genor! Then it was his ship that was wrecked?"

"If a ship really was and if the priest was not telling you a tale." Paon's voice grew hard. "It is really he, the murdering swine!" He laughed aloud and shook his fist at the body.

"He came a long way to die." Lia said the words half musingly, half in pity.

Paon caught it. "There is no need to feel sorry for such as he and those with him. They are, after all, pirates, and I have seen the sorrow they cause, the carnage they bring, the destruction to a peaceful trade. You do not think they would have spared the daughter of the man who helped them, do you? Brutes, all of them!"

"We are all brutes at one time or another, Paon!" She did not know why she spoke so; certainly there was no reason to quarrel. Paon had fought against lawlessness for Crete. He had been a mercenary and had seen all manner of cruelties, both in those close to him and strangers. His wounds had festered long. Lia knew all this and yet she could not endure this pleasure in yet another death. She had not known the horror of the stones; that would color all her life.

"If we are captured by any of these tribes, especially the 'Dians, we shall have reason to know brutality." His tone was sharp but she saw the color on the high cheekbones. He glanced past her and spoke to the others. "We must try to find out what has happened. Split into two groups and go carefully in opposite directions. Try to see if you are followed. Return before the light fades. Lia remains here with three of you to guard her. If all seems quiet we signal the *Lily Flame* this night and hope that she comes."

"But, Paon, I want to come! What good is it to remain here and take up those who could be scouting? We need the eyes of everyone!"

He rounded on her, eyes freezing. "I command here. Have you not caused enough problems?"

"Forgive me, Lord Commander. I wished only to help." She turned her back on him and looked out to sea. The gray waves and rain melted together in zigzagging lines as the rocks seemed to tilt together. Surely she was not going to weep right here in front of them all? And over what? Paon knew her too well to think that she had ever had any dealings with the pirates; they had even discussed the matter. But he had retreated from her again and with no real reason.

Lia heard him giving low-voiced orders once more. She blinked and tried to get the rain out of her eyes. Something large rose up on the horizon, flashed and faded back into grayness. She thought something must be wrong with her eyes and dashed her hand across them, trying to recall if she had hit her head in the scuffle with the priest. There was another flash. Her hands fell to her sides.

"Paon! Look yonder! A ship!" She screamed the words as the wind threw them back in her mouth.

They whirled and strained to see. The flashes came again and again almost as if there were some reason to them. Paon put his hands up to his eyes and squinted as he moved closer to the roiling water. Lia saw the long prow now and the battered shape that once was the goddess before the lines of rain closed down once more. She could not safely say that it was the *Lily Flame;* it could be the pirates. But who could land in this weather and on those rocks?

"It is the *Lily Flame!*" Paon's voice rang out and sobered almost instantly. "Build a fire. She must be told that we are here." The way he spoke told Lia that this was not the good news for which they hoped.

They had little that was not wet but the great crag faced out onto the sea and the space directly under the point was fairly dry. Once the men ranged themselves so that the wind was deflected and one began to work with sharp stones in the hope of striking a flame, the others contributed bits of clothing, pieces of wood flung up under rocks, anything to start the fire. They fanned out in the search but it was clear that the fire, provided it could be started, would have little enough fuel.

"Ah! Hurry, feed it!" It was Speo, huddled over the tiny blaze, as he gave it bits of a damp loincloth that threatened to smother the flickers. Someone contributed a pouch, another a length of crumbling wood and a belt. Speo skook his head and fanned with both hands.

Paon stepped into the shelter to stand watching them. "They flash a code I have often used. My understanding of it is obscured by the weather and the tossing of the ship. She is too far away for it to come clearly; those rocks could tear her bottom out." He was telling them things they already knew as if preparing them for the worst. All except Speo turned to watch him as he slammed one hand into the other.

Lia felt her throat close up. The smoke was burning her eyes and she stepped toward Paon, wanting to be near him. His look warned her back.

"We are pursued, my friends, both at sea and from the land. The pirate ship is ravaged, true, but those aboard her are still able to seek the *Lily Flame* and are doing so. They managed to avoid her and come here but for a short time only. They say the cliffs are filled with searchers clearly visible to their eyes. Some wear the blue and yellow paint of war. Others are slender and dark. It will not be long until they will be upon us. Our ship cannot come until the tide favors it and the passage is plain. There it is—the shape of our fate."

"What are the choices?" The speaker was a thin man of middle age with a lean, expressive face.

Paon lifted his shoulders eloquently. "I can tell them to go out to sea and try to return when the tide is right but there is the danger of the pirates catching them if they linger. We can fight and scatter, trying to return if we can get away from the tribesmen."

"Some of them will be the 'Dians who want their treasures back." Lia took the pouch from her waist and opened to show the glittering contents.

"Commander! The fire will not blaze up!" Speo was still fanning as he talked.

There is one other thing we can do and we may die in the attempting of it." Paon put his hands on his hips and faced them, challenge leaping in his eyes. "I can send one message only to the ship. We must decide now. Swim for her as best we can. Those who cannot swim must cling to the ones who do. She will stay where she is if I bid it. We face certain death in any of these choices. I leave it to you, my men, and to the priestess of the goddess."

They looked at each other and, over the howling of the wind and the roar of the surf, heard a maniacal howl that was picked up by other throats. Their fate was closing in.

"Tell us, Lord Commander!"

"Stay and fight!"

"Swim for it!"

"We'd be dashed to pieces! I say fight!"

The babble of voices rang in Lia's ears. She thought of offering the jewels back to the 'Dians in some way but they would only kill them all anyway. The idea of facing the currents and towering waves was fearful but not so much as what she knew would happen otherwise. She lifted her head. "I say swim for it!"

The argument lashed back and forth for a few moments longer. Then Paon cried, "This is a matter of personal choice! I shall swim for it and those who wish to come may do so. Those who remain to fight another time know the chances of life. You are all no longer soldiers of Crete but your own men with free choices to make. You are not bound to me in obedience."

They ringed round him then, some twenty men in all, the entire group, and said with one voice, "We follow the commander!"

Lia was near enough to see the sheen of tears in Paon's blue eyes and heard the unashamed shaking of his voice as he said, "I pray you live to do so. And I thank you." They clasped his hands and muttered casual words that belied the moment of camaraderie.

Lia would not intrude. She crossed to the tiny fire and

motioned Speo back. He took the opportunity to rush at Paon, offering his own loyalty. Under the shelter of the cloak she bound the pouch of jewels tightly around her waist, stripped enough of the cloth loose so that she could fashion a loincloth and breast band, them wrapped the rest of it around her once more. She held the thin tunic, now nearly dry, up close to the damp wood.

"Here is the means of our signal! Give it quickly while you can! The wood will burn a little while with this to ignite it!"

At her words they all faced toward her and Paon cried, "We are agreed! I can shape the direction of the fire and the *Lily Flame* will hold as long as she can. Together we shall try!"

"Together!" This time Lia's voice rose with theirs in the affirmation of life.

Chapter Forty-Two

DAYS OF OUR DOMINION

THEY STRIPPED DOWN to the barest essentials and gathered around Paon as he drew rough pictures in the sand of the rocks, the direction of the currents and the position of the *Lily Flame*. The dead fire had blazed up in long, brilliant flame that, fanned by them all, had elicited one feeble light in response from their ship. It went without saying that their pursuers must have seen the fire as they would have in any event. They truly had little choice in the manner of their dying.

The sea still beat and the rain still poured but they could see the lights on the cliffs in the afternoon gloom; to many the sea was the better thing. Paon clasped their hands in turn before he came to Lia and stood looking down at her. There was so much to say, so much more than there was time to say it in.

His words were for her ears alone. "If there were love remaining in me, Lia, it would have been for you. As best I could, I have cared for you. Forgive me the manner of it."

She drank in the sight of his long, clean-limbed body, the dark, tossing curls and high cheekbones. Never again. "You have showed me what love is, Paon. I . . ."

He touched her lips briefly. "If we live, I will try to see you safe. Let there be nothing between us but that. If the goddess pleases and there is another life, perhaps we will be free there."

Then he thrust her toward the savage waters, he remaining to urge the rest of his men. Lia glanced upward and saw the

314

tribesmen on the cliff just overhead. One saw her and drew bead with his arrow, howling to his fellows as he did so. She whirled and ran into the waves but not before she saw Paon, sword brandished, start the upward climb. One man against the hordes! Now she knew why he urged them on. She thought to go back and fight with him but that would negate everything he had struggled for and the men might attempt to return. Resolutely, forcing her mind to acceptance, Lia plunged into the icy waters.

Now there was no time for thought, only struggle. She went far under, seeking the protecting ledge of rock Paon had mentioned. Once she gripped it and clung, the strong pull of the current was lessened and she was able to move ahead at a fairly rapid pace. Far in the distance she could see the shape of another person and could only hope that those before her had had managed as well. She kept to the rock, touching the protuberances from time to time, and thrust herself on. There was no way to know how far it went but her head was beginning to ring and lights were exploding behind her eyes. She would have to surface.

When she rose the great waves caught her, spinning her over and slamming her down into a trough that mercifully held no jagged rocks. The breath left her completely as she came up on top of another. The shore was very close but the pointed rock was off at a distance and a range of crags rose out of the stormy water close to her. She was being swept rapidly toward them. When she was tossed up again she tried to look for the *Lily Flame* but only water and crags met her gaze. She came down again, this time so close to a saw-toothed rock that her side was numbed by the force of her brushing it.

Lia summoned all her strength, caught air and held it. Then she made a long sliding dive back in the direction she came. Feet and arms and legs thrust in all the power she had used and learned on Pandos when powerful swimming and holding her breath underwater for long stretches of time had been a game. The current pulled her down into an underwater maelstrom and spewed her back. The heavy, cruel teeth snatched at her again but she thrust around them and found the ledge once more.

"Follow it out as far as you can. Stay low, coming up only when you are desperate. It will go down as if to the bottom of the world. Let go at that point and swim as hard and as straight

ahead as it is possible to go. There are quiet areas in all this
wild water. The *Lily Flame* will be close at hand to one of these
if I have been correct.''

It had sounded simple enough as Paon explained it there on
the beach with their pursuers above them. Here it was a
different matter. Even very strong swimmers could easily
perish in these waters and the rocks waited to take those who
did not drown.

Lia's hands grew raw from gripping the ledge and her breath
was giving out once more. She fought the need to rise until
everything began to grow bright and dark by turns. She rose,
snatched a gulp, was thrown back and down on her face. She
fought free to go deeper. Still alive but for how long?

There was no end to the battle. Lia knew that she had been
fantastically fortunate to escape serious injury against the rocks
and the great battering waves. If not for the ledge there would
have been no chance at all. She wondered how many of the
men were surviving.

The icy, choking water was gradually numbing her body,
vigorously though she moved. She felt her strokes becoming
shorter and her legs felt as if they did not belong to her. The
struggles upward for air were so hard that she believed each
one would be her last and was beginning not to care if it were.
Her touch on the ledge was weak as she balanced herself there.
It was thrusting deeper into what appeared a bottomless black
pit. From here on there would be nothing to guide her.

It seemed to Lia then that she saw Paon waiting for her at the
depth of that pit which seemed to lead into a garden of flowers.
His hand was held out to her and the brilliant eyes were eager.
He was calling to her, promising all the delights of love. She
opened her mouth to reply and the water gushed in. She
released her hold and hurtled upward, knowing just how close
she had come to death.

The air was the most delicious she had ever smelled or
tasted. The waves were still high and strong, but after several
blessed gulps, Lia found that she could go underwater and
swim more strongly than ever. She hoped that she was
swimming straight as he had told them to do. Was Paon dead
on the beach and even now in the netherworld, calling out to
her? Would she have joined him there? Life was still what she

wanted; Lia knew that with all the determination in her and she
would continue to fight.

She swam on and on, rising now and then to look for the
ship. There was only the lifting sea and the rain. When she
turned back to look at the shore, she could see only the great
rearing rocks and the spume of the waves.

Something brushed against her, something cold and heavy
with blood streaming from head and mouth. One of their men
whose name she did not know! One of those who had so
eagerly acclaimed Paon's idea and who now lay floating on his
back, dead in the pitiless sea. He had not missed the rocks.
Even as she floated, the body was pulled away and sent on
toward shore. Anger filled Lia but there was nothing she could
do for one already dead. She ducked down and flailed on, her
endurance lifted by what she had seen. It was as if his spirit
went with her, given another chance to survive.

Now the waves were crushing her down. Her body was
weighted with stones. It was amusing, really, that the stones
would get her after all. She started to laugh but her mouth was
buried in the heaviness around her. There was no end to it and
there never would be. She had to go on, of course, the dead
man would expect it. This swimming and floating in circles
might be taking her back to the rocks, the jagged coast, the
pressing stones.

Lia rose to the surface and forced herself to lie inert in the
waves as she drew in air. The twisting, contradictory thoughts
faded but her weariness did not. The very real possibility of
drowning was closer than ever. The rain had lessened but was
still coming in thin gray sheets. She would swim until she
could no longer do so and then go down into the depths. Was it
an easy death as she had often heard?

A huge rock was looming up just ahead. She had not thought
she was that confused. Try to pull up on it and rest? Likely this
was the shore again and the entire thing to do over. She could
not do it. Her hands slapped the water feebly as she tried to
turn her body away from the rock and back out to sea.
Something trailed across her arms and floated around her face.
When she looked down, not really caring what it was, she saw
that it was a piece of rope.

The rock was a ship that bore the carving of the goddess and
the rope came from her, thrown out by men who leaned from

her decks, straining to see in the tossing waters and rain. It was
the *Lily Flame* and Lia had won her battle.

Her cold hands wound around the rope. She jerked it and
called at the top of her voice which sounded as a mere squeak.
"Help me! I am Lia! Take me up!" She pulled herself along,
waving one hand. A man glanced down, called out something
that was whipped away by the wind and then he was diving
into the sea while, far above her, the rope ladder came down.

The sailor reached her in a few moments, saw her condition
and ordered, "Be still so that you will be able to climb." She
managed to nod and let him tow her. She was never to know
how she struggled up the ladder with her numbed hands and
feet, but the man was directly behind her, calling encouragement just as those above her were doing. Eager hands hauled
her the rest of the way and she sprawled on the deck of the *Lily
Flame*, unable to move while tears dropped on her face as
Walan, servant girl and near friend, bent over and wailed.

Lia was shortly placed on cushions in the main cabin, dry
robes around her and hooded candles giving both warmth and
light to her chilled senses. Wine burned down her throat and set
up explosions in her stomach, which found the small bits of
seed cake Walan brought more to its liking. She tried to talk
and felt her throat constrict with the effort. Walan threw yet
another cloak over her shoulders, dried her hair with a soft
cloth and spread it over her own fingers to polish each lock.

Lia jerked her head around and croaked, "Who? Who else?
Must know?"

Walan burst into tears and ran out. Lia had always been
surprised that this woman had been a bull leaper, for she was
fearful and timid now, yet the accident and penalties she had
suffered must have made her so. Her courage had surely
departed with her power of speech. Lia realized now, more
than ever, that this could have been her own fate had she fallen
before the bulls. Crete was not merciful to those who failed.

There was a sound in the doorway and she looked up to see
Nes, brother of Kra and Edon, the first traitor and the second
lost to the tribesmen, standing there. She had not been as
friendly with him and now she felt strange before him. His
brown eyes were desolated but his mouth tried to smile.

"Ten have returned, Lia. Several were beaten on the rocks
and lost much blood. They may not live. I know about my

brothers. One of them told me." He shook his head as she tried to speak. "Drink more of that wine near you. You will be all right. There is no sign of the lord commander. I think we must believe that he perished in the sea."

Lia's hand went to her mouth to ward off a cry. "No!"

Nes said, "The pirate ship remains active. She ventured too close to shore and was damaged but she can still function and is dangerous to us. Those ships are built to be quickly repaired and for best speed. We must leave with the dawn. The tribesmen have boats, too, and they know these waters. If any of us are to survive, it must be."

"Not without the lord commander! He was holding off the tribesmen as he made the rest of us go in the water." She drank several gulps of the wine and felt her throat loosen. "He cannot be dead! And what of the others? Morb, Speo. . . ? We must look for Paon!"

"Morb is well and resting. Of Speo we know nothing as yet." He came and knelt so close to her that she could see the slight puffiness of his eyes. "Paon could say little with the flashes but he gave the order to sail at dawn. Regardless of who was on board. Regardless. Bado is in command and I second. Such was the chain of command after Qeno and the lord commander himself. The last order will be obeyed."

Lia stared at him. He was her friend and he had lost two brothers. He could speak so to her and hope that she might understand. She was the priestess of the great goddess on the *Lily Flame* and the hand of that great one had preserved her for something. So Lia believed in this moment when she must hold to some vestige of help. One last thing she could offer up to the man she loved was that faith. Her chin went up as she put her fingers over those of Nes.

"The great goddess shall honor him in her halls forever. His name enters with those of the immortals and King Minos shall speak it with awe before the bull god in the Hall of Shields." Words that meant nothing and cost much to say, for they signaled a life devoid of Paon, a world in which he no longer moved to enhance it and give it meaning. "I intend to speak his name and acquaint the goddess with his feats all this night." Ritual words for the dead. She would weep for him and for herself but Nes need not know that.

"Lia. Lady priestess. We honor you." He spoke formally,

inclining his head, and then as her friend. "When you feel it is time, ask Walan for a potion to make you rest. It is a long journey to Crete and we have no means to fight the pirates. We need all the intervention of the gods that we can get. But for now, rest. We must make all speed and I am needed above. Do you wish Walan sent to you?"

"No. I must be alone."

He tried to smile and failed. "We were Paon's men, Lia. Loyalty must have seemed slight at times but to those who truly followed him, he was the model we chose." He turned swiftly and left. She heard him calling ordors on the deck in a loud voice.

Lia had thought to find the release of sleep but it would not come. It was as if what Paon had commanded out of her after the escape from the 'Dians was all she possessed. She tried to sleep but could not in spite of all her exhaustion and she wanted no dulling potion. The great image of the goddess in Knossos rose against her eyelids; the crystal eyes bored into her own as she tossed. She rose to walk about but her legs shook so much that she was forced to sit back down. The weakness was a challenge and she began to practice the stretching exercises along with the twisting motions that she used before the bull leaping. Everything reminded her of the bull arena, she thought wearily.

When the exercises palled, Lia threw herself face down on the robes and deliberately forced herself to remember every facet of her relationship with Paon. The passion, the tenderness, the battles and the misunderstandings, even his involvement with Hirath, the sharing and the cruelties, the love and the hate—all the things that made up her feeling for him. At the end she was vaguely comforted. She had known that they could never build a life together, that he belonged to Crete and Minos, if not actually to Hirath. She hated to think that his splendor had departed this world but so long as Lia of Pandos lived, so would Paon of Crete and Knossos.

She rose and went outside to breathe the fresh air sometime in the late reaches of the night. The *Lily Flame* stood off the far black mass of land as she swayed in the waves. The rain continued but it was gentler. Lia tried to identify the coast but could not and was forced to assume that they had already begun the effort to get away from the pursuing pirate ship.

Even as she watched, the distant sky was red with flames. "The land is afire with war." She could hear Paon's voice in her ears as he said it. There would be no trade here for many seasons to come.

Must she think of him constantly? His life touched hers and changed it. The very shadows reminded her of him. Had he not once kissed her there? Argued with her at that rail? Now someone limped slowly toward her, the very familiarity of the shoulders a haunting reminder. She would see him in every movement, that she knew.

The figure came closer and peered at her. The voice that could not be was saying, "They said you slept. I should have known better. When did you ever do what was expected?"

Then they were in each other's arms, welded together, mouths blending in a union beyond the flesh. In that moment the *Lily Flame* lifted her anchor and set sail for Crete.

Chapter Forty-Three

A TIME TO SHAKE THE HEART

THE ELONGATED, PRECISE characters and forms slipped down the long sheet of the scroll. Soon a fresh one must be started just as three others had been before this one. The eye was captured by phrases, smoothly written in places, twisted and curving in others. "The crew is vastly decimated but their hearts are high." "No pursuit, only the open green sea." "High, hot days in endless circles, blessed of the goddess." "The sufficient treasure." "The pillars are far past us now." "Landfall and battle. There was plague and destruction." "The sea fair before us."

"You can always tell my writing from yours. I will never make a scribe." Lia stretched, her body smooth and supple under the loose green robe the color of her eyes. She smiled across at Paon who rose and came to her as she lay on the raised couch of his cabin, her fingers tracing the lines in the latest scroll.

He bent to kiss her upturned face. "I agree. But there are other roles for you to fill. Let me see." He cupped her face in one hand and let the other stray down to her breasts. "The lord commander's lady. Ruler of the heart of Paon. Sea witch. Queen of love. My love goddess. Will those do for now?"

"As ever, the lord commander has a tongue of honey." Lia sat up abruptly and put her fingers on the hardness of his stalk, which was already rising through the brief loincloth. "And the power of a tusk of ivory. Say then that he might fill the role of lover and lover and lover. That he is the commander of love as well as of the seas. How does my lord find those roles?" She stripped away the cloth, lowered her mouth to him and drew gently, so lightly that he shuddered with eagerness.

"I want you, Lia." He whispered the words so softly that she could bearly hear. "I repeat that, do I not?"

"Again and again. And I you." "She released him and spoke so that her breath blew on the full pink tip so near her lips. Their eyes locked in darkening passion as she took him in her mouth once more; this time she used lips and tongue as she worked expertly to bring him to the first level of longing. Her fingers moved under him, massaging and pulling so that he came longer and harder with every motion. He swayed toward her as his body began to jerk in the first spasm.

Lia moved back a little, letting go of him with a practiced slowness that was nearly pain. The film on his tip shone as she touched it with her little finger. Then, very deliberately, she loosed the robe and allowed it to fall. Paon reached over and, without holding her, kissed and sucked on her nipples as she had done to his stalk. They rose, hard and turgid, while the great pulsations began to beat in her.

Paon drew her close then and their mouths fastened together, tongues writhing and twisting as their bodies wove a rhythm of hunger. Lia's hands squeezed his buttocks. His worked in the wetness of her triangle to coax, push and lure. She felt the drowning sweetness and struggled against it. She did not want it to come too soon; it must be prolonged to the very last instant of endurance.

Now he was turning her so that her buttocks faced him. His mouth trailed kisses along her back and sides, returning to her neck and coming down. Then he held her firmly, spread her and entered, thrusting gently at first and harder until the strange spasms shook them in a sensation that was fullness, pain and pleasure. He withdrew still hard. The core of expectancy held them.

A tub of cool water scented with spices awaited them and they plunged into it, washing each other and kissing at the same time. He kissed her nipples, buried his face in her hair and sat very still while she tickled his back and rained kisses up it. Her hand touched his firmness and the power of her fingers caused him to writhe.

"I can hold only a little longer." His smile was wry, his eyes so brilliantly blue that they shaded toward purple. "By the goddess, you are beautiful!"

"No fairer than my lord." She used the ritual words of song and tale but they were very truth to her and he knew it.

"Come." He drew her from the water and dried them both with a length of white cloth. Then, standing, he thrust deeply into her again and again.

Lia swayed toward him, impaled and hungry for it, twisting so that he might penetrate the harder. They separated to his length and came together so hard that the flesh shivered with the impact. Then again and again until the world came down to burning fleshly passion, deep-tongued kisses and hands that could not get enough of the other.

Lia felt the rising and the final thrust that could not be held back. She was tumbling in spaces beyond her dreams, falling into darkness, collapsing and floating in the light of peace. Paon held her tightly as they slipped to the floor in total exhaustion, united in the one flesh.

Later, in the half-dreaming relaxation as they caressed each other, touched softly and murmured together in syllables of tender meaning, Lia let her mind go backward to that night when they left the shores of the cold land of death. It would never bear any other name for her. Paon had been taken on board the *Lily Flame* only a short time earlier, miraculously wounded in only the leg and shoulder. His powerful body and endurance had saved his life and those of most of his men, for he had managed to delay the tribesmen until all the others had left. They feared his swinging sword and battle cries, not knowing that only one man remained. Six of his men had drowned; five others died of the beatings against the rocks and from loss of blood. The crew of the *Lily Flame* was barely enough to maintain her and their route for Crete was planned by Paon and his officers with many stops in mind. At one of these they found the pirate ship lying in wait. There was a slight skirmish and prisoners were taken. The plague had broken out among the remaining pirates, many of whom died in agony. The *Lily Flame* waited until all danger was past and the prisoners were then used as oarsmen. After that better speed was made. The pirates told them of the fate some of their members suffered, burned in cages of wood that were hoisted into trees and slowly set afire while the occupants yet lived. That horror haunted their nightmares as well.

"What are you thinking to lie so quietly, Lia?" Paon rose on one elbow and twisted her golden hair around his fingers as he smiled down at her, white teeth flashing against his tanned skin.

"Of how very fortunate we have been, after all." She sighed. "So many dead, but we have mourned them, spoken their names before the goddess and will do so before Minos. We still live, my love, and we bring treasure with us as well as a great tale. And there is still much time ahead of us, is it not so?"

He sat up and clasped his knees. "We have so much to remember, Lia. Those islands where we swam and made love on the beaches, the sunrises on the edge of the forests, the calm here on the ship and our times together, the unity we have all known—things to remember always." Paon turned around to face her. "You have to know. We are not far from Crete. The winds have been good and the pirates are good oarsmen."

She could not speak for a long moment. She remembered as he did. There was the memory of his face over hers in the early light as he spoke of their passion, the golden noons when they ran and played together as the *Lily Flame* rose at anchor against the horizon, their secret forays into the woods in search of herbs and flowers, the times when they were young together as they had never been before, the nights when they wrote in the scrolls that would be set before Minos as the historical account of their journey, the camaraderie when they and the men sang, drank and laughed on this slow, easy journey to the homeland.

He had called her brave. Nothing would test that bravery more than the words she would now say. Nothing would be harder to keep than the assurances she must now make. Her chin went up as always when she had to face the unbearable. Paon's eyes grew an even darker blue as he watched and she took an instant to be thankful that he reacted so toward her.

"I know what you must say, Paon. I will say if for you so that there can be no misunderstandings between us. You must deal with Hirath in your own way for your son's sake and that of Crete as well because of the responsibility the king has placed in you. Her power is great, I know, and you must be free."

He held up one hand. "The difficulty is that I have not fulfilled the mission. There is no trade established and Crete must look elsewhere for her tin. We bear the jewels of the 'Dians, fabulous as they are, and the strange story of them and the marvels we saw, what we endured, all that, but there is little honor in Crete for failure. Minos is my friend but he laid duties on me from the very mouth of the bull god and the great goddess. I have enemies." He lifted an expressive shoulder. "That is the danger. I will see you safe, Lia, but I do what I must with Hirath and for my son."

"I understand, Paon. When we land in Crete, it is done between us."

"It must be, Lia." Their eyes met and did not waver. Then he rose to dress while she lay staring at the ceiling.

Lia had thought herself resigned to what must be but the passion and sharing of their many days together left her bereft now that reality had come. Paon spent long stretches of time gazing out into the sea or pacing up and down on the deck. He took many turns at the oars as they all did, for the *Lily Flame* was still short-handed even with the help of the prisoners. Lia envied him the escape of hard work; she practiced the exercises of the bull leapers for lack of anything else to do and wrote in her ever-improving Minoan on the scrolls of their long journey. When she and Paon came together now in lovemaking, they sought each other hungrily, desperately and with no time for the lightness that had helped to make them comrades. Now since they were man and woman who must part, every sensation and every emotion of the flesh must be savored, drained, sucked dry. The nights ran together in fevered eagerness. They spoke little; mouths, hands and bodies sampled, drew and returned to stoke the mounting fires that were never to be slaked. Lia and Paon bore the stamps of each other in the softly bruised flesh under their eyes and the occasional marks of their lips. They were haunted by the ending that approached and still they knew the inevitability of it.

They still played together with the old gaiety now and then. One hot afternoon when the wind was calm and the ship was propelled slowly by the oarsmen taking their turns, some of the men jumped overboard to chase others in the water and shout challenges to those watching. These were not thought to be shark waters but a careful guard was maintained by Paon's order. He, like his men, felt the need for release before Crete and duty.

Now he encouraged Lia to jump into his arms and laughed when she shot straight through them into the green depths. Her golden hair spread out around her and the thin tunic was molded to her form. He came in pursuit, a dark water god in search of the nymph who eluded him. They swam back and forth in a game that was also not a game. Lia surfaced and found the men taking bets on how long it would take him to catch her. She took the air and went deep, pretending to drift there, watching the ship, a far shadow on the sunlit surface.

He came down, reaching for her. She dove at him, circled and rose. He touched her ankle and his fingers slipped away. Then she was climbing up the rope ladder and rushing to take shelter before the carved figure of the goddess. Paon caught her just before she could place her hand on it. He whirled her into his embrace, kissing her before them all.

"Mine by right of conquest!" The words were for her ears alone, and for an instant the laughter was back in his voice.

"But the fortress was free to you long ago!" She took his hand and they ran to his cabin, heedless of the amused laughter that followed them.

That afternoon their love was protracted and tender, filled with gentleness and slow kisses as they drew the heart from themselves. Lia dared to use the endearments of "dear love" and "darling"; Paon returned them to her and in this time apart from both loss and gain they came to be the richer. Past and future were held in abeyance. There was only time for the present. They slept and loved, woke to love again. The *Lily Flame* lay on the green waters, so did they lie with each other in the matchless fulfillment they did not expect would come again.

It was late the next evening when the call came for Paon. The lookout bawled for all to hear, "Lord Commander! Lord commander! The mainland is yonder! We are for Crete! Crete!"

Paon turned to take leave of Lia and saw that she had risen to stand beside him. She was pale but composed; part of her had already retreated. He, too, had retreated, was now the lord commander of the *Lily Flame*. No longer lovers nor gamesters, they were people who would do what they must.

"How far now, Paon?"

"He means the first landmark but I must go and be sure. I would say another three days. We must make all speed, of course."

"Of course." She kept her face a mask. No emotion must show.

It was natural and expected that the commander of a voyage such as theirs would bed the priestess of the goddess; the reverse would have been thought strange. Reports going to Hirath and Minos would reveal that Paon had acted properly. He had been seen to be angry with Lia, thinking that she had thrust herself into the voyage, yet he had overcome his antipathy to her. The men would speak of it in this manner also. Only to Minos would Paon reveal the truth and demand protection for Lia. This much he had revealed to her of his method after he knew how he stood with the ruler, his friend. "The less you know, the better. That is for your protection. I may seem to cleave to Hirath, Lia, but you have given light to my days. Remember that in the times when the shadow of the snake seems to dominate all. It may be that Hirath and I must fall together. So be it."

Paon had spoken those words to her early one morning in the days of their drugging hunger. He had forbidden her to speculate or answer him, and seeing the depths of his pain, she had obeyed. She recalled those words many times in the short time before the *Lily Flame* approached her home waters. The truth of them was hard to admit. It was easier to think that this was the near declaration of a love that Paon must not admit. Only in the legends was true love ever actually won, Lia thought bitterly.

The night was still dark when Walan woke Lia. She had slept alone this last night before Crete and they had selected her clothes the day before. Now she put all thoughts of Paon and what they had shared from her mind. She entered now on what might prove to be a struggle for her own life and she must be ready.

With Walan's help she washed and dressed in the deceptively simple white gown, which left arms and slim legs bare but showed the slenderness of her waist and the full bosom. A green cloak of shimmering gauze, taken from the pirate ship, hung over her shoulders and gave back the exact shade of her eyes. Leather sandals set with green stones were on her feet. Walan bound the golden hair back from her forehead and fastened it in a crown of braids that emphasized Lia's straight nose and curving lips. When she looked into the small section of copper that was her mirror, Lia saw the new maturity of her face, the high arch of her darkened brows and the faint shadows of her cheekbones. The goddess had reason to think her servant fair.

Paon, clad all in blue, dark curls rioting above his carved, impassive face, nodded correctly at her and returned to his duties. The men, eager for home as they were, were silent at this moment of return. Lia went to stand beside the figure of the goddess just as the last curtain of darkness lifted and they looked ahead over the shimmering water.

Lia's heart rose up in exaltation at the beauty of this land. The great mountain lifted white into the sky and the green forests poured around the base. Valleys folded into each other, houses were white smudges in the distance and the harbor was filled with ships of all sizes.

While yet a long distance off, Paon commanded that the golden and white banner of the goddess be broken out. As it streamed over their heads and into the flower-scented wind, his eyes locked with Lia's in an unspoken salute. The first rays of the sun touched the banner and moved on to Lia, then spread over the *Lily Flame*.

So it was that the expedition of the great goddess returned to Knossos of Crete after many trials and vicissitudes.

Chapter Forty-Four

THE ROSE CROWN

ONCE AGAIN LIA went over the road to Knossos from the harbor village. The first time she had traveled in caution and secrecy; this time she came in honor with the men of the *Lily Flame* behind her and Paon striding ahead of the procession formed of excited people of the two towns. Some hastily assembled priests walked with them. There were drummers, pipers and players of the lyre as well as some tumblers and dancers who went before the banner of the goddess, hastily taken from the ship so that it could be borne with honor before Minos.

When she glanced about, Lia saw that there were signs of a recent upheaval in the earth. Several houses along the road had tumbled into each other and a gaping crack in the ground was visible nearby. An inn she vaguely recalled was now only a pile of rubble and a huge stone lay in the center of it. Trees were twisted back on themselves, some of their branches appeared burned. Now that she thought of it, the stones of the harbor had been just off balance enough so that the *Lily Flame* had to be left farther out in the deep water than was convenient for landing. Some of those who cheered them had bruised hands and faces. She listened to the calls and was vaguely disturbed.

"It is a sign of her returning favor! The goddess has brought them safely back. A good omen!"

"Great Minos will intercede for us!"

"The bull shakes himself! He is angry and must be fed!"

They went on over the paved road, through the hills, always to the sounds of cheers, and looked at last on the House of the Labrys, shining and serene above the lesser dwellings of Knossos and the ones of the nobles. The mighty columns surged upward in red, black and yellow, glowing against the paler stones. Flowers, vines and trees melted into the whole. Palace, hill and grounds seemed to grow out of each other—a place where the gods might dwell. But here, too, were signs of the displeasure of those gods: a colonnade shifted awry, part of a roof slipping down, a tumbled flower bed, uprooted trees. Slaves worked on these but they were slow and overseers stood by.

The people were held back by guards as the palace was neared. Now a tall priest robed all in yellow with snakes of gold climbing up his arms paused before Paon. Others moved slowly out to join him and guards walked behind.

"Who comes to the court of Minos of Crete?" The question was low in tone, picked up in chorus by the priests.

Paon crossed both arms over his chest and inclined his head. "I, Paon, sent by the king on a mission to the cold lands and returned, by favor of the goddess!"

There was a long silence then. Lia stood very still, her chin raised. The feeling of discomfort was growing. Her head ached slightly and the air seemed heavy, yet the day was golden and beautiful with a soft wind blowing. She was nervous about their reception by Minos and the dread of seeing Hirath, that was all. These were only ritual responses. Soon they would be admitted. She shifted from one foot to another and it seemed that the ground went with her. No one else had noticed but she was reminded of the earth movements she had known on Pandos. The signs of that activity here made her uneasy all over again.

"Have you accomplished that for which you were sent forth?" The priest had a long, thin face and a corpulent body but he gained a certain awed respect as he gazed at those before him and then toward the sky as if to speak with the goddess herself.

"Great Minos laid the charge upon me and it is to him that I shall answer." Paon's voice was respectful but hard.

"You accept his judgment in the matter? You will obey him in all things?"

"Yes. I swore an oath to him in the Hall of Shields."

Lia would have sworn that there was jubilation in the priest's words. He called loudly, "All of you have heard the proper obedience of Paon, Lord Commander, Friend of Minos, Harrier of the Pirates, Royal Friend! Let him enter!"

Paon moved forward and she started after him along with the rest of the men. The guards moved forward in one simultaneous motion, swords instantly raised. The tall priest said, "None but the lord commander may enter. All others remain outside."

Paon snapped, "What foolishness is this? When he is not in meditation King Minos has always allowed the people access to him and his court! These are my people who have suffered and endured with me. It is their right to come!"

"Not so. The king has been forced to moderate his own liberality; he has to consider his health and the demands on his time. I will allow the woman to come with you. The others remain." The priest folded his arms and gazed at Paon. "That is the decree."

Paon turned to Lia and said, "Come, Lady. We must obey." To his men, he called out, "Await our return. It may be that the king will come out to you after I have told him of your bravery."

They shouted with pleasure and Paon laughed with them. Only Lia did not smile. The sense of doom was pressing down upon her more heavily than ever and the air burned in her nostrils. She thought, strangely, of all the many times she and Paon had made love in the past moons and wondered if she might be with child. That would account for these feelings. But she had been perfectly well on the *Lily Flame* and at the harbor.

They were all staring at her as if expecting her to speak. Hastily she said, "I am eager to pay our respects to the great king and to honor the goddess in her temple."

"Most wise. Most commendable." The priest smiled at her in a way that reminded her of Zarnan and stood aside, motioning them to come. The guards and priests fell into perfect lines and together Lia and Paon entered the House of the Axe.

A slender, dark-haired young man immediately descended upon them. Several serving maids were behind him. This part of the palace was dim after the brilliance outside and some of the life-size frescoes on the walls seemed to move in the shadows. The man, dressed in yellow and gleaming with golden ornaments about his small waist, cried, "You must be prepared to meet with the king! The dust of travel has to be removed and you are wearing no jewels! Shocking!"

Paon smothered a spurt of laughter. "It does not matter to the king. He thinks little of such things. The tale we have to tell will be jewels enough, although we bring those also."

"You must be prepared." He came close to Paon. "That is the rule, new since your time."

Paon allowed them to lead him away. Lia, following her own escort, felt a pang. He was the only familiar thing in this place of danger. Something was wrong and she knew it. She only wondered that he did not feel it, he who had lived and worked here for so long.

Lia was taken to an anteroom where servants waited with warm water, chests of garments and sparkling jewels. They came toward her in a quick rush, chattering as a flock of birds might. She waved them back, remembering what she carried in the green pouch half concealed under her cloak.

"If you must bring something to me, get bread and wine. I am faint with hunger." She was not but she did not want to stand there under their watchful eyes until the time came for her to be called. "I go as I am, unadorned, to stand before the king. It is a vow and a promise, made in adversity."

They protested, but only slightly, eyeing her with no little suspicion. Lia gazed at herself in the long polished mirror that had been brought and knew that, whatever others thought, she was fairer than she had ever been. Excitement made her skin pink and the green depths of her eyes were bright. Her long slender form showed well in the clinging robe and her breasts rose high, quivering with her movements. Her face was a clear oval marked by the determined chin.

"Lady, look at this jewel. See how fair it is and how well it would become you." The serving girl held out an emerald set with pearls into the design of a lily. "Only one jewel."

Lia lifted her hand to take the bauble and the floor suddenly rocked so that she had to struggle to maintain her balance. The servants glanced at each other with horrified expressions. Lia's mouth went dry and her temples hammered with pain. The great bull was stretching; the gods were angered and the land would turn over. She had never seen a truly large quiver of the earth but the old legends were frightening. Sweat beaded her forehead and the young servant came to touch a damp cloth to it.

"Has this happened often lately?" She was amused to see that they did not press anything else on her. Perhaps they believed the goddess spoke through the ground. Perhaps she had. The errant thought flickered through Lia's mind and was gone.

"Many times in the last moon. The time of the judgment of the gods is near, or so says my husband's old father who has seen Minos come and Minos go." The girl spoke abstractedly, realized what she had said and backed away, her face thin with fear.

Lia wanted to ask what she meant but there was no time. The door swung back to reveal four priests, immaculate and remote in white stamped with gold, and five ceremonial guards, double axes in their hands.

"Great Minos awaits you!" They called out as one.

"I am ready."

Lia had thought to be taken to the throne room with its alabaster throne and representations of mighty beasts, but instead they wound through dark passages, up and down several stairways, around an open area and crossed a sunken yard to enter a doorway set in solid stone which opened with the touch of a finger.

The room beyond sprang into bold relief. Snakes twined with fish, lions and maidens walked together, bull leapers continued their deadly games, strange and fearful beasts copulated, the bull god roared soundlessly and the great goddess watched a savage sacrifice with joy on her face. The frescoes were so real that they dominated everything at the first glance. Columns of red and gold supported the ceiling which was painted the exact shade of sea foam. A gold-ornamented throne with a high back and arm rests of alabaster stood near the fresco of the goddess. Several priests stood close to it, their faces pale in the flickering light of many candles which shone off the jewels they wore. One of them, his small eyes triumphant, was Zarnan.

But Lia's gaze could take in little except the figure on the throne. Minos was shrouded from neck to feet in a cloak of shimmering golden cloth worked in so many jewels that the very eye was blinded by them. The bull mask was set on his head and the crystal stare did not waver. His hands wore hoof gloves woven with pearls inlaid with rubies. On his head and circling the onyx horns was a crown of what first appeared to be actual roses. Instead it was made of rubies, so cunningly wrought that each petal stood out in perfection, and the gleaming centers were of solid gold. It was the loveliest thing Lia had ever seen. She could almost smell the sweet odor of the flowers. Almost against her will she looked up to the fresco of the goddess and saw that she was crowned with that same rose crown. She had never seen the goddess so.

Now Paon entered from another door. His face was set and proud against the white mantle that had been flung over his shoulders and a headband of brilliant blue stones held back the unruly curls. An armlet of blue and gold had been set on his left arm and a sword set with the bull image hung around his waist. He started forward but was held back by Zarnan, who stepped before him.

"Where is your respect? Kneel before the king!" His thin face was sleeker than it had been and his grin was savage. He exuded power.

Lia, standing in the background with those who had brought her, saw the surprise cross Paon's face. He would not protest before the king, although he must have expected a private audience and welcome from his friend. Now he murmured something and sank to the floor. A hand pushed on Lia's shoulder and she did likewise.

"Rise, Paon. Rise, girl. Tell me, has your mission been fulfilled? You were not gone the allotted span of time that you were given. Speak, my time is short." The voice was hollow, booming with an odd cadence doubtless caused by the bull mask. Paon hesitated and it came again. "Speak out. All here are to be trusted. Obey!"

Thus ordered, Paon stood erect and gave a swift version of their voyage, the storms and the perils encountered. As he spoke the earth trembled and the frescoes seemed to come alive. Lia saw the sudden stiffening of those around Minos but he paid no attention and they were forced to remain quiet. She felt the horror rise again when Paon mentioned the stones but he moved swiftly over the 'Dians to come to the failure to complete the contract with the tin traders. He was frank and open in front of the priests; it was as though he were alone with Minos. Lia saw Zarnan grin wolfishly and feared for them both.

Then Paon turned and called for her to come forward. "Here is the treasure we bring." He sketched out the tale of the 'Dians as Veret-Sant had told it to Lia, imbuing it with a fascination that could not fail to lure the dullest. Then he paused and Lia drew out the jeweled collar with the radiating stones and the magnificent interlocked ruby. The ring with the eye and the snake shone up, a symbol of the power of dead Jies. The black 'Dian ornaments that told the tale of those wanderers and waited to be deciphered glittered in the mixture of the packed treasure of that race.

"Specific charges were laid on you Paon and on this woman. You have not performed as you were bidden." Zarnan stepped to Minos's side and held up a hand. "I know you have explained and you were always swift with a tale. But the gods are affronted that you did not keep to the letter of the mission. The matter will be weighed and you may be punished. The woman will go into the temple of the snakes in the hills. Such is the decree."

"Is that the will of Minos?" Paon stared straight into the eyes of the bull mask. "I obey, of course, but I have served Crete long and faithfully. Perhaps it would be as well if I retire from the court and from the hand of my king. I am no longer lord commander, nor do I wish that again." He kept his voice low and soft; it was as if he thought aloud and there was a hint of wonder in his voice. Once he glanced back at Lia and she was surprised by the gentleness in his face. "Once I saved the life of the king. You will remember, my friend, and later I fought for you in the councils. I would ask favor now in two things."

"Speak on." The hollow voice was lower now. The amusement on Zarnan's face was fading. The air in the ornate room was heavy and dry.

"That I be allowed to leave the court and live apart as the other noblemen do. That I may be allowed to wed and rear my children in peace." Paon bent his head once, then lifted it and faced Minos. "That I may have the woman of my choice and none oppose it. Three things, actually." He smiled into the crystal brilliance. "We spoke of these things before but now I find that I am less ambitious for power. I have made a choice as all men must."

Lia felt sickness roil in her stomach. He spoke to soothe the priests and Zarnan who hated him. Paon was one of the lodestones of this court, she knew. He had chosen Hirath and all she meant for his own power.

"I grant all that you ask, Paon. You shall wed the lady Hirath and serve me still. There was no need to speak of leaving. I am well aware of all that goes on here."

Paon said, "The king has given his word that I shall have the woman of my choice?"

"I have said so before the great goddess!" Minos rose and one gloved hand went to the bull mask. "It is done!"

"Then, Lord Minos, I claim your royal word! The woman of my choice, the woman whom I claim to be my wife, is Lia of Pandos, whom I love!"

Lia felt the world tremble as she looked at Paon. He came to her and took her hands in his. The blue eyes were clear and steady as she nodded, unable to speak for the choking in her throat.

The bull roar of thwarted rage rang through the chamber and the priests as well as the guards dashed for safety. Zarnan alone moved nearer to Minos as he rose and lifted the rose-crowned mask from his head.

King Minos of Crete was Hirath.

Chapter Forty-Five

THE DOUBLE AX

LIA STOOD AMAZED as Hirath set the mask down and drew the gloves from her hands. Her blue-black hair was wound with rubies and the pallor of her skin was accentuated by the touches of white at her temples. The magnificent breasts were bare, captured in a harness of gold underneath. Snake bracelets were wound on her arms. The short skirt was emblazoned with the bullhorns. She seemed authority incarnate as she surveyed them, lips curling a little, the brilliant eyes icy with rage.

"Where is the king? Where is Minos?" Paon's hands bit into Lia's shoulders.

"You speak to King Minos at this very moment." Zarnan's gaze flicked to Hirath and back again to Lia.

"Where is he?" Paon put his fingers on the hilt of his sword just as Hirath waved Zarnan to silence.

Her deepened voice rang through the room as though it were some fearful bell. "The Minos whom you knew and whose friend you were is dead, Paon. He was sacrificed to the bull god and the great goddess on the mountain not long after you left. The earth tremors had begun, the poisons of the land flowed out and the sacred herds were decimated. The crops began to fail and there was no rain. The court factions plotted more than ever and all he did was retreat. The goddess spoke to me and I acted. In the night we took him and at dawn he met the death. I was designated in his place and now rule as Minos;

338

my authority is absolute. I am upheld by gods and the priests alike. I am Minos!"

"You murdered him!" Loathing rang through every fiber of his voice.

"Performed the will of the goddess." Her smile was terrible. "I will forget all that you said regarding this girl here and she can go to the temple unharmed. You, Paon, may become my royal consort, giver of the seed, honored of the ruler. Naturally I shall take other men to my couch; I am fruitful as Minos should be. But you, bold one, are first. If you choose to command the fleet you may do that; if you wish to sit one head lower than I myself in my councils you may do that also. I plan to build up the power of this land and send her men forth to conquer. We shall take the tin mines! We shall go to Egypt and the lands beyond! The power of Crete can be unlimited and my sons shall rule after me! Come, Paon, are you not glad that I have taken my true destiny?"

"I know you, Hirath. Lia would not live to set foot in the temple. Her life is safe nowhere in Crete while you have power. Your given word is as a wine bladder punctured by swords. I call you liar and murderess! I will have none of it!"

Hirath gave a sharp order and the guards flowed back in to ring Lia and Paon. She said, "I think you forget something you hold most precious and I do not speak of this woman. I can give the orders for . . ."

"Our son is dead. Naris told me just after I arrived in the palace. We only had time for a quick word. In my grief I brushed him away. I think he wanted to tell me of your assumption of power." He raised his voice so that all could hear. "The so-called virgin who bore a child while she served the goddess and sought thereafter to threaten me with his death. Did you kill him, Hirath?"

The lovely face grew ugly. "With my hands I strangled him! As I should have done with that hideous Naris! I hate ugliness, Paon! I thought you would turn eagerly to me when the old Minos was out of the way and all that foolishness about the child was done. I kept Naris about for baiting and he found out. Ugly, useless thing!"

Paon let his eyes drift over Zarnan and his lips quirked downward. Lia sensed the coiled fury of him and put her hand on his arm. His composure was a mask that would fall at any instant.

Hirath burst into laughter. "Ah, no, Paon. You miss the mark there. Zarnan is my half brother. He is also my lover. He saw your interest in the outlander girl from the first and tried to warn me. I must confess that I did not believe it. I still cannot. But I am Minos now and that is sufficient."

"Let Lia go, Hirath." Paon shook Lia's hand from his arm.

"No. She goes to the goddess. It will please the people and it will please me!"

"Set her free and I will remain with you." The words were flat but there was no doubting his sincerity.

She laughed again. "What bargain is that? I can do what I please with both of you." Zarnan whispered in her ear and both laughed harder. "My brother has some fascinating suggestions of great concern to the goddess. I believe we will try them on the girl."

The faint tremor came once again and they righted themselves as if they were growing used to it. Lia tried to believe that all this was happening but it was unreal here in this gorgeous room face-to-face with her enemies and the man she loved who had declared his own love.

"Of course you can do what you please, Hirath. King Minos." Paon deliberately corrected himself and then walked closer to her. "But how would you command passion, the desire of the body that breeds strong? If I walked willingly at your side, lay so in your bed and assumed the role that you ordained, what then? When I give my word, I obey it."

Desire swam in Hirath's eyes and her full mouth went loose for the briefest instant. "Would you do so?"

"Will you free her?"

"Answer me first." She put a long finger on his cheek and scratched lightly. He did not flinch.

"The *Lily Flame* waits in the harbor. My men are just outside. Let that ship take her to Eqypt and return safely. My men will bear witness that she will not be harmed and will have enough coins or jewels to keep her well. Then I will swear loyalty of body and mind to Minos of Crete."

"By the gods! Do not do it! Give them both to the goddess in sacrifice! He flouts your authority!" Zarnan shrieked with rage.

Lia found her voice. "I cannot accept such a sacrifice of you, Paon. Your life would be destroyed if you were forfeit to this murderess who dares to call herself Minos! The goddess is profaned by her service!"

The bull roar rang again through the chamber and a dagger flashed by Lia to fall on the floor with a ringing sound. Hirath's laughter spurted out. "How amusing it would be to kill you slowly, very slowly!" She stepped down from the throne and walked slowly over to where Paon stood. In one hand she held the mate to the dagger she had thrown at Lia. Now she lifted it and lightly touched the glittering point to Paon's chin. "Your little outlander does not wish to live without you, it seems?"

Paon said, "Then you and I will escort her to the ship and make sure it sails. When I know from my captain that Lia is safe in Egypt, I am your man, heart and mind, forever." He turned his head under the thrusting blade and Lia saw the cords in his neck stand out with the effort to remain calm. "Go, Lia. Tell me that you will."

The earth swung slowly again and righted itself. The ache in Lia's head intensified. Never had she felt such hatred for any mortal as for this woman who had warped Paon's life, destroyed his son and now wished to rend Crete apart. She said, "You are an abomination to this land, Hirath. Do you think that he could hold you in his arms and not remember that you stink of the death you have wrought? How do you know that you can bear strong sons? The child breeds of the mother and often takes her nature. What monster might you bring forth, Hirath?" The unease that Lia had always felt around Hirath or at any mention of her had suddenly come clear for her. That high-strung nature, the swings of mood into laughter and cruelty, the rolling eyes and the continual excitement she exuded: the face of an old woman in the mainland village came back to Lia and she remembered what the children had done and enjoyed doing. She also recalled her father's words. A long ago incident. How could it help them now?

"Lia, be silent. I order it." Paon had dared to lay hands on Hirath but she jerked away from him and now swayed back and forth, smiling as the rage built in her eyes.

"I take no orders from you, Paon!" Lia made herself stand boldly, a little suggestively, as she touched her breasts and stomach. "We have lain together, Hirath, many times in the voyage from the cold land. I may even now hold his child inside me. Do you think you are the only woman who has lured him? Who can lure him? I called him to me as I wished and he came even when exhausted from the night's passion. You must command him; I made him wish to come. Ah, yes, Hirath, I think you will breed monsters!"

It was enough and more. The beautiful face collapsed into such a mask of violence that the guards near them drew back. Hirath screamed, "Take her, destory her! The vile slut!"

Lia let her voice ring upward in a high call that made her own ears hurt. "Monster and bearer of monsters! With your own brother you will lie and produce them! Abomination!"

Hirath started for Lia who stepped back. Her eyes rolled back in her head and she began to jerk. Her hands flew out as she collapsed on the floor with groans and her heels hammered. Foam emerged from her lips. She was limp in one breath and stiff the next. Zarnan gazed at her in horror. Then he rushed to her side and, with the skill of practice, began to loosen the clenched teeth. He was moaning under his breath.

"You both will die for this! Guards, I command you in the name of Minos to take them!"

Paon's sword flashed out and he leaped in front of Lia. Their glances met and clung in an intimacy so strong that the violent scene before them seemed to fade. There was no reality now but their mutually acknowledged love. Then the guards were upon them and Paon's sword was slashing out in the fruitless struggle that could have but one end.

A guard caught Lia off balance and she tumbled to the floor. Zarnan still knelt over the prostrate Hirath but his savage eyes told their destruction. Her fingers closed on the dagger Hirath had thrown earlier and she came up with it, thrusting deep into the arm that tried to pull her away.

"By the goddess, you shall not take me so easily!"

There was a sudden roar from above, the floor rose slantingly and the wall of frescoes with the figure of the great goddess watching the sacrifice tilted inward to fall on Zarnan and Hirath. Several of the priests and guards who had not ventured close were also consumed in the pouring stone.

Paon flung both arms around Lia and rolled to the very edge of the doorway. They clutched each other, expecting their lives to end with the next rumble of the earth. Instead there was the crackle of flame and some wailing matched with curses. One of the guards who had been fighting them sat up close by and stared with fear.

"Leave them alone! The goddess protects her!" Then he was crying out the words and laughing at the same time as he wiped blood from his arms.

"We must go!" Paon whispered the words in her ear as he helped Lia to rise.

"Where?" Her head was clearing now and the air was fresher even in this rubble.

"Away from this place!" His hands were urgent as he drew her on into the corridors of the palace.

There was less damage here but people were running and screaming, some pausing to cry aloud to the goddess and the bull god, all those of heaven and the netherworld. Some were stunned and quiet as they looked at the cracked walls of the palace which might crumble at any moment. In the scurry it was easy for Lia and Paon to move out into one of the courtyards that had sustained little damage. Just beyond them was the wide expanse of grass and flowering shrubs and beyond that was the road to the harbor.

They rested together for a brief instant. The smell of smoke was rising and from somewhere back in the palace there came another crash punctuated by screams. The wall beside them swayed as the earth rolled. A ragged hymn to the goddess was begun and then abruptly snapped off.

"Lia, we have to leave Crete. My king was all that kept them from warring among themselves; the dissolute and the purists, the decadent and the aggressors will blame each other and there will bloodshed, sacrifices. Those who supported Minos will die." His face was haggard and covered with dust but the brilliant eyes were intense on her face. "You do understand?"

"I will go with you anywhere, Paon. You know that." She would not state the obvious, that much of his life was spent here and the ties binding him were still powerful. There could be no disputing the truth of what he said.

"Leave this place. It is dangerous. Hirath and Zarnan are dead under the goddess. There will be many omens to make of that." The rich, warm voice spoke at their elbows and the familiar, hideous face of Naris shone up at them.

Paon started to speak but Naris beckoned them on. He was hooded but there was a strange authority in the small figure which made him taller. Once out in the open air, they headed for some flowering bushes at the edge of the road. From this place it was easy to see the damage the Palace of the Labrys had suffered and also that the city of Knossos had been severely shaken.

"Things will settle down. This proves the goddess was angered by Hirath's assumption of power." Naris pushed back his hood and grinned at Paon. "In fact, now may be the time to pass along information to some of those who were her rivals. . . ." He sobered abruptly at their expressions. "It is a way to survive and I am very good at survival. Life here has not been easy since Hirath ruled. Friends murdered, ears listening to the slightest conversations, all done in the name of the goddess. She was evil, that one."

The day was warm and clear now. The flowering fronds blew against Lia's face and she raised her hand to pick one. In the midst of death, she and Paon still lived. All her senses expanded in deliverance.

Paon was saying, " . . . go. It is best. We will be blamed for this, I am sure.

Lia turned toward them. "Where do we go? And how?"

"The *Lily Flame* still waits in the harbor. Our journey back was easy enough and I am sure that those of my men who are unwed and seek adventure will come with us. Egypt is a wide land and another pharaoh sits on the throne now. It will be bitter to leave Crete but there is no choice."

The pain in his voice twisted Lia's heart. The old longing to comfort came to her but she thrust it back and spoke boldly. "The madness here will pass and Crete will still rule the seas. When that time comes, my dear love, we can return."

Naris looked out at the road and back at them. "I know many of your men, stout fellows. Go to the ship and I will send them to you." His voice took on a firmer timbre and rang with pride. "You have not always trusted me. Why should you now? I am one of those who works for the time when this fair island will no longer be torn as she has been, even under your friend, King Minos. I have not always found the things I had to do pleasant but when I call, will you come, Paon, and you, Lia?"

"We will." It was Lia who answered for them both. Neither doubted that day would come.

After Naris vanished in the crowd, Paon and Lia walked swiftly along the road that led to the sea. They mingled with the crowds, seeing that the damage of the earth tremors was less extensive than it had at first appeared. The palace still shone on the hill but now the glow was baleful. After one look backward, they did not turn again.

"Why did you taunt Hirath so? She was capable of having you killed in that moment." Paon held her hand as they moved and tenderness, now allowed freedom, shone in his eyes. "I wanted to make sure you were safe and after Naris told me about my son, I felt there was little to lose since she took the power. The true king would have understood. I wanted to ask for you before them all."

Sometime Lia would tell him just what that asking had meant to her. When they were alone she would show him with all the stored-up love of her heart. Now she said, "When I was a child in the mainland village, there was an old woman who could be provoked into having such episodes as Hirath did today. She had that same wild look, the swings of mood and the glittering eyes. She would go completely out of herself, foam and toss. We thought it funny at the time. It was thought she was possessed of the gods. My father, Medo, said she balanced between madness and sanity in those spells and could be tipped in either direction. I simply wanted to distract Hirath with the piercing voice and those accusations, wild as they were. It was a measure to gain time, another moment of life, Paon."

He smiled down at her and his eyes took on a far-seeing look. "Perhaps the worshipers of the great goddess are not wholly wrong, Lia. She is life and death, giver and destroyer, love and hate. She has been all things to us."

Lia thought of the crystal eyes of the image at the Palace of the Labrys and half agreed. "We will take her with us into our new world."

There in the crowded road with the smoke rising from the palace and the people rushing by, he took her in his arms and kissed her.

"You are my world, Lia."

When her mouth was free, she whispered, "And you are mine. Always."

Later that afternoon the sails of the *Lily Flame* were lifted for Egypt. As Lia stood beside Paon and looked back on Knossos of Crete, she knew that their son lay in her womb and she was content.